Secrets
Of
The
Bending
Grove

◆

N. MARIA KWAMI

Dede
MultiMedia

Published by Dede Multimedia | *www.DedeMultimedia.com*

First paperback printing: U.S.A. 2014

CONTACT

For information on bulk ordering,
for permission and reprint information
and to contact the author's representative,
please consult the following web page:

www.MariaKwami.com/Contact.html

Cover illustration by Jesse daCosta
Author's photograph by Dudley M. Brooks

Acknowledgements

My gratitude must first go Upward, from where I was endowed at a very young age with the desire to write books. Many special people, some of them from the very beginning and others as I approached the finish line, cheered me on during this long overdue yet infinitely rewarding process of completing my first novel. They too deserve my gratitude.

To my greatest encourager, my maa, Selina Patience Kwami — who, very early, introduced me and my siblings to the hundreds of writers that lived on our book-shelves and in all those boxes underneath the stairs, who taught me how to think and write boldly, and also edited each draft of this work — you always said that I would become a novelist, and I only wish that I had done this sooner. Percy Kwami clarified several words in the glossary in the first draft; Xoladem Ayittey read the second draft and gave me constructive advice on architecture and setting; and Kafui Kwami copy-edited the final draft. I must also acknowledge the Kwami family of Ho and Amedzofe in Ghana, whose true family history, in part, inspired the fictional family background and hometown setting of my main character. I also thank my husband and kids for tolerating me during my long season of procrastination.

Several of my friends played various roles that enabled me to arrive at this point. Edith Kotei and Selete Avoke both read my first draft, and I was greatly encouraged by the fact that they did not shoot it down; in fact, Selete called it 'a brave attempt' and Edith has been nagging me for years to 'get on with it.' Clement Chela graciously gave me a crash course on viruses and opportunistic conditions; Christine Asare helped me to understand the words I needed to name the two mountain towns; and Dudley M. Brooks shot my classic photograph. I thank all of you. To James and Eleanor Afful, for bringing Charles daCosta into my circle, and also for our lengthy discussion about names, which led to 'Bediako'; to Charles daCosta for his artistic direction on the cover illustration; and to the talented young lady, Jesse daCosta, who skillfully captured the essence of my heroine in the perfect cover illustration — I'm grateful to each of you for the role you played. And to Nana Sika Achampong, who came back into my life at the right time and spoke just two words; to Brenya Twumasi, for our many hours of empowering phone conversations; and to Mina Otoo, who believed and sowed a seed — your votes of confidence sustained me more than you know. Be blessed, all of you.

-- N. Maria Kwami

To the memory of my father,
WOGBEMASE,
on whose shoulders I sat and first viewed the world.

About the author

N. MARIA KWAMI is a Ghanaian-born writer, interactive journalist and communications consultant who migrated to the USA in 1989. She holds a master's degree in communications from American University; she also has degrees in international affairs and journalism.

She lives in the Washington DC-area with her family.

WEB SITE: www.MariaKwami.com

BOOK CLUB: MariaKwami.com/Bookclub.html

Secrets
Of
The
Bending
Grove

With a complete GLOSSARY beginning on Page 309

PROLOGUE

Everybody is here. People we have not seen in twenty years, all come to say one last farewell to Sefa. Easily one thousand people, but who counts heads at funerals?

I cannot look my aunt in the eye for fear that her sorrow will claw its way into my soul and suck out of me even more than I have already given. And so I stay by her side, holding up her right elbow to make it easier for the people filing past to shake her outstretched hand.

Me, I have not shed a tear yet — not since he died, anyway — but oh, how I mourned on that fateful day six months ago when I received his note from Amsterdam, in which he entrusted me with the most difficult assignment I had ever undertaken. The note said:

I have been diagnosed with a malignant brain tumour. I'm coming back home soon to receive a miracle, I hope. If not, then I'm coming to die. Shishi, please prepare my mother for my return.

I would much rather have been skipped over, but there was no one else to perform this task. His mother, Daa Nenor Gameli, is my mother's elder sister. We affectionately call her 'Tassie' and Sefa is her only child. My brother Kobla and I were brought up to think of him as our brother. And after our own mother's death a few years ago, Tassie became, for all practical purposes, our mother. So no, there *was* no one else to do this.

As soon as I received Sefa's message, I enlisted the help of our uncle, Fo Kofigah, to go and break the news to Tassie.

'Go with Shika, this load is too heavy for her to drag all the way to Togapeme by herself,' he told his two eldest sons when he dispatched them to accompany me. I would not have been able to face Tassie alone.

I will never forget the day we went. It was a complicated process, to be sure. Tassie had no telephone in her house, so I had placed a call to the post office in her village the day before and begged one of the workers to take her a message informing her that we would be coming the next day, and for her to stay put.

'I thought that you had finally found a husband, and you were coming to introduce him to me,' she later told me.

That day, it was as if we had launched another funeral in this woman's life.

*

In her mid-twenties, my aunt had been married off to one Mr B.T. Dodzi, a prominent businessman; and although there had been a quiet, amicable divorce after six years, it was generally understood that the marriage ended over her inability to produce a child.

Then at the age of thirty-seven, she got married again — to Professor Elorm Gameli — and wouldn't you know it! The following year, she did bear her miracle child. But, alas, Uncle Elorm died on the sixth of March 1966. Sefa was only two-and-a-half years old; and Tassie, who was by then six months pregnant with a second child, suffered a miscarriage when they told her the news.

'O God! Keep Nenor in the palm of your hand, for we do not know how she will survive this double tragedy!' This was the constant prayer of my mother, Lebene, as she nursed her sister back to health in our house.

Tassie and Sefa lived with us from March until Sefa turned three that August. Then his mother took him with her to Togapeme, where they stayed for six more months with her father, my grandfather, the Reverend Gottwin Sosu.

'How could God be so cruel as to inflict such pain on the daughter of one of His own?' This was the question on everyone's lips, my mother told me; and so people were amazed that Tassie even recovered from that shock to be able to raise her son single-handedly. But she did recover; and when she concluded her year of mourning, she returned to the city and went back to teaching music fulltime at a local secondary school.

As soon as I got old enough to understand, my mother explained everything to me — where Uncle Elorm went, why Tassie and Sefa had stayed with us for all those months, and where they went after they left our house. She also clarified to me that Sefa was not, in fact, my twin — as I had somehow supposed.

All those who knew Tassie's tragic story had the same reaction to her son's name.

'Sefanam — how appropriate!' they would say; but it was not until my mother explained that too, that I fully understood.

'His birth erased the stigma of barrenness that hung over her head for almost ten years, so his existence is restitution for her lost identity as a real woman; and now that he is all that she has left, not only does the prospect of his bright future empower her, but it also justifies her continued existence.' My mother's explanations were nothing if not comprehensive.

'But dadaa, what is the meaning of his name?'

'Sefanam? Ah, it means, "God has given me peace."'

Sefa grew up having the best of everything that a schoolteacher's salary could afford to give him. This boy *was* the very breath in his mother's lungs, her raison d'être, and she tried hard to strike a fine balance.

He and I attended Saint Francis Catholic Primary, scored very high marks in the Common Entrance exams, and went on to the prestigious Christian Academy For The Advancement of Knowledge, popularly known as 'Caftak' in the Volta Region.

'The world will not give you anything except judgment,' his mother told him when he was preparing, at the age of twelve, to leave home for the first time. 'They are watching to see if you can stand on your own two feet. And if you fall, do you think they will remember that you have no father? No. But if you succeed, they will say, "Ah — is that not Nenor

Gameli's son? All he had was a poor widowed mother to raise him, yet look how well he turned out." So, Sefanam, I beg you, do not bring any shame to my name!'

From all indications, this widow had done an outstanding job. When we arrived at Caftak, Sefa became a charismatic, star athlete who was very popular with the in-crowd.

'*Buul-let, Bullet! Buul-let, Bullet!*' they would chant as he sprinted his way into record after record, all the way to the nationals, year after year. Yet he never fell prey to those youthful vices such as wee smoking, or scaling the school fence and running away to the one nightclub in town — except maybe once or twice. All the teachers loved him because he also excelled academically. And the girls! Ah, that's another story.

After doing very well in the O-level exams, Sefa and I stayed on at Caftak for two more years to study for the A-levels. It was the same story with him — flying colours, sports prefect — and then on to the university where he studied international business. After that, he went on to obtain an advanced degree in business administration. He quickly landed a cushy job with a multinational pharmaceutical corporation with operations in West Africa, which soon afforded him luxury vehicles — German, of course — and a posh house in a gated community in the beach town of Nuinui.

'I need to be able to see the water from my bed,' he had said in response when his mother objected to his proximity to the ocean.

'I understand, but must you live in this *particular* neighbourhood?'

'It's a good location, dadaa, the perfect place to invest my money.'

Although Tassie did not raise the topic again, she never set foot in Sefa's house until she moved to our hometown, Togapeme, a tiny town hidden in a pristine mountain range in the heart of the Volta Region. There, as soon as he could afford to do so, Sefa had had our grandfather's house renovated into a modern villa so that his mother could retire there; and all this before he turned thirty.

He travelled back and forth constantly between Europe and West Africa. This last stint in the Netherlands was his longest stretch of time away. His employers were grooming him, during a six-month period, to fill a regional management position that was going to become vacant in a year. After being away for two months straight, he came back home on a short break.

I did not see much of him on that visit because I myself was getting ready to leave on a business trip when he returned to town. But in the brief time that I spent around him, he'd seemed tired and overworked, more chiselled since the last time he was home.

'Oh, by the way,' he told me casually when he dropped me off at the airport the night I left town, 'my migraines are back. I have some treatments scheduled as soon as I go back. Pray for me, Shishi.'

My heart sank into my bowels, but the timing was hardly conducive to get the details I wanted to know. I simply swallowed the uncomfortable lump that this news deposited in the back of my throat, and walked into the airport. Then I completely purged the information from my mind so that I could concentrate on my assignment.

When I returned from my trip, my aunt greeted me with unpleasant news.

'Sefa has broken up with Cynthia. The engagement is off.'

He had met Cynthia, a pharmacist, three years earlier at a conference hosted by Euro-Medische, the multinational drug-manufacturing giant that he worked for; they immediately became inseparable. The chocolate coloured beauty was a surprising but pleasant departure from his preferred type. His mother had wept for joy the day he brought her home.

Tassie sent a delegation to Cynthia's family with *drinks* to declare Sefa's honourable intentions, right before he went on this extended job posting. The traditional marriage was set to take place a month after his return. Now — poor Tassie — she would have to notify our extended family about this change in plans.

'Did he say why?' I asked.

'Nothing. All he told me was that his constant travelling had placed an unbearable strain on their relationship, and that the decision was mutual.'

Since Sefa had already left town, I did not get the chance to sit with him and find out what had gone wrong between them. A few weeks later, Cynthia's family sent a delegation to return the drinks.

And then his letter came.

It was I who had met him at the airport, scarcely daring to hug him for fear he might break. I had to work hard not to gape. How gaunt he had become since the last time I saw him!

I greeted him with a *'woezo.'*

'Shishi.' He squeezed my shoulder. He never called me by my given name, only by this childhood nickname for me.

'Do you want me to carry you?' I asked, trying to lighten the mood.

He laughed at the thought of my trim five-foot-eleven frame dragging his six-foot-four through the airport, and placed his arm about my shoulders as we walked out. That booming laugh gave me hope. It was as strong as ever! Surely this was not the sound of a man afflicted with a deadly brain tumour?

Yet, it was I who had watched as the remaining days quickly became so painful that I had to manage his care fulltime. And it was I who had eventually had to give up my job in the city — when his suffering became unbearable — then pack his things from his bungalow and move with him to the village where his mother lived, so that we could care for him until the end. We had nobody, and it fell to me to do it.

'I'm not giving up hope,' he had assured me, 'but if I must die, then I would much rather die in my mother's arms, in our grandfather's house.'

I took turns with his mother as we mopped sweat off his brow, or held him while he shivered. On many mornings, I walked into his room to find his mother asleep on the mat at the foot of his bed, where she had come to sit at dawn, and then have to wake her up: 'Come, Tassie, you must go back to bed.' I knew that I could handle the rigour better than her seventy-three-year-old frame could.

Most of all, it was I who had been sitting there on the better days also, when he would come out of a bad spell and need to talk; and so, I would listen while he talked. We had always had that between us, and not even his ailment could change that. He told me everything.

'Do you remember?' he would start, and I would go back with him to wherever he needed to be at that moment. He did not have to swear me to secrecy. I knew that he simply needed to unburden himself.

*

Now here we are, staring at his closed casket, hardly believing that fate could once more be so cruel. Perhaps it is a hoax?

I keep my left hand firmly against my aunt's ribs, and her elbow in my right hand. I can feel her heart beating furiously: *P-tm! P-tm! P-tm! P-tm!* With each heartbeat, I am transported back to Sefa's last days; I hear his voice telling me everything.

My mind drifts back to the present and I hear Tassie whispering her disappointment as she rocks back and forth in the makeshift church pew, her eyes closed as if to block out the pain. She only has one lamentation, which she repeats every few minutes in the same shocked tone.

'He did not even leave me a grandchild!'

'I know, Tassie, I know.'

This is no hoax. Sefa *is* dead. And the news has even made the obituary pages in all the major newspapers:

Snatched away by a malignant brain tumour… only child of his widowed mother… leaving no descendants… in the prime of his life… Sefanam Sosu Gameli. Dead, one week after turning thirty-two.

But time soon passes. Even the deepest pain eventually loses its edge in the more vivid reality of the present; then, what once was unbearable becomes strangely familiar. And after much familiarity, it assumes the insignificance of just another milestone, ever marking the journey to higher ground.

SEASON

OF

DROUGHT

ONE

By the time Sefa arrived, he was already experiencing problems with his hearing and vision, and would tilt his head in an awkward manner when engaging in conversation. He was also prone to bouts of extreme weakness brought on by his excruciating headaches, which would leave him bedridden for days at a time.

I hired a fulltime live-in housekeeper, who brought along her eight-year-old child, just to make sure that there was always somebody there with him. Since he was no longer able to drive, I also hired a fulltime driver to run his errands and take him places. In any case, he hardly went anywhere anymore, only for his appointments with the radiotherapist.

Thanks to the flexibility of his employers, he was able to stay productive from home in the beginning. Not only was this good for his psyche, but it also provided his employers with the justification they needed to extend his health insurance coverage, which paid for the slew of expensive drugs that he required.

'Sef, I will always be here for you,' I told him. I still had to work but I had made him that promise, and so I tried to keep it. I stopped by every evening after work to check on him and spend the evening with him.

The doctors had him on some very potent medications that seemed to keep his aches and pains in check and to relieve him of his terrible headaches. He received a package from Europe once a month by special courier delivery, which I picked up from his employers' offices on Liberty Avenue in Accra. In the three months following his return, this became part of my routine.

Although his employers had been gracious enough to continue the health insurance benefits for those three months, that grace period, along with the medications it provided, would eventually run out and he would be on his own. Sefa had made the decision early on not to continue with conventional medicine once this happened. He said that he would focus on local alternatives and simply resign himself to his fate.

'That way, if I'm meant to live, I will; if not, then so be it,' he had said matter-of-factly over my horrified objections.

He also embarked on a regimen of traditional herbal medicines. Every other week, I would go to the home of our uncle, Fo Kofigah, to pick up that box, which contained several packets of specially formulated herbs from the many medicine men that Fo Kofigah consulted on a regular basis.

Our uncle did not believe in so-called Western medicine. He rejected the somewhat unchallenged notion that traditional medicine was in some way in conflict with his Western education and Christian upbringing. Rather, he subscribed to a holistic outlook to receive insight to perform his multiple responsibilities as Lieutenant Colonel Gerwig Kofigah Sosu, Retired — pillar of the community — and his main focus these days was to get to the bottom of this latest incidence of bad luck affecting his elder sister, in time to reverse it and save *her* only son from its grip.

When I brought Sefa that final package from his employers, I realised that I didn't even know which doctor was managing his care here, since I had never actually been with him to any of his appointments. In the beginning, when he had returned looking so frail, I tried to go with him to his doctor visits, but he discouraged me from doing so, preferring to let the driver take him so that I didn't have to miss work. He would become periodically weak and then bounce back, but I was fully aware of the fact that he could not go on like that forever.

'What are you going to do at the end of the month after you swallow the last of the medicine?' I asked. 'What is the doctor saying? I mean, shouldn't you be following his recommendations?'

I saw uncertainty in his demeanour for the first time.

'I'm not sure what will happen, Shishi, but I do know that unless I receive a miracle, this tumour is eventually going to kill me. Look at me, half my brain has already been taken over by it; and everyday, I have to convince myself that something will change if I just hang on long enough. One month, Shishi, one month; then I'm done fighting this.'

I suggested to him then that I should move in permanently with him; but he was fiercely independent, and did not want to intrude on my life any more than was absolutely necessary.

'Shishi,' he said, 'you worry too much. As soon as the time comes when I need you fulltime, I will let you know. In the meantime, focus on yourself and save up for when you have to take that break.'

He had sounded so reasonable that I pulled back a little. Besides, I told myself, we lived in the same neighbourhood, just five minutes apart; the housekeeper could always send for me in case of emergency. So far, there had been none; he had held his own quite well. And as the days went by, I came to rely fully on the hired help to make sure that he was taken care of.

But now, things were about to change and we did not have in place anything resembling a contingency plan.

Sefa's packages from Amsterdam were always sealed and I'd never had any reason to open them before handing them to him. I was saddened by the realisation that I didn't even know what drugs he had been on all this time. I felt a rush of guilt followed by a sense of urgency to figure out how I was going to save him from his stubborn self.

And then it came to me! His driver, Mr Enoch, would be coming to my house at the end of the week to collect his pay; I could simply find out from him everything about Sefa's doctor visits, and at least go from there. Hopefully, before the end of the month, I would have come up with an alternative plan of action.

That day, as soon as Enoch arrived at my house, I began questioning him. His reaction completely threw me for a loop.

'Oh, madam, please!' He backed away from me and threw up his hands. 'Boss specifically told me that if I discussed this with you, he would kill me with his own two hands, and that I shouldn't assume he's weak just because he's ill.'

'Enoch! What are you saying, that there's some *kuluulu* between you and my brother? Ei, who hired you for this job?'

'Madam, you yourself hired me. There is no kuluulu; as for me, I don't know anything oh!' He continued to gesture in an imploring manner.

'Enoch, I'm asking you again — who hands you your pay at the end of every week?' The more I tried to control my volume, the faster my anger rose.

'Please, madam, I'm not arguing with you, it's still you.' He was kneeling and wringing his hands by this time.

'So what is your problem? Did I hire you to drive my brother around, or did I hire you to come and play games with us?'

'Oh, madam, please don't shout; people will hear us. We've been going regularly to the radiology department at Capital General Hospital so that he can receive treatments. Sometimes when he's too weak to walk, I even have to carry him to the car.'

'I know all this, that's precisely what I hired you to do, remember? Enoch, I'm warning you, don't play games with me. You know that's not what I'm referring to. Where else have you been taking him?'

'Once every two weeks, I take him to this other place, I think it's some type of private clinic. I only know this because the first time we were going there, we got lost and boss called for directions from the car phone. But there is no sign in front of the building; nothing is written on the door, and I've never been inside. He always tells me to wait in the car. Even when he's weak, he insists that he'll go in by himself and that I should just wait in the car.'

'*Hoh!* So how do you know it's a clinic if you've never even gone inside?'

'Well, I've seen other people going in and coming out. Many of them look okay, but some of them look really sick, just like boss. But all of them come out carrying the same litres of medicine. Just like boss.'

I sat down, completely confused.

'And where is this place?' I finally managed to ask. I just sat there and listened as he gave me detailed directions.

'Madam, that's all I know, I swear on my father's grave!'

I counted out his pay into his hand and he left. Then I held my head in my hands and continued to sit for several minutes. But I couldn't get my brain to function properly, or maybe it just didn't want to go where it needed to go in order to process the information it had just received.

I picked up the telephone and dialled. If there was one person who could talk me through the stress it was Sweetie.

'Sefa's insurance has expired and he has less than four weeks' worth of medicine left. And he has decided not to continue fighting when this supply runs out,' I told her.

'Ah, Mawusi-Shika Amenyo, as for you! So *this* is what is stressing you out?'

Sweetie used my full name whenever possible. The way she would just rattle the whole thing off as if it were one word used to irritate me to no end when we first met; but time had made the sound more palatable. After all, that *was* my name, and it was kind of nice that someone took the time to fully acknowledge me.

'He won't let me help him and I don't know what to do. *Challey*, can you get Bronze to step in?'

'You should have let me know sooner; Bronze is out of town. All the same, running out of medicine shouldn't be such a big deal. Just get me a detailed list of what he's on. I'll show it to Bronze when he returns in a few days and let's see what strings he can pull. In the worst-case scenario, it might be kind of expensive paying out of pocket; but how do you suppose the rich and connected manage to survive in this country? My dear, everything is available — for the right price, of course! And Sefa has money, so *that* can't even be the issue.'

'No, he's just using the meds as an excuse to throw in the towel. He has never quit anything before.'

'Don't worry, my dear; Bronze will hook him up and that'll take away his excuse.'

I closed my eyes and let out my breath. It wasn't just that Sweetie was well connected, but if she said she would do something, she did it, and without expecting anything in return.

*

Sweetie Bediako and Miyo Mensah were my best friends; we went back a long way. The three of us used to be roommates in Atlantic Hall at the Business and International Studies University, where people nicknamed us 'the three poshes'.

Miyo and I were very disappointed when Sweetie moved out to a single room in a more popular residence hall during our final year. And then, after she had obtained a bachelor's degree with honours in economics, she left BISU. Miyo and I stayed on to pursue advanced degrees in our respective fields. Miyo attended law school and I got my master's in sociology. But Sweetie's departure did not weaken our friendship at all. If anything, she made herself more accessible to us, even as she went on to establish her own business with start-up capital legitimately earned by working hard for her politician sugar daddy.

I had definitely made the right call.

Although I could just as well have reached out to Miyo, I knew that it was out of the question to do so right now.

'I don't want her to see me like this,' Sefa had said, when Miyo had wanted to come and visit him after he returned from Holland. It had been my unpleasant duty to convey his sentiments to her, so that she could understand why he refused to have her visit; and although it had been really hard for her to hear, she'd had no choice but to respect his wishes.

Miyo had attended Caftak with Sefa and me, so our friendship went all the way back to the beginning of our teens. Sefa had had a major crush on her in secondary school. He used to write sweet nothings to her on graph paper, then braid blades of raffia into a thin rope and tie it around the note. And then he would send me on a fool's errand of trying to win her heart with his silly notes. They were all different, but they followed the same theme:

Anyemiyoo Mensah, I'm dying for your love.
If you make up your mind to return my move,
Then show me a sign and send back this rope.
Anyemiyoo Mensah, will you comport?

Miyo would fume, and huff and puff, but she would always keep the note and hand me back the rope — after she had unravelled it and viciously shredded it.

'Yeah, take that to him and tell him it's nope!'

'She's thinking about it,' I would always report back to Sefa, never once returning the shredded fibres to him.

He must have written at least one note per week to her for the first two years of secondary school. But Miyo could not be moved. Still, she was my best friend and we were always in and out of each other's houses. So, although Sefa moved on and began going out with other girls, he and Miyo eventually developed a great friendship as well.

I always believed that she too cared deeply for him, just was not capable of expressing it in the way that he would have preferred. That she thought the world of him, however, was obvious to everyone else and I suppose, in some convoluted way that only a man's ego could perceive, Sefa was sure that if Miyo saw a more vulnerable version of him, it would somehow cause her to think less of him. Everyone in our family knew that the reason why he remained attracted to copper-coloured girls all his life was because he kept trying to find a substitute for Miyo. Even his mother knew this.

*

By morning, commonsense had toned down the panic I felt the night before, but I still had a problem to solve. I couldn't understand why Sefa was being so cagey; all I knew was that I was not going to let him just give up like that without a fight. I had to go at once to see him.

I knew nothing about this so-called clinic either, had never even heard him refer to it. Yet, it seemed key to his survival. What brand of poison were they peddling there? Narcotics? Could it be that Sefa was turning to recreational drugs in an attempt to ease his pain? Why else would he go to the extent of threatening Enoch, just to keep his dealings with this clinic secret from me?

Sefa stuck to a regimen like a monk. He would be waking up soon to take a shower. I grabbed my purse and keys. I stuck my feet into my *challey-wotey* and jumped into the car. I made a quick stop at Auntie Rose's pastry stand. Sefa loved the consistency of this woman's *bofloat*, the way they were always dry and pillowy with a crispy brown coating. But I was a little too early; the first batch wasn't ready yet, so I placed an order for a dozen and left. When I got to Sefa's house, I just parked outside, reached over to unlatch the gate, and let myself in. Emilia, the housekeeper, popped her head out of her doorway when the gate creaked.

'Morning, Sister Shika,' she said. Then she waved and went back inside.

Using the duplicate set of keys, I entered through the kitchen and went straight to his bedroom door. I stuck my ear to the door and listened. The shower was running. Perfect!

He kept most of his meds in a little fridge. The rest were inside a cabinet. Everything was in his bedroom. I crept in and gingerly pried the cabinet open. For the first time, I looked at his bottles and packets, really read the names. Nothing jumped out — a bunch of weird, long names that I couldn't possibly memorise, that's all. But I hadn't brought anything with which to write, so I grabbed a pen from his bedside table and scribbled the names in my palm. Then I opened the cabinet, scribbled *those* names on my forearm.

The water stopped running. I headed for the door.

'Emilia, is that you?' he called out just as I made it out to the corridor.

'No Sefa, it's Shishi. I stopped by on my way from the boflaot stand.'

'Ei, so early? Is everything okay?'

'Yes, everything's fine. I went to bed early and woke up at the crack of dawn, that's all. I also brought you the newspaper. Finish and come out to the back porch so that we can have breakfast together. I can only stay for an hour, then I have to leave for market.'

I called out to Martha to go and pick up my boflaot order.

'Shishi,' he said as soon as he joined me on the porch, 'remember?'

For weeks after his return, it seemed as if all Sefa did was talk about the past. When he had an occasional good evening, we would even go for a walk on the beach along the back of our neighbourhood so that he could watch the tide come in. Perhaps this was his way of holding on to all that he was before he should begin to lose his memory. The doctors had warned him that with the progression of his tumour, for sure, that day would come. And so, I continued to humour his fixation with the past.

'Of course,' I said, and he took us both back in time once again.

What butterfly could forget the first time it ever ventured from the cocoon? We were sent to school together. I was older than Sefa by just eleven days and my brother Kobla was three years older than us, so Sefa and I had marked several of our milestones together. We got the measles around the same time; we attended the same schools and had the same friends.

People had thought that we were twins throughout primary school. Kids at that age do not retain each other's surnames, so it made no difference to them. All they knew was that we were siblings in the same class — Shika and Sefa — therefore we must have been twins. It seemed pointless to explain to them exactly how we were related, especially since we frequently addressed each other's mothers as 'dadaa' and Sefa had also called my father 'papa' until *his* death when we were nineteen.

Our teen years would turn out to be another story, though. Secondary school was a more sophisticated atmosphere, and it would impact the rest of our lives in unimaginable ways.

I can still remember the day I received my admission letter. It was a Monday. The fourth of August 1975, to be exact. Sefa had received *his* letter the previous Thursday, and it felt as if I had been overlooked, especially since that Thursday was also the day on which I turned twelve. And then, mine arrived. I too was going to Caftak, surely the most sought-after boarding school in the whole of Anglophone West Africa at the time!

'Remember so-so-and-so?' he asked me several times, recalling various characters, trying to guess what had become of them.

We tried to predict how and where they might have ended up in life based on what we could recall of their character traits. The bona-fide geniuses who had made it there purely on braininess, unlike those other ones whose rich parents had obviously bought them a place in the school. The juvenile delinquents, the star athletes, the politicians' children; the foreign kids with unpronounceable names; and those snobs whose fathers turned out to be nothing more than international fugitives, their names double-underlined with black ink on the Interpol watchlist.

Who could forget the odd couples and the wicked seniors? The religious fanatics; the bullies, cliques and groups; the wannabe bourgeoisie and their legions of hangers-on; and us, the regular kids?

And their nicknames — I reminded Sefa of 'leapfrog', that window-climbing, wall-scaling, disco-trotting mulattress; the bed-wetter nicknamed 'faucet'; the loose girls collectively referred to as the 'school mattress brigade'; and of course, the 'kleptocrat' — all in all, a colourful and unforgettable bunch. The images conjured up by these recollections had not been erased with the passage of time.

But it was still a relief when my early morning visit came to an end.

'I have to leave now, otherwise they will be out of fresh produce by the time I get to market,' I told him.

He went back to his bedroom and returned with money for his portion of the shopping. As usual, it was far more than he needed to give, sufficient for our two households. Then I called out for Martha to dress up and accompany me to market.

TWO

Thank goodness for this rare opportunity to let out my breath and focus on myself for a change, I thought, as I squeezed into the tight parking spot and handed the man a tip to watch my car. Although there had been a last minute change from our usual chop-bar to a more upscale restaurant, which set me back by some ten minutes, I hoped that I would have ample time in which to catch up with Sweetie and Miyo.

When Sefa first returned home, I drove him straight to Togapeme. He needed his mother. After a two-week hiatus, the serene environment worked wonders for his constitution and he returned to the city quite invigorated. Since then, he had not been back to the village, but every other week, his mother came to town to spend a few days with him. She always had to return to Togapeme before the weekend so that she could be there for Saturday choir practice and Sunday service.

Whenever Tassie came to town, although it was just for a couple of days at a time, I was able to catch up on my social life. It was not as if I had much of one any more, but these treasured connections were all that were sustaining me emotionally, and every now and then, I felt that they were deserving of some engagement on my part.

'How's Sefa doing? And Auntie Nenor?' Miyo said as soon as I sat down.

'He's hanging in there, and Tassie is her usual unshakable self. She sends greetings to you both.'

'What about you, my dear, how are you coping? You've been really scarce lately.' Sweetie gave my shoulder a shove so that she could take a better look at me.

They always regaled me with such questions, but on this particular day, my responses were a bit strained. I had told them the last time we chatted that Sefa was running out of his drugs, but I hadn't seen or talked to either of them since then. I tried to fill them in now, but I kept picking at my food and losing track of the conversation. Then I apologised and tried to mask my confusion by sipping my cold drink. They were worried, I could tell from the way they kept glancing at each other.

'Let us know what we can do to help; we're here for you. You shouldn't be doing this alone, you know?' Miyo reached across the table and rubbed my little finger.

'Yes. And what about that list you were supposed to send me? I know you have a lot on your plate right now, but the clock is ticking. In fact, you know what? We're going to find you a man,' Sweetie said, slapping the surface of the table for emphasis. 'That's what you need — some rich man to take care of everything so that you don't have to keep going up and down like this anymore.' She firmly believed that a man with deep pockets could fix anything.

'Leave her alone, she already has a man and doesn't need you to find her another one,' Miyo fired back, and then, 'By the way, when is your *obroni* returning?'

I laughed. It never failed to amuse me whenever she referred to a white person in the vernacular, considering that *her* mother was also one, and anyone of her own complexion was loosely classified as such.

'My obroni is almost done with his Calabar project. Then he'll go to Lomé for a week before returning home.'

'So, you're taking a little break and going to meet him there, right? Don't snooze and let some Efik or Ibibio woman use her *mami-water* magic to snatch him away, that's all I'm saying,' Sweetie said.

'*Haabah*!' I swatted them both with my napkin. 'You know you two would be the first to hear if anything were to change.' They seemed determined to have me hitched before the end of this date, but I refused to bite.

Jean-Marc Charbonneau was a Canadian environmental scientist at a major oil company in the region, and he and I had a somewhat unclear relationship, according to these concerned observers. Miyo and Sweetie regularly fished to see if 'this thing' between Jean and me was progressing in any noteworthy direction.

Yes, it sure would be nice to be able to take a break and also to see Jean again, I thought. The job of being a primary caregiver was proving to be emotionally taxing, requiring more of me than I had anticipated.

'Sweetie, what about you? Your voice message was rather mysterious, as usual. What's going on?' I quickly deflected the focus from myself lest I should succumb to self-pity.

Sweetie's life read like a soap opera. You never knew what drama was going to unfold next. Every time she invited Miyo and me to one of these power lunches, we assumed that she was going to announce the final unravelling of her longstanding love-triangle, which began during our college years, and was as confusing to us as it was addictive to her; but we were always wrong.

*

She had a long-time sugar daddy, one Samuel Tebi Dompey, an egomaniac with a better reputation as a very effective politician. True, Sammy had been relentless in his pursuit; but in all fairness, Sweetie really did try to resist his advances when he began chasing her during our third year at BISU. He was, at the time, a mid-level civil servant in charge of some committee or other, and he regularly attended meetings on university campuses as part of his job.

As soon as he set eyes on Sweetie, it was show time! And who could blame him? Her flawless coffee-bean complexion — combined with her large eyes and thick, black lashes — contrasted dramatically with her perfect set of ivories, thus making her one of the most striking visions on campus.

And it was not as if having a sugar daddy were unheard of. In fact, about half the girls on campus gave in to the pressure. Practically all the lecturers on campus were lechers; they made it plain, as soon as first-year students arrived, that they fully expected you to sleep your way through their classes. But it really takes two to tango, and while some girls evaded this unwanted attention as if they were navigating a minefield, there were plenty more who made it obvious that they were not only willing but quite enthusiastic to service the entire faculty, if need be. In fact, this latter group was so large that it took the pressure off those of us who were not willing to use *bottom-power* to pursue academic success.

And then there were the heavy hitters, those select few on that higher plateau, worthy of being wooed by outsiders — politicians, businessmen, respected professionals, and arrogant-looking men with questionable sources of income — who stormed the campus in their flashy cars and flouted the stipulated visiting hours with impunity.

Some of these girls, even the lecturers did not dare to approach, while others juggled the lecturers alongside the outside suitors with acrobatic precision. It looked like a butcher's shop outside Pacific Hall on Friday and Saturday nights. That residence hall held the dubious record as warehouse of the finest meat in the entire nation; and some mothers would have even sold their souls to have their daughters assigned there.

People always seemed surprised to learn that the three of us had not yet yielded to the pressure.

'You mean to say, you haven't *comported* to any advances?' they would ask.

'Those three poshes — it's unnatural for them to be so fine and yet be celibate; they're probably *supis*,' others would snidely comment, as if we were somehow prohibited from fostering close relationships outside a sexual context.

What none of them knew was that we had made a deal in our first year to protect each other from stupid choices, at least until the end of our second year. It had by no means been easy, but we'd held solidly to our prolonged fast and helped each other to withstand the continuous onslaught.

'I've decided to go steady with Bronze,' Sweetie told Miyo and me as soon as our self-imposed season of abstinence expired.

This 'Bronze' was one Bronsford Anomar-Bilson — a pre-med student a year ahead of us — who had meticulously and patiently wooed Sweetie for two years. And although they snuck off regularly during our dry season, Miyo and I always pretended not to know that Sweetie was breaking our fast.

Bronze was a real gentleman, born to a proud family from Windy Bay. His maternal great-grandfather, a quarter-caste directly descended from a Portuguese slave trader, was the first person in his hometown to board an aeroplane. It was a matter of public record that the old man changed his original family name to Anomar in homage to that big bird; but popular legend held that he did so more out of a desire to obscure his ancestor's detestable role in world history. Even so, the Anomars were still considered the crème de la crème in their hometown, carrying themselves above the dregs as if their flatulence did not stink. What with their straight noses, their old colonial family house, and all the access they had continued to enjoy over the decades, it was kind of hard to detect any remorse in their bearing over their family skeleton.

True, Bronze had the personality of a stick of *twapia* — as boring as wood and as efficient as toothpaste — but that, after all, is considered good husband material, and Sweetie was definitely thinking ahead. Miyo and I were thrilled to bits for her.

'Hm, that Bronze has class oh!' I said.

'Perhaps he can polish her rough edges and she, in turn, can liven him up a bit,' Miyo said.

When we returned to campus the following term, you couldn't separate them. Sweetie's self confidence had gone up several notches, and she had stopped obsessing over her physical flaws. We also found out toward the end of that term that Bronze had made the shortlist in a nationwide academic competition. If he got selected, he would be one of only four students in the entire country to be awarded a full scholarship to attend medical school in the U.S. That first term of our third year was a good one for Sweetie and Bronze.

But the next term, along came Sammy Dompey in hot pursuit, riding in his government-issued, tinted-windowed, black Mitsubishi Pajero, pompously flashing his government money and giving the broke medical student some stiff competition.

'Didn't you know? Sammy Dompey has a girl or two, or so, on every university campus in this country, in addition to having a woman that everyone knows is *the* girlfriend,' people said when we tried to dig into his background. In fact, his reputation was so bad that they referred to him behind his back by his given initials. There wasn't a more appropriate acronym for this dog than STD.

Sammy first caught sight of Sweetie at a campus meeting, which he had convened to explain some new government policy. The following weekend, he drove back to our campus and cruised around, randomly asking people for Sweetie until he found a student who knew her. Then, he parked in front of our residence hall and waited.

'You have a visitor, Sweetie Bediako,' the young man came upstairs and told her.

Sweetie went downstairs in some confusion, only to discover that her visitor was Mr Dompey from the Ministry of Education. She just stood there politely listening to him until he left; and then she came upstairs, rolling her eyes and loudly sucking her teeth in irritation.

That was the beginning of Sammy's weekly visits. The next Saturday, while we were returning from the cafeteria, we noticed his vehicle tailing us. When he realised that we had seen him, he pulled up beside us as if he had just happened upon us by chance, and began to chat Sweetie up. She would not even approach his vehicle; just stood there, arms folded defensively, pretending to laugh at his boring jokes. After he drove off, she caught up with us. We were quite sure that she was going to explode.

Sweetie said that Sammy was the most unattractive man she had ever laid eyes on; she felt that he lacked the physical attributes and social graces that she would have preferred in *her* man.

'*Bush* man! Look at his face, it's as if a truck just drove over it. And I can't stand the way his trousers wedge up into his butt when he walks. But I suppose, when he looks in the mirror and inspects his portrait, he concludes that it qualifies to be seen next to mine.'

'And why not? He's ambitious and, clearly, has good taste. The trouser problem can be easily corrected with the help of an expert tailor, I'm sure; and the *bushiatics* too can be reversed — eventually. But as for that face of his — eish!' Miyo took delight in stoking the fire.

Sweetie evaded Sammy after that by leaving campus before he showed up, or hiding and begging us to lie and say that she was away. After several rounds of this cat-and-mouse game, he seemed to have taken the hint and stopped coming around.

After midterm, Bronze found out that he had won the national scholarship for which he had been shortlisted the previous term. In just a little over two months, he would be leaving for Illinois and would be gone for four years.

'Don't worry, Sweetie. I'll fly home once a year at least, and in between, you will come and visit me,' he told her.

His confidence plumped out Sweetie's cheeks and deepened her dimples. The prospect of travelling back and forth to America to see him only served to elevate the level of her excitement, and it carried her through the rest of the term on a cloud. Bronze was finally on his way to becoming a doctor, just like his mother had always wanted.

Even after he handed in his final paper and was officially done at BISU, he still hung around campus for another couple of weeks, spending every possible moment with Sweetie. For those two weeks, they stuck together like bread and butter. At the beginning of *our* exam week, he went home to prepare for his upcoming trip.

When school let out, Sweetie came home with me to Kanda so that she could remain in the city until Bronze left town; and then, she travelled back home to Ahemekrom.

During that long school break, she stayed away from the city and kept a very low profile, but she did call to wish me happy birthday.

'Sorry I couldn't make it down for your twenty-first bash. I didn't want to risk coming across Sammy Dompey by chance,' she said. She had already heard from Bronze. 'As soon as he arrived in Illinois, he sent me a postcard. And he's already telephoned me twice at the post office to tell me everything about his trip and his first impressions about America.'

'I'm glad. You seem to have adjusted well to his absence.'

After we chatted a bit, I excused myself and put Miyo on the phone so that they could carry on while I went back to my guests.

Two days before we were due to return to campus to begin our fourth year, Miyo telephoned me at home in quite a state of excitement.

'Quick, Shika! Turn on the TV.'

I did, but I only caught the tail end of the news item. All I heard was '... *for the vacant parliamentary seat in the new district of South Aheme.*'

'Ah, isn't that Sweetie's home district? What did I miss? What has happened there?' I asked.

'It's Sammy Dompey! He's going to run for MP of that new district.'
'What!'

'I can't believe it either. Should we try calling Sweetie?'

'No, we'll see her soon enough. Let's just wait until Saturday when we return to campus,' I said.

Hm, Sammy about to go into politics, I thought, how about that! I couldn't wait to see how Sweetie would react to the news.

'I can't believe this!' she said when we caught up with her on campus. 'In my district, of all the places he could have picked. I didn't even know that he was also from South Aheme. What bad luck! I hope he doesn't start coming around here again, now that he's switching careers!'

If her fairy godmother had been listening to grant that wish, godmother's wand must have run out of batteries, for no sooner had we settled into our final year than the black Pajero began reappearing in the parking lot in front of Atlantic Hall. Six forty-five sharp, every Friday evening.

This time around, Sammy Dompey had upped his game. He must have taken lessons while he was away — he did not come empty-handed. He always brought Sweetie a gift of expensive treats. Every Friday it was something else, each new treat more exotic than the last. Sweetie stopped dodging him, but she would still only stand by his Pajero and smile politely while he did most of the talking. Then, after he left, she would come and toss the box of treats onto the bed and we would have at it. *She never ate any of it.*

As if to add insult to injury, she had not heard from Bronze in over a month. He had only been gone four months but, already, his phone calls had slowed down.

'I'm about to begin my program,' he had told Sweetie by way of preparing her for the change in their communication pattern after his second month away.

So, Sweetie called him once. She had had to pay an exorbitant rate to use the phone in the post office; but it had been worth it, she said. And then, just before we returned to school, she'd tried calling him one more time. After paying the non-refundable charge and dialling his number, she encountered an automated voice: *The number you have dialled is out of service. Please check the number and dial again.*

And now, here was this man with his unsavoury face, flashing his exotic treats and obviously going to great lengths to become more palatable to her discriminating tastes. All of a sudden, Sweetie became very confused. She began wondering out loud about Bronze.

'Will he even come back after he completes medical school? I don't want him to take me for a ride oh! I mean, it hasn't even been a year, and he's already changed his phone number on me; yet, he expects me to sit here and wait for him, right? For four whole years.'

She was so torn about this that she told her mother about her dilemma when Eno came down to visit.

'You should release that small boy and let him focus on pursuing his studies abroad,' Eno responded. 'You just wait until he meets *one* American woman — that will be the end of your dreams. I hear they are very aggressive in pursuing successful black men. This Sammy sounds like a more stable option. A whole politician, and from this same South Aheme where *we* also come from — it's a sign from above! What are you confused about?'

'Well, he's quite old, and they say he already has a woman in his life that everyone knows about. Besides, he's not as refined as Bronze.'

Sweetie's mother, Eno Bediako, was driven. She had acquired her brand of wisdom exclusively from the school of hard knocks — gutter side, to be precise. She could barely write her name, but what she lacked in classmates, she more than made up for with unrivalled sagacity and a hunger for advancement that bordered on sociopathic. Eno was determined to find someone with clout who would elevate her family to another social stratum; and Sweetie, her only child and the first person to go beyond elementary school in her entire family, was the medium through which this ambition was to be realised. Eno quickly straightened her daughter out.

'Is there a legal document backing Sammy's so-called relationship with this other woman? And what do you mean by *refined*? Have those haughty roommates of yours been filling your head with this stupidity? Remember, we don't have the same connections that *they* have, and you're already two years older than them. If you're not careful, you'll end up an old maid. Ahuofeh, this is our one chance oh!' Eno had it all mapped out, and what Eno wanted, Eno got.

After the heart-to-heart talk with her mother, Sweetie quickly progressed to sitting in Sammy's Pajero and chatting with him. And from the minute her butt touched his spotless, white leather upholstery, he began inviting her to go away with him. Every weekend he would ask, and every time she would decline his invitation.

Miyo and I tried; we fought hard to discourage Sweetie from leading him on, and she maintained that it was all just a harmless game to keep her from losing her mind while she waited to hear from Bronze.

'What if something happened to him?' Miyo urged her to try and find out from Bronze's family if he was still in touch with them.

'Then you would at least know for sure before getting in too deep with this Sammy,' I added.

'I'm not going to go running to Bronze's family who already think I'm not good enough for him,' she said. 'Don't you suppose we would have heard by now if something bad had happened to him? Don't worry, I know what I'm doing.'

As midterm approached, Sammy invited her again to go out of town with him. Her birthday had fallen earlier in the week and he said that he wanted to take her to a resort near Ningo for a quick break to celebrate. After his visit that day, she came back to our room and dropped the bombshell.

'I've decided to go away with Sammy for the weekend, and the next time I get hold of Bronze, I'll break up with him.'

Miyo and I were too stunned to say anything. We just stared at her while she packed a bag and borrowed Miyo's swimsuit for the upcoming tryst. In the end, her mother's encouragement had prevailed over our warnings, and Bronze's silence had not helped either. Right before our eyes, Sweetie was about to cast the die that would set the course of her life on an unanticipated detour. We had no choice other than to accept that

Sammy Dompey was about to become a fixture in her life, and by association, ours. The next morning, she left with him.

When she returned from the midterm rendezvous, she was strangely silent. It was not as if we were expecting a blow-by-blow commentary on what had transpired between them, but at least we thought she might give us some description of the resort — the food, the amenities, the ambiance — anything but this uncharacteristic silence. Whatever transpired there must have shaken her to the core, but it would be months before she disclosed the details. At any rate, it seemed that the vacation had been successful in other ways.

Sweetie hit us with the good news: 'Sammy is going to pull some strings and get me into a single room in Pacific Hall.'

This was no small feat. It could only be accomplished with some serious *palm grease*, especially since we were already halfway through the term. The following Saturday, Sammy did not come to see her, but he had managed to get her transferred into the new room, as he promised; so, Miyo and I began helping her pack her belongings.

While we were still going back and forth moving her things, she got summoned downstairs to take a phone call in the residence office. She was gone for about thirty minutes and when she returned, she looked as if she had just seen a ghost. Bronze had resurfaced with a very reasonable explanation for his long silence.

It was as if Sweetie's fairy godmother finally remembered to replace the batteries in the wand, and then decided to swing it really hard just to clear the backlog.

Now that she had crossed the line and spent a weekend with Sammy, surely, our Sweetie had broken up with the medical student. But I was in for an eye-opener.

'I changed my mind,' she told us, 'I'm not giving up Bronze anymore. He still has serious plans for our future, so he's my insurance policy. After all, it isn't as if I'm going to marry Sammy.'

When I warned her against two-timing Bronze, she defended her decision; and Miyo seemed to agree with her.

'Hey, she's a big girl, right? She's capable of making her own decisions. And it's her life. Obviously, there's a right way and a wrong way to play this game and Sweetie is, as you can see, more clued in than we are.'

Sammy must have promised her the world; he proved that he could deliver too by furnishing her new room and everything; and he gave her *chop money* on top of that! Her wardrobe dramatically improved, and she was the only one of us who ever really lived up to our original nickname. All the same, Sweetie was generous to a fault; and so, in spite of the fact that she was now in a whole different class all by herself, nothing else changed between us.

We still hung out together, and although Sammy still came by to see her on Friday nights at her new hall, for some reason, Sweetie never went away with him anymore. He would bring her gourmet carryout food and they would sit in his vehicle eating and chatting, while the exotic treats continued to trickle down to us. And all that time, Bronze was doing *his* part to uphold their long-distance relationship. He continued to telephone her every two weeks like clockwork.

We soon began to dream about graduation and as final exams loomed, so did the beginning of Sammy's campaign. He had been calling on Sweetie's knowledge of economics for advice on fundraising and other financial matters. Now he was offering her a paid position on his campaign team after graduation, and she was seriously considering accepting it.

'I think I can juggle it along with the master's program,' she said.

I did not try to dissuade her. After all, it wasn't as if I could offer her an alternative, I who was now trying to figure out my own way in this tough world.

'I'm too busy studying to keep giving you pro bono, unsolicited advice that you will completely ignore anyway,' Miyo told her.

Turning up the volume on the relationship with Sammy supported Sweetie's immediate agenda. Miyo and I had no recourse other than to sit back and watch her manage her new career, for that's what it was.

Evidently, even aspiring politicians have unbridled access to significant stashes of cash. After graduation, Sammy took Sweetie to a car dealership to pick out *any* car. That's when she made her first chess move.

'I told him to give me the money instead so that I could take my time and shop around for what *I* wanted,' she told us.

'Why didn't you just pick out what you wanted and have him pay for it right there? You would have saved yourself all that trouble,' I said.

'Listen and learn, Mawusi-Shika Amenyo. Never, *ever* sit there and allow some man to bring you gifts of expensive property. Rather, get the cold cash from him and buy it yourself. That way, there is no evidence that he gave you anything, and you will also be sure that *you* own the title to it; then he can't return tomorrow and ask for his gift back.'

So, Sweetie got the cash from Sammy and bought herself a car, which she duly titled in her own name before she even hired someone to teach her to drive it. True — it was just some insignificant non-European *chenchema*, but a car is still a car, especially if someone else was going to foot its maintenance bill as well. After all, now that she was officially running Sammy's political campaign, it would be hardly appropriate if she were to ever get caught flagging down a taxi or, God forbid, climbing into a *tro-tro* in her stilettos!

We also discovered during the campaign that Sammy had dispatched his relatives to perform the preliminary rites to engage his long-time girlfriend, the timing clearly calculated to coincide with his political plans. The colourful photos made the centrefold of a popular society magazine that Sweetie brought to show us when she came to visit us on Campus. We were confused, but she seemed to take it in stride.

'It's just a strategic move meant to bolster his image before the election. It was even I who suggested to him that he should perform the *knocking rights*,' she said.

'And what exactly is that supposed to mean? They've been together a while, so it would appear to be the next logical step,' Miyo said.

'Trust me, it's all for show. Sammy will *never* marry that woman and, deep down, she knows it.'

'Explain,' Miyo said.

Sweetie stood up and began pacing about rapidly, as if she were trying to make a difficult decision.

'I can't take it anymore,' she said.

'Sweetie Bediako, what's going on?' I said.

'If I don't tell you today, I will die.'

'Just say it!' Miyo and I shouted at the same time.

'Sammy can't — erh — perform. In the bedroom.'

'Hoh! Since when?' I asked.

'Since forever.'

'What!' Miyo almost stepped on my toes when she jumped up in shock.

I quickly shut the door. I looked intently into Sweetie's face. She was not being facetious.

'O my God!' I said.

'Yah.' She nodded. 'I've been sitting on this for a whole year, and he thinks I'm so naïve that I still haven't figured it out.'

'Talk, Sweetie,' Miyo said, and pulled her back onto the bed.

*

'It was during that rendezvous last year. And to think how I tortured myself with guilt before deciding to go away with him. Anyway, we get there and he checks us into this chalet — just unbelievably gorgeous!

We go to the pool and lounge about, although I can't swim. There's no need to break for lunch. An army of waiters keep patrolling with fruit, hors d'oeuvres, grilled meats, drinks — I've never seen anything like that. He seems genuinely determined that I should enjoy the experience; plus I have to keep cool and appear sophisticated, right? So I just play along; but all I can think about is what will happen once we get back to our chalet.

After a couple of hours of lazing in the sun on a full stomach, I badly want to go back to the chalet to change from the tight swimsuit and take a nap. But he doesn't seem to be in a hurry. He keeps looking around as if he's waiting for something else to happen. When it becomes obvious that he isn't yet ready to leave, I excuse myself and go back to the chalet.

I take a shower and lie on the bed, but I can't sleep — I keep expecting him to walk into the room at any moment. I swear an hour goes by.'

'Sweetie, are we also going to have to wait a whole hour before you tell us what happened?' I said.

She just dismissed me with a toss of her hand and continued.

'Anyway, after an hour, I make my way back to the pool, but he's no longer out there; so I work my way slowly through the lounge, looking to see if he's sitting in one of the alcoves. But I can't find him anywhere. I go out front — his vehicle is still standing where he parked it when we arrived; so, I decide to go back to the chalet to see if he returned. Our chalet is in the back, and instead of cutting through the middle of the compound, I slowly wind my way around the perimeter.

As I'm strolling along, enjoying more of the scenery, something suddenly catches my eye and I turn my head sharply to the left. And what do I see but Sammy Dompey popping out of one of the doorways. He looks around sneakily, and then he slinks away in the direction of our chalet without seeing me.

For a few seconds, I'm just frozen, not sure what to do next. And then, just as I turn to walk in the direction from which he appeared, the door opens again, another man comes out of the same chalet and starts coming toward me. I quickly step out of sight and watch him go by. He's extremely attractive — much younger than Sammy, closer to our age — very well built and highly groomed, tight black jeans and tee shirt hugging his fine, sculpted body. And reeking of cologne!

As if drawn by a magnet, I walk up to the stranger's chalet and knock loudly on the door. Nothing. I quickly take the shortest route back to the lobby. Scanning the setting, my eyes come to rest on the young man. He's sitting at one of the tables, pretending to be flicking through a magazine. I calmly walk his way and sit at the table across from his and wait.

In about two minutes, a group of men walks into the lobby — Americans, I think, all of different races. They split up and go around the lobby, each one stopping to sit for a moment with similarly well-groomed young men sitting in the alcoves, all with rippling muscles bursting out of tight clothes. There are a few young women too — all in tight clothes and wearing too much makeup. Then each pair walks out about thirty seconds apart.

As I'm taking all this in, one of these men suddenly comes and sits in front of me in the same manner and says to me, "Hey sugar, how much for one hour?" I shake my head in confusion. He profusely apologises and leaves. Then, I notice Sammy's acquaintance leaving with another man just as Sammy is entering the lobby. I stand and wave to attract Sammy's attention. Then I watch closely; but when he comes abreast of his acquaintance, you wouldn't have known that they had ever met each other.

"What happened to you? I thought you had abandoned me here," I say.

"I'm sorry about that. I met a colleague; we got carried away discussing business. Shall we go dancing?" He holds out his hand and helps me up, and we walk out hand in hand.

Finally, we go back to our chalet. He turns on the television and I beckon to him to join me in the shower, but he says to me, "why don't you go get started and I'll join you in a minute?" After standing in the shower for more than five minutes, I figure he's not coming; so, I finish and get out.

As I walk back into the bedroom, there he is, hanging up the telephone. He apologises and goes into the bathroom, where he spends an inordinate amount of time flossing, brushing, showering, and Lord knows what else.

Eventually, he comes out and lies beside me on the bed. I snuggle up to him, and he reciprocates, passionately kissing me and really getting into it. I didn't know that the human hand was capable of inflicting such passion during foreplay. The hour of judgment is finally upon us.'

'Sweetie Bediako — I beg, you're killing us softly,' Miyo said. 'Can we go past his hand and get to it? What really happened in the bed that night?'

'Nothing.'

'What do you mean?' I said.

'As in "no sex". He wanted to go up my one-way street, but I didn't allow him to. Once I turned down his freaky request, he immediately lost interest and his hand stopped working, as if his fingers had suddenly fallen off. And as for his main equipment, please! It might as well have been a museum relic — impressive to look at but serving no useful purpose at all.'

'Eish, Sweetie Bediako! What are you saying?' Miyo said.

'Let her finish,' I said, 'perhaps she misunderstood.'

'Oh, I *definitely* did not misunderstand.'

'Okay,' I said. 'You do know that there is a difference between "cannot" and "will not", don't you?'

'And today, *you're* the sex expert? Look, as for me, all I know is that the man crept out of bed and left our chalet each night, okay? He would vanish for about an hour and then creep back in, smelling as if he had just taken another shower. I always pretended to be asleep. We *never* did it — not even once — and he never made another attempt to go down my one-way street, or anywhere else on my body, for that matter.'

'But, what about the next three days? You were there Thursday, Friday, Saturday, Sunday.' Miyo stood up and counted out the days on her fingers.

'*Huu. Rien.* Nah-ting; just a whole lot of wining and dancing until past midnight, and then promptly falling asleep when we went back to the chalet. Oh, don't get me wrong, the wine was really nice; but what man do you know who would rather drink wine and dance than have sex with *me*?'

'Eish! So, you mean all this time?' Miyo asked.

'Yah. One whole year,' Sweetie nodded.

'Surely, he must have said something by now to explain his incapacity. Or?' I said.

'Yah. He said I'd made him wait so long that it had now affected him, that he had fallen in love with me, wanted to do right by me — this and that — all sorts of crap!'

'Eish, this is some major, award-winning *kwasiasem* oh!' Miyo said.

'No kidding! God help us women,' I said, raising my finger to heaven.

'So what are you going to do?' Miyo said.

'What does it look like I've been doing for the past year? Relaxing and going with the flow. He's in love with me and will do anything for me, right? Well, we shall soon see about that.'

'I can't believe you sat on this for an entire year, though; why didn't you just tell us?' I said.

'You have no idea how relieved I am to be finally letting it all out. I didn't want to hear, "Sweetie Bediako, I told you so"; but now, you know. You also know why I haven't yet broken up with Bronze.'

'As far as I'm concerned, you're not doing anything illegal,' Miyo said.

'That doesn't make it okay,' I said. 'Remember, *"The fact that a horse is crazy doesn't mean that its owner is also crazy."* Just be careful your perfect plan doesn't backfire, especially with Bronze coming into town. Or have you forgotten?'

Bronze had been gone a year already and now he was coming home on vacation, just as he had promised he would. He arrived a couple of weeks later, expecting to spend every second with Sweetie, but she was in the middle of running Sammy's campaign. The timing was just unfortunate for the long-distance lovers.

As if this weren't bad enough, it seemed that Sweetie had omitted to mention to her sugar daddy that she had a *real* boyfriend somewhere, or the fact that he was coming into town. She was operating with a clear conscience, knowing that because she had technically done nothing wrong, there was no need to rehearse her moves before she made them, nor was there any reason to explain them afterward.

So, when Bronze insisted on accompanying her to a campaign event just before he left, she threw aside her usual guile, only to later find herself awkwardly introducing the two men to each other.

'Mr Samuel Dompey, meet Dr Bronsford Anomar-Bilson,' she said, and then stood aside.

'Ah, Mr Dompey,' said Bronze, stretching out his hand, 'my girlfriend can't stop talking about all the positive changes you'll be bringing to South Aheme District. I've heard a lot about you.'

'You have? I wish I could say the same. So, Sweetie is your girlfriend, eh? Sweetie, how come you haven't introduced us until now?' Sammy said, enthusiastically shaking Bronze's hand.

'Well, I'm currently based in the U.S. I'm studying medicine there,' Bronze said.

'Oh, I see. In that case, we shall take very good care of your girl for you until you return home. You are a fortunate man, very fortunate indeed.' Sammy turned on the charm, jovially punching Bronze in the bicep and putting his arm around Sweetie's shoulders — just for two seconds.

Bronze went back to the U.S. and Sammy won the election by landslide. Sweetie never registered for the master's program.

'I will not be coming home this year,' Bronze told her the following year.

'Then let me come and visit you,' she said, but he told her to wait until Christmas.

'The timing is bad right now,' he said when Christmas came.

By then, she was calling him more than *he* was calling her, and half the time she was talking to his answering machine. The following summer, she couldn't get hold of him at all. She found out after the fact that he came home for a few weeks without her knowledge. She had travelled out of town with Sammy and his fiancée when Bronze came to town.

Her focus on Sammy's career was driving Bronze away, as far as we could tell, but she kept assuring us with the usual 'Don't worry, I know what I'm doing.'

And she truly seemed to — until the day she dialled Bronze's number and a woman picked up.

'Who are you?' Sweetie asked, to which the woman replied, 'I'm his *fiancée*; and who the hell are *you*?'

'His — just tell him it's his sister.'

It would be another four years before Bronze returned home with his American wife, the same one that he claimed he was going to marry just for immigration papers when he got on the phone and talked to Sweetie that day — that same day on which he later changed his telephone number and broke off all contact with Sweetie.

During those four years, Sammy firmly planted his feet on the political ladder. We watched in amazement as Sweetie assumed various highly visible roles in his career — from campaign manager, to spokesperson, to chief of staff — accompanying him to public events and appearing by his side in official photographs.

We gaped when her salary afforded her and her mother a two-storey house in Ahemekrom, complete with telephone line, red BMW, houseboy and cook. Sweetie also acquired a large storefront on *Oxford Street* and set up her mother there. Equipped with a dodge minivan and her own driver, Eno began trading in oriental laces and other expensive fabrics. Her days of pushing modest quantities of overripe seasonal foodstuffs were long over. Her daughter's economics degree was yielding serious dividends.

By now too, Sweetie had become fast friends with Sammy's fiancée Sheila, who was still in the picture, although a wedding date hadn't been set yet. Miyo and I remained baffled by the strange arrangement, but there seemed to be no logical reason to continue advising Sweetie against what was, quite frankly, one of the most lucrative career choices we had ever seen anyone make.

*

Now, it seemed that I had asked a pertinent question.

Miyo looked at Sweetie. 'Eheh? Aren't you going to update Shika?'

'Well, Sammy is being considered for a very important ministerial appointment.'

'Oh, fantastic!' I said. 'The rumours are true then. So, why the gloomy tone?'

'You'd think that this would be the perfect time for him to keep his personal drama under the radar, right?' Miyo said.

'But of course.' I looked at Sweetie's blank face. 'Well?'

'Do you know what my precious MP is about to do? He's about to ruin my life!'

'Why, what happened?'

'Sammy has dropped Sheila like yesterday's banana peel.'

'Hoh! How?' I leaned forward, almost hanging off the edge of my seat. 'Is this a joke?'

Miyo looked at Sweetie. They huddled closer to me.

'Sheila paid me a visit. Alone,' Sweetie continued. 'She parked outside the gate and sent the houseboy to get me. I was surprised, of course. I mean, she's never been to my house; I didn't even realise that she knew where I lived. I invited her in, but she refused to enter my house.'

'Eheh, eheh?' I waved my hand impatiently.

'Don't interrupt! She's just getting to the good part,' Miyo said. Apparently, she was already in on the scoop.

'Anyway, she stayed in her car and told me, "Ahuofeh Bediako, now that you've figured out how to solve Sammy's chronic problem, your true motives have come to light. You can stop pretending to be his chief of staff, you home wrecker!" I asked her what she was talking about, and she said that she and Sammy had had a fight the previous night. She'd asked him to tell her if and when they would ever sleep together so that she could try to have a child, or else stop wasting her time. And guess what he told her? He said, "If you think that you're wasting your time, then move on. After all, unlike Sweetie, you don't even have what it takes to be a suitable wife for a serious politician."'

'Ei!' I abandoned my lunch, which was stone cold by now.

Sweetie fished out her nail file from her Italian designer purse, leaned back and crossed her legs.

'Yah. Can you imagine? I've sacrificed a lot by allowing him to hide his secret behind this Don Juan façade at the expense of my reputation; but to *actually* use me as the excuse to get out of marrying Sheila, that's just cruel! She had some pretty serious expectations, which is why she stuck with him for this long. But she's been in denial all these years and would rather stay there than admit the truth to herself; I didn't even bother pointing out that he was lying. Besides, I need time to decide how *I'm* going to play this hand.'

'Has he himself said anything to you?' I asked.

'No, not a word; but if he thinks that I'm going to volunteer for a life sentence without so much as a conversation about it, then he really hasn't studied me well. After all, we've kept up this charade for over ten years; it was the perfect arrangement — perfect! Why couldn't he just give Sheila the usual excuse and leave things the way they were?'

Miyo sarcastically explained, 'Because, Sweetie dear, he's ambitious and he figured out long ago that it would be beneficial for him to marry an articulate, educated woman; that's the only thing he ever wanted from you. He played Sheila, obviously, but *you* didn't seriously think that you were the only genius with an agenda in this arrangement, did you?'

'Well, the other genius must be delusional if he thinks that he can outwit me. Pretending to be the other woman is one thing; but I never volunteered to become an actual *wife* in a sexless marriage.' Sweetie was quite agitated and gesturing wildly with the nail file as if it were a dagger.

Miyo looked at me and rolled her eyes. I shook my head and took a sip of my drink.

'So, what are you going to say if Sammy should propose? And what about Odum?' I didn't think that she was seriously going to entertain the thought of perpetuating this drama, but I asked anyway.

'Well, that's why we're discussing it now, isn't it? I don't know what I'm going to do; but I have to move fast and make sure that Odum is safe before I'm forced to make a decision. I need to have a serious discussion with Bronze.'

Miyo started sneaking glances at me. I knew that she would want us to analyse this latest development as soon as we should find ourselves alone.

'Hang in there, girl. We'll think of something,' Miyo said. Then she gave Sweetie a pat on her hand and prepared to leave. I looked at the time and also said my goodbyes.

As soon as I got home, Miyo rang.

I put her on speaker so that I could change my clothes while we talked. 'Eheh?' I said.

'Challey! Sweetie is really losing it; is she seriously going to consider marrying this man?'

'I know, I can't believe what I just heard either. I really don't get it. Why didn't she walk away long before it came to this?'

'Well, power is a drug and she's hopelessly hooked. She's been calling the shots all these years, but now the rules are about to change. I warned her when she reached the six-year mark to cut and run; after all, she had made quite a fortune from this arrangement by then.' Miyo was very rational, down to earth, and completely unsympathetic to Sweetie's current predicament.

At this point, I was more concerned about Sweetie's little brother, Odum, than anything else.

'I hope that Bronze can at least do something about Odum,' I said. But I could not shake off the bad feeling.

THREE

There are certain days that will stand out forever, no matter what else happens in one's life. At thirty-one years old, I had already experienced more than my fair share of such days, but I could still count them all on one hand. The twenty-seventh of May 1995 was one of those.

I received a voice message from Sweetie the night before that said: *Mawusi-Shika, this is urgent. Stay home tomorrow afternoon. Miyo and I are coming to see you.*

Good, I thought, she has kept her promise to look into Sefa's list of medications and she's coming to discuss her findings.

*

It's a very busy Saturday morning. I have come to Sefa's early so that I can help him sort and box his clothes, those expensive suits and custom outfits that he used to wear before he fell ill and started looking like a scarecrow in them.

While I'm sorting, he supervises. I hold up an item and mention a name, and he either nods in agreement or corrects me. Other than that, he is strangely quiet — just sitting on the bed, leaning back and not saying much. I keep looking over in concern, but nothing seems amiss.

When we have finished, I sit crossed legged on the floor and begin stuffing bags and boxes, labelling them with the names of who will be getting what after I have had them laundered.

All of a sudden, he sits bolt upright and pats the bed. He is strangely calm, almost robotic.

'Sit, Shishi. Please.'

O God, here it comes, the farewell speech. I rush to his side.

'What is it, Sefa?'

'I have to really talk to you, Shishi. I've been trying to find the words all this time to prepare you for today, but I realise that there is nothing I can say that will soften what I have to tell you; and besides, I don't think there will be another chance.'

I'm still standing, ready to flee if I have to. He pats the bed again.

'Sit. Please? Last night I had a dream in which I was turning in my grave unable to rest because I had not parted from you in good standing. I cannot undo my dying, but I would like to have a good rest when I get there — wherever I'm going. Look at me, Shishi.'

I sit on the edge of the bed and hold his hand, staring intently into his twisted face.

'Shishi, I'm dying from a cancerous brain tumour, yes; but that's not all. Shishi… Shishi, I have AIDS.' He shuts his eyes and a tear falls from the corner of his right eye as he releases this information, as if the process has inflicted torture on his soul.

I continue to stare into his face; my breathing does not change. In fact, I cannot tell if I'm breathing at all. I sit calmly in stunned silence.

He lets out his breath slowly through his lips, opens his eyes and holds my gaze.

'Shishi, Shishi! Are you all right? Shishi!' I feel his hand patting my cheek firmly; he looks really concerned.

It takes a full minute or more for the magnitude of his announcement to penetrate my consciousness.

'You mean, as in HIV AIDS?' I try to stress the syllables one by one in my croaky voice, as if there's any other way to say it.

'You did not hear wrong. Forgive me, Shishi. I just couldn't figure out how to tell you.'

'But your people in Amsterdam — they know?' The oxygen is flowing again to my brain; I can think.

He nods.

'And the office here?' My breathing is picking up pace.

He nods again.

'So, all these people have known all this time? And you're *now* telling me?' By this time, I'm gasping.

'I have not told anyone else. For sure, dadaa does not know, and I'm begging you to keep this from her. All I have is you. Shishi, please — I just couldn't find the right time to tell you.'

Now I can feel the bile rising. It's starting from my gut and working its way upward, festering in my chest.

'What about Cynthia, does she have it too? Did she give it to you, or have you given it to her? Ei, Sefa! When exactly were you planning to tell me?' The questions are rolling out at a hundred words per second, competing with my heartbeat. 'O God! I think I'm going to be sick.' I run through the bathroom door and reach the loo, just as the bile climbs up my throat and spills out of my mouth.

I have already come to terms with the fact that he is going to die, but I could never have imagined worse news than that. AIDS? But that's a foreign disease! You hardly hear people talking about it, other than on television — the media campaigns, the documentaries. Every now and then, you might hear of someone who knew someone else that *you* didn't know, who was *suspected* of having it — but not Sefa. O God no, not our Sefa!

The tears will not stop flowing. I sit on the loo for several minutes, just sobbing. After I'm able to breathe again, I rinse my mouth and creep back in. My knees feel like rubber. I cannot look at him. I just grab my purse and keys.

'Need air,' is all I manage to blubber.

'Shishi! Shishi!' He is calling out to me, reaching for me; but I must flee the oppressive atmosphere. I stumble into my car and back out as fast as I can.

Drive! Drive! That's all I can think. No destination in mind. Just need to keep moving.

I drive around in a daze for several minutes and then head home. I'm so dizzy that I can barely get out of the car. I stagger to the kitchen and pour myself a glass of water; and then I go into my bedroom and draw the curtains.

Just get under the covers, that'll stop the shakes, I convince myself.

I lie there quietly, floating in and out of awareness. My tears are soaking into the pillow without any instigation from me. From far away, my phone is ringing persistently. But it is of no consequence.

*

Miyo and Sweetie came and found me there like that. They arrived ahead of schedule because Miyo had received a call from Sefa that said: Find Shishi urgently. She badly needs you.

'Shika! Shika!' Miyo shook me and peeled the covers off.

'My dear, are you okay? You left your keys in the lock.' Sweetie was speaking to me gently; she was feeling my neck and forehead, wiping tears from my cheek.

I took one look at them and started sobbing again.

Sweetie gently placed my head on her shoulder. Miyo rubbed my back. They did not utter a word until I finished sobbing.

'You found out, eh?' Miyo asked me bluntly, 'Sefa finally told you the truth?'

I nodded and smiled weakly.

'That's what we were coming here to tell you,' Sweetie said. 'Bronze just took one look at the list you sent and recognised the antiretroviral drugs; he knew at once. I was wondering how to face you by myself with this horrible news when Miyo called to say that Sefa had just spoken to her. We both headed out at once.'

I nodded again.

'Who is there with him now?' Miyo was frowning; she was concerned for *him*.

'Just the housekeeper and the maid,' I said.

'That can't be good. Why don't I drive over there quickly, check on him and come back.' She left.

Then Sweetie prepared a bucket of scalding water and gave me a hot towel massage. When she was done, she rubbed me down with raw Shea butter. I ached all over as if I had been in a boxing match.

'Don't worry,' she said when I winced under her firm hand, 'by the time you take your next bath, it would have done its job.'

My head was still throbbing, but I had a guest. I had to get up and be polite, so I reluctantly dragged myself out of bed and threw on my dressing gown.

Sweetie had taken over my kitchen.

'What are we having for lunch?' she called out from the depths of the fridge. 'Leftover *light soup*? Oh, Mawusi-Shika Amenyo!'

'There's some *fufu* and fresh *palm nut soup* at the other house; I forgot to bring it.'

'Relax, I'll take care of it,' she said; then she called Miyo. She told her to get the dish from Emilia and bring it along. But Miyo wanted to spend more time with Sefa. 'She says she will ask Emilia to send the food thru Martha.'

She made us tea while we waited for the meal. Five minutes later, Martha arrived, gingerly balancing the basket of food on her head.

After lunch, Sweetie quickly got to the crux of the matter.

'I'm quite concerned about your emotional state, Mawusi-Shika Amenyo. What are you going to do about Sefa's care in light of this new information?'

'I can't believe he kept this from me.'

'Well, my dear, you're going to have to get your head out of the clouds quickly, okay? Regardless of what is going on with Sefa, you need to take care of *you* — physically and emotionally. Have you seen yourself in the mirror lately? I mean, just look at your nails! And I bet it's been over a month since you went and had your hair done. Half the time, in the middle of a conversation, your mind is wandering; and now, you've developed this God-complex too. Do you think you can be a one-woman hospital? Get real, Mawusi-Shika! Once he runs out of the meds, it's going to be a different ballgame.'

'But I thought you were going to get him some more.'

'I told Bronze everything, about the brain cancer and all the other symptoms. Apparently getting more HIV drugs is the least of your problems. As long as Sefa continues taking them, they're going to do what they're supposed to do; and yes, Bronze can arrange for Sefa to get some more privately. Look, you're going to have to talk to Bronze yourself at some point. He's even willing to come to the house because I told him that Sefa was practically bedridden.'

This was really going nowhere. I just shook my head and held my forehead.

'I'll have to talk to Sefa first, I can't think right now,' I said.

'You should talk, and not just to him. This really ought to be a family burden, not yours alone; but I get it, it's *his* secret to tell. So maybe the two of you should discuss it quickly and decide how it should be handled. Mawusi-Shika, look, *you're* the preacher's granddaughter; better start praying oh! As for this one, it's only God who can give you the wisdom you need to go through it.'

'I know, I know.'

'I almost forgot. Here,' she said, and dragged a box across the floor.

'Thanks, but what's all this?' I rummaged through the odd assortment. The box was full of latex gloves, surgical masks and all sorts of sanitising agents.

'Start using these, please! And find a way to have the servants also use them.'

'Oh, how? Isn't that a bit drastic?' I recoiled at her suggestion. 'How will it make Sefa feel?'

'Wait! Let me understand this, Mawusi-Shika Amenyo — so, you're worried about hurting *his* feelings, at the expense of your health? How will *he* feel — is that what you're asking me? Really?

Nonsense! I know that he's your flesh and blood, but don't you think he could at least have told you earlier, since *you're* the one who's stuck here taking care of him? This is potentially life threatening for you, hardly the time to be cradling his ego and being politically correct. Wipe your tears and put on your fighting shoes, my dear. You're going to have to be strong to get through this.'

Sweetie was ruthless; but we had never shared a moment of dishonesty, and we weren't about to start now. In fact, I had always depended on her for the truth, and so her hard talk was just the kind of therapy my soul badly needed. I sat holding up my head a little longer, trying to think my way out of this nightmare.

After a few more minutes of this brutal honesty, she said she had to run.

'I have to go pick up Odum from karate. Are you going to be okay? Miyo should be coming back soon. Be strong, my dear. Now is the time to stand and fight. You can lick your wounds and weep after it's all over.'

After she left, I curled up in the armchair and hugged myself. I contemplated my situation and realised just how pitiful it was:

At least Sweetie has Odum to live for, not to mention having two men fighting over her, neither of whom she wants. Miyo does not need any man, or want any children, or require social validation; she's incapable of feeling sexual passion, and finds fulfilment in trotting across the globe, fighting other peoples battles for them.

Yet, here I am, beautiful, accomplished, nurturing, and what do I have? None of the things I want or need. All that I ever had, I have lost — my father and my mother, my brother Kobla who is as good as dead to me, and now Sefa. I'm just on the verge of sacrificing what little career I've built, for the sake of a loved one that I'm going to lose; and all for what? So that I can win the award for 'perfect specimen of humanity' or receive a crown of glory in the sweet by-and-by?

The immensity of the past three months is crushing my spirit as though it should squeeze out my very soul. My tailbone is firmly pressed against the floor of a dirt pit and there is no lower plateau to sink to. I, Mawusi-Shika Amenyo, am nobody, I have nothing, and I have no power over my circumstances.

'I give up,' I whispered into my void, shaking from this revelation. It felt necessary to be still and not think, so I stayed curled up in the chair and simply allowed myself to breathe.

An hour-and-half went by. Gradually, the heaviness dissipated and I was left with a feeling of certainty that the next move I made would be significant in determining the direction in which my life should go from that moment forward. I had arrived at a major crossroads.

I reached for my phone, intending to call Miyo and leave her a voice message, but discovered that she had left me one: *Shika, I think you need some breathing space. Consider stepping away for a day to refocus your thoughts. Sef will be fine. Let me know if you want to crash at my place.*

I smiled. No need to call back. I was going to be just fine.

Feeling very light on my feet, I turned on the music and hummed along. I opened my address book and zigzagged my finger down the C-list until I found what I was looking for: Charbonneau, JM. Calabar. I called him.

'I have just returned from Abuja, so it's fortunate that you've called now.' I could hear from his tone that he was pleased to hear my voice, and he confirmed it by telling me so.

Although he had sent me a postcard and telephoned me twice since he left on this trip, *I* had never called him. The singularity of this occurrence was not lost on either of us.

'Is everything okay? Bullet...?'

I updated him on Sefa's state of health. Although I was trying to sound optimistic, Jean knew me well. He had always been sensitive to my unspoken feelings.

'What is it, Shika? I know that you just described a good week; but there's more, and it's bad, no?'

How could I tell him the whole truth, all the things that had transpired since he'd been gone? It was a struggle to keep my voice from cracking, but I was *not* going to break down.

So, I only told him half the story: 'Sefa has run out of his radiation treatments and the time they bought him; it's just a matter of weeks now.'

I also confessed that I was feeling overwhelmed. I couldn't have admitted this to anyone else, as I was quite sure that it would be have been misconstrued as self-centredness or ungraciousness on my part; but Jean understood my need to express such feelings. He tried to do what he could over the phone, but I could hear the helplessness in his voice.

'I'm supposed to be done in another three weeks. I was going to go through Lomé, as you know. I would ask you to take a weekend off to come and meet me there, but I know you, Shika — you will not leave Bullet's side right now; so I'm going to postpone that little holiday and return to Accra as soon as I'm done here.'

'Don't be silly, Jean.' I begged him not to give up his visit with his friends, protested that I was old enough to take care of myself.

But he insisted, even tried to capitalise on this sacrifice.

'Well, you should know by now, for you I will do anything. I'm actually touched that I was the one you called all the way out here when you were feeling like this. Maybe if I give up this visit this time, you will accompany me there soon, yes?'

We bantered back and forth for several more minutes, but he wasn't satisfied until he had made me laugh.

'Perhaps you will even pick me up from the airport? I'll let you know the details once I confirm the date and time. That would be really sweet of you.'

'Well, I don't know about that.'

'Shika Amenyo, are you running away from me again? I promise, I will not grab your butt in public, kiss you vigorously up and down the arm, loudly profess in a foreign language my undying love for you, or do anything else that would make people stare and point the finger.'

Ah, this man knows me so well, I thought. I couldn't stop giggling. He had me cornered.

'Okay, Jean, I'll pick you up when you return. Happy now?'

He also made me a promise before hanging up, 'Chérie, I will speak to you every night until I return.'

*

For the first time in three months, I slept through the night. In the morning, I drove to church. It had been a long time since I attended service. I went, not because I was looking to fill some void. I just needed to be plugged in, to subject myself to the discipline of that environment in order to retain a sense of control; and only after that was I able to drive back to Sefa's.

I found him by the back gate, sitting in the wheelchair. He was looking out to sea, as if he had an appointment to keep with a merchant ship. He turned toward me as I approached, searching my face eagerly, like a child looking for reassurance after a scolding.

I smiled at him and squeezed his shoulder.

'You look nice,' he said. 'Church?'

I nodded. I leaned against the wall.

'Did you sleep well?' I asked.

'I did okay. It was rather pleasant having Miyo over yesterday. We had so much to catch up on. I shouldn't have shut her out for this long. She stayed until bedtime, you know?'

His eyes were gleaming. He appeared to have resolved some issues within himself.

My heart was overflowing. I could afford to be generous again. I reached over and patted his shoulder.

'We have some planning to do,' I said.

He nodded.

We went back indoors. Martha had set the table for two as usual — Emilia always cooked enough to include me; but I unwrapped the *waakye* and *wele* that I had brought along and settled down to eat.

This put a gleam in Sefa's eyes. I knew what he was thinking but I didn't want to lose my appetite, so I tried not to focus on it. He had often teased me that if I ever got squashed, a gooey stuffing of waakye would seep out of me, for sure.

When we were done, I sat on the leather cushion at his feet.

'Shishi,' he said, reaching down and placing his hand on my head, 'I'm truly sorry that I hurt you, of all people. I don't want you to think for a minute that I've taken you for granted. It has just been a confusing time for me, and although that is no excuse, keeping it bottled up inside was the only way I could react to what I was going through. I did not want my family to shun me, could not bear the thought that you might recoil if you found out — '

'Hush, Sefa!' I patted his hand. 'I'm not going anywhere. Let's stay focused and see this thing through, okay? If you're not up to talking about it, we don't have to discuss it now. We can just set some dates and fill in little details every day until we have a plan.'

'No, Shishi, we must talk now. I will stop if I need to. First of all, you are fine, you can't catch it from me by taking care of me or anything like that,' he said matter-of-factly.

'I know.'

Even after Sweetie's dramatic donation of the disinfectants yesterday, I had not for a second entertained the notion that Sefa could be so careless as to even inadvertently endanger the lives of the people who were so selflessly caring for him.

But this was 1995. To me, this blight did not yet have a personal face —
I had never even heard of anyone who had been diagnosed with it. If he
hadn't told me, I could not have guessed. It would never have crossed my
mind that this curse could land on his doorstep.

Now, several small details that had not made sense before confirmed
what those of us close to him already knew — that Sefa was a meticulous
and responsible man. I understood why he himself had spent a fortune
keeping his house well stocked with the same types of products that were
in Sweetie's well-intended box.

At the time, we had assumed that he was merely protecting his fragile
constitution from our germs, which did make sense too. After all, what did
we know about cancer? But now, it was clear that those precautions had
been intended to protect not just him, but everybody around him as well.

'So how long have you known?' I said. I was ready to listen. It was
going to be a long afternoon.

*

'Soon after I returned to Europe last year, I realised that the headaches I'd
been experiencing for over a year had suddenly become really unbearable.
I was losing my balance and having problems sleeping. When I went to
the company clinic, they recommended that I go for a brain scan. The scan
revealed a large-sized mass; it was so embedded within the surrounding
tissue and blood vessels that operating wasn't even an option. You can
imagine my shock. But it was nothing compared to what was coming.

They kept me in the hospital and immediately ran more tests, including
routine blood work to prepare me for a brain biopsy. When the test results
came back, the doctor came to my room, accompanied by a woman that he
introduced as the psychologist. He explained that the shrink needed to
administer a questionnaire. "This is routine," he said.

The shrink then began to ask me very probing questions about my
health, social activities, and habits — in effect, everything I had ever felt in
my body, done with it, or put into it — over the past three years or even
longer, if I could remember. As soon as she began to dig further into my

past, I realised that this was far from routine. At that point, I asked them what was going on.

"A couple of the tests we ran have come back positive for the HIV virus," the doctor said.

I just stared at him as he explained that the tumour in my brain was an opportunistic illness. And even though I had shown no signs of infection, the HIV virus had been steadily multiplying to the point where it had now damaged my immune system badly enough for me to develop the tumour, as well as Hepatitis; it was also responsible for the skin problems I'd been having and the sores in my mouth. In fact, my T-cell count was so low that it was a wonder I didn't have any other illnesses, he said.

This was all gibberish to me, of course, but what it meant was that I'd been carrying the virus undiagnosed for a while; at least two years.

I immediately thought of Cynthia. She'd always been absolutely fine, not a cold or cough since I'd known her. When we began seriously dating and decided to become intimate, we got carried away the first few weeks; but then commonsense prevailed, and we began using protection so that she wouldn't get pregnant.'

'Sefa,' I interrupted him, 'so, what about Cynthia?'

The arduous task of caring for him had consumed all my focus and I had not had time to think about her all these months. Looking back on it now, it *had* seemed strange that she herself had never attempted to contact Sefa. In fact, she appeared to have vanished from town. I was discovering that there was more to that chapter of the story.

'Cynthia? Hm.' He paused as if he had to think for a minute before speaking about her. 'Shishi, I do not know her status.'

'So, what you're saying is that she does not know? Didn't you tell her so that she could also go and get tested?' My volume went up a tad.

'Calm down, hear me out. That's why I'm opening up to you now. Can you imagine going through this torture, not knowing whom to discuss it with, and all the complicated reasoning that goes with it?'

'Sorry — go on, go on!'

'In any case, Cynthia does know; I had to tell her at once. I begged the doctors to release me, as I urgently needed to travel back home to break the news to my fiancée. But that was out of the question, of course. They did the biopsy and it confirmed the worst — the tumour was malignant. The diagnosis was primary lymphoma of the brain. They immediately booked me for several rounds of low-dose radiotherapy, the only treatment they were willing to even attempt. It was only after I underwent these that they released me from the hospital. I even booked my trip while I was still in the hospital.

As soon as I arrived home from the airport that day, I sat Cynthia down and broke the news to her. But she refused to go and get tested. In fact, she responded quite hysterically, accusing me of cheating on her, and thanking God that we had been using protection all this time. I tried to reason with her. I told her that the doctor had said that she could possibly be carrying the virus and yet show no signs, but she was adamant: "I'm not going to get any test done, Sefa, because I *know* that *I* don't have anything."

She began throwing her things into her suitcases. I begged her to stay so that we could figure it out together, but she told me that it was best if we broke off our engagement at once. I left it up to her to decide what to tell her relatives.

I flew back to Europe to continue my regimen of radiation and anti-retroviral therapy, and also to begin undergoing psychological counselling. I also had to tell my employers at once.

After being on the meds for a while, my various infections and ailments subsided, and the doctor said that my T-cell count was now normal. My status would remain stable as long as I continued taking my meds. And then this past January, after my usual battery of tests, I got hit with the dreaded news — the radiation treatments were pointless because now there were more tumours. The cancer had also metastasised.

Shishi, it's over. I *am* going to die. Please protect my mother from ridicule, that's all I ask. You know how people will react if the truth were to ever come out.'

'Don't even think about that, Sef. I will not allow us to be put to shame.' I was crying again, frustrated at how I felt, yet unable to stop it. 'Let me bring you some herbal tea, your mouth must be dry.'

All I could do was to stare at my sad reflection in the kitchen window and try to make sense of this nightmare as I waited for the water to boil...

It has been a very stressful month so far. He has spent every breathing moment talking, trying to hang on to all his memories and obsessing over missing important details. I know now that he has told me everything there is to tell. If anything else remains, then it will have to be left hidden because his memory has begun playing tricks on him, and soon there will be nothing left of the past.

Now, everything I do is going to be motivated by the urgent need to help him put his house in order. It's no use pretending anymore that he will have time to do so later. I have come to terms with the fact that I will be quitting my job in two weeks. He is fighting a losing battle, and although no amount of vigilance on my part is sufficient to alleviate his torment, the time has come for me to drop everything and focus entirely on his care.

He has sworn not to try anything that might only serve to prolong his pain and delay his departure, but that is a selfish stance and not entirely his call to make. What about those of us who love him and want to hang on to him a little longer? What about his mother who has nothing to live for besides him?

Surely, there is some combination of herbs somewhere, in some grove in one of our jungles, which holds the secret to purified blood and longevity? Some prophet somewhere who has the healing touch needed to rid his body of the tumours? Perhaps one of Efo's medicine men will come through for us after all?

The kettle whistled, rudely interrupting my thoughts. I wiped my eyes and ran my hand across my eyebrows to straighten them. Then I brought him his herbal tea, sat on a cushion at his feet and opened my planner. It was time to make some hard decisions.

FOUR

We gave ourselves until the end of July to leave for Togapeme, so I had to find a way to squeeze in everything that Sefa needed done before we left town. Gone were the days when I could just take off on a whim to indulge in some random moment of camaraderie. It was as if I had just given birth to a grown man.

The more I witnessed the painful changes that marked his decline, the more vigilantly I watched to keep my own soul afloat. I clung fast to those symbols and rituals that buttressed my sense of balance, lest in my effort to save him from drowning, I myself should become completely overwhelmed by his desperate state.

And as soon as I began having daily chats with Jean, life acquired a new attractiveness to me. I began to care more about my own feelings; I spent more time taking care of my body, and invested more effort into maintaining my vitality. I chopped my life up and neatly arranged its segments into set timeslots, being careful to allot adequate amounts of time to spend with my friends. They kept me focused and held me accountable for the commitment I had made to myself to stay above the fray.

But this weekend, it was going to be Miyo's turn for some attention from me. Her birthday had fallen during the week, so her mother was making dinner that Saturday. I hadn't seen Auntie Tati in several months by this time.

*

Tatyana Mensah was a vibrant woman — very versatile and industrious — and funny as hell! She was born in Tiraspol in the USSR, and had met Tawiah Mensah in Moscow, while he was on a Soviet scholarship at the university where they were both engineering students. They got married and she moved to Ghana with him when they were done with their studies.

When they arrived, they stayed with his relatives in the family house for a few years, and she had survived the experience — much to the befuddlement of every woman that had ever had to perform this suicidal stunt.

Mrs Mensah insisted on being addressed by her first name, but it was a mark of our acceptance of her as one of us for people to precede it with the customary, deferential 'auntie' or refer to her as 'Miyo mami.' Funnily enough, her kids referred to her as 'Tati'.

Tatyana had really assimilated into our culture. She spoke three indigenous languages fluently, with the correct accents and inflections, in addition to her native Romanian and Russian. It was only when she spoke English that you detected her Eastern European accent.

She knew more about our history and traditions than did most of the traditional rulers, and had been involved in more local business ventures than anyone I'd ever met. She had even sold *kenkey* before, I heard!

'She cooked it herself,' Miyo told me. 'People would line up in front of our family house; some even drove all the way there and parked their cars bumper-to-bumper, just to buy Tati's kenkey. Of course, half of them came just to see the white woman with a child tied on her back street vending; but it was good for business and Tati really milked the publicity while it lasted.'

Her husband, Tawiah Mensah, hailed from that long line of macho men who needed to establish their superiority over their womenfolk by grinding them into the dirt. Such men didn't even have to think of their behaviour — it was second nature; and everybody around them validated their being that way by going with the flow instead of holding them to a higher standard.

He treated Tatyana as if she were just some common woman that he had picked up from a street corner, subjecting her to an assortment of indignities that were, alas, all too familiar to women from around these parts — affairs galore, a *pikinabodo* or two on the side over the years, no respect whatsoever. His behaviour, as expected, went unchallenged, as if it were written into the marriage contract.

Over the years, Tatyana had had to develop a reputation as a tough bitch in order to set some boundaries. I heard that any floozies who had ever had the temerity to telephone her home and ask for her husband never called again. Nobody knew what exactly it was that she said to those dung beetles, but whatever picture it painted was enough to deter them from completely overrunning her life.

'Don't worry; she won't call here again. I had a chat with her,' she would declare after any such encounter with one of her husband's strumpets; and then that laugh. Tatyana was a blast!

Yet, behind that vivacious façade, there was an undercurrent of misery only detectable to those of us in their inner circle. Her husband was also a violent man prone to fits of uncontrolled rage directed at his wife and three daughters.

From what Miyo confided to me over the years, I gathered that the emotional abuse had escalated gradually and turned physical after her mother got pregnant the last time. And all this inflicted by a man who didn't even drink alcohol! For sure, he was mentally unstable, if you ask me.

Tatyana suffered an eight-month long nightmare before undergoing a premature delivery. As it turned out, she had been carrying twin boys. One was stillborn; Oko survived.

Once Oko was born, Tawiah Mensah began spending more time away from home, supposedly consulting with out-of-town clients. He was an engineer, and really milked the 'I'm going on trek' excuse to the max. But everybody knew that he was running the streets like a common fowl, indiscriminately dropping his hot shit every two or three steps. He made no attempt to pretend that he respected his wife or cared what his kids thought.

'He would be gone for days at a time, then strut back in whenever he pleased, and pick up right where he'd left off, without skipping a beat. And nobody — least of all, my mother — held him to account,' Miyo told me.

Miyo was twelve and getting ready to go away to boarding school when Oko was born. She arrived at Caftak a very cautious and reserved kid, emotionally inaccessible, unwilling or unable to open up to anyone, and seemingly unmoved by the novelty of the boarding school experience. All she did was bury her head in her books. I was the first friend she made, and I've remained her closest friend all these years.

Tatyana had known me since forever. She thought that I was a good influence on her daughter, and had told me as much many years ago: 'I like you, Shika, you have your head in the right place. Miyo is very lucky to have you as her friend.' I must have been fourteen or so when she made this declaration.

I remember how everybody in the house would walk about on eggshells whenever I went to visit them in their home. Tawiah Mensah was very charming at first, but after several visits, when I had become a familiar face, he let down his guard and proceeded with bullying them in my presence.

This was foreign to me. I had never before heard a man address his wife and kids like livestock. The first time I witnessed him barking an order at his wife, I became so upset that I rushed off in confusion to the ladies' room, where I sat on the covered loo for the longest time until Miyo followed me there, profusely apologising and explaining away his behaviour.

'Please don't leave, Shika.' She sat on the floor at my feet, sobbing and begging me not to tell anyone.

That sealed our friendship. After all, what was I going to do? Run away and never come back? That was the first time I saw her cry, and I never saw her shed another tear in the twenty years that followed.

Really confusing to me though, was the fact that Tatyana was a foreign national. I remember asking, even at that young age, 'Why doesn't she simply hop onto the next plane and go back to her country?' To think that she was a *white* woman to boot! And *we* thought that *they* had it better than the rest of us. I knew right then that I would never forsake Miyo.

Everybody needs someone, and boy did they need God Himself to come down the side of this mountain!

*

Auntie Tati almost knocked the breath out of my lungs with her mama-bear hug. She was a well-built woman, stood about five-nine, every muscle exuding life.

'Ah, Shika! Let me look at you again. How's Bullet coming along? And your aunt?'

'He's actually doing well; he sends greetings. Tassie just went back to the village after paying us a visit. I told her that I'd be seeing you today and she said to say hello.'

What a refreshing change it was to have dinner with Auntie Tati! She liked to entertain us with tales of the antics her husband had pulled over the years, trying to balance his numerous affairs. It had been a long time since I enjoyed such whooping laughter and loud conversation while eating a delicious meal. It was just like old times.

'Eat, Shika,' she kept urging, 'You look as if you're the one who's been sick!'

'Mm, Auntie Tati, your meat pies are getting better over time, I swear. This is really amazing; you must give me your updated recipe.'

'Hm, I became an expert overnight ages ago when I had to suddenly stop buying them from the corner bakery.'

'Why, what happened?'

'Miyo never told you about the meat pie *ashawo*? Tell her, Miyo.'

'After my father had the affair with the first housekeeper and Tati fired her,' Miyo said, 'he started screwing the daughter of the woman who ran the neighbourhood bakery down the street.'

'Hoh! You've got to be kidding! He stooped that low?' I said.

'Oh yes,' Tati said, 'haven't you heard of Tawiah Mensah's affinity for the gutter? If it has two legs and crawls in the sewer, he will chase it. I used to order pastries from that bakery every week for two years until the day I found out.'

'Ei! They could have poisoned you and your children oh, and nobody would have been any the wiser!'

'Hm, are you telling me? Miyo, *boss* her what happened.'

'That day, as Tati got out of the car and approached the shop, she heard the woman yell out to her daughter in Ga, "Adokor, here comes your lover's wife with her angular *tin-cutter* jawline and chunky legs. What did he even see in her that convinced him to marry her?" to which the daughter quickly responded, "Careful, mother! He told me that she understands our language." Tati was stuck for a second, but she did walk into the shop, and picked up that last order.'

Miyo then looked at her mother and gave her the cue to finish the story.

'And then, instead of paying them,' Tati said, 'I snapped my fingers and sweetly told the girl in Ga, "Hey, ashawo, when my husband comes to sleep with you next time, why don't you add the cost of this order to your fee." And that was the last time I bought anything from them.'

'Eish! Auntie Tati the Great! O my goodness!'

'I know, right? And that night, guess what I served him for dinner? Two meat pies, two sausage rolls, two scones — all arranged nicely on the plate and accompanied by two glasses of water. He sat at the table confused and asked me, "Hey, Tatyana, what the hell is this?" and I said to him, "Why, Tawiah, it's the food you've been paying for — *two-two*, just the way you like it." Shika, you should have seen his face.'

I laughed so hard that I fell out of my chair and spilt my drink. Eating pastries was definitely going to take on a whole new meaning after this visit.

Miyo pulled me up from the floor. She looked at her mother for a moment and said, 'Today, we're able to laugh over all this, but it was real hell back then.'

Tati smiled and patted her hand. She said something to her in her language.

Suddenly, the mirth was gone and there was a lump in my throat.

I couldn't even remember the last time I actually saw Uncle Tawiah. He was never there any more. Inevitably, there'd been rumours of him having kids out there. He had to have had at least eight over the past twenty years, if the whispers were anything to go by. And *still*, his wife stayed.

As always, I wondered why Tati stayed, since she had been self-sufficient for years. And then I remembered: she was still caring for her youngest, now twenty.

'Where's Oko?' I asked, looking about expectantly. 'He hasn't come out since I got here.'

'Today you must go to his room to see him, he is feeling not so good, and trying to pick a fight with me all day. He gets like that when he misses his father. He will be back from trek, maybe tomorrow, I already told him; but no, still we fight. Maybe you will cheer him up when you see him? Go on, you know the way; nothing has changed.'

I went upstairs to see Oko. He was watching cartoons, leaning back in bed with his hands folded across his chest, and scowling as if there were some palaver between him and the figures running across the screen.

Every time I saw him, I tried to picture him with the maturity level of my cousin Emekor, who was around the same age as he, and I always had to swallow the overwhelming sadness I felt over the apparent fruitlessness of his existence.

I used to feel even worse for him and treat him differently, but once I'd hung around them long enough, I learnt to stop thinking of him as mentally handicapped and instead as a regular kid of whatever age bracket he fell into whenever we met. It usually required about five minutes with him to be able to place his age and then adjust my interaction with him accordingly.

Right now, we were at maybe four years old. Not so bad, considering what I knew it could be. I tried to give him a high-five but he made rude noises and turned away.

'Well, in that case you don't have to see the pictures of Napo that I promised to bring you last time; besides, I will be leaving soon and not be back here for a while. Bye!' I left him to his cartoons and went back downstairs.

Three minutes later we heard the door creaking upstairs. He stood on the landing, weighing his options, I guess. In another minute he started shuffling down the stairs reluctantly. I didn't turn around when he came and stood behind my chair, breathing down on my head and covering my eyes with his large, sweaty hands.

'Hi Shika, you here.' We all laughed as he gave me my high-five in exchange for the pictures of Napo.

*

Oko Mensah was a strapping young man; must have stood about six-one, barefooted — a child in a giant's body.

One day, when he was six years old, his father had beaten up his mother again, even more brutally than usual, until she'd passed out. The two older girls were away at school. Ten-year-old Shayo ran to fetch the next-door neighbours, who came to intervene by carting the near-unconscious Tatyana away to their house; but she refused to let them call the authorities.

The neighbours kept her in their home for several hours until later that night when her husband drove away to his mistress. Then she snuck back home, where she found Shayo still hiding in the bathroom with Oko.

Something changed that day. That was the last time Tawiah hit Tatyana. And that was also the last time Oko functioned normally. He was so traumatised that he did not speak for weeks. And when he finally started opening up, his communication skills were diminished. He was barely coherent, and over the months that followed, he regressed further into childhood, retreating deeper into a world of his own. His mother pulled him out of school and began teaching him at home.

A lot changed that day. Yet still, Tatyana stayed.

What with their father's demons and their mother's determination to see that none of them ever had to depend on any man, I often wondered if any of the girls would ever marry.

Manye, the one after Miyo, left the country right after A-levels and never returned. She settled in Moscow, and had a fairly successful career as a model in Europe, but she had stuck to her vow: 'The next time I return to Ghana will be to attend my father's funeral, if for no other reason other than to verify that he is in fact dead.'

Shayo, the third girl, had stayed in Ghana. She had barely managed to graduate from secondary school by the skin of her teeth; yet now, she was the public face of their mother's contracting company — thanks to Tatyana's foresight in training her to run the business — and at only twenty-six, she was already building a reputation as a very savvy contractor. Yet the two of them hardly had a personal relationship outside the walls of their offices.

'You cannot come to my house until you divorce him or you bury him, whichever occurs first,' she had told her mother. 'If you want to be in my life outside of business, we can visit each other on neutral ground, because I'm never stepping into that house again, not even to come and see Oko.'

She visited Miyo often so that she could see her brother regularly, and Miyo would facilitate the visit by bringing Oko over. Sometimes Tati came too.

Yet, of all of them, Shayo was the one who most resembled their father. She seemed to be possessed by the same vagabond spirit that tormented him. She travelled frequently to procure supplies for their business from all over the world. She knew everyone who mattered from here to Timbuktu, and had a pile of dirt this high on every self-righteous, pompous bloke up and down the Gulf of Guinea. This was her trade secret. Consequently, she breezed through customs with minimum aggravation.

She had vowed: 'I will not allow some self-important twerp to hijack my business by refusing to do a job that he's already being paid to do unless I pay him with cash or my vagina. I simply refuse to succumb to that level of intimidation. Any woman with half a brain in her head ought to know how to get men to perform their basic responsibilities without giving them anything extra in return.' That Shayo? Hm. Talk about tough!

*

I sat bemused, resting my head on my folded hands, watching the interaction between mother and son as these thoughts flitted through my mind.

Miyo kept darting critical glances their way.

'It's getting late; let's clear the table so that Shika and I can leave. Come, Oko, help me.'

She threw her mother a look and rattled something in their language when Tatyana attempted to do Oko's share of that chore. Tatyana sat back down.

I was hardly a stranger to their family and so I was used to these spats over Oko. Miyo basically disapproved of the way Tatyana treated Oko; said she babied him too much, and he took advantage of it by staying locked up in his head. She felt that her mother subconsciously needed Oko to stay the way he was because it gave her an excuse to remain in this sham of a marriage. They were equally hot-blooded but Miyo invariably won over her mother when it came to the question of how to treat Oko, probably because Tatyana knew that her daughter was right.

We cleaned up and were soon on our way to opening night at a new upscale jazz lounge, which was my birthday present to Miyo. Sweetie was initially going to be there as well, but cancelled at the last minute because she had taken Odum out of town for a karate tournament and had not made it back in time.

'These outings are wasted on you,' I teased Miyo in the car.

Still, I never lost hope that she might meet someone who would ignite a spark in her heart, but it wasn't for want of eligible men that my hope had not yet materialised.

Whenever we went out to socialise, she always held court; and Miyo Mensah sure knew how to work a crowd. She would make her dramatic entrance and then cut through a packed room as if she expected all the men to pause in the middle of whatever they were doing, move out of the way, and stare at her flat arse as she breezed through. And boy was she right — every time! It was like watching Moses part the Red Sea.

All the warm-blooded men who were not intimidated by two tall, attractive women brimming with confidence would invariably gravitate toward us. Those who preferred caramel, which was at least sixty percent of them, would head straight for Miyo without giving me so much as a passing glance. The chocolate-loving minority, as expected, would make a beeline for me. When Sweetie accompanied us, the numbers rearranged themselves somehow, and we all ended up enjoying equal amounts of attention. But boredom was never an option. At the very least, we knew that we would have an entertaining evening.

Tonight was no exception. The attention was like fuel to Miyo's brain. She drove these men out of their senses with her charm and wit; then, she handed out her special business card — the one displaying the fake contact info — to half of them, and we left. This seemed to be sufficient to keep her going until the next time. Once her emotional tank ran out of fuel, it would be time to go out again.

After we left the lounge, we went back to her place to unwind. We changed our clothes, then we sat on her balcony and I listened through the cigarette smoke while she blew off steam about her father. Her issues with him came up whenever she spent time alone with me, since she could not discuss him with anyone else.

Miyo never drank in public, no matter the occasion, and she was not a habitual smoker; but she would invariably light a cigarette and pour herself a glass of brandy to unwind anytime we talked about her childhood in detail. It seemed to be the only way she could go through those chats.

'Do you know he hasn't been by the house in over three months?'

'So he has completely moved out now, has he?'

'Practically. He has built a house for his latest ashawo and moved in with her. I ran across her in town two weeks ago, and as expected, she eyed me up and down while I stared straight through her as if she were a glass partition. Shika, she's younger than us! Can you imagine?'

'Why do these home wreckers always think they're immune? If he can do it to his wife, the mother of his four children, what makes her think she's that special?' I asked.

'She's feeling empowered because she has my father's relatives on her side. They think they're going to win by using my mother's foreign heritage against her — you know how that game is played. Can you believe they're still trying to find a loophole they can use to have Tati deported, even though she's been a Ghanaian citizenship for more than twenty years? She burnt all her bridges and made that final commitment as soon as *her* mother died, so she has nothing to go back to over there and everything to lose here.'

'Ei! So, how did you find out?'

'One of Shayo's connections at the Office of Government Accountability alerted her to the fact that OGA has been snooping around Tati's business activities, looking for an excuse to possibly deport her — after she has invested thirty years of her life here! Can you believe it?'

'The most annoying thing is that if he should die right now, you would be expected to foot the entire bill as if he had added any value to your lives,' I said.

'Tati is definitely better off without him, that's for sure. At this point, the only thing tying them together is their shared guilt over Oko. Oh, and the marriage certificate. If he wants a divorce, he's going to have to ask for one and we know that will never happen because of his family's deep roots in the Methodist Church. He would rather take a second wife and attend Sunday service with her than properly divorce his real wife.'

'Oh, the hypocrisy!' I said, 'It just drives me nuts to see how quickly people invoke religion when it suits them.'

'They wear and discard it like underwear. Now, you see why I don't go to church?'

'Sometimes you just have to wonder what brand of Christianity these people are practising.'

'Well, Tati won't initiate a divorce either. She is also hanging onto *her* brand until the day he dies, and then we shall see,' she said calmly through the cigarette smoke.

'But, I thought Tati was your grandmother's darling.'

'When my parents lived in the family house, you'd have thought Tati was a goddess. I remember how they used to croon over her and treat her like gold, especially when we first arrived from Moscow, and even up until Manye was born.

Then something happened. My memory is fuzzy and I draw a complete blank when I try to remember that time; but all of a sudden, things changed. There was a lot of drama — Tati crying a lot, my dad quarrelling with the rest of his family — and we quickly moved out of the family house.

For a few years, we were very happy. Tati stopped crying and my father was even affectionate. Until Shayo was born, and then hell began.

'So when did things go downhill with the extended family?' I asked.

'Even through all the women who came and went, they had remained civil to us kids. So, as soon as they started being hostile toward us, I knew that something major had changed. As it turned out, he had finally got himself a hometown girl. Cousin Nii-Boy has been supplying Shayo with inside info; but you know me, I don't encourage those games.'

'Oh, just wait and see. The day he dies is the day she will smell real pepper. They'll show her what she's worth by throwing her out like three-day-old trash,' I said.

'When he first started beating Tati to a pulp, I told my grandmother and my aunts; they all knew, but never once lifted a finger to help. My grandmother told me, "Stay out of it, you don't know the whole story." My aunt essentially implied that Tati did something to instigate the abuse. She said, "Some women think they can drive a wedge between a man and his family, so he is probably just trying to clip her wings a little to let her know who is in charge" — all sorts of stupid comments like that.'

'No kidding! That respected church elder, and this is the drivel that flows from her mind?'

'Well, it's drivel to you and me today, but Tati bought into it for years. We all had clearly defined roles and we played them well, as if we were in a school play. Whenever he started with Tati, I would intervene and try to deflect some of the slaps. Manye would quickly grab the two smaller ones and take them upstairs, lock the door and turn on the telly.

Poor Shayo, she assumed the role of protector whenever Manye and I were away at school. She was too small to ward off the blows, so she would lock Oko in the bedroom. Sometimes she would stay there with him; at other times, she would come downstairs and try to save Tati by jumping up and down, tugging at that devil's arm and begging him to stop hitting Tati.'

What was it with some of these men, I wondered for the billionth time? Why uproot somebody's daughter from her country and bring her all the way here? And if you didn't want her anymore, why beat her too? But I had to wonder, would it have descended to this level if Tatyana had put her foot down in the very beginning, maybe even pulled his bluff and tried to take the kids and leave him? Clearly, she herself had deep-seated issues that compelled her to sacrifice her humanity like this.

'It isn't as if Tati needs him; but I worry about Oko — you know?'

'Hm,' I responded. That was all I could offer. I had never even told her about the one time when her father tried to grab my breast while giving me a lift home after I had visited them. Nor did I tell her how I had quickly thanked him for the lift and jumped out of his car the moment he stopped at a traffic light, or how I had walked the remaining five miles home. We were fifteen at the time. Not all truths require telling.

They say these dysfunctional behaviours tend to run in families. Tawiah Mensah was an only son with four sisters, and nobody had anything bad to say about *their* father, a respected retired police inspector from a prominent family which, going back many generations, had donated acres of land toward church establishment all over the region. But who was to say what went on behind closed doors, or what strain of mental defect mocked their noble lineage?

Still, I simply could not picture any of Miyo's aunts permitting any man to so degrade them. On the contrary, the prominent Mensah clan would have sniffed out any scandals even hinting at histories of disease, mental illness, or physical abuse in the families of any potential suitors of *their* daughters, early in the courtship process.

But, having met and married Tawiah Mensah before moving into this society, Tatyana did not benefit from the same kind of thorough family background check that might have revealed any such issue in that family before she married into it. One thing was certain, though — no man would have laid a finger on any of Uncle Tawiah's sisters and lived to defend that action.

I reached over and took the cigarette from Miyo's hand just as she started to light it.

'It's enough, Miyo; now you're going to kill both of us.'

Now that we had got the preliminary details out of the way, we were ready to revisit her deeper issues. I had been through this birthday ritual with her for years. It was her only outlet for an entire year of gnawing pain and I wasn't about to leave her halfway through her annual purge.

Years ago, I'd begun suggesting that she seek professional help from a psychological or spiritual counsellor, but she had been dead set against it.

'I'm not crazy or possessed by demons, Shika,' she had responded, 'and I'm not going to allow myself to be labelled as such. I just need to talk about it every once in a while, that's all.'

So my role slowly evolved over the years to encompass the duties of shrink-guru.

'Come,' I said, pulling the cushions off her sofa and arranging them on the floor. I sat down, comb, brush and jar of pomade in hand; she stretched out on the cushions and placed her head in my lap. I took the comb, slowly parted her hair, and applied pomade.

'And how are *you* doing? Talk to me, Miyo. Has it stopped?'

For as long as she could remember, she had been having the same nightmare. Sometimes, it even happened twice in the same night. We were thirteen when she first told me about it:

'There is a little girl of maybe three years old lying in bed hugging her pillow tighter as an approaching monster's footsteps keep time to her escalating heartbeat. The monster draws closer to the dark bedroom, until she can see his shadow underneath the door. Then, the door slowly creaks open, the light in the corridor framing the monster's silhouette for a brief moment before the door closes once more. The child can hear the monster's claws scratching about on the bed, inching toward her. She buries her face in the pillow to feel safe. But soon, she can feel the hairs on his arm brushing against her thigh. And then, right when she opens her mouth to scream, light floods the room, a woman shouts something in Ga, and the monster vanishes in a pouf, just like the Cheshire cat. But unlike the cat, the child never sees this monster's face. I

cannot tell if I am that child lying there, or if it's one of my sisters. And I've never been able to recognise the woman's voice or make out what she screams.'

Every time she had this nightmare, she would wake up to find her bed in disarray. She would immediately throw up. By her teens when she went away to boarding school, she was no longer throwing up in bed, but she still experienced the gag reflex every time she had this nightmare.

Over the years, we had dissected and analysed several times, every second of her childhood for possible clues as to what this nightmare might indicate. Some repressed memory, perhaps, of an unspeakable act committed against her or one of her sisters that was fighting its way up from the recesses of her mind; or maybe the disturbing visitation was just an exaggerated representation of a less diabolical childhood experience that had left a major imprint.

'It's down to once a month or so, but as my birthday approached, it picked up again to maybe once a week. But it's been getting better, really,' she said.

'Do you think this might be the year when you finally buck up enough courage to ask Tati if something happened during your childhood, which might explain this nightmare and the gaps in your memory around the time that you moved to Bujuazee?' I asked.

'I don't think I'm ready to know yet,' she said, turning her head rapidly from side to side as she tried to control her agitation.

'Shhh! Miyo, it's all right,' I whispered. I massaged her neck and scalp to help her relax even further. I waited until she calmed down, then I tried again.

'Miyo, this has *got* to be the year; you cannot continue dragging this weight around. I haven't bothered you all year because you promised to take it to the next step and talk to Tati. You're not being accountable.'

'But I am. I've really made progress; at least I've been trying to find out why she stayed and permitted the abuse. She wasn't very receptive at first to my probing questions, but I persisted,' she said.

'Oh, good! And did you find out anything new?'

'She finally revealed that for years, my father had told her that he had people at airport immigration on the lookout to make sure she didn't leave this country with any of his children. That's when I realised that she had stayed because she hadn't wanted to leave us behind.'

'Well, that's good, that's really good,' I said.

'Really?'

Lord, have mercy! The things women will go through for their children, I thought.

We had pulled another all-nighter, just as if we were back in school, and Miyo's eyes looked like they were about to pop out of their sockets. I had nearly given up on my plan to go to church in the morning; but after this, I definitely would need to go and recharge my spiritual battery.

'Yes! Really,' I said, 'this is definitely a step forward. Come on; let's get some sleep. I'll have to leave here early so that I don't miss church.'

FIVE

I marked my last day at work with no fanfare. Now that I was free, I could begin ticking off the urgent things on my to-do list in preparation for the upcoming trip. Sweetie had been an angel, making good on her promise to set up an urgent home visit for Sefa with Bronze, and it was only after Bronze's first visit that Sefa and I fixed a definite date for our move to Togapeme.

Everyday, Sefa's illness brought on greater challenges that taunted him in the mirror. Even as the tumour began to take over his senses and aggressively rearrange his facial features, his increasing helplessness pushed the limits of his sanity, so much so that he wrestled with bouts of depression and intense solitude.

A couple of weeks after she first came to see him, Miyo sent him a wheelchair so that he could use it whenever walking wore him out.

Time had really run out now. Sefa had lost all vision in his left eye. It was now pushing outward, making it hard for him to shut his eyelid so that he had to wear goggles or an eye patch all the time; he had also lost hearing on that side of his body; and there was a pronounced slur to his speech. We were down to the last few dozes of his medications. When Bronze graciously brought him another thirty days' worth, he made it quite clear to us that this was a favour he would not be repeating.

'Being in a family setting when the meds run out again is not an option, because you would be subjecting yourself and everyone around you to a very high risk of exposure to any number of infections, including herpes and hepatitis, not to mention tuberculosis and pneumonia,' he told Sefa.

'Of course, I don't want that to happen. But if I go to the hospital they will detain me, and I need to be with my mother. I will not die in Accra,' Sefa said.

'You don't have to. Bremen Clinic is less than thirty minutes from Togapeme. It's a top-notch facility, and I will make sure you get placed in a private room. You will have the best care available, and Shika and your mom will be allowed to visit you. So, two weeks with your old lady, and then you *have* to go to Bremen. Shika and your mom are just not equipped to handle you beyond that point,' he said emphatically.

When I walked Bronze to the car, I asked him to tell me honestly what I should expect.

'You're really pushing the boundaries; I'm not going to lie to you. But we have an overloaded medical system as it is and honestly, as long as he continues taking the meds, staying at home wouldn't be a problem. But in his particular case, we have the opportunistic condition to worry about. Even if they found a cure for HIV today, it wouldn't help Sefa. What is killing him is the cancerous tumour that he developed as a result of having a severely compromised immune system, and at this point, that tumour is out of control; and there are now secondary ones also. He could suffer seizures, even a massive stroke or heart attack, at any moment. If he really wants to spend some time with his mother, you ought to take him to the village *now*, Shika. *Now!* Quite frankly, he's been really fortunate so far, but he will not make it past one month. I'm sorry.'

'So there really is nothing at all that can be done?'

'Nothing. Not with the tumours he has. The radiation treatments only helped to lessen his discomfort by trying to contain the original tumour for as long as possible; but there really was nothing more that could have been done about it because of its location. It's a ticking time bomb, and we're counting down now. Sefa never stood a chance.'

He insisted I give him a verbal promise that we would leave town as soon as possible.

'Call me in a couple of days, by then I should have made the necessary arrangements with the staff at Bremen Clinic,' he said.

Miyo also stopped by a couple of times after work. Sefa had asked her to help him with his will and some other important documents. They spent hours poring over paperwork. I was concerned that he might be over-extending himself, but he brushed away my fears.

'If I had spent time trying to prevent myself from using my brain, I would have been gone already; but there are just a few important things which I have to do before that time comes. I don't want dadaa to spend her last days in poverty and then die in disgrace. I should have done all this sooner, but thinking about it was too depressing.'

Tassie was due to come down for her fortnightly visit in a week. This time, she was arriving earlier in the week and would be staying until Thursday or Friday.

'I promise to sit with her at some point during her visit and prepare her for what lies ahead,' I told Sefa. I was not looking forward to this at all, but what choice did I have? There was no way around the bitter truth anymore.

'Be strong, Shishi. This is going to be the hardest thing you will ever have to do for me; it's almost over.'

When I went to pick up his supply of herbs from Fo Kofigah, I discovered the reason for Tassie's early arrival in town. My uncle had intricate plans laid out for her.

'I will send the driver for Daa Nenor on Monday night,' he said. 'We have an appointment with some powerful people on Tuesday; we are going to enquire about her situation from a spiritualist. I've already purchased the required items for the rituals. She knows all this; just remind her to fast that day.'

'Is Emekor back from school yet? Maybe she can visit with me while you and Tassie are gone, so that she spends some time with Sefa.'

'Yes, that's a good idea. Daa Nenor and I will return from our journey by Wednesday.'

This would give me a long overdue break from the routine and I would get to spend some quality time with my younger cousin, Emekor, who had been away at school all this time and had not seen Sefa in more than a year.

*

My uncle had gone and had Emekor outside his marriage, and then brought her into his home for his wife Jane to bring up as her own. Daa Jane's father, a prominent headmaster, had given his daughter away in holy matrimony at Resurrection Cathedral, so theirs was not a polygamous marriage that would have tolerated the existence of a second wife. As a matter of fact, the disgraceful liaison had been with the wife's maid, so polygamy was hardly the issue. After all, what self-respecting polygamist married his wife's fifteen-year-old maid just because he got her pregnant?

I was about twelve when Fo Kofigah sullied our family's name with this abomination. All I remember were the whispers surrounding the topic of the maid's pregnancy, and how she had been sent quickly and quietly back to her village with a lump sum of money. And then, out of nowhere, this fully formed toddler appeared a couple of years later — although Daa Jane had not had a baby, nor been pregnant that anyone knew of, for at least eight years.

They already had five boys, the youngest of whom was about seven by the time Emekor came along. She was the only daughter.

She had been brought up very strictly and somewhat isolated from the rest of the family, probably in a subconscious attempt to obliterate Fo Kofigah's indiscretion. At any rate, the whispers had quieted down over time. Now, no one even talked about it anymore; but those who knew, knew.

Daa Jane was a good Christian woman, the firstborn daughter from a prominent family, and once she had grappled with the dilemma and come to terms with it, she understood the role she was called to play. She did her best to treat the waif as if she were her very own; but she never exuded any warmth toward the child — no excitement over her achievements, no scolding over her failings — in fact, no display of passion whatsoever toward Emekor. In any case, what did it matter? Daa Jane was the closest thing to a saint that you could ever hope to meet on earth, both in comportment and in outlook.

Now Emekor was almost twenty, completely clueless about life and quite scatterbrained. She did not yet realise how pretty she was, thank goodness. Still, she could use some positive input from caring women in her life. It was dangerous out there for a naïve, young lady.

My heart felt just a little lighter as I slowly drove back to my house, planning how to entertain my young charge.

*

Monday came soon enough. I picked Tassie up from the station at around midday and brought her to Sefa's. She spent all afternoon with him while I ran errands.

I returned in the evening to find her waiting anxiously for me. Sefa had hinted that I had something important to discuss with her.

I sat beside her in the living room and told her that we had decided to advance our planned trip to the beginning of the following week.

'But that's two whole weeks ahead of time. Will you come right back here, and then make the final trip as originally planned?' she asked.

'No, Tassie. It is that final trip that I'm talking about. The doctor has advised me not to wait any longer, but to bring him to Togapeme *now* so that you can have enough time to spend with him.' I gently placed my hand over her clasped hands to quell their trembling.

'You mean, he will not be returning here?' She searched intently in my eyes for refutation, some assurance that she had misunderstood.

Unable to agree or disagree, I just held her stare until her understanding opened.

'Oh... I see.' The light slowly left her eyes.

We just sat there like that, weighing the significance of this decision together in silence. She kept fidgeting with her hand, and her left leg would not stop shaking.

'How long?' she finally asked.

'Two to four weeks.'

'Hm. That is good. It is better than nothing.' She patted my hand. 'Go Shika, go and take care of yourself; we'll be fine. See you in the morning.'

I left her with her son and went back to my own house, where I spent the night.

I returned to Sefa's around five the next morning and lay on the sofa waiting for Tassie to finish getting ready. She was already up; I could hear her walking around the bedroom, reciting Psalm Ninety-One. Taking a bath, pacing again. I cannot say that I know what went on in her mother's-heart as she weighed her options.

Over the years, her faith had become stronger following each loss in her life. She seemed to pick herself up, shake her shoulders, and bounce back stronger as she got over each encounter with grief and pressed on.

She was the choirmaster and church organist, a pillar of the Christian community in the entire region. I can only guess at the desperation that now drove her, against character, to go in search of help from her brother's alternative sources of spiritual revelation. But how could anyone who knew her story judge her harshly for that decision? I applauded her courage and prayed for the ability to one day have a child, and the capacity to feel for that child on such a profound level that I would willingly go anywhere to find a solution, if only to buy him a little more time here on earth.

I went and knocked on her door. She bade me enter.

'I just came to see if everything was okay,' I said, 'you've been pacing up and down for a while now. Maybe you need to talk a little, or pray with somebody before you leave?'

She sat on the bed, removed her spectacles; she rubbed her eyes. I suddenly noticed how tired and older she had become lately.

'Oh, don't worry about me, dear. I made peace with God long ago. My pacing is not a reflection of confusion or hesitation. I know that I *must* go and find some answers. That would be better than sitting here and wondering tomorrow if, perhaps, there could have been a way out. So I have crossed that bridge; but thank you for your concern.

I thank God for you every day. You are definitely an angel sent to this family for this trying time. Come, sit and let's read some Bible, eh? It will do you much good. I sense that you will need more courage in the days ahead. I know that Sefa has been pouring out his every thought to you. You two always had that between you. It's as if you were twins in another life.' She smiled as she said this.

I smiled back but my heart was pounding erratically. I could not trust it to keep its most haunting secret from this pure-hearted woman who deserved to know the truth instead of going off looking for solutions in the wrong places.

'Tassie, let me pray with you,' I said; but my throat was so dry that I could barely get the words out. The guilt from keeping her son's secret was weighing my tongue down. Fortunately for me, we heard the *pi-pimpii* of the Range-Rover as Efo's driver arrived with Emekor, just as we held hands and closed our eyes.

My stomach churning, I was only able to get out a short prayer: 'May the Lord grant you wisdom during this quest, and may He grant you safe travel.' I squeezed her hands. Then I grabbed her bag and escaped into the sitting room.

'Ei, Tassie! Daavi Shika!' Emekor hugged her aunt, then me. It took a full five minutes for Tassie to go through a complete recitation of greetings and responses with her. My uncle's strict adherence to order extended to matters pertaining to culture and tradition, so Emekor was schooled in the proper protocol. She had been raised well.

'Where's Fo Bullet? Is he awake?'

Oh shucks! I had not thought of that. I quickly grabbed her elbow before she could dash off to look for him.

'Wait, he's still asleep,' I said, 'he will wake up soon enough, and then you can go in to see him. Actually, he's been feeling much better lately, so he himself will probably come out when he wakes up.'

She laughed. She hadn't seen Sefa for more than a year by now and I had to somehow prepare her for the shock of meeting his shadow.

'Don't expect him to swing you around like a monkey or do any acrobatics like that, okay? He's not the same person anymore, and neither are you. Why don't you put the fish away while I see Tassie off, then you can update me on the latest news in Tema.'

I went outside bearing Tassie's bag and a mug of hot tea for the driver. Fo Festus had worked for my uncle in different capacities for almost thirty years and was just like family. I asked him if he would like to come in to get a bite to eat before driving back, but he declined because they had a strict deadline. He only drank the tea.

Tassie settled comfortably in the back seat. I bade her farewell and asked her what meal she would like me to cook for her return. She said something gracious about my culinary skills and left it up to me to decide.

'Take good care of my son oh, and do your magic with Emekor. I know you will have your hands full. See you tonight. If not, then tomorrow before noon.' She waved as she was driven off into the early morning mist.

My mind racing, I shut the gate and went back into the house. I lingered on the porch for a moment, trying to figure out how to prepare Emekor for seeing Sefa like that. I needn't have bothered. I heard noises coming from his bedroom.

I walked toward the sounds. His door was ajar. Emekor was kneeling on the floor at his feet, sobbing. He was sitting up in bed with his hand on her head, his eyes closed and tears silently trailing down his cheeks. I quietly shut the door.

Hugging myself, I returned to the kitchen. I checked to make sure that she had not left the fish out; then I got out the ingredients to prepare us breakfast.

Haunted by the sound of her sobbing, I could not focus at all. After several minutes, it became quiet again. She came out of the bedroom dry-eyed but quivering-lipped. I avoided making eye contact.

'Daavi Shika, it's really bad, isn't it? I had no idea he was this sick, I didn't even know that he had cancer. And nobody told me, not even *you*?' She sounded like a wounded animal.

I felt like a traitor. I feebly embraced her.

'Sometimes, we try to protect you too much and in the process, we rather hurt you. We forget that you're no longer a child and that you could actually handle some of the things we're afraid to expose you to. Forgive me; I should have told you. Come on. Wipe your eyes, eh? Let's sit down. I'm making breakfast, why don't you set the table? If we're lucky, Fo Bullet will sit with us and drink his horrid teas while we dine like royalty.'

While I cooked, she set the table and updated me on everything happening in her city. They were really catching up with civilisation, it seemed — fancy cars and big-dos, drug dealers, armed robbers, guns and all. The only thing missing was the well-equipped, incorruptible police force to handle it. It was scary, but she seemed to take it all in stride.

'If it isn't your lifestyle, it won't come near you,' she quipped. Such profound insight from a nineteen year-old! I was rather impressed.

'What about boys? I notice you steering away from that topic. What are you hiding from me?'

She giggled self-consciously.

'Ei, do you want my father to kill me? Even when the neighbourhood boys come too close to our front gate, he opens the front door with the dog beside him and shouts, "Eheh? Are you lost?" They've nicknamed him "Centurion" in our neighbourhood.'

'I can just see him.' I burst out laughing but she was not amused.

.

'You have no idea. I have to sneak out the back gate when he's napping, just to go to my friend's house down the street.'

'But that's ridiculous! Does he follow you to work?' She had just begun her National Service, and I couldn't imagine him allowing her to enjoy that much freedom.

'More or less. I've never taken public transportation to work since I began. Fo Festus drops me off every morning and at five o'clock on the dot, is waiting for me in front of the office. Once, I even tried to sneak out early to pass by the store with my friends; and there he was, waiting. Can you imagine? At four-thirty! It made me wonder if he had stayed out there all day or what? My friends have started really resenting me because they think I'm just some *dadaba* who really doesn't want to rub shoulders with them at all.' She was quite livid.

My mouth was still hanging open in amazement over the picture she was painting, when Sefa's boyish laughter jerked us out of this serious conversation. He must have overheard us. He wheeled himself in. That lowered the temperature in the room.

We all laughed at the ridiculous picture and the new name for Fo Kofigah, and then we sat down to eat. Centurion. How befitting!

'Did you bring the newspaper?' Sefa asked.

'Actually, Fo Festus saved me the effort by bringing it; let me see where I put it.' I went and rescued it from the corner of the sofa. 'You look really well today. Hey, we might be able to tackle some *akple and fetri-detsi*.' That was a far stretch, of course, but I was still happy to see him in a good mood.

'Not a chance,' he said. 'Actually, I'm expecting a guest around ten. Please make yourselves scarce, as I need some privacy.'

I knew what this meant. He was going to be fitted today for a custom-made tuxedo. Sweetie had recommended a tailor and sworn that the man was an expert. Sefa wanted to be laid out in style, even if it was going to be in a closed casket.

'You never know what could happen,' he had teased me when I suggested that one of his designer suits should be altered by the undertaker. 'What if the hearse were to take a sharp bend and I toppled out of the casket? I can just see the caption accompanying the photo on the front page:

Sefa Gameli's corpse, clad in oversized suit by stingy relatives, escapes hearse in embarrassment.

Emekor and I packed the car with half of the foodstuffs that Tassie had brought; then we drove to my place, where we spent a leisurely day washing and braiding each other's hair. She wasn't as feather-brained as she had been the last time I spent any significant amount of time with her; she was no longer that little kid.

She did not think that her A-level results were going to turn out that well. The results were due in a couple of weeks and she was wondering what to do as an alternative to attending the university. I discovered that her strength lay in languages.

'That was my favourite subject too! You *do* know that my first degree was in Linguistics, right?' I was thrilled. 'We can go through some of my books when we're done with braiding. What other plans have you made anyway, if you don't think the results will be that great?' I was sitting on a pillow on the floor while she sat on a chair behind me, braiding my hair.

'Well, I have this friend named Hadiye Abu. Hadi's dad is a dentist, and they live on the next street over from us. Her older sister, Hassana, followed some guy to Brussels and found a really good job there. Within like three months, she returned home with all these nice things — cars, electronics, clothes — you name it! Now the guy has married her and they travel back and forth.

He opened a car dealership in town and Hassana has also opened a high-end boutique. Hassana is making documents to take Hadi with her in less than a month, and they are recruiting some of the girls in the neighbourhood who want to go along. I think she said that they would train you to work in fashion, cosmetology, or European cuisine, whatever you decided *you* wanted to do. I want to be a fashion designer. She said I would be perfect.

Their middle sister, Rahma, also left for Brussels; *she* actually settled there and owns a business that employs most of these girls. They even brought some of their poorer relatives down from their hometown. It was better for those girls than ending up as the third or fourth wife of a seventy-something-year-old man.'

'And what are the neighbours and other people in the community saying about this sudden influx of wealth among Dentist Abu's daughters?'

'You know how people are; the envious ones are spreading rumours that the money is probably from carrying *on-the-body* or doing two-two. On the other hand, a couple of the neighbourhood girls have already agreed to go; *their* parents are happy for this chance, but you know my situation already. I haven't even bothered to broach the topic with Papa. I know he would never give his consent for me to go. I'm at the point where I'm seriously considering getting up and vanishing with Hadi, you know? Just leaving him a long letter explaining everything. Once I return in three months or so with all these obvious signs of progress, he would have to admit that I made a mature decision after all.'

I was hardly breathing by this time, but I didn't want to come off sounding like a parent and losing her trust, so I tried to stay calm.

'So what are you going to do about Hassana's offer?'

'Actually, I told Hadi that when I returned from this visit, I would give her sister my definite answer. Her sister thought that it would be a good idea if I just left; that's what *she* had to do as the first girl to leave home. She said their father used to always whip them with a cane and fire his pistol in the air to scare off boys! But now that he's driving around in the latest Mercedes-Benz S-Class, which they imported for him for his sixtieth birthday, he's not complaining anymore. They outfitted his clinic with modern technology, new equipment and everything. Now, he charges his patients twice what they used to pay. He just wanted to see his daughters doing well, that's all.' She spoke with the conviction of a damned soul who had just seen a flicker of light beckoning from the depths of hell.

This was major. I had to think with a clear head but the tight braids seemed to be blocking the oxygen from flowing to my brain.

'Why don't we take a break, eh? Let's find something to eat,' I said. 'There's some *palaver-sauce*, which I made yesterday. I will add to it some of the *smoked fish* that you brought. Why don't you boil us some *puna* to go with it? We have all afternoon to finish my hair. Come on, help me up.'

She almost pulled my arm out of its socket. She laughed at me and teased me about getting old.

'When are we going back to Fo Bullet?' she sounded concerned. 'I'm really worried about him. Should he be by himself? He seems so weak.'

'I know what you mean, but he's fine. He has his good days and bad days. We've been having a good week so far, and he has some really important things to attend to, which only he can do, before we leave town.'

'Hm. I guess I didn't think of it that way. So how do you feel about all this? I know you are very close to him. My mother always says that you two were raised like twins.'

'I think that I've finally come to terms with it but everyday it hurts more, especially when he goes through a bad spell. And when I see Tassie watching him, that's the worst pain of all. Do you know I still haven't seen her cry? Her well is so dry that no tears would come out even if she tried to cry. No woman should have to watch her child dying like this, one day at a time. It must be hell. So my pain is nothing compared to hers.'

'So many young people are dying these days,' Emekor said, shaking her head sadly. 'Do you know that about three people my age have died in our community alone within a four month period? Now, every time you ask about someone, it's "oh, didn't you know he died three months ago?" And the cause is always TB, or cancer, or some major disease like that.

A young man in Papa's office died two months ago followed by his nine-month old baby that same week. The day after the baby's death, the wife drank poison and killed herself too. The lady was only twenty-eight. Their five-year-old is left behind for their relatives to take care of. Papa didn't talk about it at home, but people are saying that the man was sleeping around and got AIDS and spread it to his family, except the five-year-old. It's really sad.'

'Speaking of which, since you raised the topic, I have to talk to you about sex,' I said, tugging at her ear.

'Again? Oh, Daavi Shika, you're going to ruin my whole visit! Nothing has changed since the last time you talked to me about it. I'm still a virgin. How can I be anything else living under the control of the Centurion? Hey, I think the yam is ready.' She escaped through the steam from the boiling yam, so I decided to wait until we should be sitting behind the food; it would be kind of difficult for her to switch topics while she had hot yam in her mouth.

We sat across each other, the dishes of food between us as we dug in. There is nothing quite like *koobi*-flavoured palaver-sauce with puna yam. We ate like marooned sailors. Emekor's eyes remained glued to her plate and she ate quickly, as if she planned to run away from our impending discussion as soon as she was done.

I felt sorry for her. I remembered myself at her age. At least, *I* had been close to my mother, and had learnt many of the intricacies of life from our conversations in the kitchen, or on the way to market, made all the more special because of the long periods of separation while I was away at school. Really, Emekor had no one. I could not picture Daa Jane discussing sex with this child, especially considering the circumstances surrounding their relationship. So, I decided to let her be for now.

'Finish up and let's go and look at the books and some clothes. I have some nice suits that will just be sitting there now that I've stopped working, and I bet most of them would fit you perfectly. By the time we're done, the food would have settled; then we can finish braiding the front of my head. I'll go and open the boxes while you do the dishes. Come to my room when you're done.' I left her at the table and went into the room where I kept my boxes and suitcases.

I pulled out my old *chop-box*, in which were stored most of my old textbooks, and dragged it into my bedroom. I opened the box and looked over those old, familiar friends that had served me so well. Maybe now they could help me save Emekor. I dusted the books off tenderly with a cloth and stacked them against the wall.

Emekor knocked and came into my sanctuary. She headed straight for my dressing table.

'Ei, Daavi Shika; look at all these designer perfumes and cosmetics! It feels like a Parisian boutique in here. And they aren't just props either; they're all more than half full. Mmm...' She closed her eyes in ecstasy with each sniff. 'My mother says you bring her expensive perfumes every time you travel. I thought she was exaggerating but now I can see how. Which one is this?' She sprayed and sniffed every single bottle on the dresser before coming to plop onto the floor next to the books.

'Well, now that you're smelling so good, we might as well look at the clothes before we get to the books. Go to the third bedroom and bring my old school trunk, I've stored all those clothes in it.' She left and came back in a flash.

'Eh? You mean all the clothes in this trunk don't fit you anymore? Look at this one. Ei! It has a designer label and everything. I've never seen a designer suit in real life, only in magazines. You mean I can have this?' She was out of her clothes and into my outfit before I could say 'jack!'

'Go on, try on some more, then we'll decide.' Her enthusiasm was infectious. I giggled at the speed with which she went through the trunk. 'Careful, don't rip the skirts!'

'So, how many can I have, how many? Oh, say I can have all of them. I'll do anything!' she gushed.

Ah! I had not expected to hear that.

'Really? I tell you what, why don't we strike a deal right now? They'll all fit you anyway, the whole bunch of them. So, pick out the three that you like best — go ahead!' I said.

She chose the three that I would have picked myself. They also turned out to be the most expensive three; this girl had impeccable fashion sense.

'Now, set them on the bed beside me and pick two more.'

She looked puzzled, but she followed my instructions.

'Here, take these last two and go put them in your luggage; then come back so that I tell you about these three.'

She came back quickly and sat on the floor, still looking puzzled.

'Eheh? I'm back,' she said.

'Come on, sit on the bed beside me.'

'You chose well,' I said 'I knew you would, because you have a good eye and know better than anyone what compliments your good looks.'

Then I told her when I had bought those three outfits. It was during my first trip abroad. We had gone to Geneva for a summit. My first job straight out of college was a two-year stint as an interpreter. I told her how much I had been paid for the ten-day trip, not counting the paid-for roundtrip tickets and hotel accommodations.

'In *foreign* currency?' Her eyes popped as if they would drop out in another second when she heard the figure.

'In U.S. dollars, my dear. It was a routine assignment to do my usual job of interpreting the summit's proceedings from French to English for one English-speaking delegation. If another group had also hired me — and they could have done that — I would have been paid double for the same amount of work. But this was my first major assignment, and I didn't know how to negotiate for extra bookings. That is the lowest I ever got paid while doing that job. After that, I quickly figured out how the system worked.'

'And this was just to do interpretation at the summit for ten days?' She was still shaking her head in disbelief.

'Actually, it was one week, but we left for Geneva in the middle of the first week and the weekend fell in the middle of the trip. That's when my friends and I went to explore the shops. Emekor, I'm telling you all this because you can be in that position too, in charge of your own destiny.'

'But *you* are so intelligent, *you* grew up in Caftak! How does that compare with *my* abilities? I know enough to know that I can't make that kind of money without a bachelor's degree, at least; and *you* have a master's degree! I'm not even sure how well I'll be doing on my A-levels.' She sounded really old and pessimistic right then.

'Just listen to yourself. I've worked with a lot of people who did not have advanced degrees but developed the skills required to make themselves marketable in the workforce. True, you would start off probably not making as much money in the beginning, but acquiring a marketable skill will open doors for you. Besides, if you don't make it into the university immediately, you can always retake the subjects you need to make the cut and go in a year later. Either way, I will be back in Accra by then, and I'm willing to talk to your parents to see if you can come and stay with me while you attend classes.'

'You would do that for me? What about Sister Hassana, what should I tell her? Her offer looks so promising; and if I lose this chance, that might be it.'

'How well do you know this Hassana? I realise that Hadi is your best friend and all, but think about it carefully. In the first place, do you believe that Hassana cares more about your future than I do?'

She quickly shook her head.

'Secondly, what does she stand to gain by recruiting all these girls, even going as far as to the village to bring girls down and send them abroad with her own money? Did she indicate how she expected to be paid back for this magnanimity?'

She began defending Hassana, but I wasn't about to lose this argument.

'No-no-no!' I wagged my forefinger at her. 'Shut up and listen to me! Thirdly, have you sat down and done any research or talked to anybody, other than the Abu sisters, *anyone* at all who actually went *and* came back, to find out exactly what it was that they did when they got there?'

'No…' she said in a weak voice. She was beginning to look faint.

'Well, I happen to know for a fact that girls your age and younger are being rounded up and sent to these foreign countries with the promise of something extraordinary; but most of them go and end up as prostitutes in Paris, Amsterdam, Brussels and other European cities. And Emekor, guess what? Yes, they do find something extraordinary and bring it back home.'

I was holding her hand by now and almost whispering, but the intensity of the discussion had tears rolling down both our faces.

'It is called AIDS, Emekor. There is no cure for it, and people are dying from it. Are you hearing me? Eh?'

She had one hand over her mouth, eyes shut tight, as if to block out the images I was creating. She was shaking. I so desperately wanted to shake her even harder, pump some sense into her; but she was really vulnerable right now. One wrong word and I could lose her forever.

'Listen, you have me. I want you to be rich and happy and all those good things too, but most of all, I want you to stay alive. Even if you don't strike gold, at least there will always be that second chance, but not if you're dead or dying. Eh?'

She had my hand in a tight grip and kept nodding vigorously, but I wasn't done. 'Wouldn't it be a shame if, after you left with Hassana, your exam results came and you had in fact made it into the university after all?'

I seemed to have touched a raw nerve. Her grip on my hand tightened and the sobbing escalated for a moment. I didn't make a sound. My right hand was too small a price to pay for her deliverance. I rubbed my other hand over her back until she was done. I was sweating and panting as if I had been in labour.

Strangely enough, the only person I could think of right then was Jean. Perhaps, it was because I needed a familiar but disinterested sympathiser, someone with no stake in my view of the world, to lend an unquestioning shoulder to my exhausted head. And in that moment, I realised that Jean was, without a doubt, the most qualified person to do so; yet we had not spoken to each other all weekend. I had been so busy that I hadn't even given him the courtesy of a reply to the long message, which he left on my machine, assuring me of his love and expressing concern over my silence.

'Fo Bullet and I will be coming over this weekend; you've heard, right? I can try to talk to your father then,' I said to Emekor. 'That way, he will have enough time to get used to the idea before I return to Accra. And guess what, I will bring along these three suits that you first picked, as a sort of celebration of your first adult decision about your future. Deal?'

She nodded.

'Thank you, Daavi Shika,' she said. 'I promise, as soon as I get home, I'm going to decline Hadi's sister's offer.'

I smiled at her. I could see the relief in her eyes. The prospect of making such a momentous decision as leaving home without her father's blessing must not have sat well with her.

She started to put the books back into the chop-box. I went into the dining room to catch my breath and dip my hand in iced water for a few minutes. I shook my head to delete the picture of what almost became. There was hope yet.

When we had finished braiding our hair, we went back to Sefa's place to have dinner with him. He had had a full day and was quite tired, so he left us sitting there and turned in early. Tassie had said we should expect her the next morning if she was not back by nightfall, so we waited until nine. Then, we went back to my place.

I had promised Emekor that we would stay up to chat, but Jean called as soon as we turned in, so I kicked her out to the living room while I talked to him. When she came back into the bedroom, she was like a frisky puppy.

'Ei, Daavi Shika! Look at you,' she teased, 'it must have been a man on the phone.'

'Why do you say that?' I asked.

'Because you're all glowing, curled up like that on your satin sheets! You're suddenly young again. Wait till I tell my mother! She thinks you won't find a husband on this entire continent because you're too polished for your own good.'

'Your mother talks too much, and so do you,' I said. 'She's stuck in that *colo* mindset that considers a woman to be worthless unless she is married by twenty-five and bears a child by twenty-six, no matter what else she may be accomplishing with her life or contributing to the world. *I* don't think thirty-two is too old. Besides, your mother is wrong about me.'

'If she is, then how come you still don't have a man at this age?'

'How do you know I don't already have one?'

'Well, do you?'

'Or maybe, I just haven't found the *right* one yet. Most of the ones who have come my way want a shorter woman, preferably one with a more subdued personality, or someone who comes off as unintelligent. Although, if I were foreign, all my traits would be considered attractive — I would be perfect, in fact — and they would be fighting each other just for the chance to hear me say "good morning" to them.'

'Why is that? Maybe you should water down your personality. Then, as soon as you snag one, you can be yourself again.'

'And you think that would work? Emekor, any relationship that would cause you to have such low self-esteem is not healthy, to begin with. And any man who would require that of you has an inferiority complex himself. He probably doesn't have any examples in his own family of accomplished women who look like me, or you.'

'Or maybe his mother felt that she needed to dim her own light in order for his father's light to shine brighter.' There was a discerning smile on her face when she said this.

'Exactly,' I said, 'so when he thinks "successful woman", the picture that flashes in his mind does not resemble his mother. It does not have brown skin, high cheekbones, full lips, curly hair, or wide hips. And in that case, no matter how many things you try to change about yourself in an effort to measure down to the lower standard that you are accepting, he will never value you or treat you the way every woman wants to be treated.'

'Ei, Daavi Shika, this philosophy of yours is really profound oh! No wonder these men are so scared of you. For the record, I'm on your side — I don't think thirty-two is too old, and you deserve a man who will treat you well — but there aren't any more men like that left on this continent, are there? Maybe if more of us women also married foreigners, just as our men do, that would even out the playing field a little.'

'You naïve girl! If only it were that straightforward. Any number of factors could complicate a relationship.'

'But at least you would eliminate most of them — the interfering in-laws, especially. For that alone, I would even *pay* somebody to marry me, if I didn't have to deal with his relatives.'

We both laughed.

'So was this a fruitful visit? Are you glad you came?' I asked.

She hesitated for a second before responding.

'You know, I think I was meant to be here this week. I cannot imagine how next week would have turned out if I hadn't come. Thank you. But you aren't going to tell my parents about my plans, are you? If you are, I just want to know so that I can prepare myself for the inquisition.'

'You should know me better than that.' I gave her hand a squeeze.

SIX

We woke up early, packed Emekor's things into the car and drove to Sefa's to wait for Tassie. The late-morning pi-pim-pii ushered her in, laden with enough supplies to stock a cruise-liner. I could tell that she too had had some kind of epiphany. Her mood was very telling. She practically danced in, hugging and kissing us all, as if she had been gone a whole year. I knew that it was going to be a long night for me on the bedroom floor, picking every juicy tit-bit she would throw my way.

I gave Emekor my word that I would speak to her father on Saturday afternoon, and then we sent her on her way.

'How's my son, any emergencies while I was gone?' Tassie asked when we were alone.

'You have no idea what an unbelievable day he had yesterday. If I didn't know better, I would argue that he was never ill. He drank a lot of light soup, with yam, mind you. No headaches, no dizziness. Tassie, it was amazing!'

She placed her hand on her chest and opened her eyes wide. 'Ah, are you sure? Where is he?'

She went to his door and pressed her head to it, knocked lightly and entered. She came back out immediately. He was still sleeping.

'He looks well rested, almost like his old self. And what about you, my dear? *You're* looking so young and carefree,' she said, placing her hand on her hip and tilting her head, the better to see me.

'Oh, Tassie! Maybe it was Emekor's visit and this new hairdo that she gave me. Look,' I said, and pulled off my protective scarf.

'The hair is very beautiful; but no, that's not it. I actually noticed it when I arrived on Monday; something has definitely changed,' she said; and then she inspected me from head to toe, as if the events of the past few days would have left an imprint. 'It must have something to do with that Frenchman of yours. Has he been here? He's the only man who has this effect on you.'

I backed away as if she had just stung me. We had never discussed Jean in any detail, although she had met him a couple of times when she still lived in the city. I had updated her once about his growing interest in me, but I'd also made it quite clear that while I valued his friendship, I was keeping him at arm's length. Occasionally she would ask about 'the Frenchman' in a general way, as she did about my job or my other friends. I had never thought that I sent out any vibes regarding him, and she had never implied that I did — until now.

'Tassie, what effect does he have on me? Tell me, what have I been doing?' My heart was beating erratically and I was finding it difficult to breathe.

'Well, for one thing, while you're saying very little with your mouth, your eyes always speak volumes on the few occasions that you've mentioned him to me. You have this "close friendship" with him that you don't want to lose; he wants more but you won't give him a chance; yet, you don't allow other men to come near you. Everyone can see it but you, Shika. I don't think any other man stands a chance.'

I heard the familiar tapping of the cane behind us.

'And then you stay awake past midnight, chatting with him while he's abroad,' Sefa said.

'Oh, Sefa, I could kill you!' I reached up to swat him on the back of his head.

'Too late! Dadaa, woezo! You seem happy too. Have you also found a Canadian somewhere?' He turned toward his mother, still laughing.

'My son! Let me look at you, your sister really took good care of you, I can hardly recognise you.' She hooked his arm with hers and walked with him into the sitting room. I could hear him telling her that he had a surprise for her.

I snuck away to the bedroom and crept to the mirror. My spine was tingling and there was a burning in my cheeks. I looked at my hair, my face, my clothes, but I could not look into my eyes. I just stood there and blocked everything out of my mind until all that remained was Jean — the sound of his voice, the shape of his face... All those countless occasions when we had gone out with friends and seen couples being affectionate... How our chatter would dwindle and our laughter would fade away as we watched those couples...

I could feel the goose bumps going from the tips of my fingers all the way up my arms. My heart skipped a beat. I needed to know the truth; but I still could not look into my eyes.

And then, I remembered the details from that horrible day almost three weeks ago, when I had felt compelled to call him in Calabar — from the sound of his voice when he had picked up the phone, to when he told me, "well, you should know by now, for you I would do anything."

I closed my eyes and held my breath; I could almost feel him gently but firmly taking my heart in his hands and tilting it just so. The sensation was so real that I placed my hand on my left breast. Jean-Marc Charbonneau was shifting my heart back into place. I did not need to look into my eyes to know the truth; I knew. I slid to the floor in front of the dresser, still clutching my left breast.

I do not know how long I sat on the floor in front of the mirror. Maybe five minutes, maybe ten? And then I heard the tap-tap, Sefa's voice in the doorway.

'Shishi, get up. It's okay. You know now, don't you? You love this man. I was hoping that you would discover this while I was still here. I need to know that you will be happy. It's no secret how *he* feels about you, the whole world knows. But I wasn't quite sure about you; you've always been so strong and independent, so generous to other people's needs. I didn't know what it would take for you to slow down and hear your own heart.'

'I'm so scared, Sefa. I'm so scared to let him in. I feel as if I would lose charge of myself, and I have vowed never to let that happen. Not since —'

He did not let me finish the thought.

'Don't you see,' he said, 'it's too late. Jean already has your heart. You will never be complete unless you *do* lose charge of yourself and trust that he will not hurt you. It's time to let the past go and release your future. Come, Shishi.' He held out his hand.

I shook my head and continued sitting on the floor.

'Stand up, Shishi,' he whispered. 'Look in the mirror. Tell her that she was just a girl, that it was not her fault.'

'I know, I know. Just let me be.'

He closed the door and limped away.

Courage, Shika, I heard my own voice. I trusted the voice in my head, so I summoned everything in me and stood up in front of the dresser.

I slowly opened my eyes. I held the gaze in the mirror for what seemed an eternity. It had been fourteen years since I last looked into those eyes.

I did not recognise the girl staring back at me. But I could see her pain; it was still raw. And yet, I could also see a glimmer of strength hiding behind the pain, wanting to be released. That strength was something I did not feel right now. But I refused to close my eyes. Instinct told me that if I did, she might stay locked up forever, and it was way past time to set her free and let her go. So I held her gaze, and we both remembered...

*

It is 1981 and I have just turned eighteen. My brother's friend, it appears, has a huge crush on me. I know this, not only because Kobla has been teasing me nonstop about it, but also because every time I venture past his house, this guy conveniently pops out of the side gate.

'Perhaps if he made an attempt at ordinary conversation, he might actually stand a chance,' I tell my brother sarcastically.

But his friend never says anything. Instead, he always pulls out a cigarette and lights it, trying to look cool. His vice comes as a surprise to me, secretary of the Scripture Union, and offends my youthful sense of morality. His sophistication fails to impress me. My admirer has just killed any chances he might have had of *ever* winning my affections.

And then, toward the end of that long vacation, the young man — Bacchus is his nickname and he's twenty-one like Kobla — suddenly begins to pay all this attention to me. It appears that my brother has gone and blabbed to his friend, and it seems that their other friends have also heard something.

It's embarrassing and exciting all at once — except that *I* am the one who feels all the embarrassment. I assume that Bacchus is excited about whatever my brother told him, because every time I venture into the neighbourhood, he shows up and tries to chat me up. His fans egg him on with whistles and catcalls, along with the occasional shout of 'Bacchus *alomo*!' But their excitement does not move me. It only becomes an irritating inconvenience that prevents me from walking about freely in my own neighbourhood.

A few days before they are due to return to college, Bacchus comes by our house unexpectedly. My parents are out of town attending a funeral, and Kobla is off somewhere chasing a girl.

I tell him, 'Kobla is not here; I thought he went to your house?'

But he says, 'I didn't come to see Kobla, I brought *you* some *kelewele*.'

'You can't come in,' I say after he puts his foot in the door; but he comes in anyway. Instinct is cautioning me, my mind is racing ahead for a way to place myself between him and the door, but the aroma of the kelewele has begun to interfere with my reasoning.

'I told Daavi that it was for you; see how much she gave me to bring to you?' He opens the paper and offers it to me.

I reach for the kelewele, but in a kind of playful cat-and-mouse move, he snatches it back so that I have to stretch for it. The paper falls from his hand. There are pieces of kelewele flying all over my mother's marble kitchen floor.

'You twit! See what you've done now,' I say.

He thinks it's funny but I'm not amused. I get on the floor and start picking up the pieces of kelewele. Now I will have to clean the floor all over again.

Suddenly, he grabs me from behind and jerks me off the floor.

'Bacchus, put me down! Are you *crazy*? Let me go,' I say with all the authority I can muster; but he still thinks it's a game.

'After I've gone out of my way to your favourite Daavi and bought you kelewele, is this all the thanks I get? Can't you even give me a kiss? Like this… ' He tries to reach around to kiss my face, but I thrash about wildly, trying to loosen his grip around my body so that I can escape from the foulness of his cigarette-flavoured breath.

But it is a futile attempt. My arms are trapped against my back within his grip.

'Let me go! The housekeeper is napping in her room and my parents will walk in at any moment.'

'I thought your housekeeper's father died and your parents have gone out of town with her to attend that funeral? Do I really look that stupid? Or is it just that you think you're too good for me? And whom are you saving your fine self for, anyway — the king of Arabia?'

'Let me go, you cad!' Even though it is hard kicking backwards, I give it my best shot. But all it achieves is to infuriate him.

He partly hoists and partly drags me, as I'm kicking and fighting, through the kelewele and onto the stairs. He uses his knee to pin me facedown on the marble steps. His one hand keeps my hands behind my back and the other hand pulls my panties down to my knees in one swift motion. I cannot thrash about anymore.

Tzia! He unzips his jeans.

His movements are quick and efficient. It suddenly dawns on me —
this son-of-a-bitch must have done this before, he intends to follow
through!

I make one last appeal to his humanity: 'Bacchus, I'm warning you; my
father will kill you. Let me go!' But I'm speaking out of the side of my
mouth to a marble step. It does not answer me. It cannot.

I tune out completely while he grunts like a pig and finishes doing
what he came here to do.

The door slams and I open my eyes. I am alone once more, just the
marble floor and I.

I feel the urgent need to get up and clean up the kelewele. But I cannot
feel one side of my face, and it hurts too much when I try to stand.

I *must* rise up to my knees, at least. My mother's marble floor can have
no stains. It is imported marble.

It's as if I'm standing aside watching and telling me what to do: *Quick,
Shika, crawl! Pick up every piece of kelewele, and every speck of spice. Grab the
sponge. Splash a little Dettol. Wipe the grease. Don't miss a spot.*

I sit back on my legs and inspect my handiwork. The floor is perfect
again. My mother will be pleased. I reach up with the back of my wrist
and wipe my brow. A drop rolls down the side of my nose into my mouth.
It tastes of tears or sweat... I'm not sure which. The smell of kelewele
mixed with disinfectant is nauseating.

I drag myself to the bathroom, grab the towel, and drape it over the
mirror so that I do not have to look at my face. Then I run the bath and
climb into the tub of steaming water. Now I do not have to think about
what has just happened to me.

*

Rape. That word is part of my consciousness now, but I did not even have
it in my vocabulary that day. For years after my brother's friend raped me,
I dragged around an albatross of guilt and confusion: I should not have
opened the door — in spite of the fact that I had fought him all the way —
although I had played no part in his appearing at our house that day.

I guess he went back to school and bragged about finally deflowering Kobla's holier-than-thou virgin sister. A few days later, my brother travelled all the way back home from Kumasi, just to come and confront me over 'rumours going around campus'. He did not ask me anything or tell me the specifics of what he had heard; he just put it to me that I had played the slut and embarrassed him. *Him*!

He was so furious! He called me a liar and struck me across the face with the back of his hand when I told him that his friend had forced me. I fell to the floor.

That was the first time — the only time, in fact — that he had ever hit me. Not even throughout childhood, fighting over toys or for attention, had he *ever* laid a hand on me, other than to push my head with his finger or elbow me once in a while. Now that I needed him most — after he had failed to protect me as my parents had instructed him to do when they left me in his care that weekend — *he* rather had turned against me.

I started to get off the floor but I cringed and fell back down when I saw that Kobla had raised his hand to strike me again. The sound of the slamming door interrupted him. It was Sefa.

Were it not for our cousin's fortuitous arrival, Kobla might have beaten me senseless. Instead, he straightened up, turned right around, hopped on the next bus and went back to Kumasi. Our parents never even realised that he had travelled home that day.

To this day, I still wear the small scar left by the impact of his knuckle breaking the skin over my cheekbone. It looks like a tear streak down my left cheek.

It did not help that people immediately began linking my name to Bacchus around the neighbourhood, openly addressing me as 'Bacchus alomo', as if they had ever so much as seen me standing in the shade of any mango tree, or beside any milk bush hedge, exchanging a 'how-are-you' with him.

I could not tell my parents that Kobla's friend had forced me. My father had always warned my brother: 'I will kill you if you ever bring any riffraff through my gates to come and even breathe the same air as your sister.' Papa was a man of his word. I didn't want my brother to die.

So, I kept my secret shame and went back to school a few days later, as if nothing had happened. Besides losing my appetite and starting to take multiple showers a day, everything was fine — for a while, at least — until the end of the month arrived and my period did not show up. I panicked and almost had a nervous breakdown. I turned to the one person who knew my secret.

'Maybe your body is in some kind of shock,' Sefa said when I told him. 'Why don't you wait another month and see if it comes, eh?' He sounded so confident. I believed him.

During that long vigil, I could not eat. I hardly slept. I considered — several times — various chemicals that I could swallow either separately or in combination to either trigger my period or kill myself, it really didn't matter which. But I always discarded the thought out of fear that the attempt might only maim me and leave me stuck halfway between death and life without the ability to complete the process. This then, I concluded, is what it feels like when one is on death row waiting to be executed.

All I had at that time was Miyo to lean on. Unbeknownst to me, Sefa had told her what happened and asked that she keep an eye on me; so, she followed me one day when, armed with a metal coat hanger, I headed for the bathroom in the middle of the night. She burst into the toilet and pried the device from my hand. Then she sat on the terrazzo floor with me and held me till dawn.

When another twenty-seven days came and went with nothing to show, I marched to Sefa's dorm early in the morning of the twenty-eighth day, and sent someone to get him.

'What am I going to do, what am I going to do? My life is over!' I was shaking and crying, just falling apart.

'Don't cry, Shishi. I told you not to worry. Pull yourself together; just trust me, okay? Tomorrow we must skip classes and go to town without permission. Bring along all your pocket money. Can you survive till tomorrow?'

Sefa was preparing for the national inter-school athletics competition and he was on a very strict training schedule. We had to leave early so that he could be back in time for practice. I was a senior, so no one was going to miss me in the dorm; but I still asked Miyo to cover for me, in case any staff member noticed my absence.

We snuck out of campus by dressing up in regular clothes and cutting through the bushes bordering the athletics field. He took me to the back streets of a suburb near our school, where this 'midwife' had a 'clinic' that catered to the predicaments of unfortunate teenaged girls. Once we had paid the money, I lay there. I did not feel any emotion. Four tablets of painkiller and one hour later, they had solved my problem.

It cost us both our entire pocket money for that school term, but we paid so much more for this, both of us.

About a week after my visit to the midwife, I came down with a high fever, chills and shortness of breath. I keeled over in terrible pain. Miyo sent for Sefa. They called a taxi and rushed me to the hospital.

It turned out that I was suffering from an infection to which I almost lost my life. I spent three days in the hospital.

'Go, Sefa, go! Just leave me here; I'll be fine now. Do not skip practice. You can just come back here after practice everyday,' I told him when I was able to talk.

But he wouldn't leave my side in those three days. He just sat there shaking, sweating, almost pissing on himself, and praying. I don't know what strings he pulled but he managed to get the hospital papers signed, supposedly by my parents. I lay there wracked with guilt for those three days, knowing that I was probably robbing him of the most rewarding experience of his youth.

'It was a family emergency, my grandmother was dying,' he told his coaches when he eventually showed up three days later; but they were not moved.

'Rules are rules,' the senior coach said; 'the last thing I need is for you — the sports prefect who should know better — to set a precedent. And I am definitely not going to be accused of favouritism.'

As a result of deserting the team with no explanation, Sefa got disciplined. Due to his otherwise impeccable record, and because of the gravity of his family emergency, they did not suspend him or strip him of his post. In fact, they allowed him to continue taking part in practice. But it had already cost him. They cut him from the team that made it to the nationals.

This was to have been his last competition for Caftak. The following year we were going to take the A-levels and the rule was that final year students were not allowed to participate in competitive sports so that they could focus on their studies. It would have been his most glorious season as an athlete, representing not just our school, but also the entire region.

The pain of these recollections was almost more than I could bear. I really missed my mother in that moment and, as I thought about it, I realised that I had never actually mourned her passing. I tried but could not recall shedding a tear over it. All I remembered was the sense of betrayal I'd felt when she died.

How could she leave me like that? And how had she not noticed, when she returned from the funeral of our housekeeper's father on that Sunday, that there was something the matter with me?

This realisation opened the last floodgate. I wept until I only had enough strength left with which to climb into bed.

When I opened my eyes about two hours later, Tassie was sitting at the foot of the bed reading.

'Ah, you're awake now! I enjoyed the akple very much; but I could tell, as soon as I tasted the amount of salt in the soup, that *you* didn't cook the meal.'

'At least she can cook rice and fry an egg; there's still hope,' I said in a croaky voice. It was a relief to hear the sound of my own voice. Although I was still drowsy, I felt well rested. I couldn't remember the last time I had indulged in the luxury of an afternoon nap.

Tassie touched my face.

'You miss your mother, eh? I miss her too. I remember when I was getting divorced from that man. I cried more over my mother's absence than over the crisis facing me. I felt robbed. I suppose it may have been because I never really loved him; and I knew that if my mother had not died, Papa would not have pushed me into marriage to a man who was so much older than I.

But when I met Elorm, now *that* was something else. We were on the same level intellectually and spiritually. He treated me as if he had just struck gold. And you know what? Those three short years that I spent with him were worth all the pain that followed. But then, just like that, he was gone. I didn't feel anything for several months.'

She stared into the distance for a moment, a soft smile on her face. 'Lebene was there for me every step of the way. My little sister became my mother. It was as though she carried my soul on her back to cross over that patch of time.

Now, when I think of Elorm, I don't see his body lying in a casket. I only remember the sound of his voice and the ridiculous colour of the shirt he was wearing on the day we first met at Accra Polo Club. And I still dream of him making love to me, after all these years. Those are happy memories, a place to which I can escape when the need arises. You're fortunate, Shika, times have changed. You're an independent, enlightened woman who will make your own choices. Choose wisely, my dear.'

I closed my eyes and rested my head on her shoulder for a moment. There was no need for words. My mother's spirit was alive and well, and sitting right here beside me. I had never felt more whole.

'So, when do you start bossing me about this trip, do we wait until he's asleep?' I whispered after a few minutes.

'Come, let's go and see what he's up to; maybe I can start with part one right now and we can continue later. Hopefully I'll finish bossing you everything before I return to Togapeme tomorrow.'

Sefa was almost done laying out some sheet music for his mother. This was the surprise he had shown her earlier. He had brought her these from Europe and forgotten to give them to her all these months.

When he was done, he went to sit on the back porch. He had taken to spending several hours a day there, just breathing in the crisp, sea breeze. It seemed to keep his spirits up.

I fixed myself some of Emekor's akple and fetri-detsi and made myself comfortable at the dining table. Tassie came and sat by me while I ate. She was even more eager to share than I was to hear what she had to tell.

*

'Ei, Shika! Kofigah is really a man of many connections. He took me to this place behind Afloa Market, not far from the Togolese border. Evidently he has been soliciting help from a spiritual advisor there for some years now.

It was hidden behind a palm grove away from the rest of that town, a one-room structure, just as I expected.

As we approached the building, Kofigah picked up his car mobile phone, dialled a number, and said "we're here" to the person on the other end.'

'Ei, telephone! They're really keeping up with the times, eh?' I laughed over the image.

'That was my exact thought also. Anyway, Kofigah had already bought all the required supplies — a white hen with no blemishes or deformities, same thing with the she-goat. I had never seen a completely spotless, white goat until this weekend. There were some other things in a box. So many symbols and rituals that I never before subscribed to; in fact, I almost backed out. But, having gone all that way, I thought about my son back at home dying, and decided to stay and find out what the spiritualist had to say.

Festus deposited the required items, including the goat and the hen, half way up the path leading to the front of the structure. He seemed to know just what to do. Obviously, it was not the first time he had accompanied Kofigah to this place. Then a young boy appeared from the side of the building and beckoned to us to follow him.

There was no entrance in front. We removed our shoes before entering the building, and once inside, we deposited any electronic devices in a bowl just inside the doorway — Kofigah's pocket watch, my wristwatch; it was as if we were about to go through a border security checkpoint.'

'Maybe they were worried you might record the proceedings or take photographs or something, like in the movies!'

We laughed.

'Perhaps. But this is where it got really interesting and made a sharp departure from what I was expecting. Shika, this was no dark, smoke-filled mud-hut oh! No mysterious voice beckoning from the shadows, nothing spooky. It was a long, open space with the door on one end and a large window on the opposite end. There was a wooden table in front of the window and seated at it, with his back to the window, was the man we had come to see.

Although his features were partially obscured because he had his back to the light, I could see enough detail to realise that he was no bare-chested, mat-haired *juju man* as I was expecting, but a bald-headed, well-groomed, educated man in his mid-to-late fifties; sixty, at most.

Kofigah and I sat on folding chairs while we consulted. Although this was *my* problem, I was equal parts client and clueless observer, never having gone to such a place before.

Standing between the table and us was a second man, obviously lower in rank than the one sitting at the table, and it was this second man who asked me, "Do you understood Ewe, or will you require an English-French interpreter?"

I told him that they could proceed in Ewe.

He then introduced himself as the *otsami*. Imagine that! Of course, that didn't make sense, since we could clearly see and hear the spiritualist communicating in Ewe, and the linguist was merely repeating the same words in the same language. Anyway, he was acting as the spiritualist's otsami, so Kofigah had to act as mine.

He told me, "Your son is dying because you offended someone many years ago by taking possession of something belonging to that person; all the misfortunes that have befallen you since then are retribution for that seizure, because the offended person has a protective covenant with a powerful oracle."

I was completely puzzled, not recalling ever having waylaid anyone to steal anything.

"But, I don't understand," I said, and he spelt out the details to me.

Apparently, my first marriage to B.T. Dodzi was the bone of contention. His first wife was supposedly offended because I had stolen her husband, hence my string of bad luck since then.'

'Eh? You stole him from his wife?' I asked.

'I was amazed too, not that I accepted any culpability, mind you. I knew the man had been married before, but he *had* properly divorced his wife long before I arrived on the scene. My father sent people to investigate all these details before he gave me away in marriage. No, my amazement was over the fact that the spiritualist knew *anything* at all about my life prior to meeting me, and in such specific detail!

I had my suspicions, of course, but how could I accuse a spiritualist of being in cahoots with my own brother, perhaps, or someone else feeding him information about my life? I couldn't prove it, and even if I could, I didn't know what the established procedure was to level such an accusation. Besides, I was curious to see what else they had on me. And so I just sat there.

Anyway, to reverse this curse so that I should experience no further bad luck, the otsami produced a written list of items to be used to placate the woman's oracle. He checked off each item when we confirmed that we had it. These were the items we had brought along, which the young boy had already transferred from the front of the building to the back of the room. Sacrificing them would insure me against future calamity.

But as to my current state of distress, the spiritualist said that he did not possess the power to reverse it. The only one who held that key was the former Mrs Dodzi herself. I would have to search for this woman and beg her for forgiveness.

"But, where am I to find this woman? I have no relationship at all with her — I don't even know her," I said to him.

"That is where my part ends and yours begins," he said. "It is out of my hands now. If in fact you want your son to live, then you will have to do what you need to do to complete the redemption process."'

At that point, I began gagging over the last morsel that I had placed in my mouth. It sat in there for a little while. I finally swallowed hard. I coughed and took a gulp of water.

'Ei, so what did you do, Tassie?' I asked. I held my breath for her answer.

'Wait, I'm coming to the best part. Careful you don't choke on your akple. Before he sent me on my way, the spiritualist told me that if I failed to do what was necessary to redeem my son and he ended up dying, I would have established my identity as a witch, with a preponderance of evidence backing that claim, namely, the quadruple-calamity record which I would have under my belt.'

I looked puzzled, so Tassie clarified even before I could ask what she meant.

'Being labelled "barren"; then losing my husband; and my baby; and now, losing my son — in other words, I owe a debt to some woman that I don't even know, and so I may have to sacrifice my son in order to honour that debt.'

As soon as she uttered the last word, Tassie's voice cracked.

Could it be? Finally? I dropped my morsel of food and ran to wash my hand, making it back to her side just as the first sobs shrank her noble shoulders and bowed her proud head.

'Tassie!' I rushed to her side and knelt by her chair. I had watched a long time for her to release some of the stress I knew she must have been under all these months; but not like this, not under such an ominous cloud of condemnation piled on top of her pain! I could not manufacture any words with which to comfort her, and this was a place where she needed to be right now. So I placed my hands on hers and just waited.

We stayed like that for a while, long after she had finished sobbing. She sat with her hands still folded together and the most wounded expression on her face, just staring off into space. This was hardly the time to press her for the rest of the story.

When I heard Sefa shuffling toward the door, I patted Tassie's hand gently to bring her back to the present.

'He's coming in now,' I said.

She collected herself and went into the bedroom.

The next morning, I came to pick her up and took her on a couple of errands. She finished telling me about her trip to the spiritualist.

'When we left the palm grove, Kofigah told me that he knew where the lady in question lived, and offered to accompany me there. I wasn't surprised at all. When we arrived at the woman's house, we were ushered in together. After the greetings and introductions, we stated our business with her.

The lady, Mrs Grace Amuzu, politely expressed the desire to meet with me alone. Kofigah declined her invitation to wait in another part of the house where he would have been well entertained. After he left with the driver, Mrs Amuzu explained to me that she hadn't wanted to discuss my private business in front of my brother because the topic did not appear to pertain to him.

We got to learn more about each other that afternoon. After I poured out my heart and explained the events that had led me there, Mrs Amuzu told me that she had never harboured any animosity toward me. She told me how her first set of in-laws had driven her out of that marriage, after blaming her for the lack of children during the short span of that union.

"All I heard was that, after that foolish man divorced me, he kept marrying one unfortunate young woman after the other," she told me. "You were number three, and came along fifteen years after he had divorced me; and although I had never met you, I felt sorry for you, knowing what was in store for you. You see, I knew from day one that *he* was the one who was sterile. But as you know, in this society the initial reaction is to blame the woman. I remarried two years after leaving him, and had four children of my own. Do you really think that I had time or energy to focus on B.T. Dodzi or wonder about his other victims? *Pswii!* My sister, that man did me a favour by divorcing me. Why would I hate you? *You're* lucky you got away so easily, with a divorce settlement and all. They probably suspected by then that their son was the one with the problem and not you. *I* left with the clothes on my back."

Then I also shared with her the last details that I had on our ex-husband. I had heard that after me, it took two more marriages for him to have children. That last woman, she was fresh out of the university when they married her for him. She was one-third his age and gave him three children, none of whom looked anything like anyone in his family; but he *had* managed to prove his manhood before he died — he had fathered three children. And then, they tried to fight his widow in court over property, but couldn't quite explain why they thought that his three children should not inherit him. Needless to say, she won, hands down.

Mrs Amuzu also showed me her family album. She revealed that her youngest daughter, Afi, had died ten years earlier in a car accident and empathised with me over my present agony. She said that she was a staunch Pentecostal who chose not to mix traditional religion with her faith. She encouraged me not to allow Kofigah to bully me into compromising my beliefs, especially since he was the younger.

Apparently, she went through the same thing with *her* brother when her second husband died many years ago, and again when her daughter died. Her brother also wanted to take her, against her will, to some shrine. Each time, she told him to take the lead and be sure to greet the fetish priest when he arrived there.'

'Now they're trying to clean up their image by using technology and labelling themselves with highfaluting titles,' I said, 'but they are all charlatans, Tassie. They thrive on lazy and greedy fools who feel entitled to the fruits of other people's labours.'

'That was exactly what Mrs Amuzu said. But in her case, she didn't have to worry that her in-laws would come to fight her over property when her second husband died because he did not leave behind a half-penny; besides, his relatives were very cultured people. But, just to be sure, she didn't leave anything to chance. The experience with B.T. had really toughened her, and she had vowed never again to give anyone, least of all in-laws, that kind of power over her life. So, she took all the necessary precautions along the way.

Her husband, God rest his soul, was a good, kind man, she said; but he seemed to be satisfied with his modest, civil servant's salary, even though adding her paycheque was barely allowing them to get by. Yet, there they were, with four little girls to bring up. It fell to her to do something so that their girls wouldn't grow up and end up having to sell their bodies just to have a decent life. And *she* certainly wasn't going to just sit there and allow herself to end up in poverty during her old age.'

'What a tough woman,' I said. 'So what did she do?'

'Hm. She borrowed money and went into fabric trading at a time when people had money to spend, unlike today. She threw off her nurse's garb on her days off, donned her *wrapper and duku*, and did what it took. Her two older girls helped her during school breaks. They did this for two years before she made the final commitment.

Right after she gave up her nursing job and sank what little money she had saved into the business, they woke up one morning, and there was her beloved husband in the bed, dead from a heart attack. They lost his modest income overnight. Imagine what would have happened if she hadn't had the guts to pursue her own dreams,' Tassie said.

'Or if she had been cursed with a husband who felt threatened by her ambition,' I said.

'She was luckier than most. She said that her older girls gave up the chance to further their education. They joined her fulltime after secondary school. By the time the last two were old enough to join them, they had already broken through, and there was no need for the younger daughters to also give up their dreams of going on to the university. They worked very hard for everything they ever acquired. So naturally, all their properties are legally in her name and her daughters' names.'

'Now, none of their children, or their children's children will ever go hungry,' I said.

'Never again,' Tassie said. 'Even her dead daughter's children are none the worse since their mother died. All three grandchildren are in European universities. One is on full scholarship; as for the other two, their grandmother pays for their tuition in hard cash with monies that she has sitting in European bank accounts.'

We finished our ride in silence. I couldn't stop thinking about Tassie's encounter with that remarkable woman. I wondered how it was that women like Tassie and Mrs Amuzu became conditioned to overcome obstacles, while others only crumbled under less trying circumstances.

SEVEN

The whole clan was there — Fo Kofigah's three married sons and their wives; the two younger sons; Emekor; all the grandkids. It was unforgettable. Daa Jane had outdone herself by preparing a feast befitting royalty. And Sefa was amazing. He seemed to have discovered a panacea from somewhere, such that by Saturday morning he was able to drag himself around the house without the aid of his walking stick, making it unnecessary for us to bring along the wheelchair.

He had everyone at the family gathering highly entertained by his jokes, and I watched in awe as the body language of the in-laws, none of whom had ever met him, changed from near-horror over his extreme emaciation and distorted features to a comfortable camaraderie as with an eccentric but familiar friend.

There was ample opportunity to talk to Emekor alone and find out what had happened.

'Eheh? I'm listening,' I said. We had escaped briefly to her bedroom so that she could try on the remaining clothes that I had brought.

'You know, Daavi Shika, you must be psychic. You won't believe what their reaction was when I went to their house and told them that I was no longer interested in following them to Europe. It was quite hostile. Sister Hassana told me that she didn't expect such ingratitude from me, of all people, considering how close her sister and I were, and how they considered me one of them, this and that. I was stunned! It was almost as if she wanted to force me to change my mind on the spot.'

'And what about Hadi herself?'

'I haven't yet spoken to her alone. I went back to their house yesterday, but the houseboy came to the gate before I even got to it and told me, "They're out!" I tried telephoning her all afternoon, but she wouldn't come to the phone. It wasn't until this morning that I got her on the line; and it was very brief. She was very civil, as if she were talking to a stranger. She said that she was busy packing because she would be leaving to her sister's tomorrow and flying to Europe next week.'

'Oh, Emekor.' I patted her shoulder.

'It was really hard holding that last conversation,' she said. 'It seems that I have to face the ending of a life-long friendship. As soon as she gets to Europe, she will cut all ties to me, I can just feel it. But I kept thinking about what you told me, and it just made sense to stick to this decision.'

'I have never been prouder of anyone in my whole life,' I said. I squeezed her hand. Not until she reached out her other hand with a whimsical smile and brushed a tear from my cheek did I realise the weight of the burden I'd been carrying around for the past few days, praying that she would do the sensible thing. Still, she *had* attended kindergarten with Hadi; this couldn't be easy on either of them.

'Yes, I know you are. I'm feeling quite proud of myself too.'

'It's okay to mourn the loss of a friendship because every friend is precious and has a place in time,' I said, 'but not every relationship is meant to last forever. Each has a purpose, and if that purpose has been fulfilled, you need to release it and let it go. New ones will come along. In time, you will discover that it isn't the duration of a relationship that defines it as real friendship, but rather the quality of a relationship that determines how long it will last. Just wait and see. Who is to say that your paths will not cross again later when you've both gained greater wisdom about life and can contribute more to a real friendship that will last forever?'

She kept nodding vigorously, as if to keep my words from evaporating. But I sensed that her mind was made up; she was merely experiencing a little anxiety over the impending separation. I was concerned all the same about that final split, hoping that it would go well.

'So are you going to try to meet Hadi or talk to her again before Tuesday, a final goodbye or something like that?' I asked.

She shrugged one shoulder; again, that whimsical smile.

'Tuesday will come soon enough,' she said, 'we shall see. Come on, let's go downstairs; they must be missing us by now.'

The mood outside had undergone a drastic shift. Sefa had begun vanishing with one cousin at a time to conduct a one-on-one farewell session, as became apparent as soon as they returned to the gathering. There were a lot of red eyes, and more hard liquor flowing.

I looked at my watch. I had to be at the airport by seven-thirty. We would be cutting it close if we didn't start winding down. And it was about time I cornered Fo Kofigah and had my chat with him. I found him inside with his pipe, taking a break from the heat.

'Ah, Shika, come and sit down beside me and let's chat,' he said. 'Whenever you come to visit during those fortnightly intervals, you're always in a hurry and we never get the chance to talk. Now I see why. Sefa's situation appears to be more serious than I thought. And now, here he is bidding everybody farewell. Funnily enough, apart from looking pale and thin as a ghost, and not counting his obvious physical defects, his spirit is intact. He can still captivate an audience. Just listen to him.' He shook his head in disbelief. 'Ah, what bad-luck is this? Whose toes did we tread on, eh?'

He looked at me, but I too just shook my head sadly.

'Hm, God knows everything, Fo Kofigah.'

He rocked back and forth, puffing at his pipe while I sat quietly beside him digesting the scene through the window. Finally I asked his permission to discuss something important concerning Emekor.

He waved his pipe and told me to dispense with the formality and cut to the chase, this after I went around in circles for a couple of minutes.

'You *book-long* women — always with something to discuss. Now it's stuck in your throat, and I bet you practiced in front of the mirror for hours. Well, I'm listening. Carry on.'

His comments irritated me a little bit more than usual, especially following Tassie's account of her adventure with him; but I checked my attitude. After all, the objective was to get him to be agreeable.

'I had a chance to talk to Emekor when she was with me, and it seems that we have a lot of interests in common,' I said. 'I was thinking that once I return to Accra, I would like to help her in any way that I can, in case she wants to follow a similar career path.'

'Did she ask for your help?' He cut in before I could finish. 'Is that what she's been doing behind my back, plotting to escape from the disciplined atmosphere in which she is being brought up and submit to *your* influence?' He thrust with his pipe for emphasis. 'And exactly what help is it that you think *you* qualify to give her, living in that Accra with no husband, going and coming as you please?'

I seemed to have opened a can of worms, and the free-flowing whiskey was not helping either. I tried to reason with him, but he had a lot on his heart, it seemed. He proceeded to drag me through a litany of grievances that I had apparently committed over the years against his sensitivities. It was pointless.

Finally, I was able to steer his attention off Emekor's supposed role in the 'plot' before I gave up the attempt.

It was time to say our farewells. Fortunately, everyone had been preoccupied all this time. I escaped outside. One look at my face and Sefa himself initiated the goodbyes. It was another ten minutes before we were done shaking all the hands, exchanging all the hugs, lingering by the car, and finally pulling away.

'After church tomorrow, I will probably hang out with Jean for the rest of the day; will you be fine?' I asked Sefa when we were driving home. I had less than an hour in which to pick Jean up from the airport.

'I'll be fine,' Sefa said, 'but if he isn't too exhausted from his trip, you don't mind asking him if I can meet briefly with him at some point this weekend, do you?'

Although I didn't mind, I asked him why, considering how carefully he had avoided being seen by almost everyone we knew.

He said that it was very important, and assured me that he could handle it, so I agreed to mention it to Jean.

*

It had been almost three months since I last saw Jean, and things had been quite different between us then.

Our paths had crossed professionally several years ago, and it was no secret that he had had a thing for me from the first time he saw me, or so everyone said. Even before I knew of him, he had been surreptitiously asking questions about my private life from everybody around me.

Over time, we became very comfortable with each other and regularly socialised, but I never allowed it to go beyond my comfort level. And then, about a year ago, Jean told me that he loved me and wanted to take our friendship to the next step, even marry me on the spot, if that's what it would take. I had been quite touched by his admission and flattered by his proposal, but I told him that I was not ready to change the status of our relationship.

At any rate, he had responded to my rejection by telling me that he was content to wait for me. He seemed confident that things would progress between us, as if he knew something about the future that *I* could not see.

And so, Jean and I had become even better friends. He made me feel light-hearted and carefree.

*

As it turned out, his flight was ten minutes behind schedule. I was really nervous. I kept looking in the opposite direction and did not see him approach. And then, there he was, right behind me.

129

He startled me by speaking straight into my ear: 'What does a guy have to do around here to get noticed by you?'

I spun around, and he caught me by the waist. He just clasped my hands with one hand and kept the other firmly around my waist. We stood like that it seemed forever, with our noses touching. Actually, barely, since I am an inch taller than he, and my slippers added another couple of inches.

I could hardly breathe. I closed my eyes for a moment and rubbed my face against his.

When I opened my eyes, he was staring into them. He made a funny face and pulled my nose. I pursed my lips and smiled back. Without saying a word, he placed my hand in the crook of his arm, and pushing the cart, he strutted out of the airport with me hanging on his arm.

All my usual inhibitions flew out the window. For the first time, I did not look about me to see who was staring at me in the company of a white man — one shorter than me and balding, at that — nor did I try to assess people's expressions. What a relief it was to let go and just live in the moment for a change. I must have walked to the car, although I do not actually recall executing the motions.

I had remembered at the last minute to bring Sefa's four-by-four in case there was a lot of luggage. Jean insisted on driving.

'I've been sitting around all day, and flying first-class is hardly labour-intensive. I know you've had a long weekend already. How nice of Bullet to let you borrow his vehicle. How is he, by the way?'

'Ah, speaking of which… ' I was just about to convey Sefa's request when the shrill sound of the car phone interrupted me. Jean picked it up — it was Sefa.

After Jean said hello, there was a lot of kidding around and laughter, and then finally, 'Here, why don't you tell her yourself.' He handed me the clunky handset.

'Shishi, don't hate me for this,' Sefa said, 'I don't mean to put you on the spot. But listen, I'm really tired and I don't think that I can stay up for

even ten more minutes. So, just scrap my earlier request to meet Jean
tonight, and spend that time with him. He says he can come by tomorrow.'

'But I thought — ' I was going to say that he hadn't asked to see Jean
tonight, but he didn't let me get the words out.

'I know that you're in good hands,' he continued as if I wasn't trying to
speak, 'and you two have a lot to talk about. Shishi, whatever you decide
to do is fine. Just listen to your heart. So, I'll see you sometime tomorrow,
eh? Goodnight.'

Oh, shucks! What now? I sat for several seconds, the bulky device still
held up awkwardly to my ear, unable to hang up. Jean was looking at me,
trying hard not to laugh.

'Ah, good! At least one of us finds this funny,' I said.

'Listen, Shika.' He took the phone from my hand and replaced it on its
stand. 'We have a to talk about, more than anything. You do agree, yes?'

'I know.'

'The way I see it, these are our options: me continuing to sit beside you
here in the dark in the airport parking lot; you sitting across from me in
some watering hole; or us sitting beside each other in my house — which,
by the way, is just ten minutes from here — eating and talking, with
nobody staring at us. Which option should we pick?'

The choices were so preposterous that we were both laughing by the
time he was through. I conceded.

'Drive, Jean.'

'Good, I will stop for some kelewele.'

We went to his very own Daavi to buy it. He walked to the fire himself
to get it because he was a regular customer and she would top it up once
she saw his face. He picked up some kenkey and fish as well.

While he drove, he regaled me with tales from Calabar and beyond,
and had me in stitches by the time we pulled up to his gate. His watchman
let us in after verifying that it was indeed his boss driving the unfamiliar
car. I had been to his place a couple of times, but always in other company.
I had also been out with him several times, just the two of us. But this

would be our first time together in such an intimate setting. And it was only eight o'clock.

'Woezo!' he said when I walked in.

It was very thoughtful of him to welcome me in my own language. He must have practised for this moment, I concluded. I kicked off my slippers and plopped onto his comfy sofa. I was ready to relax, and that brought a glint to his eyes.

'Give me a minute, let me drag this *portmanteau* out of the way,' he said and vanished around the corner. I ambled about comfortably, looking at his artwork and photographs of him in different parts of the world. His parents were dead, but his only sibling, a sister, still lived in Canada.

'You're meeting my relatives?' he asked, touching the photos of his parents and his sister. 'Colline. She's all I have left, you know. She's still in Canada with her family. I saw them last Christmas.' He smiled. 'Don't look so sad, she's more than enough family. For starters, she's a Gemini, so that's like having two siblings. And she has three sons. She's finally expecting a girl — she's pregnant again.'

'What!' I said.

He laughed at my shocked expression, 'Yes, Shika, some obroni women *do* have more than two children a-piece! Ah, but the food will grow cold. Come on, let's eat!'

I shook my head in amazement. People were just people when it came down to it.

He had some music playing in the background. We ate slowly and in silence, but it was a comfortable silence. I was thinking ahead to 'the talk' after the meal, and wondered if his mind was on that too. We snuck smiles and glances at each other every now and again. I stayed off the kenkey, which would not have gone down well for me this late in the day, and stuck with the fish and kelewele.

This was the longest it had ever taken me to eat a serving of kelewele. I had not eaten any since the day I picked the scattered pieces from my mother's kitchen floor, and it seemed somehow appropriate that this should be the occasion on which to purge the bad memories that had turned me completely off this delicacy for fourteen years.

When we were done, I followed him into the kitchen. We washed, dried, and played with each other's hands like little kids. He would not let go of my fingers afterwards. He leaned against the counter and wrapped his arm around my waist, holding me to him. He looked at me — just like that.

'I'm so glad we're finally here, Shika.' He kissed my fingertips, then raised my hands to his chest and placed them there.

There was no escaping it. I could feel the *ptm-ptm-ptm* of his heart; I could also see his eyes glistening. I looked deep into them. I had never looked in them long enough to notice their colour. They were a dark, rich shade of green, like a Star Beer bottle. I swallowed.

'So am I, Jean, so am I,' I whispered.

I closed my eyes; it seemed right to do so just then, as I had in front of my own mirror a couple of weeks ago. He held my head in his hands and kissed me ever so slowly. Neither of us was breathing. It was as if the entire world held its breath, waiting for us to come up for air.

Afterwards, we just continued standing with our faces together, slowly feeling each other breathe again. We opened our eyes at the same time and he led me back into the living room. The choreography was perfect. We sat on the couch with our hands shaking like teenagers, laughing and whispering all at once, while he showered me with endearments and tenderly touched my face.

'So what excuse did you give your friends in Lomé for not showing up?' I said when I could form the words.

'I told them the truth, that my heart was calling and I couldn't refuse it. Now they can't wait to meet you. They've known your name for years.'

I marvelled at this man — at the depth of his faith and the power of his perseverance in spite of my rejection. I needed to understand this whole process.

'So, how is it that you believed, after all this time, that we would be sitting here today? I mean it's been a long time since we've known each other.'

'Five years, eleven months and fifteen days — and two-and-half hours, to be exact — and you've done an excellent job keeping me at arms length. I always knew, Shika. I could see it in your eyes, hear it in your voice and feel it echo in my heart. It had to be mutual. You just weren't ready to acknowledge it. Sure, there was a wall but I was prepared to wait until you were ready.'

'But, forever?'

'If need be. Yet here we are today, no? And it didn't take forever, did it?

'Only my whole life — thirty-two years is a long time,' I said.

'Make that thirty-eight. Across two continents and an ocean. Yet worth every mile, and every second too.'

We talked and talked, as if we hadn't already been friends for years, and were just now discovering new things about each other. It was healing and revealing at the same time.

Somewhere along the way, he urged me to get more comfortable by changing into one of his nightshirts.

'I never use it,' he said, 'I just have it because one ought to have a nightshirt among one's possessions.'

We did the sensible adult thing by transferring to the bedroom. We continued talking, finally falling asleep, I suppose. I woke up in the middle of the night to use the loo, and found myself alone in the bed, all covered up nicely and everything. When I finished using the bathroom, I tiptoed out of the bedroom and discovered that he had gone to sleep on the couch. I lingered for a moment, just watching him sleep and resisting the urge to touch his face and his shirtless, muscular chest.

'Shika.' He reached for my hand and whispered my name just as I turned to sneak away.

'Jean, there you are. I didn't mean to drive you from your comfortable bed.'

'Don't apologise, it was my decision. I could not fall asleep lying so close to you. Of course, I could have slept in one of the other bedrooms, but that also would have been too close.'

'Oh...' It had not occurred to me how he might feel. 'I suppose I should go back in there, then.'

He jumped off the couch and hooked my waist. 'Don't be ridiculous, it's about a mile to the bedroom, and you have no slippers on. Here, let me at least give you a lift!' He scooped me up and carried me the short distance, depositing me at the door. I could see his eyes really gleaming like a wild cat. He was shaking. I touched his lips and opened my mouth to say something but nothing came out.

He kept his one arm around my waist and with the other, kept my hand held up to his mouth.

'Go, Shika,' he whispered into my fingers, 'I will see you in the morning. Maybe you should lock the door.'

He made a growling sound as I slid into the bedroom.

I reluctantly shut the door and leaned against it. After a couple of minutes, when I did not hear him leave, I slowly opened the door a crack and peeped out.

He was pushing against the opposite wall with his fists and forehead, his back turned to me. He did not see me.

I left the door cracked open about three inches, tiptoed through the darkness to the bed and slid back in. I turned on my side, facing away from the door and went to sleep.

Some sleep! I must have lain there maybe thirty minutes, waiting for his footsteps to either walk away or walk in, before I drifted off. But it was a fitful sleep. I kept turning and reaching out across the bed. Something was missing. Every time I looked toward the crack in the door, I thought I still saw his shadow there; but how could that be? It was more than an hour later by now!

'Jean?' I finally whispered his name, just to be sure.

'Mon coeur!' he responded immediately, as if he had been waiting to hear me beckon. He slowly came into the bedroom and closed the door behind him.

In the morning, I drove back home to prepare for church. Jean was still sleeping when I left. By the time I arrived at my house, he had left a groggy-sounding message on my answering machine to say that I should meet him at Sefa's after church, and to bring along my swimsuit.

I still had no idea what Sefa wanted to discuss with him, but they had a decent enough relationship and they were grown men capable of interacting without my help; so I focused on church.

After service, I went back home to get my swimsuit and change into casual clothes; and then I drove to Sefa's to meet Jean so that we could go on our date.

Miyo's car was parked outside when I drove up.

'Hey girl, I didn't know you were coming by,' I said to her.

'Yeah, I bet you didn't,' she said, looking at me slyly. 'No wonder you didn't pick up your phone all evening, you weren't home,' she whispered in my ear.

I smiled but said nothing.

'Sweetie will also be stopping by with the tailor to deliver my suit later this afternoon,' Sefa said, 'I'm going to have a full house.'

'You lovebirds run along then; call me later, Shika,' Miyo said. She winked at me mischievously and waved us off.

Jean and I left in his car. I was curious about his visit with Sefa, but he seemed to be quite focused on driving so I just stuck to small talk and tried to guess where he was taking me.

'Now, you're going to have to close your eyes for maybe twenty minutes and not ruin the surprise,' he said after we left the hub of the city. But he knew that I would definitely cheat. I hated surprises.

Through my partially closed eyes, I found out soon enough when he turned onto the road leading to Hippo Lodge. But of course! I might have known!

I started giggling all the way to the parking lot.

'I already made reservations for the entire afternoon,' he said when he came around to help me out of the car.

I had only been to Hippo Lodge once, but as soon as we walked in, it all came back to me.

We sat next to each other in a cosy corner of the restaurant, hanging right over the beach. I cuddled up to him and gave him a peck on the corner of his mouth.

'You are so sweet and thoughtful, this is really special,' I said softly.

He smiled back at me, and put his arm around me. He was now in a talkative mood.

'Ma pauvre, how you must have suffered!' he said, and held me close, with more sensitivity than I thought the occasion warranted. 'I'm going to come and see you every weekend for as long as it takes to finish what you've been doing.'

I was puzzled. I started to sit up, but he shushed me with a finger to my lips.

'I know, Shika. I know everything. Bullet admitted it when I asked him outright if he had AIDS. The next thing I asked him was whether he had told you.'

'Oh?' I sat up and looked at him.

'I just took one look at him and knew. Actually, he seemed relieved that I had asked him. He told me how he had hurt you by keeping it from you for too long, and asked me to thank you for your selflessness. He said that he wanted to leave you in good hands, to make sure that I still have noble intentions toward you, and all that good-brotherly stuff. We actually covered everything.'

'And do you? Have noble intentions, I mean.'

He pulled my nose and laughed.

'Let me think about it for a week, and when I come to see you in Togapeme, I'll tell you what intentions I have. But first, I have to decide how long I'll be able to keep lying beside you without jumping over the pillow that you placed between us.' He laughed again when I rolled my eyes. 'It was quite charming actually, and I knew to expect that. You didn't disappoint me.'

I looked at him coyly and pouted.

He winked at me.

I looked down at the menu. This man never ceases to amaze me, I thought; I can't believe he remembered…

*

I had just been assigned to a new project. I came to Hippo Lodge for a work retreat organised by my employer and the two organisations with which we were partnering.

The seven members of the leadership team were here to meet each other to brainstorm. I was the last person to arrive that Friday, so I didn't even bother checking in. Dragging my overnight case behind me, I went straight to the introductory meeting. I tried to look composed as I entered room 205.

A shaggy-bearded white man in spectacles was addressing the group, but he stopped as soon as I entered. He came up to me, took my case from me, and stashed it out of the way.

'Scoot over one seat, everyone, so that the lady doesn't have to climb over to the empty seat,' he said.

This placed me right next to him, and he made sure that I was seated comfortably before he sat down again. For whatever reason, this generated amused reactions from the rest of the team. I only recognised two people in the group: Sylvester Boye, the other programme analyst from my office, and Valeria Malloy, an American technical expert from one of the other organisations. Valeria and I were the only women in the group.

After we had tackled the last item on the agenda, a waiter came to escort us to dinner. Sylvester, Valeria and I strolled together to the restaurant, and I secured a seat between the two of them when we got to our table.

'Since we still have some fifteen minutes to play with, I'm going to check in quickly and freshen up before dinner,' I said. Then I dashed off.

Everyone was seated again when I returned to the table. I noticed at once that the seating arrangement had been slightly adjusted. Valeria had moved down one space and in her place, next to me once again, was the rugged looking obroni man with red hair.

Valeria and Sylvester were pokerfaced. My two friends could not look at me, and I got the distinct impression that there was a conspiracy of sorts afoot. It was a little annoying, but that was neither here nor there because we were there to do a job and I didn't want to be distracted.

'Could we go over the introductions again? I'm sorry that I came in a little late to the opening meeting.' I started the ball rolling by introducing myself to the group.

They all took turns and it ended on the annoying man sitting to my right.

'And my name,' he said in his unusual accent, 'is Jean-Marc Charbonneau; but everybody calls me 'JM.''

'Ah.' I smiled and nodded politely.

I had first heard about this JM when my boss called me into his office a couple of weeks earlier to tell me about the assignment. Apparently this man was the project lead and *he* had made the final selection of who would be on this team.

'I hear the guy asked for you by name,' Sylvester had told me when he and I discussed our new assignment over lunch the day after we had been selected.

'Really? I didn't know that I even made the shortlist, and they never pick a woman anyway, so I knew that I wouldn't make the final cut,' I said.

'Precisely — you didn't. But JM turned down the guy who was their other recommendation with the excuse that there were enough men on the team. Then I hear he skipped over the other two women who *did* make the shortlist, opened the next page, and circled your name on the original long list. I'm just glad it wasn't I who got turned down.' Sylvester had a smug look on his face.

That explained why so many cold stares followed me around the office when the final selection was announced; but I went on my mettle and prepared for the new assignment with gusto, grateful for the opportunity to prove that I was a capable professional in my own right.

At no point during the project did JM Charbonneau ever do anything out of line, or exhibit any behaviour that lent credence to the office gossip. He was the perfect gentleman throughout the assignment.

I found it quite preposterous that a man I barely knew could possibly be attracted to me, as people were insinuating.

*

'Hm. Table sixteen,' I said, looking at him. 'Was it a coincidence, or did you specifically request it?'

'I bribed and cajoled to get table sixteen, just for a chance to start over,' he said.

'Okay, you have a captive audience now. One, two, three — go!'

'My name is Jean-Marc Charbonneau; everybody calls me 'JM' but I would like to hear you call me 'Jean' in that sexy voice of yours.'

'Uh — in your *dreams*, Monsieur Charbonneau!'

'And by the way, I would also like to ask your permission to begin glaring at other men who look at you when we are together, and to begin kissing you noisily and excessively whenever we go out, like a proper Francophone. Do we have an agreement?' he asked.

'You mean like this?' I leaned over and planted a kiss firmly on his lips, much to his delight, and to the discomfiture of the waiter who had just arrived with our lunch.

The rest of that day passed like a sweet dream. Hippo Lodge was going to occupy a special place in our relationship going forward. I just knew it.

EIGHT

Looking back, I now see how much effort it must have taken for Sefa to go through that last weekend in the city. It was as if he had saved up enough energy to hang in there long enough to do the things that he needed done in those few days.

When Jean and I returned to his place after our day out on Sunday, I called Emilia to make sure that all Sefa's daily needs had been met. Then I chatted with him briefly. He sounded as if he was in very good spirits.

'Sweetie did stop by with the tailor, as promised, to fit my tuxedo,' he said. 'The quality of his workmanship is superb, and he has taken it back to finish it.'

'I would have expected no less from someone recommended by Sweetie. Anyway, I'm still at Jean's. I just wanted to check on you.'

'Don't worry about me, Shishi. I don't need anything, just stay where you are,' he said. 'I'll see you in the morning.'

I had not heard him sounding that carefree in a long time. I almost didn't recognise his voice. And so I relaxed and spent another night with Jean.

On his way to work in the morning, Jean dropped me at Sefa's.

'Happy birthday, mon coeur,' he said and handed me a box. 'I hope you like it. I thought of you as soon as I saw it.'

My mouth formed into a silent 'oh!' I stared at the flat, square package. I hadn't even remembered my own birthday.

'I'll stop by to have breakfast with you before you leave tomorrow,' he said when he came around to let me out.

'I'll let you know if I like what's in the box. Thank you.' I kissed the corner of his mouth.

He unlatched the gate for me to enter; then he waited for me to close it again before he drove off.

Miyo's car was parked in the courtyard behind mine.

She must have stopped by early to see Sefa, I concluded.

I entered through the kitchen and walked through the house. There was no sign of anyone. Puzzled, I walked to Sefa's bedroom door and listened, but I heard nothing. I hesitated a moment, then I knocked lightly.

'Come in,' Sefa said. He sounded drowsy.

I went in about two paces and stopped. Sefa was still under the covers and there, curled up in the curve of his body, fast asleep, was Miyo.

'What time is it?' He yawned; then he sat up and rubbed his eyes. He looked confused.

'It's almost eight.' I pointed to Miyo and asked, 'What the hell?'

He just made a dismissive gesture with his hand and completely ignored me.

'Miyo! Miyo, wake up!' he said, shaking her.

'Oh drat! I'm going to be late for work,' Miyo said. She sprung out of the bed.

I heaved a sigh of relief when I saw that she was clothed — well, she had on panties and one of Sefa's t-shirts. No bra, as far as I could tell. I was at a complete loss for words. I just stood there staring after her as she walked into the bathroom to quickly gargle with his mouthwash and wash her face. I was still standing there when she came out of the bathroom and pulled on her jeans.

'Shika, close your mouth before an insect flies down your throat,' Sefa said.

Miyo laughed. She put on her slippers and ran her hand through her hair.

'I'll talk to you before you leave, Shika. Thanks Sef, these are really special,' she said, hugging a couple more of his t-shirts and his very first trophy.

He smiled; then he reached out his arm. She bent toward him. He rubbed her face affectionately with his hand and she kissed his palm tenderly. I felt that I shouldn't be there, so I turned away, closed the door gently behind me, and went to wait for her in the living room.

I walked her to her car and held the gate open so that she could back out. She was smiling and humming! Miyo didn't engage in useless pastimes like humming and singing, I reminded myself. But she was *humming*. Her face looked more beautiful than I had ever seen it. She paused before pulling away.

'We just needed to write this chapter well, you know? It's all good, Shika.' She sounded unguarded.

'I know, Miyo, I know. Drive carefully,' I smiled at her and watched until she turned the corner.

I went back in and found him preoccupied with his thoughts. I packed his remaining personal effects so that I could transfer them to my house. The only items I left behind were in the small suitcase that he would be taking with him to Togapeme. I kept looking at him closely, trying to read his mood to be sure that he was able to handle his last day in this house where he had once been so happy, and yet now was so pained.

The burst of energy that he experienced last week was still evident, with some other quality that I hadn't seen in him before. The heaviness had lifted, and there was no reason for me to be unduly concerned.

Around eleven, I drove home to finish packing my own things. It was unlikely that I would be travelling back down any time soon, so I would definitely be taking more than the one box that I had already packed.

As soon as I got home, I sat on the bed and opened my birthday present. I gasped.

He must have got me these in Nigeria, I concluded, not because I hadn't seen such beads here before, but because the address of a popular

Calabar boutique was printed on the bottom of the box. I put on the gold-accented coral necklace, matching earrings and bracelet. Then I raised my bejewelled wrist up to my shoulder and considered my aspect in the mirror — from all angles — and drew the only possible conclusion: these beads were a suitable decoration for my distinctive features.

I looked confidently into those eyes and recognised *me*. Then I gingerly removed the pieces, put them back in the box, kissed it, and tucked it into my vanity case. I cast the vixen in the mirror another knowing smile as I turned away slowly.

Sweetie arrived around noon with lunch. I hadn't seen her in more than two weeks, and I wasn't going to just leave town without saying goodbye. She wasted no time getting to the heart of the matter.

'Mawusi-Shika Amenyo,' she started as soon as she had slammed the car door, 'don't tell me that you let that white boy into your goldmine! No, not you!'

I tried covering her blabbering mouth while I pulled her inside.

'Oh, shut up, you crazy girl,' I laughed. 'No, he didn't get into my goldmine; but it wasn't for lack of trying.'

'Good girl!' she said, clapping happily, 'I'm so proud of you. *Never* give a man *anything* until he invests in you. And I mean *heavily*! That's the only language they understand.'

'Haabah! Would you stop with that foolish talk? It's a relationship not a transaction,' I said.

'And who's the economist, you or I? Anyway, I hope you at least checked to make sure that his engine is intact and working properly?'

'Oh, believe me, everything's in tiptop condition, battery fully charged,' I said.

'But, why am I even asking you?' she said. 'You wouldn't know the difference.'

'I remembered your situation, so I made sure that I checked! But he and I have an understanding. We're proceeding cautiously.'

'And he's fine with this understanding, right?'

'Sweetie, the man loves me, okay! What do you want me to say? In any case, since he has already waited this long, what's a little extra time going to do to him?'

'And these are *his* words, or *your* opinion? This longsuffering gentility in anticipation of a woman's love is definitely not African. Ah, excusez-moi, I keep forgetting oh! Anyway, listen. All kidding aside, you remember the rules, right?'

'Yes, Miss Bediako! One: no HIV test, no sex. Two: if I don't feel like participating in some freaky behaviour, I'm a grown woman and I'm allowed to tell a man, "Look here, mister, it isn't by-force, okay?" And three: if a man ever hits me, hit him back harder, preferably in the crotch; *then* call Inspector Yamboni — in that order, if possible.' I recited her self-preservation credo, laughing so hard that by the time I was done, tears were running down my face.

After I stopped laughing, we ate the lunch that she had brought. She updated me on the logistical arrangements she had made for Sefa's house and mine. Our neighbourhood was gated, so I had no security concerns; but I would need the grass cut and the gardens tended while I was gone, and she had agreed to arrange it.

I requested an update on her love triangle drama, but all she said was that she had managed to stave off Sammy's proposal for the time being. I pressed her for details, but she wouldn't budge.

'You have too much on your plate right now,' was all she said. 'I'll update you at the right time.'

'But did you talk to Bronze? And what did he say?'

'I can take care of myself, so don't worry about me.' And then she quoted me a proverb in her native tongue: *"When a single tree tries to withstand the force of the wind, it breaks."'*

'Oh, Sweetie! This proverb of yours is way beyond me, as usual.'

My understanding of Akan was rudimentary at best and definitely did not cover idiomatic expressions; but Sweetie insisted on lacing her advice sessions with carefully placed nuggets of age-old wisdom in her language, which inevitably underwent translation into English for my fuller edification.

'Mawusi-Shika, all it's saying is that you alone cannot do everything for Sefa, for me, for Miyo, and for everyone else that needs you. Allow others the chance to do their part. I will solve my problems, okay? And I will have Lawyer Anyemiyoo Mensah to help me figure things out. Don't worry, eh? Knowing that you care is going to have to suffice for now. Focus on yourself for a change.'

That was easier said than done. They'd always teased me that I wore my heart on my sleeve, that I was too 'deep'; but somebody had to be the thermometer for our group. I suppose I fit the bill by providing the necessary emotional counterbalance in our friendship.

Sweetie's insecurities had led to a few stupid moves that had brought her to this point in her life, but I still didn't want to see her get hurt — she had been through enough already. The next bad decision would only serve to perpetuate the cycle of dysfunction in her life. She needed to break the pattern before she destroyed the only person she had ever cared about.

*

Miyo and I first met Odum when Eno brought him to visit Sweetie in college. Eno had referred to the toddler as 'Sweetie's little brother', which immediately struck us as odd, since Sweetie herself had already told us, when we first met, that she was an only child. Other details of her life's story did not add up either, like the extra two years of secondary education that she seemed unable to account for.

And then there were her issues with body image, like her obsessive preoccupation with her breasts. I mean, who wears a bra to bed *every* single night? And inspects the barely visible stretch marks flanking her underbelly, just above the bikini line, *every* single time she stood in front of the mirror?

Even Miyo, as skinny as she was, had the unforgiving streaks that garnished most women's torsos in strange places. But Sweetie's stripes were actual scars, clearly nature's medals of honour, reserved for those warrior princesses who had made it all the way to the battlefront and back on behalf of the human race. Maybe a man would find it hard to tell the difference, but *we* knew.

'Look,' the outspoken Miyo had eventually put it to her in plain English, 'we're all women here, bound together by this roommate experience. Relax.'

'We all have our baggage,' I added, 'whenever you're ready to let go, we'll be here for you.'

It took a good while; but eventually, Sweetie levelled with us and told us her horror story.

After attending primary school in the small town where she was born, Sweetie had moved to the city with her mother so that she could have access to a good secondary education. Although she herself had never even completed primary school, Eno Bediako recognised the potential in her extremely intelligent and exceptionally beautiful child.

They lived for free in the *boys' quarters* of a relative, and Eno would travel back and forth to the countryside, trading in foodstuffs and other essential commodities.

When Sweetie was thirteen, their relative's college-aged son began routinely raping her whenever he was home.

'If you don't know and you go and breathe a word of this to anyone, my father will kick you and your mother out, back to your little, bush village,' he would always threaten her. And so Sweetie never told. This continued for two years.

Never having missed her period, she was still too naive to realise that she was pregnant when, at fifteen, she began putting on weight around her waist. As luck would have it, her school was not a boarding school, so no one noticed it or teased her about it. She was already several months along by the time her mother detected that she was pregnant.

'Are you trying to ruin your chance at a bright future? Look at all that I'm doing to get us out of poverty!' Eno had ranted at Sweetie, almost clawing her eyes out when she could not or would not say who was responsible for her condition. To this day, Eno still does not know who got her daughter pregnant.

Sweetie said that as soon as she finished her last exam, Eno packed up and moved with her back to the village, where she went and had the baby. Then she stayed home for the remainder of that academic year.

'It's time to go back to the city so that you can finish school,' her mother told her as another school year approached, 'I will stay here and take care of Odum; nobody needs to know that you have had a child.'

'All by myself? But mama, where will I stay?' she asked.

'What do you mean by "where will I stay?" You will go back and continue staying in your father's house, and pick up from where you left off.'

'And that is how I found out who my father was,' Sweetie told Miyo and me. 'That was also the day on which I discovered that my rapist, the father of my son Odum, was my own half-brother. At that point, I realised that I was on my own and had to take my destiny in my own hands.'

So, she had opted to stay in a students' hostel while taking evening classes to prepare for the O-levels. She aced the exams, and went back and forth for two more years so that she could take the A-levels and apply to BISU.

As to how she had sustained herself during that time, Sweetie never supplied us with a definite explanation, and Miyo and I did not find it necessary to press her for one. We were just overcome with shock that anyone as young as that could have already gone through so much and still made it into a university.

Those disclosures elevated our friendship to a different level. I think it needed that for us to actually let her in as one of us and not just see her as the 'other' roommate.

Personally, I couldn't help wondering where *my* life would have been if *I* had not made a different choice when I was eighteen. The extra dose of protectiveness that I developed toward Sweetie was definitely a symptom of survivors' guilt, which I secretly bore within my soul.

Although Sweetie was initially a little wary of Miyo's sharp-tongued, caustic approach and highly amused by my sensitive, nurturing style, we all learnt to adjust to each other's strengths and shortcomings. We soon forged an unbreakable bond of interdependence and loyalty. It became quite clear to Miyo and me that the poor girl was just a pawn in her crazy mother's overriding ambition.

Yet, here she was, ten years later, on the verge of fully morphing into her mother. If we didn't do something urgently, Sweetie might very well fulfil the adage: *'A crab does not give birth to a bird.'*

*

For now, all I could do was nod in agreement and try not to cry as I said goodbye to my tough-shelled nut with the loud mouth and big heart.

'You know already, as for me I don't pray by heart; but I know that *you* do, so I wish you the strength you will need in order to finish well,' she told me.

'Ahuofeh Sweetie Bediako, I'm going to miss you so much,' I said, hanging on to her hands. 'You promise you will try and drive up my mountain to see me in two weeks?'

'I will *try*, but honestly, I can't promise. You have no idea how complicated Odum's calendar is becoming. I know that you will not have a telephone in the house, but try to call me from your post office whenever you can, eh?'

After she left, I lingered by the gate for a moment, basking in the energy that she had brought, and appreciating having her as my friend.

Truly, I reminded myself, this crazy chick empowered me in a way that no one else did.

By mid afternoon, I was done. I called for Enoch to bring the SUV around so that he could load it with my luggage. Then I locked up my house and drove back to Sefa's. We were leaving first thing in the morning.

That evening, Miyo called to remind me to leave the keys with Emilia. She also confirmed that she would be driving up to Togapeme at the end of the week.

'I have not finished preparing Sefa's documents which I've been working on. So, I'll pick up his completed tux from the tailor and bring it along with the documents next weekend, I promise,' she said.

Sefa and I spent a quiet evening, looking at photos of happier times spent in his house, and remembering how excited we had been to discover this housing development.

It was just three years ago when he came to me and encouraged me to invest in my own place in the same community where he had purchased his house just the year before.

When he learnt that the second phase of development had begun, he pushed me to seize the opportunity, and we were quite excited to discover that I could get a property close to his if I hurried. But at the time, I was unable to come up with the full down payment. In the end, it was he who had loaned me the balance I needed to make my dream a reality. I did not get the property that was close to his but I was quite satisfied to secure one on the next street.

He had thrown many unforgettable parties in this house, and it was a shame that his last memories of it should focus on its quiet, empty rooms and the lonely, pain-filled nights of these past few months.

As bedtime drew nearer, I saw his mood undergo a drastic shift.

'Do you want to call Miyo?' I asked him.

'No, I already told her not to come. I don't want her to see me like this,' he said.

He wanted to sleep with his bedroom door and all his windows open. After listening to him struggling to breathe, tossing and turning for a couple of hours, I gathered the covers from my bed and stumbled through the darkness to the living room. Grabbing the cushions from the sofa, I brought everything to his room and prepared myself a place on the floor by his bed. I went to the bathroom and brought a damp face towel to wipe his face and neck. Then I turned on the fan and rearranged the covers about him. I sat and patted him on his back for several minutes. When he stopped struggling and started to breathe evenly, I lay down on my cushions and went to sleep.

In the morning, I allowed him to sleep in for an extra hour before reluctantly waking him up. His mother was expecting us around noon, and She would worry if we didn't show up by one. Emilia had been up early to make sure that we would have something to eat before setting out.

Jean arrived at about seven-thirty to have breakfast with me, just like he had promised. All the sadness and worry I had felt overnight evaporated when I saw him. And when he rubbed my shoulders and assured me that everything would be fine, I felt that I could indeed handle whatever lay ahead.

Sefa walked out and greeted us; then he sat down and had some porridge. I packed his medications into an insulated bag and set it beside his suitcase in the living room. Then I went into the kitchen to hand Emilia the keys and give her last-minute instructions. When Sefa finished eating, he also came to the kitchen to thank Emilia and bid her farewell.

'God bless you for everything you've done for me; you are a good woman.' He handed her a fat envelope.

'Ao, Mr Sefa! May God accompany you and watch over your soul,' she said, kneeling and gripping his hands tightly.

He just smiled at her sadly. 'Make sure Martha finishes school and does something with her life, eh?' he said. Then he patted Martha on her head.

I went back to the dining room. Jean held me close and assured me that he would come to see me every weekend.

'I have to go to Calabar this weekend, so I will come next weekend,' he said.

'You would do that for me?' I asked.

'I've finally won your heart after all these years; believe me, I'm not planning to lose it again. Of course I'm going to come up there every weekend.'

'Wrap it up, love birds, it's time to go.' Sefa said.

Jean folded Sefa's wheelchair and carried it to the vehicle. Emilia and I followed with the remaining luggage.

'Bullet!' Jean shook Sefa's hand and gripped his shoulder; then he helped him into the car.

'I will be expecting you on Friday next week.' I run my fingers down the side of Jean's face and across his mouth.

'I'll be there. Je t'aime, Shika Amenyo. You should go as often as possible to the post office to use the telephone so that I can tell you that when we chat. Be kind to yourself, ma chérie.'

'I love you too,' I said. It no longer felt strange, but I looked forward to the day when I would be able to say it to his face everyday.

He deposited me in the driver's seat and kissed my upturned palm; then he closed my hand over the kiss before waving goodbye. I drove away, overflowing with wellbeing.

The ride to Togapeme was rather pensive. I had expected that during the trip Sefa would want to talk about the weekend, about Jean and me, about Miyo — anything. I tried to convey to him that it was safe for him to communicate his thoughts and emotions to me. But he said that he was feeling drained. And who could argue with him? It had been an emotional weekend for both of us.

I drove nonstop for the three hours. Sefa leaned back with his eyes closed most of the way, as if he could not bear to see those familiar sites along the route for the last time. I played soothing music as we drove further inland, and occupied myself with my thoughts, hearing over and over in my mind Jean's parting words to me. Those words kept me company all the way and enveloped me like a warm blanket against the cold mountain air that met us as we began the ascent toward Togapeme.

SEASON

OF

RAIN

NINE

'*Mia woezo!*' They welcomed us warmly and brought our luggage in. We arrived just before one o'clock to find Tassie anxiously waiting for us. With her were Reverend Anani and a couple of our relatives who had come to help her prepare to receive us. D'Amavi, Tassie's cousin, had even dispatched her daughter Irene to move in with us for as long as necessary to relieve us of some of the housekeeping.

My stomach growled in reaction to the aromas emanating from the kitchen. We dispensed with the lengthy formalities and held hands for the pastor's quick prayer of thanks for our safe arrival. Then we washed our hands and dug in.

The three nights that followed were the most gruelling we would go through with Sefa. Our arrival in Togapeme immediately drew the stark reality of his situation to the fore, and he experienced a complete emotional breakdown that first night.

For three days, Tassie and I took turns sitting by his side and watching over him through the night while he curled himself up in bed and groaned like an animal. Unable to shed tears, he cried out to the universe with questions that we could neither decipher nor answer.

More challenging for me was the fact that he refused to take his medications, and I was faced with the difficult task of calling Efo David, one of the neighbours, to come and help me physically restrain him so that I could force-feed the medicine to him.

After two days of this, his depression began to transfer to his mother and me, and I could not take it anymore. I didn't sleep that night.

On Friday morning, I went to his room and told him in no uncertain terms that I was not going to put up with his self-centred behaviour any longer.

'Everyday people die, Sefa. But they don't deliberately torture those around them in the process, especially the people who care about them and are trying to ease their transition. I've put my whole life on hold for you. Do you think I have nothing else to do with it, other than to sit here and watch you torture all of us, as if we were somehow to blame for your situation?

When Miyo arrives on Saturday, I will return to Accra with her and leave Tassie to take care of you by herself. Perhaps, when you see your mother going through your misery with you, it will restore that sense of control that you feel you have lost. Oh, and don't worry, I *will* come back for your funeral.'

I left him lying there without attempting to give him his medicine.

'I'm going to town to use the post office and stock up for Miyo's visit,' I told Tassie; and then I drove off.

When I returned, he was propped up in the wheelchair under the cashew tree, with Napo lying at his feet. He did not look at me. I said nothing either, just carried the supplies in and unpacked them. Tassie was in the living room taking a nap on the sofa. I spent the rest of the day tidying up in preparation for our guest.

Sefa's energy level was much higher by the next morning, and although we were both under strain from Friday's confrontation, we tried to maintain a veneer of civility in front of Tassie while we eagerly waited for our dear friend. By the time she arrived, things were almost back to normal.

Miyo got there just in time for lunch, bringing along the documents and the completed tuxedo. Sefa's fitting of the crimson brocade suit was the highpoint of the day. He twirled around with the aid of his walking stick, primped and bowed to our cheers.

He had derived a perverse sort of pleasure from the process of planning his burial outfit down to the finest detail; and the irony that he would be laid in state in this flamboyant monstrosity that he would never be caught alive wearing only seemed to heighten that thrill. It was a good thing that his mother had gone for choir practice. She would not have found anything to laugh about.

I left them discussing the documents while I went to iron Tassie's choirmaster robe and my church outfit. Miyo declined the invitation to accompany us to church in the morning.

'I have to leave early tomorrow, but I can go with you this afternoon to run errands,' she said.

I had already placed a special order of *abolo* and *abobi* to send to Auntie Tati. Togapeme was known for having the fluffiest, freshest abolo in the entire region and no visitor left here without a hefty supply of our 'manna from the mountain'.

In the late afternoon, I circumnavigated our little town with Miyo, pointing out its landmarks to her.

'There's the post office, my lifeline to the rest of the world; and next to it is our department store,' I said.

'Ei, by the way,' she said, 'how's his royal highness doing? Does he know you're back? I'm short of corned beef. Any supply coming soon?'

I flashed her an irritated look but her eyes were clear pools of innocence. I tried to laugh at the joke but my laughter came out as more hostile than amused even to myself.

*

I had caught the eye of this man-about-town during the two weeks when I accompanied Sefa here after he first returned from Amsterdam. My unlikely suitor was one Efo Yao, the well-known and respected owner of our only department store, whose direct approach to courting me had been the brunt of much entertainment for Tassie and Sefa.

161

I met the gentleman for the first time when I walked into his store to pick up some supplies for Tassie. He very helpfully followed me about the store chatting me up — in English, of course — and gave me a huge discount; and then he carried my box of supplies to the car for me.

Two days later, he sent someone to bring Tassie a gift of one carton of Exeter brand corned beef with a verbal message informing her that he was interested in courting me.

Bristling with indignation, Tassie asked the messenger, 'Hoh! So, is that why he has sent me this *box* of Exeter? In exchange for my daughter's affections?'

The messenger hastened to sooth her vexation by clarifying that the corned beef was totally unrelated to the expression of interest; the presence of the canned meat was a mere coincidence, in fact, and solely intended for Tassie's nutrition, with no strings attached — whatsoever! And so, Tassie kept the corned beef and sent him a rather crisp response thanking him and informing him, 'Shika is a grown woman who makes her own decisions.'

After the messenger left, Tassie laughed and teased me until she wept.

'Just listen to this arrogant buffoon!' she said. 'It really takes some audacity to approach the choir-mistress of your church and ask to court the granddaughter of a priest.'

'And then, to add insult to injury, bring along a box of corned beef, no less! Where are the other ingredients? Does he expect us to eat the corned beef by itself?' Sefa chimed in.

As far as I could tell, Efo Yao had not even completed primary school. Not that *that*, in and of itself, was an issue; but his insistence on displaying his limited English vocabulary that first time he addressed me had been an immediate turn-off. For some reason, he had felt that chatting with me in really terrible English would impress me better than if he spoke in our own language, as I was doing.

Yet, as bad as that was, it was hardly the cause of Tassie's indignation. His greater offense lay in the fact that he was already married to a woman his age, the mother of his children — his six grown children. Who said I deserved somebody's chenchema with excess baggage in tow?

After that, I stayed away from his store. But every time I went into town to do anything, he or his relatives would pop up out of nowhere and try to slay me with charm. Nothing came of their efforts, however; and when I returned to the city at the end of those two weeks, that was the end of my encounters with the bunch of them. Miyo and Sweetie nicknamed him 'Prince of Exeter' when I narrated the hilarious details to them.

Since I returned, I had kept a low profile, being careful not to draw attention to myself whenever I visited the post office. But just the day before, when I went to market to stock up for Miyo's visit, I came across one of his relatives. My polite greeting froze in my throat when she made a big fuss and referred to me as 'in-law' in front of people, as if the deal were already carved in stone.

*

'Come on, let's go and pick up your abolo,' I said to Miyo, driving by cautiously as if I expected Efo Yao or one of his relatives to jump out in front of the vehicle at any moment.

'Ei, Abolo Factory! Is she still alive? I remember her from way back when we came for your mom's funeral. Even then, she looked really wizened.'

'I think you're confusing D'Amavi with her mother, who was my grandfather's sister,' I said. 'The old lady died maybe four or five years ago. In fact, hers was the next funeral in town, right after my mom's. Her daughter Amavi moved back to the family house to run the operation after the funeral. Nothing has changed, it tastes exactly the same and the business is really thriving. They've stopped vending it by the roadside, though. The other vendors now come and buy it from her at wholesale, so it *has* become a real factory, with a signboard and everything — Amavi's Abolo Factory — imagine that!'

'Good for her!' Miyo said. She was always delighted anytime a woman took charge of her finances.

We stayed up chatting deep into the night about Sefa. I told her how he had pushed me to the point where I had threatened to go back to Accra with her.

'Don't be silly. You're not leaving,' she said. 'You'd never forgive yourself, and we would have a basket case on our hands after his funeral. He's changed in one week, you know. He's too calm and carefree. I think it's a sign that it's over. He seems to be at peace or something.'

I slept on her words, not sure that I agreed with her because I had not noticed any such change.

In the middle of the night, I felt her sneak out. She went to lie beside him until dawn. By the time we woke up in the morning, she had left without saying goodbye. And on Sefa's pillow where her head had lain was a bracelet fashioned out of braided strands of raffia. The bracelet was looped about a piece of rolled up graph paper. I found him sitting up in bed staring at it with tears in his eyes. He handed me the paper. I unrolled it and showed it to him. Written on it were just two words: *I comport.*

I wiped my own tears, and then I took his hand and placed the bracelet around his wrist.

I went alone to church. Today's service was going to be the last one in the main sanctuary for a while and everybody was going to be there. Tassie was to conduct the whole choir, so she had left early for choir rehearsal before service.

'Don't forget to take along the camera,' Sefa said.

'Why don't you come along?' I urged him, 'we can just sit in the back.' But he wouldn't.

'Just be sure and take pictures of everyone,' he said, 'I want to see all their faces.'

I knew what he was thinking. It was where we had all been christened; where my mother had been laid in state; where he probably would lie if he tarried a while, God willing, and the renovation picked up pace. It was a sobering thought. I squeezed his arm without saying a word. Then I left him under the watchful eye of Efo David.

I always felt a sense of awe whenever I entered the sanctuary in Togapeme, and it was clear that this service was going to be one to remember. Walking through the doors and sitting in our family pew connected me with my heritage as nothing else could.

*

The church had once been a thriving mission house, initially built circa 1830 by four German brothers, missionaries of unknown denomination, who would be instrumental in bringing Christianity and Western education to the small towns and villages nestled around Togapeme. It is not known if they were active elsewhere in Togoland before coming to settle in Togapeme.

However, the brothers Gottlieb of Togapeme ransomed countless African captives who were being transported by European slave traders along the Volta River toward the Gulf of Guinea. The brothers used this strategically isolated mission house as a secret haven where they sheltered and educated these rescued men and women for more than sixty years. Three of them also married local women. As a result, the town's population is made up entirely of the descendants of rescued captives and the German missionaries, and their unusual dialect is a blend of Ewe interspersed with traces of German vocabulary and several West African languages.

Around 1894, a decade after the entire Togoland nation became a German protectorate, the last surviving brother died. The local people abandoned the mission house out of fear, a fear that materialised when German soldiers quickly took over the property and used it as a munitions warehouse.

In 1922, when German Togoland was partitioned in two, Togapeme fell under British rule in the new nation of Gold Coast that would later become Ghana. Three years after the partition, Gottwin Sosu, descendant of a ransomed Gurushi captive and a German missionary, approached the British government on behalf of the town of Togapeme and requested to purchase the sixteen-acre property. After a tedious process of negotiation that lasted two years, he finally acquired the mission for sixteen shillings.

With help from the townspeople, he rebuilt the mission house, expanding it to include a chapel, church offices and a twelve-room guest hostel by 1940. In line with the wishes of the people of Togapeme, he kept it nondenominational.

The mission campus is by far the most illustrious landmark in our small town. The hostel serves double duty as an income-generating hotel, and the sanctuary occupies the highest elevation in Togapeme.

Now, that campus was about to undergo its first renovation since my grandfather built it. A famous daughter of Togapeme, a prominent architect of no small international repute, was going to oversee the renovation. The modernised, expanded facility promised to be the heart of our community and a major tourist attraction in our entire district, once completed.

*

The sanctuary was packed. There were folks standing in the back and crowding the doorways, their attention riveted on a very young, visiting preacher who seemed to be directing his sermon at me — about heavy loads and burdens; crosses and crossroads; responsibility and commitment; about hard choices, and love, and victory — it was poignant.

At the end of the service he asked people to come forward to receive special prayers for strength, for guidance, and for revelation.

I was reluctant to go in front of all those people. So I waited until he had shaken all the hands and patted every child's head. Then I made my way to the vestry to speak to him privately.

He seemed to be expecting me.

'My sister, you have a puzzle to unravel?' he asked.

'*Osofo*, does God still heal like he used to do in the days of old?' After I had asked him this, I waited for his response.

'This is not your entire question. There are many parts to it, are there not?'

I looked at him; but how could he know?

'Well, I know — I believe, rather — that He *can* heal, and I also know that He doesn't always heal, not every single time. It all seems random. I want to know what exactly it is that will cause Him to heal one person over the other, and what I can do to obtain such favour from him, so that I am the one He heals when He decides to heal.' My request fell apart and my courage fizzled under his focused stare.

'Do you ask this for yourself or for a loved one?'

'I ask for a loved one. I fear that it may be too late for him.'

'It is never too late with God but you should know one thing: the power of life and death are completely in His hands. God shows that favour to whomever He wills; it is called Grace. He gives to one and takes from another. In the final analysis though, His plan for your loved one will be compatible with His plan for you, for the next person, and for some stranger that has not even been born yet. Our lives are intertwined from His point of view in such a way that everything makes sense to Him.

Unfortunately, you and I don't occupy that vantage point to be able to see things His way. All you are required to do, therefore, is to trust that the good and the bad fortunes alike will work to achieve His purpose.'

'So there is nothing I can do for my loved one, then.'

'Ah! But there is. You should play your part in this matter to the best of your ability so that your role in the eventual outcome of God's plan is complete and unquestionable. If it is time for your loved one to die, allow him to do so with dignity. *He* must settle in his own heart with God concerning his healing or death; you cannot assume that task for him. It is just like eating, or drinking, or breathing or dying — he has to do it himself.

Your role is to live, so live fully and love this person unconditionally. That is all that is required of you. Let me pray with you, my sister. I sense in my spirit that it is rather *you* who will be in need of spiritual sustenance.

There will be difficult times ahead because you are carrying the weight of an entire family on your shoulders. That is your calling, but only for a season. At the end of that season, the sun will rise once more on your horizon.'

He covered my shaking hands with his and prayed for me. It was a simple prayer, nothing dramatic. I did not see lightning. I did not hear thunder; but when he was done, I felt peace.

For the first time I was able to accept my role in Sefa's life, in all our lives:

Perhaps, on some level, we are soul mates — twins from somewhere — just like everyone always says. We have to run this parallel course part of the way; and then I'm to carry on by myself and cross the finish line alone. Ah, I see it all clearly; it makes sense. Yes, I see it now...

I came out of my momentary reverie to find the preacher looking at me intently.

'You have received the revelation, have you not? I see it in your eyes.'

I could barely get the words out, 'Yes, I believe I have. Thank you. I'm so glad I made it here today.'

'God bless you, my sister.'

Tassie and I left after catching up with several friends and church members. We packed the back of the vehicle with people who needed a lift. It had truly been a fulfilling weekend.

When we got home, Sefa was bursting with energy and curiosity. He wanted to know what had been preached in church.

'I sense that something has changed this weekend but I don't know what it is,' he said, even before we walked into the house.

I just smiled at him and told him not to worry because everything had been set aright. Then I handed him the Polaroid photos that I took of the service.

Inside, he had a surprise waiting for his mother. He had had her piano rolled back to its original corner in the living room. It had been tuned and polished, with her favourite sheet music ready and open on the rack.

Tassie had not touched the piano since Sefa and I came down. She had felt that the sound would be too jarring for him, so I wheeled it out of sight where it quickly became a catchall for the occasional book and other odds and ends.

'Dadaa, play for me,' he said softly. He tugged at her hand.

She looked down at him with stars in her eyes. Then she slowly walked to the piano, sat down and began to play him an old lullaby:

Tuu tuu gbovi; Tuu tuu gbovi…

He locked his hands together and placed them on his chest; then he closed his eyes, dropped his head, and rocked back and forth while she sang and played for him. I tiptoed away.

In the days that followed, Tassie cut out the unnecessary hikes she used to make into town just to go and practise on the church organ. She played everyday, and I noticed that her eyes were almost always closed now when she played. There was a new passion, never before heard, in her art. She too seemed to have arrived at a place where she had made peace with God over her situation.

And Sefa continued to bask in his remarkable lease on health. He actually looked as if he had picked up a couple of pounds by the middle of our second week in the village. This was his best week in a really long time. He ate real food, not just soup and porridge, and he was in very high spirits. He didn't use the wheelchair even once, and his slur was barely detectable.

His mother cried everyday out of joy. 'Shika, he is experiencing a miracle,' she said.

I had never seen anything like this before, but I did know that it couldn't last forever. He had only fourteen days worth of medications left and with each passing day, I had nightmares about the hour when he would shut his eyes and never open them again. I pictured how the sun would stand still while we all held our breath and counted the ticking of the clock.

He had resisted all my attempts to take him to Bremen Clinic for even a preliminary visit. Everyday was a harder struggle for me to suppress the urge to tie him up, throw him in the back of the car, and drag him by force to the clinic. Instead, I studied him like a hawk for any new signs of deterioration.

On Thursday, I sat with Tassie to prepare her for Jean's upcoming visit. She was overjoyed to learn that we had made strides in our relationship, and she immediately started planning what we should cook for him and how we could make him feel welcome.

I showed her the set of coral beads that he gave me on my birthday.

'Shika! Do you know what these are?'

'Coral. Pretty, eh?'

'Over here, *we* just consider these to be expensive beautiful beads, but in Nigeria, these Edo beads are widely referred to as "bridal beads" and typically worn by brides. Considering the fact that he travels back and forth between here and Nigeria, this isn't just a casual gift of beautiful coral beads. The man is in fact sending you a coded message. Get ready, my child!'

'He will be staying overnight, maybe we should put him up in the church hostel,' I suggested.

'And how exactly is that supposed to work?' Tassie placed her hand on her hip and put on her schoolteacher face. 'Your plan is to go visiting him there in broad daylight for everybody to see, or what? Don't be silly, dear. He's going to become part of this family soon; of course he will stay here with us.'

'I'm just trying to do the right thing oh! I don't want people whispering about how you run your household. He can have my room and I can sleep with you,' I said.

'Ah, was I wrong? Do you not love this man?'

'Oh Tassie, you were right, I do!'

'And are you not pleased that he's coming to visit you?'

'I am.'

'Then I trust that at *thirty-two* you can run your life without my supervision. Let *me* worry about how I run my household. Besides, it's nobody's business what we do under our own roof. After all the praying and fasting I've done for God to send you a man, now here comes this good man who has been waiting for you all these years, driving all the way up this steep mountain just to spend time with you; and you want to do *what*?'

That settled the matter.

That Friday was also Sefa's birthday. He had not wanted us to make a fuss, so Tassie and I passed the day quietly, only baking a small pound cake for ourselves, fearful that we might upset him if we attempted to mark the occasion in any other way.

Jean arrived as promised that evening, bringing with him adequate supplies of the joy and vitality I so badly needed to refill my depleted reservoir. He charmed Tassie with his humour and his affectionate ways, but he definitely stole her heart with the Champagne that he brought for us to toast Sefa with. Sefa did not drink the alcohol, but he graciously smiled as we sang 'happy birthday' while his mother played the piano.

Tassie in turn made sure that she fed Jean well. I watched in amazement as she called him 'my son John-Mark' and found out every last detail about his family, his work, and his life before he moved to Africa.

Jean also insisted that I at least learn the route before the time came when I would be compelled to take Sefa to Bremen Clinic.

'You can't just wait until the last minute when you're in the middle of the emergency and then hope to find it,' he told me when we were alone that night.

So, after breakfast the next day, he and I made a test run to Tovidzi on the other side of our mountain range to locate the clinic. It only took us twenty minutes to drive there, much closer than we had anticipated. It was a pleasant surprise to see such a modern looking facility in the lush setting. We decided that we should go in to get a better feel for the type of service one could expect.

To say that we were floored would be putting it mildly. The enthusiasm with which they welcomed us, and the speed with which they attended to us assured us that Sefa would be well cared for here. After they had given us a tour of the clinic, Jean sat in the waiting room while I conferred privately with the resident physician, Dr Klenam Hofmeister.

'Dr Anomar-Bilson did call from Accra and preregistered one of his patients, a Mr Sefanam Gameli, and you *are* listed as the authorised contact person. My staff and I have been expecting you to come in all week, at least for an initial visit,' Dr Hofmeister said. He sounded irritated until I explained to him why we never showed up.

I told him about Sefa's reluctance and stubbornness, and he explained that this was the natural reaction of most terminal patients to the prospect of hospice care. He also informed me that his clinic offered counselling services to families and caregivers of terminal patients for free, and urged me to avail myself of those services.

'Doctor,' I asked him, 'do you also perform HIV testing here?'

'Yes of course. We draw the blood and send it away. We get the results back within two weeks. If there is a genuine concern due to high risk of exposure, we recommend repeat testing after three months, and again after six months, just to be sure.'

'Can I book an appointment and come in to be tested?'

'Sure. But it's a good idea for any current or future spouse or sexual partner to be tested as well,' he said.

'Oh, I see.'

I went back to Jean and sat beside him.

'What took you so long?' he asked.

'I talked in detail with the doctor.' I turned to face him, 'Jean, I'm going to book an appointment and come back for an HIV test. I think we should both be tested.'

'Of course,' he said. 'I'm glad you've brought it up. I've taken one before; there's nothing for you to be nervous about.'

'You've taken an HIV test before? You never mentioned it. Should I be worried?'

'I'm a grown, single man, Shika. You should be more concerned if I'd never been tested before. Book us both for next Saturday. When I return, we'll come back here together.'

When we went back to Togapeme, I walked around my hometown with him, telling him every memory associated with every tree, person and building, as I eagerly shared my proud heritage with him.

I cut behind our house and headed for the stream where we used to play as kids whenever we came to the village to visit our grandfather. Although it ran along that entire border of our property before curving sharply to flow steeply away from the village, there was a path running along it that directly connected the village on the lower end to the church premises on the top end.

Right in the bend, where the stream turned away from the path, stood the sprawling flamboyant tree that we used to climb. I sat on the carpet created by its tiny leaves and pulled him down beside me.

'What is that sound?' he asked, looking toward the tree line to the east of our property.

Then I remembered Tassie's whispered recommendation to me as we were leaving home that morning: 'Don't forget to show him the waterfall.'

'Come,' I told Jean. I held out my hand and pulled him up; then I led him down the stream away from the direction of the village, until all we could see were the roots of the giant trees.

'Close your eyes, Jean; give me your hand.'

I stood in front of him, placed his hand on my shoulder and descended a few more yards through the foliage until we appeared by the bubbling brook at the foot of the waterfall, across from the curtain of water.

'Sh! Listen, Jean,' I whispered, 'just breathe.' Then I stood still and placed his arms around my waist. 'Now look!'

'Oh... Shika! This is heaven!'

He pulled me down into a nook between the buttress roots, where we cuddled and watched the light flirting with the water. And there, under the spell cast over us by the sound and the glimmer of falling water, we bared our souls to each other and stopped just short of making love, right there between the tree roots at the foot of Paradiso Waterfall.

'I now know why you are so intoxicating. Togapeme has saturated your very soul with its beauty,' he whispered to me after we could think clearly again. 'Shika Amenyo, I'm not going anywhere. I may be insane by the end of the process, but I will wait for you for as long as it takes you to be ready. I swear.'

His eyes were boring into my skin, threatening to strip away my resolve. I closed my eyes under the intensity of his gaze. My flesh quivered while he held me and proceeded to stamp every visible inch of my body with his lips.

The next morning, he insisted on going with me to church before leaving. We walked slowly upstream with the other churchgoers, responding to the friendly greetings of all the folks who walked briskly past us. By the time we arrived at church, he had memorised the words in the lengthy salutation process, and he pleasantly surprised several people with his fluent responses to their greetings.

He went back to the city after lunch, leaving my body tingling in anticipation of his next visit, and a new melody firmly vibrating in my chest.

TEN

I could feel myself getting more nervous as I waited for Kobla. There was no direct bus to Togapeme from the North, so he was passing through Kumasi. His telegram had said that he would be on the last bus from there. That bus should have arrived around seven but thirty minutes later, I was still waiting.

It had been fourteen years since I felt my brother's hand on my face in a backhanded slap, yet thinking of him still made me reach for the scar on my cheek.

*

Ever since Kobla's friend violated me, there had been bad blood between my brother and Sefa.

Kobla seldom came home after that incident. When school let out and he did come back to town, he would be gone all day, hanging out with his friends; and he would spend days at a time at Fo Kofigah's, whose older boys were closer to his age anyway.

Sefa had always spent most of *his* time at our house, so that did not change. It was just that they ceased to get along after that. Oh, they never *fought* to my face, but you could have cut the tension with a knife, could almost smell the blood! By that time too, Sefa had grown a little taller than Kobla and was better built. All in all, it was a sorry arrangement of circumstances.

The following year, we lost Papa in an automobile accident. It was a crushing blow to all three of us, since he was as much Sefa's father as he was ours. But whereas Sefa and I seemed to bounce back more quickly from that blow, things were never quite the same with Kobla. It was as if his remaining reason for even stepping into that house had been taken away.

He came home for maybe one more Christmas, and he telephoned quite often from Kumasi to see how dadaa was doing. But once he graduated, that was that. He immediately found a job there and never came back.

When Kobla got married, I did not accompany the family delegation that went to perform the traditional rites on his behalf. I later heard that he had moved up north, become a preacher, and started a church. Dadaa went to visit him when he had his first daughter, but she died before the second one was born, the one who was named after her. She had always had a bad heart, and it got worse after she lost Papa. My mother put up a valiant fight, but she lost it.

The last time I stood next to Kobla was by our mother's deathbed almost six years ago. We knew it was coming, so we were all there — Kobla and I, Fo Kofigah and Daa Nenor; a couple of older cousins that she had been close to; and her pastor — except for Sefa, who had gone on a job related trip somewhere.

I was in shock and Kobla was devastated, so we clung to each other. We didn't even speak, just held hands tightly while he prayed through his tears and I stared, dry-eyed, at our mother lying there dying.

When it was over, we never once sat down to discuss her, clear any past misunderstanding, or chat about his family or my life. Sefa had made it back in time for the funeral, but the two of them never exchanged even one private word. After the funeral Kobla bade us all farewell and left.

Ironically, my brother was the pastor of a thriving, charismatic, Christian church located in Moslem territory. We had thought that he would become a career diplomat, and in a way, I suppose that you could consider him an ambassador of his faith. Yet here was this fourteen-year impasse with his own blood, which had isolated him from everyone.

We had relatives and family friends who had never once seen him since he completed secondary school and left for the university. Whatever it was between him and Sefa, his moving so far away had not helped his case.

Everybody in our family came to look up to Sefa's leadership; *he* was an ever-present force at all family gatherings. He could be counted upon to contribute the most to every funeral fund. It was to the point where if anyone asked, 'How is your brother?' or said, 'Greet your brother for me', I knew that they were referring to Sefa and not Kobla. It would have been nice to just relax and be the little sister sometimes, instead of always having to make excuses for his absences, as if I were his mother.

Kobla and I no longer communicated directly, although I still received a monthly tract in the post from his church every now and then. I guess I was on his 'sinners' mailing list.

*

The bus pulled into the station almost forty-five minutes behind schedule. I was not sure what our initial reaction to each other would be — even worse, how we would make the ten-minute ride back home in the close confines of the car.

Ah, but there he was, clutching his luggage, clean-cut in his pastoral collar, looking about him to see if I was anywhere in sight. I honked and waved.

'Kobla, woezo!' I opened the boot so that he could toss his luggage in.

'Ei, look at you; a proper lady. *Atuu!*' He embraced me awkwardly.

We made small talk — I enquired after his wife and children, his church, the people of his congregation — anything to keep the conversation general. Just for ten minutes.

'So how is Sefa, truly? Is he really as ill as your message insinuated? I mean, for you to move to the village with him, and then send me an urgent telegram asking me to come down as soon as possible, surely it must be serious.' He looked concerned, I'll grant him that, but not having seen Sefa in over five years, and having no clue that he was even ill, it was obviously hard for him to perceive the gravity of the situation.

Sefa had expressed the desire to see him before the end. I thought it prudent to give them an opportunity to settle their differences, now that Sefa was still lucid, before they lost that chance. My summons had been short and to the point, and had not specified the nature of Sefa's ailment. On Monday morning, one of the boys from the post office came to knock on the side gate and asked for me. Kobla had sent me a reply: *Arriving Monday 7pm last bus from Kumasi.*

Now, as we approached the house, I felt that it might be wise to prepare him for what lay behind the gate.

'In all honesty, he is at death's door. He was diagnosed with a malignant brain tumour almost a year ago. I'm sorry to confirm the fact, but Sefa *is* dying. He wanted to see you before he went. You will not recognise him and at this point it's just a matter of time.'

'Terminal cancer! Ah!' He touched his fist to his mouth for a moment, before Christian discipline took over. 'I wish I had known before now. But we are here anyway, let me focus on the present.'

He got out himself and opened the gate, still shaking his head in disbelief. I carried his bag and led him indoors.

'Tassie! Kobla has arrived!'

She came out of the kitchen, wiping her hands on the corner of her wrapper.

'Kobla, atuu! But I smell of fish, I have been preparing you something,' she said.

He gave her a bear hug anyway and promptly went to sample her *kanami*. He wiped his hand and hugged her again.

'It's your brother! I have released him into God's hands. *He* knows best,' she said. Then she threw her hands up in resignation and used the corner of her wrapper to wipe a tear from under her specs.

Ever since her visit to the shrine with Fo Kofigah, she had become less inhibited and would wipe away a tear or two every now and then, or pat her chest and shake her head when she thought that nobody was looking.

'I have placed your luggage in the middle bedroom, that is where you will be sleeping,' I informed Kobla. 'Would you like to change from your suit to be more comfortable? I can draw you some water for a bath? Anything?' It was a shame that I had to stand on such ceremony with him, but truly, his ecclesiastical bearing and garb demanded nothing less than the civility due an important guest.

'Oh, let him change and eat something first, then he can think of other things. But first — where are our manners — let's give him a proper woezo. He has come a long way. *Bring him water.*' Tassie was insistent, ushering him into the living room even as he hesitated over what to do next.

They sat down and I brought fresh spring water for Kobla. We went through the greeting procedure, with me serving as otsami while she inquired after his family. He updated her on their progress. Then he stated the purpose of his visit and Tassie also updated him on the situation here.

'Thank you for the sacrifices you have both made in taking care of Sefa since the onset of his illness,' he said.

'I didn't want to burden you with news about his condition, especially since I'm still believing that he will experience a miraculous healing,' Tassie said.

After the formalities were over, I set a place for him at the table. He ate slowly and in silence while I cleaned up. Tassie went to check on Sefa. When Kobla was done with the meal, he excused himself and went to change into casual clothes.

'He's fast asleep, but would you like to at least look in on Sefa now? Shika, take him,' Tassie said when Kobla returned to the living room.

I led him around the corner to Sefa's bedroom.

Kobla could barely maintain his composure when he laid eyes on the shell of this once-vibrant athlete. I wondered if the lost years flashed across his mind while he was contemplating the figure in the bed. He touched the back of his hand to Sefa's forehead and then snatched it back as if a wasp had stung him. All he managed to get out, halfway between a squeak and a whisper was 'Sefanam!' I left him standing there.

Tassie could not hide her relief that Kobla had made it home in the nick of time. She was sitting in the living room, leaning back with her feet up, eyes closed. I heard her whisper more than once, 'Thanks be to God!' The inexplicable estrangement between the two men must have weighed quite heavily on her heart all these years.

I went outside to make sure that Irene had remembered to lock the gates for the night. When I returned, Kobla was sitting beside Tassie in the living room. He kept shaking his head in disbelief and looked as if he had just communed with ghosts.

'Ah!' he uttered every few seconds.

Tassie was nodding her head to an invisible beat. They stayed like that, saying nothing, preoccupied with their thoughts.

I brought them mugs of hot *Milo*. Then I left them and went to bed.

I stayed in for a while before coming out of the bedroom the next morning. Tassie had gone to town, and Sefa and Kobla were nowhere in sight.

'Where did they go?' I asked Irene.

'They went to the streamside, I think.'

I ate a quick meal and then went to look for them.

I knew exactly where to find them. I headed downstream. As I approached the flamboyant tree, I could see Kobla sitting on the ground, leaning against its trunk. He looked at me with the trace of a gleam in his eyes, and pointed up. There was Sefa, perched in the cradle of the tree, just as he would have been twenty-five years ago.

'Sefa!' I gasped. 'Is this a good idea?'

'Challey, relax; this is perfect! I've never felt stronger. After all, this is probably going to be the last time I enjoy this view, so why do it halfheartedly? Kobla was kind enough to grant my wish by helping me climb up.'

'I just came to see if you needed anything. I brought you your flask of herbal tea,' I said, placing the bag down and getting ready to go back.

'No, don't leave. It's a good thing you've come to join us. Stay, Shishi,' Sefa said.

I reluctantly sat on the ground beside Kobla.

'We've been talking,' Sefa said.

'Oh, okay. Eheh?'

'Kobla has something to tell you,' Sefa said.

'This is not the right time,' Kobla said.

'There is no better time than today. Go on, tell her!' Sefa insisted loudly.

'Tell me what?' I asked.

Kobla sat up and also raised his voice.

'Sefa,' he said, 'as I told you earlier, *"All things are lawful for me, but all things are not expedient."* I will tell her in due course.'

'Hypocrite! For how much longer will you continue to hide behind your cloak of righteousness? You owe her the truth, man. I won't be here much longer and all you will have is each other. Be a man, Kobla. Be a man!'

'Sefa, don't distress yourself for my sake,' I said. I rushed to his side and helped him climb down. 'Whatever it is can wait, I'm sure.'

He was extremely agitated. He was trembling, and the slur in his speech was more pronounced than ever. Kobla too was visibly shaken. His eyes were very red and he was sweating profusely, in spite of our cool climate.

I was very worried for both of them. I tried to pull Sefa away but he refused to leave. He just plopped onto the ground beside Kobla. I quickly knelt between them to prevent the palaver from turning physical, for that is where it seemed to be headed.

'You can choose the coward's way out and walk away, but I'm not budging until you tell her what happened that day. If necessary, I shall sit here until I die,' he swore.

'Ei! What is this?' I threw my hands on my head. 'What have you done, Kobla? Say it and let's all be free!'

Kobla held his head in his hands and rocked back and forth in obvious anguish for two full minutes.

Sefa was staring up at the sky. I was kneeling. We waited.

And then, in a crackling voice, he said, 'It was just a stupid bet, that's all. Just a stupid, boyish prank.'

'What is he talking about?' I asked Sefa.

'He's referring to the day when that hooligan attacked and raped you. Go on, coward; tell her everything!'

'Bacchus and I made a bet to see whose sister would be the first to give in. I swore that my sister was a nun, and he was also convinced that I would lose the bet,' Kobla said.

'Eheh? And how did he know to come to the house when he did?' Sefa asked.

'I merely mentioned in passing that our parents would probably be out of town attending a funeral. He was only supposed to come and sweet-talk you and get you to walk hand in hand with him to *kelewele junction*, not actually *sleep* with you!'

'Nonsense! You wanted to see whose sister would be the first to get deflowered, that's all. Don't sugar-coat it now.' Sefa was fuming and heavily slurring his words.

I had been sitting on my heels all this time, with my hands clasped loosely in my lap, as if I were listening to a story about someone else's life.

'And then what happened?' Sefa asked him.

'I strolled all the way down the street to kelewele junction, holding his sister's hand, but he was nowhere in sight. We had a couple of friends as lookouts, and they declared me the winner. I assumed that I'd won the bet — until we went back to campus and I started hearing the rumours. He didn't tell me to my face, but everyone was teasing me for thinking that I had won, when Bacchus had come away with the better prize. When I asked him about it, he told me that you and he had liked each other so much that you both decided that walking down the street would only be a waste of time.'

'Did you not wonder — when you came back home that evening, and I had shut myself in the bathroom, and stayed in there for over an hour — why I refused to talk to you?' I asked him calmly.

'And when you later found out what had happened, and got on that bus, and came all the way home, did it even occur to you to ask her for her version of the story before you raised your hand to her face?' Sefa asked.

'Well, he was my friend. I had no reason to doubt *him*,' Kobla said in his own defence.

I do not know where my sense of composure came from. I had just sat there calmly all this time while he was speaking; but when he opened his mouth and defended his friend — after all these years, after all that it had done to my psyche, my self-esteem, my ability to trust men — something finally snapped. The adrenaline gushed into my bloodstream, and I shut my eyes for a moment…

My right arm is swinging in slow motion, swinging so hard that I'm about to dislocate my elbow. I have broken his skin. My open hand has landed on his righteous face in the same spot across from where he left a mark on my cheek fourteen years ago…

I opened my damp eyes and studied the contours of his face for a second — it was as though I were looking into a mirror — and I saw that his skin was intact; then I shifted my focus to gaze into the depths of his eyes.

Ah… I see where I differ from him — the empty hole where my humanity would have peeked out, the shiftiness where my integrity would have firmly vouched for him — and I now realise that birth order and gender do not automatically confer leadership ability on a man.

Today, the fifteenth of August 1995, I finally know the truth. My brother is a pitiful, spineless coward who took my virtue and gave it away on a bet — as if it were his to give — and then chose to hide his despicable act behind a façade of holiness.

I felt a rush of pity for him.

Surely, he must have suffered all these years — each time my brother beheld our similar features while he stood in front of the mirror to adjust his pastoral collar; every time my brother made love to my rapist's sister, the one that he had gone ahead and married — oh, how he must have suffered!

And so, instead of slapping him as I had just pictured myself doing, my hand inclined gently toward his cheek of its own accord.

'But, am *I* not your *sister*?' I asked him — as if he could give me some sort of assurance of what I was now beginning to doubt.

He had nothing to give me, however, and my soul could not yet afford to extend to him anything more than those words. I suppressed my pity and dropped my hand just short of actually touching his face. He was not yet ready for my forgiveness, and I wasn't going to just give it away like that. I had lost too much already.

Carefully, I brushed the debris off my clothes and picked up the bag. Then I reached out my arm to the other. Him, I had never had reason to doubt.

'Come, Sefa, let me take you home,' I said.

I pulled him up and draped his good arm around my neck. I held him firmly about the waist. He leaned more on me as we began the slow journey back to the house. His limp was more pronounced today and his body more lopsided than it was yesterday. He was getting heavier by the minute.

Ah, I should have brought him the wheelchair, I thought.

He faltered; I paused so that he could catch his breath. Then I looked at him and I knew. He had finished fighting.

He went to lie down as soon as we got home. I went to wake him up in the middle of the afternoon to give him some soup, but he had no appetite. He just drank herbal tea and went back to sleep.

Tassie slept in his room that night. I found her there at dawn, lying on the mat by his bed.

By Wednesday morning it was undeniable. Something was very wrong with Sefa. He was conscious but quite delirious, and his mother was very distressed. I suggested that we take him to the clinic at once, but she wanted to first summon the priests.

'Sefa, shall we take you to the clinic now, or shall I call the pastor?' she asked him. He was barely conscious, but he could hear her. He nodded that we should bring the priest.

Tassie sent for Osofo Anani. And he came with company.

Irene brought water for the guests, and the gathering went through greetings and introductions. Osofo Anani welcomed Kobla home and introduced me to his companion, Reverend Winsome Addo. The young pastor and I had already met. Yes, Osofo Addo was none other than the gifted visiting preacher who had so refreshed my spirit with his words of encouragement two Sundays ago.

Osofo Anani said that he got worried when he did not see Tassie at choir practice.

'I knew there had to be good reason when you sent a message yesterday to say that you couldn't make it.'

'I don't think that I will be able to meet any of my obligations this week,' she said.

Thankfully, the church renovation was officially underway; and since services were now being held outdoors under a canopy, Tassie would not be needed to play the organ. A piano was in use outdoors, and there were a couple of capable young musicians who were more than willing to avail themselves of this opportunity to hone their skills and contribute their share to the church body.

We got to know a little more about the young reverend from his proud mentor. He was officially on posting to our congregation as an assistant pastor for several months. We marvelled at his fluency in Ewe, although not in our local dialect, because we assumed that he was a Ga man, as his name suggested. But he explained that he was only half Ga.

'My mother is actually Ewe, her father having been an Anlo and her mother from Tsito.'

He said that he had attended seminary right after college. He was also fluent in German, Latin and Swahili, and his first mission had been to a small church in Tanzania. This was his third posting. And he was only thirty-six years old.

'But don't let his youth fool you. This is a brilliant young man with a wealth of experience belying his youth, and the Lord has truly blessed us beyond words to have him assigned to us for six months. Many larger congregations were fighting to have him; in fact he is very popular in East Africa.' Osofo Anani was beside himself with pride. I could only imagine the strings he must have pulled to snag such a prize.

Kobla was also quite impressed; he and Osofo Addo seemed to have hit it off nicely. It was interesting to watch their interaction and catch snatches of their conversation — this charismatic missionary, and my brother the conservative evangelist. Somehow their roles seemed mismatched with their personalities. Yet each was, no doubt, vital in his own way to his calling.

The senior pastor then followed Tassie and Kobla to Sefa's room. This gave me a chance to exchange a few words with the younger pastor. It was easy to relate to him.

He did not know exactly what the situation was, so I briefed him. I explained to him what it was that ailed Sefa and impressed upon him the gravity of his condition, leaving out the HIV aspect.

He listened without asking any questions.

'Thank you for your words of encouragement to me last time; those words have sustained me this far and made my task more bearable,' I said.

He reiterated his encouragement, and in his usual discerning manner, advised me not to reject help from well-meaning friends and relatives. He asked about our family.

I explained the relationships to him.

'There were five siblings in all, but my two older aunts died decades ago during childhood. Tassie is the middle and oldest surviving child; then came my mother, and then Fo Kofigah. My parents died several years ago, and so here we are.'

'And Kobla?'

'What about him? As I just told you, he is my elder brother; our parents only bore the two of us.'

'That's not what I meant. Forgive me,' he said, 'but I sense in your interaction with him a disconnection. I know that family relationships can be complicated; yet, somehow, this rift seems to be deeper.' His honest eyes were kind but unflinching. He leaned forward and seemed to focus his eyes on my very thoughts.

How could he have discerned all that in one visit? I hardly knew how to react or what to say. It was so easy talking to him. He exuded none of the formal distance projected by the clergy. It was an easy camaraderie, just like talking to one of my cronies, so I felt the urge to go on and unburden my soul to him. But I barely knew him, and so I hesitated.

Sensing my reticence, he backed off.

Just then, Kobla beckoned for us to join them in Sefa's room. Osofo Anani anointed Sefa with oil and laid his hands on him. Then the rest of us stretched our hands toward the bed, and the pastor committed Sefa's soul into God's hands.

The priests said their good-byes and left.

The rest of the day was very stressful for me. Sefa had been unable to swallow his meds, and I could not convey to his mother, without disclosing his secret, how urgent it was that we take him to the clinic at once. But I did not give up trying. The weekend was approaching again and I knew that Kobla had obligations to his congregation.

'Kobla, I will not be able to transport Sefa to the hospital by myself after you leave town. Can you not try and convince Tassie?'

He eventually agreed that before he left town on Friday morning, he would help me take Sefa to the clinic. At that point, Tassie had no choice but to agree.

Kobla did not appear to be able to stomach the situation as well as one would have expected. It was one thing, I suppose, to minister to the spiritual and material needs of the living but quite another to minister to those of a dying relative. So Tassie and I took turns with Sefa during the day, in addition to our usual responsibilities. Kobla took the night shift for a change, which allowed Tassie and me to finally catch up on our sleep.

On Thursday morning, when Tassie was taking her turn with Sefa, Kobla came to lean against the doorpost while I was cooking.

'Sefa has done some talking since I've been sitting with him,' he said.

'He has?' I placed the knife down and looked at him.

'Yes. He came out of it around midnight with perfect clarity. While I was reading, I felt him staring at me intently; then he called out my name, which means he recognised me as well.'

I wiped my hands and turned to face him; then I leaned against the counter and folded my arms. 'What did he say? Was he coherent?'

'Quite. The first thing he asked me was if I would officiate at his memorial service. I agreed. Then we had a very cogent conversation about the past; it was brief but important. He needed to confess something to me before he left.'

I did not much like his tone, but I tried to stay calm.

'*He* needed to confess? To *you*?' I actually let out a laugh after I asked him this.

He paused and looked at me — really looked at me well — as if seeing me for the first time since he arrived. I held his stare until he looked away.

After a few moments of apparently considering his next move, he resumed his stiff-necked stance.

'Look, little sis, I didn't come here to generate any discomfort; I just came to do my part. Besides, you begged me to come, remember? In any case, whatever Sefa and I discussed was confidential and will remain between us. But, just for the record, he wasn't a saint.'

'Begged you to come? Hah! *Begged* you? With all due respect, Kobby, I didn't force you onto that bus.'

He flinched at my use of his childhood nickname.

I myself was surprised. I had not uttered it since the day he gave me that backhanded slap fourteen years ago. For a moment we both stopped and held our breaths; but I was not done. Slowly, I looked him in the eye and continued my delivery.

'Also, for the record, I'm no longer your *little* sis. You may not have noticed, but I'm a grown woman now with a load of responsibilities on my shoulders; the least you could do is give me some acknowledgement for standing up to *my* obligations.'

I turned back to the counter and stared down at the knife. I could not take my eyes off its blade. I closed my eyes and waited until he walked away. Then I picked up the knife calmly and resumed cutting the meat.

A strange peace overtook me and I finished the cooking actually humming.

After lunch I went to relieve Tassie. As I approached the bedroom, I could hear her reading. I pushed the door slowly and saw Sefa propped up against the pillows. Although I hadn't made a sound upon entering, he turned his head toward the door. His good eye fixated on the distance, with no focus.

I stared with open mouth. I had wondered why Tassie didn't emerge from the room all morning, not even to use the bathroom; but I had been too busy to check on them.

I rushed to his bedside and fell to my knees, whispering his name over and over to see if he would respond. I held his hand and felt him squeezing gently. I looked up and saw a tear falling out of the corner of his eye. Tassie and I looked at each other and smiled. Then she left the room.

I continued reading from where she had left off in Psalm 91.

After twenty minutes or so, Kobla knocked on the door and stuck his head in to say that he was taking a walk to the post office. I told him to take the car, but he said that he needed some fresh air.

'Kobla… sorry…' Sefa said after Kobla left.

'I know. You talked, he told me.'

'Kobla… sorry…' His speech was slurred and laboured but in that moment, he was quite coherent.

I patted his hand.

'Hush! Don't try to talk, save your strength. You have done nothing wrong.'

'Kobla… sorry…' he repeated.

'He is not God. You do not need his approval to live, and you certainly do not need his permission to die.'

He continued to stare vaguely, and kept repeating, 'Kobla… sorry…'

I wiped the corner of his eye and plumped up his pillows. I took his pulse. It was very erratic. I kept talking soothingly to him and stroking his hand until he calmed down and stopped the rambling.

I read silently and monitored him every now and then.

Other than Tassie's popping in a couple of times to check on us or for me to use the bathroom, I stayed the rest of my shift without incident and handed over to Kobla.

*

At dawn, I am awoken rather early to a commotion outside; it sounds as if the cat is agitated. It's not yet six o'clock, so I go outside to see to the pets. Irene is already there in quite a fluster. She seems relieved to see me.

'Oh, Daavi Shika, I was just now coming to wake you up! It's the cat,' she says, 'he started behaving strangely, going around in circles as if he was chasing his tail, but it wasn't the usual game. Then, after several spins and somersaults, he just threw himself on the ground. He's not moving, I don't know…'

I stand there, transfixed over the stiff, outstretched body of Churchill. The cat is dead all right.

As if in slow motion, I turn to Irene and ask her, 'Where's Napo?'

'The dog has crawled underneath the loose boards behind the house and will not come out,' she says. 'I was actually trying to get him to come out when the cat started displaying.'

The blood drains from my head as I stand and digest this information.

From far away, I can hear her asking if I am all right, if she should get Tassie.

I tell her to run as fast as she can and fetch the priest. She asks me which one. I do not recall my response. She takes off.

I walk stiffly and slowly like a zombie back into the house, through the living room and toward the bedrooms. Even before I turn the corner and touch the doorknob, I know.

I stand just inside the doorway and take in the scene in slow motion — Tassie on the mat at the foot of the bed as she has been on many a morning, arms folded under her head, fast asleep; the electric fan making its regular, whirring sound as it sweeps across the room and back — nothing seems out of place.

A copy of Mary Baker Eddy's *Science and Health with Key to the Scriptures* lies facedown on the floor beside Tassie. She probably read to him until she fell asleep. I remember hearing her tell Kobla not to worry about taking last night's shift, because she wanted to finish reading to Sefa. I pick up the book and turn it over. It's open to the chapter entitled 'Footsteps of Truth.'

I hold his wrist and check for a pulse before running my open hand down his face to shut his eye. Then I look at the clock ticking away on the windowsill. Five forty-five. Today — the eighteenth of August 1995 — Sefa is gone…

*

Without any success, I tried to wake Tassie up. Tassie had never been a deep sleeper. I left her there and went to knock on Kobla's door. He did not respond, so I entered. I could not wake him either. After shaking him several times, I gave up and went back to Sefa's room.

I brought a pail of warm water and wiped him down from head to toe; then I pulled out a pair of brand new underpants from his drawer, and changed his underwear. I removed the pillows from under his head and rearranged his facial features. Then I wrapped a scarf around his head and tied it under his chin in order to hold his jaw together before rigor mortis should set in. When I was done, I tidied up the room, opened the shutters and pulled aside the curtain. Soft light flooded the room. It was going to be a magnificent day.

I went to sit on the front steps to wait for the pastor.

Osofo Addo was the first to arrive. He must have greeted me, but I do not recall if I responded. I only remember making the effort to smile at him, and seeing his lips move.

He touched my head and hurried past me into the house. Hard on his heels was Osofo Anani. It was he who stopped and took my hand and pulled me to my feet. I felt lightheaded and could not hear what he was saying. He placed his arm about my waist, led me into the house, and sat me in the living room.

'Make her some sweet tea,' he told Irene. 'And where is Fo Kobla?' He went to the bedroom to wake Kobla up.

I could hear Tassie in the other room, where the assistant pastor had also succeeded in waking her up. She was whimpering, as if she were too tired to generate sufficient sound for real sobs.

Everybody came out into the living room. Kobla had his arm around Tassie. He brought her to the sofa where I was already seated.

She began to groan like a wounded animal, rocking back and forth, the tears washing down effortlessly from underneath her swollen eyelids. I stared at all of them; it was like watching a movie in slow motion.

The senior pastor took charge of the situation. He dispatched Kobla to go into town to telephone our relatives and arrange for Sefa's body to be transported to the mortuary.

Kobla came back twenty minutes later accompanied by Efo Yao's driver, who had once been sent to woo me with a box of corned-beef. Apparently, my former admirer had quickly and most generously volunteered the use of his pickup truck to transport Sefa's body to the mortuary. They carried him out and away in the back of the truck.

Osofo Anani instructed his assistant to stay with us. Then I gave Kobla the key to Sefa's vehicle so that he and the senior pastor could accompany the truck to Tovidzi. Today, of all days, there was no electricity in our small six-slab mortuary, and the one at Bremen Clinic was the closest one.

I remember the house getting filled with people — women wailing, hugs and handshakes; town's folk and church members bringing food — people dressed in black and crimson, coming and going. Osofo Addo trying his best to answer questions and shake all the hands.

By midday, some of the family from out of town had begun to arrive. Fo Festus brought Fo Kofigah, Daa Jane and Emekor. Sefa's paternal uncles also arrived.

And then Jean also appeared in the middle of the afternoon, earlier than I expected. At the sight of him, it finally hit me and I felt my heart bursting. I heard myself sobbing, but no tears fell.

'But how?' I asked him. He was not due to arrive until evening.

'When you hadn't contacted me all week, I knew that something had to have happened. I called the post office, but the operator said that you had not been there since Monday. So I asked him to send someone to Daa Nenor Gameli's house to find out if everything was okay. He put me on hold for about two minutes; then he came back to say, "Erh, Efo — please — they say that Daa Nenor's son has just died."

I immediately called Miyo. She had heard nothing either, but she said she would find out what she could and call me back. It took forever, but she called your uncle's house and the houseboy confirmed it. Then I called

Bremen Clinic at once and spoke to Dr Hofmeister; I asked him to come to your aid. He told me not to worry because Sefa's body had been brought to his mortuary this morning. I grabbed my stuff and headed out. Miyo sends her love. She and Sweetie will come tomorrow.'

Osofo Addo graciously offered to entertain Jean, refusing to let him go and stay in the church hostel.

Daa Jane made sure that I took a shower. I assume she did the same with Tassie. All I could do was nod and follow instructions. It had been a long, gruelling week and it felt good to not be in charge for once. It was a relief to have people to depend on, and it was good to see Emekor. More than any other feeling, though, I felt exhausted.

The senior pastor opened up his home to any of our guests who would be staying overnight, so we sent Sefa's paternal uncles there. Of course, the immediate family, including Fo Kofigah and his clan, stayed in the family house, making themselves comfortable for the night on every sofa, mat and rug. A couple of my uncle's sons would be arriving in the morning, so we were going to have a packed house all weekend. And it was going to be a long one. We had a funeral to plan.

First thing on Saturday, I walked to Osofo Addo's place to meet Jean. He was already dressed and waiting for me. We left at once for Tovidzi. We had decided not to postpone our nine o'clock appointment with Dr Hofmeister.

When we got there, the doctor had our blood drawn as per our agreement the previous week. He also informed us that Sefa had ruptured an aneurism in his brain. This was reflected on the death certificate, which he handed to me, as the cause of death. I was grateful that we had this efficient man to rely on.

He followed us in his car back to Togapeme.

'You and Dr Hofmeister are coming to the house to officially express your condolences so that I can properly introduce you both to the entire family,' I told Jean.

'Tell me what is expected of me,' he said. 'Am I to stay and attend the family meeting after the introductions or would it be better if I returned to Accra tonight so that I don't get in the way of the proceedings? I don't want to appear to be running away but I'm not sure what the accepted protocol is.'

'Stay. I need you. You're not running away, are you?'

'Of course not, don't be silly. If you need me, I will stay all weekend. I want to be here for you, but I don't want to overstep any boundaries and accidentally offend anyone.'

'I know. And I appreciate your thoughtfulness,' I said, 'but, first things first. Let's get the introductions out the way; then we can think about tomorrow. Relax, honey, the time will come for you to be more involved. Today is definitely out. I will bring you and Osofo Addo some lunch after the family meeting.'

We stopped by Osofo Addo's to pick him up. He accompanied us back to the house and we proceeded with the formalities. Judging from the manner in which Tassie received Jean, weeping in his arms and he in turn comforting her tenderly, it was quite apparent to everyone watching that he was no stranger in our household.

I saw out of the corner of my eye, Emekor whispering in her mother's ear, clarifying Jean's identity. This clarification circulated the gathering and before long, each subsequent handshake was accompanied by a verbal annotation in our language that 'he is Shika's person.' Even Tassie smiled through her tears.

Klenam Hofmeister was received as enthusiastically and profusely thanked when I introduced him as Sefa's physician.

Kobla had to leave; he said that he would return on the Thursday just before the funeral. I wasn't about to risk having Jean offer him a lift, so I arranged one for him with the doctor.

'Fo Kobla has to return to his congregation,' I told the good doctor after his visit was over. 'Can you please drop him off at the station?'

The family meeting progressed quickly. It wasn't as if we had been taken by surprise. Nevertheless, we had never buried anyone after such a protracted and devastating illness, so we had no point of reference.

Tassie made her wishes known that he should be buried as soon as possible. There seemed no reason to argue this point since all the major decision makers were represented — his father's family, his mother's family — and all that was required was consensus, which would then be relayed to the traditional chief of Togapeme for final approval. We set the dates for two weeks later, with the wake on Friday and the burial on Saturday.

We were fortunate that this was the first death in town that month; otherwise, we would have had to wait in line for a later date. There was a funeral limit of one per weekend in effect in Togapeme.

What we had not expected was that the Gameli uncles would request their nephew's body to be transported to their hometown, being that our social structure is patrilineal, and Sefa was his father's firstborn and only child. This reasoning was hotly debated and almost resulted in blows.

'Where were you these past thirty years since your brother died, when my sister was raising the boy by herself?' Fo Kofigah asked them.

'But no one sought us out during that time, and we are especially offended that you people did not inform us when he fell ill.'

'Your suggestion is certainly reasonable. We will give you the body as soon as you pay your fifty percent share of what it cost to raise Sefa all these years.' Fo Kofigah was in his element when debating matters of this nature. There was no way they were going to win this fight.

Daa Jane, Emekor and I had been eavesdropping behind the scenes while putting away all the food that people had brought, and discussing what design of fabric to choose for the mourning attire. Meanwhile, poor Tassie had been virtually held captive in their midst while this drama ensued. But as soon as they mentioned poor Uncle Elorm's name, Daa Jane marched into the living room and dragged Tassie away from the meeting.

This served as the cue for them to wrap it up; or maybe it was the look she cast in her husband's direction that did it.

By now it was almost noon, and we knew that more people would soon come knocking at the door to sympathise with us. Daa Jane gave the signal for us to serve everyone a hot meal.

This initial family meeting concluded with Fo Kofigah handing out some friendly caution, reminding the Gameli uncles that they were in *our* territory.

'The mortuary employees know that you are not authorised to retrieve the body. I'm warning you, do not hatch any adventurous plots to spirit the body away; Sefa's body will not descend these slopes willingly.'

I took Jean and his host some food. Against our objections, Osofo Addo very graciously left for the church office after the meal. I curled up against Jean on the pastor's sofa and took a much-needed nap.

Miyo and Sweetie came up to see me that Sunday as promised. They arrived around eleven. After church, more people stopped by, including Osofo Addo, who graciously took my guests back to his place. After I had finished attending to the houseful of relatives, I took my guests some lunch and spent a couple of hours with them before they went back to Accra.

By Sunday evening, Fo Kofigah's clan had also returned to the city.

The next few days were very trying for the rest of us. We did make some urgent adjustments. We accepted help from some of the women at church, who either came or sent their daughters to help us with basic chores such as laundry, cleaning, fetching water, or going to market.

By Wednesday, there was an obituary piece in every major newspaper and Miyo had informed Sefa's employers that he had passed away. Osofo Anani assigned a couple of elders to come by the house everyday for a male presence. We were never short of visitors. People stopped by everyday to sit and mourn awhile with us. It was a frenzied whirl of preparations as the two weeks descended upon us.

ELEVEN

'I cannot understand how we went through that difficult time,' I told Tassie months later when we were reliving those dark days.

'It was as if we were caught in a foggy dream, just stumbling forward, hardly registering anything; yet looking at us, people probably saw our pain,' she said.

'I see it now, Tassie. Vividly. That, I suppose, is what Osofo Addo meant when he said that God would give us sufficient grace to bear it.'

Grace. God. Hah!

I went back to that first conversation with Osofo Addo, when I had completely understood God's purpose. Really, I must have been drunk on fatigue, eager to grasp at any limp thread of hope, such that even the nonsensical made perfect sense. How else could I have arrived at any conclusion that this pain should at any time be acceptable, even bearable, let alone contribute in any way to any good?

During that two-week fog between Sefa's death and burial, I drew a blank. I would look at my aunt, then wonder why God's grace had not extended to preventing her pain rather than allowing it, only to later seek to placate it. Surely, it would not have impacted His grand design by much for Him to extend to her that little favour?

Yet, pull through we did, albeit strenuously, eating, drinking and sleeping on the fumes from that pain.

Sefa had been a generous, well-connected man whose skillfulness in human relations extended beyond the business world so that more than a few people came out of the woodwork to pledge money toward his funeral. They were probably waiting for the night of the wake to make a public display of their generosity.

Only a few actual contributions trickled in before the funeral, these from his classmates and various organisations in which he had been active over the years. These close friends would have cut off their limbs to honour his memory if they could.

Even so, keeping the accounts straight caused much anxiety. The figures barely totalled half the budget, and no family pledges had been honoured thus far. The planning committee was completely dominated by the men, with the Centurion himself its self-appointed head, and the rest of us mere women, though technically part of it, playing no visible role.

The representatives from Sefa's company handed me a huge sum of money when they came by. Sefa had told me that he expected they would.

'Hold that money for dadaa. Under no circumstances should you let anyone know about it; and no matter what happens, do not spend it on the funeral,' he had told me. He had taken care of the smallest detail, even to the point of letting his employers know to deal with me directly and discreetly. So, I did what he had requested.

Besides, he had made some other provisions so that his funeral would not be a financial burden on the family. These provisions were clearly spelt out in a document that Miyo gave to me, along with a sum of money, when she and Sweetie came to see me. It was not exactly a will, but it did outline his wishes pertaining to his funeral and the disposal of his body.

I was sceptical about the handling of the finances but in the grand scheme of things, this was not necessarily a battle that I felt called to fight. So, I handed the document over to the committee, along with the money that he had put aside for his funeral.

One of his paternal uncles took issue with that arrangement.

'Oh, so he lived like a white man, separating himself from the rest of us; and now he wants to bury himself too, eh?'

'He did not want any curses following him to the grave,' I said; but this snide response did not satisfy the itch in my throat. Their continuous haggling over funeral expenses had really rankled. As I turned to leave, I delivered the coup de grace: 'None of you lifted a finger to care for him when he was dying; so if you cannot even give him a decent funeral, those of us who wiped up after him will also bury him; after all, he *was* ours.'

He sharply reprimanded me; attacked, actually, which opened a Pandora's box of all sorts of accusations — from questions about my qualification in presiding over Sefa's medical care, to insinuations about my self-serving motives in isolating him and denying access to his other relatives.

It was amazing! Yet, strangely, it energised me and reminded me of the importance of the role I had played up to that point, its necessity justified by the ongoing melee. Indeed, left to them alone, he could just as well get tossed into the valley in a cardboard box, or burnt Buddhist-style, down to his last tooth.

I wondered if they wouldn't do it too, if they really knew the truth about his illness. Then, would they still grill me about 'any other secret document', about life insurance money, and about property they needed to take into account during their calculations?

This was by far the worst time of my life, unmatched even by the horror of watching him die piece by piece. At least, *that* had been a gradual process, marked by many fond memories and made bearable by his gracious, grateful spirit. But *this* — this was cruel and vulgar!

I sought refuge at the post office after that by resuming my daily phone calls to Jean; I needed his shoulder now more than ever. But he was going to have to skip the upcoming weekend and put in some extra time at work, so that he could take an unplanned leave for the funeral.

'I will come on Tuesday and stay an entire week.'

'I understand, of course I do,' I assured him when he told me this, but that did not ease my pain any.

Almost everyday, Osofo Addo came by our house. He proved to be an invaluable ally, and helped me sort through a lot of the issues I was having with God, with the relatives, and with myself. He was such a progressive person, and we soon became fast friends. I asked him once why and how he had ended up a missionary, of all things. Somehow, by the end of our conversation, I was asking myself 'why not' and 'who better'. I also realised that I had access to something he wanted — Miyo.

But of course! All those questions about my childhood, my schooling, and my friendships that somehow always ended on her. Initially, I was dismayed to find out that he had more than a cursory interest in her. What did this mollycoddled church-boy think he could do for her — Miyo of the frigid, untouchable soul, who fantasised about killing her father — even if he could begin to guess at the depths of her despair? And then I decided to just tolerate his musings. After all, why rob him of this harmless delusion that would never materialise? Everybody is entitled to a little hope, even if it is through make-belief.

Tuesday came soon enough, bringing with it the only outlet for my sorrow. Jean's one week's stay would have been too much of an imposition on Osofo Addo and of course, staying at our house was completely out of the question now. I put him up in the church hostel this time; then he came to the house to sit with us and take part in the running around.

'Go with him, Shika,' Tassie whispered to me that evening. 'Go!'

Jean and I returned to the house in the morning to prepare for the return of the other relatives.

When Fo Kofigah arrived on Wednesday afternoon, he immediately reacted to Jean's presence in the house. I overheard him talking to Tassie in her bedroom. They did not see me.

'Are you going to allow Shika's person to be sitting in on the family meetings? This is not a tourist attraction,' he said.

'Consider him my guest, if it makes you feel any better,' she said. 'After all, it's not as if he will understand anything we say.'

'And what are his intentions, anyway?' he continued. 'Don't sit there and allow him to come and play with her, and then run away. '

'She's thirty-two years old; give her some credit. He wants to marry her. I'm warning you, Kofigah, don't do anything to drive him away.'

'I'm just trying to protect our interests. One day, I will be vindicated.'

'You take yourself much too seriously, my brother. It's not good for your blood pressure.'

By Wednesday night, the rest of the family had regrouped in Togapeme for last minute decisions. The next couple of days were tough for all of us. Every proposition was fraught with conflict and tested all that bound us together as family, descendants of a reverend minister. It shook the very basis of our Christian household by pitting our beliefs against the traditions of the larger society to which we belonged.

Even the two pastors got caught up in this cycle of conflict when it became apparent that the older man sided with the take-charge attitude being demonstrated by Fo Kofigah who, at this point, was even siding with the Gameli uncles. *They* were pushing for a more traditional ceremony — complete with pouring of libations, invocation and placation of ancestral spirits — and other practices that were at odds with our family's avowed religious beliefs going back several generations.

The senior pastor's justification was that these practices predated Christianity, were cultural rather than religious in intent, and formed the basis of our tribal identity. Unfortunately, his position was not seconded by the younger pastor, who humbly but firmly advocated for a more radical departure from what he defined as 'archaic beliefs that are at odds with true Christianity, beliefs that are being propped up by conservative people afraid of change and uncommitted to the Christian discipline, not to mention being a waste of financial and other resources of the grieving family.'

By Thursday morning, they were still at an impasse. The body was due to be released to us the next day and we had less than twenty-four hours to decide what kind of funeral to give Sefa. The irony was that he had not been particularly religious — not overtly anyway — nor could his outlook to life have been characterised as being inspired by any monumental sense of tribal affiliation. Yet here we were, fighting over how he should be buried.

Even more laughable to me was the fact that the morning session of the meeting concluded on the compromise that we should leave the final decision until later, when Kobla would have returned from the North, given that he was supposed to be one of the officiating ministers. We were expecting him to arrive by late afternoon. Jean had volunteered to pick him up from the station and although I would have preferred they not fraternise under such close confines, I didn't have the energy to resist that suggestion. Frankly, I didn't care that much.

We womenfolk left the men at home still arguing and went to the seamstress. Jean drove us to our fitting appointment. When we returned, Kobla had already arrived, accompanied by some of his in-laws. They had driven all the way down, and he had set them up in the church hostel. It was a relief to see that he had not needed the lift from Jean after all.

The two priests had left the relatives to carry on by themselves, and the afternoon session was already under way when we entered. We greeted the men in a general way and went into the bedroom to sort our outfits.

A few minutes later, Kobla came to knock on the bedroom door, and pulled Tassie and me aside. He wanted to tell us himself before someone else told us.

'I will not be participating in any official capacity after all. Judging from the way the meeting is going, I feel that it would not be prudent for me to get mired in conflict. I believe that the two capable ministers should be allowed to do their jobs without any family interference.'

'But we have one thousand copies of the program already printed out, listing you as the officiating minister,' I reminded him, 'and you promised him.' I could not believe that this act of final betrayal was about to occur.

Tassie spun her head around to better see him.

'You made Sefa a promise? And you're backing out now? After we waited for you to arrive so that we could make a final decision?'

'I have been praying about it, and I feel led by the Spirit to make this decision at this time.' He would not look either of us in the eye.

'Fine.' Tassie was calm, resolute. She smiled at him and patted him on the arm. 'Who are we to argue with a man's spiritual convictions, eh?'

I pursed my lips to still their trembling. I looked at her and nodded. I thought about Kobla's volatile relationship with Sefa and wondered if there had been even more to their estrangement than what I recently discovered. I turned on my heel and left the room.

Tassie went into the living room and clapped twice.

'I have arrived at a final decision,' she said, 'this meeting is over. Festus, please take me to Osofo Anani's house at once.'

They stared at her. There was a certain air of command about her person that no one dared to challenge.

Late on Friday afternoon, before the sun began to set, I followed the men to Tovidzi to bring Sefa's body home. As soon as they took delivery of the body, the Gameli uncles pulled out of their pockets bottles of palm wine and the paraphernalia used to perform traditional religious rites.

All the men turned to look at me, as if they expected some show of resistance. But it made no difference to me because I knew that I had done my part. I *had* watched over Sefa's soul while he was alive, when it mattered most. I could not perceive what value could be derived now from any ceremony, be it traditional or Christian, other than to sooth the consciences of those who had given him nothing, and to comfort the hearts of those who had given him everything. All of us were powerless to change his current state. So, I just stood by and waited for them to pour their libation and commit their son back to the world of his ancestors. Then they placed him in the coffin and we took him home.

I stared at the wailing crowd of neighbours and friends gathered at the entrance to our house as if they were characters in a play. I could only make out a few faces; my mind seemed to switch on and off.

When we brought him in, Tassie was in her bedroom, surrounded by all the women — Mrs Anani, D'Amavi, Daa Jane, Emekor, the cousins' wives — all making every effort to comfort her through their own tears.

We had set up Sefa's bedroom to receive his body. The windows were trimmed with white tulle and flowers, soft music playing in the background, fit for a new bride. The undertaker was already there to complete her job of giving him his final sprucing up, crimson brocade suit and all, mahogany casket waiting to package the completed masterpiece.

'Auntie, could you do me a favour? Please tuck this note into his glove and place this around his wrist,' I told the undertaker.

'I can stick the note into the glove, but what is this dried grass? You know that they have already performed the rites; I cannot be putting things on his body by heart.'

'This is very important. He was wearing it when he died. It's a token from the love of his life; he wanted to take it with him — he told me so on his deathbed. Besides, it's going to be a closed casket; who will see it, eh? He will not rest well without it. Please.'

She reluctantly complied with my request.

Then the family crowded into the bedroom. The priests prayed over his body and the uncles nailed the coffin shut. Fo Kofigah's sons carried the coffin outside.

We laid Sefa in state under a white canopy on the grounds of our property. I did not register much of the events of the night. It was one familiar face after another — old schoolmates, teammates and teachers; ex-girlfriends with their entourages, representatives from various organisations — the welcome and the unwelcome, all come up our mountain. Each one of them took the time to step up to Sefa's coffin, to touch it and look up at his photo, before joining the queue to shake the hands of the *chief-mourners.*

The foremost feeling I remember experiencing was overwhelming fatigue. I thought that my right arm would surely fall off. It stayed outstretched all night to accept handshake after handshake. After a while, I abandoned this task, lending my support instead to Tassie. She could not keep her arm stretched out any longer without my assistance.

The night went on forever. By dawn, it was only family and close friends left. We took turns going inside to snatch a quick nap, freshen up, and change for the service. The women made sure that our guests got something to eat.

When it was time to go, we proceeded down the mountain past the stream, taking the long way through town. The advance guard comprised the brass band and the church choir on foot, all clad in black, their heads and wrists banded with strips of crimson mourning cloth. Then came the hearse. And then followed the clergy, and us, his family. People came out of their homes to wave pieces of cloth as we slowly passed by, the women wailing and ululating, dogs howling in unison.

And then we circled back up to the church.

One newspaper later likened the procession to *'the trailing of a black cloud across the Togapeme sky on that sunny day.'*

The gathering was held outside on the church premises because of the renovation already begun on the inside. We were blessed with good weather, so there had not been any complicated tasks besides extending the existing canopy. But we did have to rent extra seats because of the number of people expected.

When the service began, Osofo Anani introduced his assistant to preach what was to be the younger man's first official funeral sermon in Togapeme. I darted a surprised look at Tassie but her eyes remained shut throughout. The senior pastor explained that he himself would later officiate over the interment, but that the sermon was to be handled by

Osofo Addo in accordance with the wishes of the mother of the deceased. There was no mention of Kobla.

I looked around to note the reactions of the other relatives. Then I settled back in the seat and let out a breath of relief.

It was not a long sermon. Osofo Addo was very concise in his advice to the family to 'rally together during this time of suffering... allow only the good memories to prevail... and let your sorrow bind you together.'

Many people eulogised Sefa — old friends, newer ones; schoolteachers, co-workers — even a representative from NODA, the National Organisation of Decorated Athletes. It was touching to hear how Sefa had positively affected their lives, to know that he had enriched all our lives with his many talents.

The senior pastor called for the pallbearers. My cousins positioned themselves along the casket. Then we all stood up. I was able to squeeze Tassie's hand one last time, just as the recessional hymn began to play.

*

The recessional hymn jerks me out of my thoughts. My heartbeat is escalating and there is a stifling weight on my chest that I cannot seem to shake off. My throat is dry; I cannot swallow.

As soon as the pallbearers lift the coffin, Tassie begins to tremble and moan. The gathering proceeds to the back of the church cemetery and assembles around the freshly dug hole.

Jean is by my side, holding me throughout this graveside ordeal; my two loyal friends are standing beside me. As soon as I see the gaping hole, my knees begin to buckle; and just when the tension in my chest reaches its climax and explodes, the hot tears finally begin to rain down my cheeks.

With the repetition of the final 'amen!' that accompanies the last shovelful of soil, Tassie's groans escalate into one long, high-pitched shriek and she passes out into the arms of her brother and his two oldest sons, who have been restraining her from throwing herself into the hole.

There is not a dry eye in the assembly that witnesses this heart-wrenching spectacle. People cling to each other, wailing loudly and bidding farewell to Sefa.

SEASON

OF

BOUNTY

TWELVE

The clock on the dashboard says seven forty-five. Although I ended up leaving the city later than I intended, at least I have met my goal of arriving in Togapeme before nightfall.

The car headlights pan across the length of the front wall as I turn into the entrance and blow the horn. I roll down my window and stick my head out while I wait for Irene to open the gate.

Five weeks after we buried Sefa, people have progressed to walking past our house without stopping to look at his obituary poster that is still stuck to our wall.

Perhaps, it's because the tape has lost its stickiness, causing the left edge of the paper to fold over in a stiff curl that is now obscuring his portrait. Or maybe it's because, after it paved the way and turned our wall into a public notice board, it is now lost amidst all the brightly coloured announcements and adverts that have since sprung up around it. Either way, at least from the outside, life has returned to the way it used to be. It is time to move forward.

I roll up the car window and drive slowly into the courtyard.

The three-hour drive from Accra gave me plenty of quite time in which to go over the events of the past month…

*

At first, the endless trail of sympathisers had made it impossible to quell the tears. But after a couple of weeks, the pall hanging over the house lifted, and we were able to pick up pace. Still, it was very hard for Tassie to break out of the habit of staying up to care for Sefa. I would wake up on several nights to find her missing from her bedroom, only to discover her sitting in his room reading.

'I can't sleep,' she would say, 'and I feel closer to him in here.'

Two weeks after Sefa's funeral, Osofo Addo paid us a visit. It was hardly unusual, but we hadn't seen the younger pastor since he preached at the memorial service.

'Ei, osofo, long time no see,' I greeted him.

'I travelled to Accra to attend a conference. I just returned last night,' he said.

'Ah, that explains it; you did mention that you might, I remember now. I trust that all went well?' Tassie said.

There was an air of excitement about him.

'I had the opportunity to spend some time with my grandmother in Tema and update her on my progress,' he said. 'When I mentioned Togapeme, she immediately asked me if I had met Daa Nenor Gameli yet. I had no idea that you two knew each other. She asked me how your son was doing, and I told her that Sefa had just passed away. So, I'm conveying her deepest condolences to you.'

Tassie and I looked at each other. Which friend or acquaintance could there possibly be left who had not heard of Sefa's death until now? Osofo Addo's grandmother turned out to be none other than the gracious Mrs Amuzu, would-be ex-rival and former holder of the key to Tassie's salvation.

'You mean to tell me that Daa Grace Amuzu is your grandmother? What a small world!'

Osofo Addo was not done, however.

'Yes. In fact, Daa Nenor, she told me that earlier in the week, she had felt a strong premonition to intercede for you; this impulse was so intense that she meditated on it all week, seeking guidance on how best to help you. And then I arrived, revealing my acquaintance with you.'

Thus begun for Tassie, a definite process of healing and invigoration through what I now realise was a divine arrangement of circumstances. Indeed, so remarkable was this reinfusion of strength that she was ready to stand and fight when her brother came to ruffle her feathers just a few days later.

My uncle had telephoned the post office earlier that week, just ten days after his sister buried her son, and sent for her.

When she returned from speaking to him, Tassie was in quite a state of distress.

'Tassie, what did he have to say that has left you so upset?' I asked her.

Not that he was overly concerned about her welfare, nor even that he needed something from her. Instead, he was driven by a more pressing purpose, one that could not accord her the consideration of sufficient time in which to overcome the loss of her son. Fo Kofigah was on a mission to save his sister's soul from perdition.

I practically forced this information out of Tassie.

'Evidently, his spiritualist is predicting more doom and "people are talking" everywhere, casting aspersions on my reputation. Naturally, the only remedy he can come up with requires my immediate compliance with his suggestion that I return to the shrine to perform whatever urgent rituals are needed to avert more bad luck.'

I couldn't imagine a worse act of betrayal than to have your only remaining sibling leading the charge against you, feet astride to cast that first stone. But then again, remembering my own brother, maybe I could. Even so, this was beyond my comprehension. My issues with my uncle's hardcore traditionalist views rose to the surface once more.

'So, what does he want you to do?' I asked.

'He says that I should think about it over the weekend and telephone him with a response; if not, then he will come to Togapeme on Tuesday to convince me in person.'

'Ei! Is he coming to force you to do his bidding?'

'Don't mind him; he's a joker. On Tuesday, he will discover which one of us was born before the other. Pswii!'

Tassie paid him no mind. So he showed up on Tuesday as promised. Two strangers, in whose company he apparently hoped to exert greater influence over his aging sister, accompanied him.

'I need to talk to Daa Nenor for a couple of hours. In *private*.' That was my cue to make myself scarce.

I found it puzzling that he had travelled this far, only to stay for a couple of hours; but it was his father's house, and he had a right to visit his sister there in whatever manner he chose and for whatever length of time. I was hardly in a position to have an opinion on the matter, let alone express it.

I grabbed my bag, preparing to head off to the post office, but Tassie stuck out her arm to block my path, and told me to wait.

And then she asked him, 'Are these *boys* staying or are they going to wait for you outside while we have our discussion?'

He insisted that his companions stay.

'Shika, there are strangers present. If they are going to be part of this discussion, then sit down and be my otsami,' she said. And then, she sent Irene to go and summon Osofo Anani. 'That way,' she explained sweetly to her brother, 'there will be a balance. Since you have brought your two friends with you, I will also have two people as my witnesses.' She was poised for a showdown.

This move surprised me, but, as she explained to me later, it was an intuitive act on her part to have the elder pastor, rather than the younger, be a witness to this confrontation.

'In the first place, I didn't want to place the younger man in the uncomfortable position of publicly appearing to usurp the role of pastor. Besides, I knew that Kofigah would ascribe greater significance to the senior pastor's presence.'

When Osofo Anani arrived, I conveyed to him Tassie's desire to have him witness the discussion between her and Fo Kofigah. Tassie then recapped her telephone conversation with her brother, and I watched in amazement as she unequivocally outlined her stance to the assembled group of men. My interpretive role was rendered redundant; it also became quite clear that the pastor's presence was nothing more than a backdrop against which to establish her own position.

'I'm a God-fearing woman who is simply trying to make the best out of what life has handed me. I didn't ask to be burdened with all these calamities that I've gone through. It is between God and me. If you are not able to live with this fact, then that is *your* problem, not mine.

Kofigah, your physical existence is not tied to mine, neither is your spiritual salvation. After all, when our mother gave birth to me, I came out alone. And come that day too, I will go alone. The days when women used to bend over backwards to do the bidding of the men in their families — simply because they were men — have long been over.

How dare you presume to define what should hold my life together! Do you give me air to breathe, *you* — the toddler that I used to carry on my back when I was only eight years old, without even the breasts to hold the cloth in place around my bust? If life has thrown adversity my way, must that now rob me of all dignity? And then you show up here with these two buffoons. So that what — you can prove to them that here too, you are a lieutenant colonel? Did you remember to bring your gun? Eh?

Hey, Kofigah, I'm letting you know today, in front of all these people, that I will live through whatever new curses may follow the ones I have already endured.'

She was very calm and proper in her delivery. Not a bead of sweat on her powdered nose, not a twitch in her face. When she was done, she stood up, and in the same gracious manner, took her leave.

'Now, if you will excuse me, gentlemen, I have some pressing matters to attend to. We have nothing more to discuss. I wish you safe journey back to the city. Osofo, thank you for obliging me.' She left the room without so much as a glance at anyone.

I did not move. I couldn't breathe.

217

The two strangers would not look at me.

Fo Kofigah kept fidgeting with his hands. *He* also kept his eyes averted.

The reverend quickly took his leave and escaped.

'Would anyone like a drink of water?' I asked belatedly.

The two strangers stood up.

'Efo, perhaps we should set out now since we have a long drive back,' the lanky one said to Fo Kofigah. Then they took their leave of me and went outside to wait for him.

I continued to sit with my clenched fists held up to my mouth. My eyes remained open wide as I waited for whatever was to follow.

Fo Kofigah stood up. He looked down at me for a second, as if deciding what to say. Then he stormed out.

My feeble greeting to his wife and daughter got lost in the sound of the slamming screen door. I let out a sigh of relief and leaned back in the armchair, stretched out my legs, and stared at the ceiling. What now, I wondered.

'Are they gone?' Tassie came out after five minutes. She was armed with a broom.

Muttering under her breath, she bent over and began to purge the house of their presence. She shook out the doormat; then she *swept away their footsteps*, all the way to the gate. I just stood there, astonished.

This incident laid things to rest for Tassie. She continued to counsel discreetly with Osofo Addo whenever he came to visit.

A week later, Miyo came back up the mountain to give Tassie and me copies of Sefa's will, which she had properly filed with the courts. Sefa had named her executor of his estate.

'Don't we need the entire extended family to be present so that it is read aloud to everyone?' Tassie was merely trying to forestall any more family drama.

'There's nothing complicated in the will,' Miyo said. 'Only two names are mentioned in it, and those are the only people who need to be privy to its provisions. Beyond that, it is in the public domain, so anyone who feels the need to do so can go and request to see it.'

Sefa had left his beachfront residence to his mother to occupy or dispose of as she deemed fit; he also left her his vehicle. And he had named me sole trustee of a couple of income properties and a taxicab business, which I was to administer so that his mother could live off the proceeds. After her passing, those properties were to become mine.

Jean had faithfully kept up his weekend visits all this time. Each Sunday, it got harder for me to watch him leave. I had resisted his invitations to visit him in the city, with the excuse that I couldn't yet leave Tassie.

But, truth be told, Tassie did not need me anymore. She had gone ahead in her gentle but unwavering manner and retaken charge of her life. Irene continued to live with us and Tassie also took in the teenaged daughter of another relative. In fact, by the end of the third week, I had run out of excuses and had started feeling like a fifth wheel in the house.

'It's time you moved back to Accra,' Tassie told me that Sunday evening after Jean left. 'His birthday, and he's going to spend the night alone at home, after driving three hours from visiting you. Shame on you for not letting me know until he left, else I would have packed your things and pushed you into his car myself. That man cannot wait forever; what are you afraid of?'

I was stunned by her discernment, wondering for a moment if I had given away any signs of restlessness in my behaviour, especially since Jean and I had had a falling out that morning; but I neither agreed nor disagreed with her. How could I possibly explain to her that I was ready to move on but didn't know how to leave her?

I guess it must have been the uncertainty of what the future held. Suddenly, my fire was out. I felt safer hiding in Togapeme, and the prospect of re-entering the faster-paced setting of Accra, away from what I had become used to for almost three months, was a little daunting.

Most of all, I was secretly afraid of what it would spell for my relationship with Jean. The sexual tension between us was approaching fever pitch and I didn't know how to extricate myself from my internal and external pressures so that we could move on.

'Well?' Tassie had assumed her signature stance — arms akimbo, specs perched low on her nose — and was waiting for my response.

'Miyo and Jean are helping me look for another job; I will see what Jean has to say when he comes up here next weekend.'

But then, on Wednesday morning, while I was removing laundry from the clothesline, the sound of a familiar vehicle pulling up caught my ear. I stepped around the side of the house into the courtyard; and although the gate was shut so that I couldn't see the car, I knew that it was Jean's...

*

It's only ten o'clock, he must have left the city before rush hour, I estimate; what is he doing here on a Wednesday anyway, and why didn't he honk for Irene to open the gate?

After he unlatches the side gate and steps inside the courtyard, he pauses for a moment to find my eyes. Still holding my gaze, he walks slowly up the gravelled path toward me.

I take a couple of steps forward and stop right in front of the bench underneath the cashew tree. Then I place the pile of clean laundry on the back of the bench.

Something holds my tongue. The same thing slowly pushes me down and firmly pins me to the bench. When he arrives in front of me, slowly removes his glasses and rubs his eyes, I keep my head tilted up, my eyes still fixed on his face.

Before he even opens his mouth and says anything, I know. Our time has finally come.

He starts speaking before he remembers to take my hand. Then, almost as an afterthought, he goes down on one knee and continues rambling, long after the words have come out.

I suppose he is nervous. After all, I have rejected him before.

This time it's different. I do not require even one minute to consider what he has just asked me amidst the rambling. I place my finger on his lips to interrupt his tirade. Then I grab both of his ears and hold his head still so that he can hear my response. I articulate it to him clearly and slowly.

'Oui, Jean-Marc Charbonneau, j'accepte! Yes, I will marry you.'

There are no other words necessary. We just stay there like that — he kneeling on the gravel and I sitting on the edge of the bench, cupping his face with my hands — while we both hold back tears of amazement over the fact that we have come this far.

'This is a placeholder; your ring is on its way. I can't wait any more, Shika,' he tells me in a raspy voice; then he removes his college ring and places it on my finger.

He wants to properly ask Tassie for my hand. When she waves at him through the kitchen window, he carries the laundry and goes in to talk with her.

I stay in the courtyard, my ringed hand placed on my chest, my eyes looking ahead, a soft smile on my face.

They soon come out, Tassie overcome with happiness for us, Jean bearing a pitcher of *aliha* for us to celebrate with.

*

A week later, I drove into the city. I had urgent things to do, a new life to plan. Miyo had secured me an interview with a different NGO.

Five minutes into the interview, the job was mine. I spent the next thirty minutes filling out the necessary paperwork and meeting one or two significant people. In a little over an hour, I had moved one step closer to steering my life in a forward direction.

They gave me the sixth of November as my starting date, a little more than a month away, and I was going to be earning almost double what I had on my last job. I left the building feeling quite lightheaded and sat in the car for a good five minutes, just leaning back and allowing this latest development to sink in.

I hadn't even spoken to Jean yet, since I'd driven straight from the village to the interview. So I called him with the good news, but before I could tell him everything, he interrupted me.

'I don't want to know any details; let's reserve them for when we meet at home later,' he said.

I called Miyo to tell her that I was on my way to her office. During the urgent phone call that she made last week to inform me about the job interview, she had also hinted that she had something important to give me; so I promised to stop by her office after my interview.

Miyo wasted no time when I walked into her office. As soon as I sat down, she shut the door and drew the blinds. Then she pulled a sealed envelope out of her briefcase and placed it on the desk in front of me.

I looked at it; it had my full name, 'Mawusi-Shika Amenyo' neatly printed on it.

'You can consider this an early Christmas present from Sef. I have been working on it for weeks and it has just gone through. Go ahead, open it.'

I clumsily fiddled with the thin envelope, wondering what important message it could possibly be delivering from Sefa. I looked in it for a note, some unforgettable words of comfort from beyond the grave that would, perchance, wrench my heart. But there was nothing, only a half page of text printed on the official letterhead of some insurance company:

We were informed of the death of Sefanam Sosu Gameli by Miss Anyemiyoo Mensah, his legal representative and the executor of his estate. Following our duly mandated investigation process in such cases, we have now confirmed that all conditions have been met to our satisfaction. Therefore, it is our duty to inform you that you, Mawusi-Shika Amenyo, are identified as the sole beneficiary on the above-named decedent's life insurance policy, which is valued at—

The next thing I saw was Miyo's worried face right in front of mine as her mouth moved frantically to the beat of the loud pounding in my ears. I couldn't hear a thing she was saying, and it wasn't until I felt her helping me up from the floor that I realised I must have passed out from shock. After I drank water and composed myself, she read the rest of the letter to me.

Enclosed within the folded bottom of the paper was a cheque in the stated amount made out to me.

'Ei, Sefa! Sefa!' I gasped, staring at the figure written on the piece of paper that I was holding in my shaking hands.

'Shika,' Miyo said, 'this is going to change your life forever! You should deposit it in the bank immediately, and then take your time deciding how to invest it. I can accompany you to the bank now, and then we'll stop somewhere for lunch. Come on, let's get out of here.'

After our trip to the bank, we spent a couple of leisurely hours catching up over an early lunch. I told her that I had agreed to marry Jean, and she gave me tips on how I could make sure that I was properly protected in the marriage.

'Too many educated women who should know better, don't. So we blindly go into marriage, assuming that the standard marriage certificate is sufficient to safeguard all of our rights. I know — you love him and he loves you — but please, Shika, take a page from my mother's book; go into this with your eyes wide open. Read up on marriage and property laws in this country and in *his* country, so that you'll know how to handle your business and financial decisions in order to protect yourself and any future children. I beg, cover your behind well so that you don't wake up one day like Rip Van Winkle — wrinkled, dazed and alone — as broke as a church mouse. That's all I'm saying.'

I drove slowly to my house in Nuinui, thinking all the way there about how Jean and I could customise a marriage contract to reflect our real, individual expectations. I didn't even know until just now that there were prenuptial agreements one could use to fine-tune the marriage covenant.

My mind immediately went to Mrs Grace Amuzu and her astute planning — how different *her* outcome had been from those of so many women who are left with nothing when they either get divorced or become widowed. That lack of planning not only stifled *their* dreams, but it also ricocheted down the generations and stole their children's future. *Theirs* was not a club that I intended to join.

When I opened my front door and walked in, I sat in my armchair, closed my eyes for a moment, and took a deep breath of the familiar air. How hard I had worked to afford this place — the feeling of security that I'd always felt here, the peculiar way in which my music echoed in each room — I didn't need to think beyond those memories to know that I wasn't yet ready to let this house go. I picked up the suitcase I had come to retrieve and drove off to Atiawu.

Jean's watchman made a big fuss over me, calling me 'madam' and carrying my luggage in. It sure felt different, letting myself in with my own key.

I stopped in the doorway for a second. With the breath knocked out of my lungs and my mouth hanging open, I moved slowly around the living room. There were photos everywhere of me or of us together — even on the walls of the corridor leading to the bedrooms. This display was surpassed only by a huge oil painting of me on the wall directly facing his bed. On the chest underneath the painting was a vase that contained two red roses. Leaning against the vase was an envelope that had 'Shika' written across it; and in the envelope was a card that simply read, 'Welcome home.'

I sat on the bed and blinked away the tears. Suddenly, the blurry Polaroid photo of us that I carried tucked into the inside cover of my planner seemed inadequate, but only for a moment, because I remembered the depth of my own love for him. I felt deserving of the blessing of this good man's love, and that realisation filled me with gratitude toward the forces that had conspired to send him to my specific corner of the globe.

As if on cue, his phone rang. I waited until his answering machine picked up, and when I heard his voice asking me if I was there, I picked up the phone.

'Welcome home,' he said.

My heart skipped to the sound of his voice. I could only whisper his name into the phone.

'So, is this the sound of joy or disappointment?' he said.

'I'm just happy to be here. I've missed you; hurry home.'

'I will see you after five-thirty. You'll be okay until then? I have a special night planned, don't lift a finger to do anything, and definitely do not cook, okay? I hope you already ate lunch. Let me guess — Adabraka waakye?' He got me to laugh before we hung up.

I unpacked my things and made myself comfortable. The closet in the master bedroom was empty, which surprised me; he must have moved his things into the other room to make space for me. It was unnecessary, but I appreciated the gesture.

I went into every room — opening every door, touching, smelling and feeling the simplest things — to acquaint myself with these surroundings where I was about to become a familiar presence. I could picture my things, how and where they would fit in with his. I listened to his music, skimmed through his literature. We had no secrets anymore, at least none that were hidden behind the objects we possessed.

Before I realised it, it was four-thirty. I jumped into the shower.

*

I'm not yet done when I hear him calling out for me. It can't be past four forty-five; he must have snuck away early, I conclude.

He comes into the bathroom, pulls aside the screen, and steps into the shower. Without uttering a word, he holds my head and kisses every inch of my face and neck, as the water washes over both of us. Then he places his hands on my hips and presses his body into mine with an unmistakable message, which leaves no doubt in my mind that he's really glad to have me home.

Then he goes and sits on the loo and rests his chin on the back of his hand so that he can watch me finish taking my shower.

I'm quite amused at the degree of concentration that he is applying to watching me. I flick a handful of water at him to try to shake his focus, but he only smiles back and gets more comfortable.

Much has happened to us since I last visited this house…

Although we have stuck to our agreement to postpone the consummation of our relationship, we have, nonetheless, made a conscious effort during his subsequent visits to the village to leave no other barriers between us.

In view of the fact that I have never been in a real relationship before, I have no realistic point of reference; but from what I've gathered from my environment, I never would have expected intimacy to be possible without coitus. So, I assume that it must be a Canadian man's trait, this ability to defer gratification and develop intimacy on a completely different level.

I didn't set any definite deadlines or stipulate any conditions for lifting the prohibition when we first discussed it because, quite frankly, I didn't want to set expectations that I myself might not be able to meet. I *was* reserving my right to decide how and to whom I should dispense my affections when I felt ready to do so. After all, it's not as if I were still trying to hang on to my virginity — had it not be stolen from me by force, that ship would probably have already sailed by now. But since *I* had brought the matter up as a topic for our joint discussion, I didn't want to come across as though I were handing out ultimatums.

As it turned out, it was I who eventually found this self-imposed prohibition to be rather vexing, and my attempt to lift it had led to our first tiff.

I had been quite sure that he would happily accept my ultimate gift when, at dawn on his birthday, I took a perfumed bath, adorned myself with nothing but my waist beads, and went back to bed. I threw off the covers, woke him up with a passionate kiss and pressed my naked body into his.

But Jean didn't oblige me that day. Instead, he embraced my naked body, told me how much he loved me — and then proceeded to make a long speech:

'You made me swear at the foot of Paradiso that I would honour your decision and even though I wasn't sure that I could, I still went ahead and gave you my word. This process is teaching me how to master my appetites so that I can become *that* man that you want.'

'But, Jean, I love you! I'm ready. Today! I *know* that you love me; don't you want my body too? I'm lifting the embargo.'

'I love you so much that I want *all* of you, Shika, not just your body. *Everything!* Are you ready to also give up the parts of you that I cannot touch with my hands, the parts that you have been holding back from me? Or are you offering me this concession because part of you doesn't trust me to keep my word, and you think that you have to do this to keep me? I've been working hard to deserve you, Shika. Now it's your turn to trust that I *can* wait for you until you're *truly* ready, because you're worth waiting for.'

I let out a loud groan and covered my face in embarrassment, trying to hide my 'concession' under the covers. But he snatched the covers back, peeled my hands from my face, and kissed me tenderly.

'Don't hide now; I *do* want to feast my eyes on you.' Then he directed my hand down his body to prove to me that it had acknowledged my offer. '*That* is my birthday present. Look at me, Shika,' he said with a twinkle in his eyes, 'or are you deliberately trying to make me lose the bonus?'

Ah! The bonus.

When we were getting ready to leave the waterfall on the day that I took him there — after I had managed to momentarily break its hold over us so that we could discuss this now-problematic embargo — I had stood in Jean's embrace and made him a promise: 'This will be our reward to each other. I will throw away all my inhibitions and we *will* make love right here at the foot of this waterfall the very first time we return to Togapeme post-embargo.'

'Oh, only once?' He asked it as if I had accidentally dropped half his ice cream just as he was about to lick it.

'How many times then? This is your chance, Jean; your wish will be my command.'

'I'm rather hoping that it will be every time we return to Togapeme.'

'Then consider it done.'

'Really? In that case, let us not come back to this spot until then, because it would be too much for me. Instead, let's reserve it for that day.'

'And every time we return to Togapeme, we'll climb down here and I, Mawusi-Shika Amenyo, will keep this promise to you, Jean-Marc Charbonneau. Every visit.'

So we never went back to the foot of Paradiso. Instead, we took to picnicking under the flamboyant tree at the edge of my family's property, from where we could see the crest of the waterfall and hear its sound. And every time we sat in the orange glow cast by the shade of the tree, the green of his eyes would deepen and he would look at me with much longing tempered by his ironclad determination to earn that bonus.

Now, as I look at him watching me slowly lather up all over again, I am amazed to realise just how far we have progressed since my last visit to this house.

During this time, I have been working on my issues, discovering myself anew:

Mawusi-Shika Amenyo, the deep one—a woman of discriminating taste. Well trained in the kitchen, yet does not enjoy cooking. Taller than necessary; small breasted and wide-hipped. Might be barren. Although still evolving, previously stiff and inhibited. Yearning to be loved passionately and

*unconditionally by a man worthy of her. Unapologetic. Nonnegotiable. Ideal
candidate recently identified, all others need not apply.*

He has been teaching me everything that I never realised I didn't know
— how to receive affection from a man without feeling that I have to
reward him for that 'favour'; how to yield completely to his embrace
without cringing in anticipation that he will throw me onto the floor
against my will.

He has entrusted into my possession the key to *his* sanity — taught me
how to please him without driving him out of his senses — and in the
process, I have discovered that trust goes both ways.

Finally, I am learning that it is neither apostasy nor an exclusive
privilege, reserved for some superior woman from a preferred section of
the globe, for a man to declare boldly that he worships me and then
proceed to back that declaration up by putting the needs of my soul before
the desires of his flesh. Although I have been a slow learner, I have a better
teacher. And so I'm almost there.

And while it pleases me excessively and puts a twinkle in my eye, as I
reach out my hand for a towel, to witness the hypnotic hold that my hips
have on Jean-Marc Charbonneau, this knowledge does not fill me with
arrogance. Rather — that a man in full control of all his faculties can will
himself into capitulating to my taming in order to earn his place in my life
— *this* causes me to marvel over my own worth. It has kept me humble
and grateful, and is accelerating my process of resolving all my issues so
that I too can fully validate him, this gallant knight whose bottle green
eyes now seek to burn two holes through my flesh and strip me down to
the bone.

All the same, there is a limit to what the human body can endure,
however noble its intent. And so, letting out an agonised 'aarh!' my knight
quickly grabs the towel and hurls it at me. Complaining loudly in his
native tongue, and with his hand restraining his fiery sword, he flees from
the bathroom before I step out of the shower in all my glory.

*

True to his word, it was an evening to remember. I sat on the kitchen counter next to him and watched him cook for me 'a real Québécois meal,' as he claimed, 'except that I am preparing it from scratch with African ingredients and spices for you, my queen.'

We sat on cushions on the floor of the screened back porch and dined by candlelight to an orchestra of crickets and the smell of forget-me-nots. We hand-fed each other the *Poutine* that he made with local sweet potatoes and goat cheese, and washed down with a carafe of red wine the Ghana meat pies that he'd ordered.

'Long story,' I said, when he asked me why I was giggling at the sight of the pies.

'The Québécois version takes forever to bake, so I will make it for you another time,' he promised.

After the meal, he took away the trays and put on some soothing music.

'Come, I have a surprise for you,' he said, and pulled me into the bedroom. 'Don't move; close your eyes and count down from ten.'

I did as he instructed — I was intrigued.

He embraced me from behind and asked me to open my eyes. In his hand was a tiny leather box embossed with 'Cartier'.

'Here, let's open it together!' He kept his fingers on mine.

In the box was my engagement ring, its gigantic red rock blinking at me. He slipped it on my finger.

'A ruby, my birthstone! Oh, Jean!' I turned to face him.

'For you, mon coeur. It finally arrived this week. I special-ordered it weeks ago from Paris. It would have been ideal to have it in my hand when I proposed; but it was taking forever to arrive, and I just couldn't wait any longer. I didn't sleep that entire night and by morning, it was so bad that I cancelled all my appointments for the day and came to Togapeme at once.'

'The timing is perfect,' I said.

'Look closely.' He raised my hand up and turned it to catch the light.

I gasped. The ruby was flanked on either side by three diamonds.

'For the six children that we shall have.' He laughed at my sudden change of expression.

Children were never part of our plans from the beginning. I had told him enough for him to know that I might never be able to give us any.

'I will understand if that is a deal-breaker for you, Jean. I cannot change what I cannot control.' I had told him this on that first night when I slept in this house.

'There are medical miracles these days, or we could always adopt. Believe, Shika,' he had responded that day, but my reaction to the word 'adopt' had been far from enthusiastic. I had concluded that he was just trying to downplay the bad news with what he thought was a positive response. Besides, how could I explain to him that bringing up some stranger's child might not go down too well because we were not used to that here? And so I had left it at that.

Now, looking down at the ring, I felt conflicted. Then I searched his eyes. I was carrying all my doubts in mine.

But he didn't flinch, didn't look away or attempt to apologise for his pronouncement. Instead, he placed a finger over my mouth and shook his head before I could say anything.

'You *are* sufficient for me,' he said, 'we will leave any miracles up to God, yes? Now, may I have this dance?'

We took all the necessary steps to ensure that there would be no impediments in our way. The next morning, before doing anything else, we drove down to the municipal building to post the banns of our upcoming marriage.

Then I dropped Jean off at work, where he detained me for another ten minutes and introduced me to everybody. It came as no surprise when I discovered that all of them had already heard about me and seen my photo, which sat in a picture frame in his office.

I called Sweetie to tell her the good news and let her know that I would be returning to town at the end of the month for the traditional ceremony.

'Come with JM to Eno's shop and pick out some fabric before you leave town,' she said, 'my gift to you guys.'

I told her that we would stop by on Saturday afternoon on our way back from Tema.

I was going to try to reconnect with Fo Kofigah. I wasn't certain what would happen, as he had not resurfaced and two weeks had now passed since his quarrel with his sister.

'Shika, I beg you, do not involve Kofigah in your marriage plans; go and seek out your father's brothers instead,' Tassie had warned me before I left Togapeme, but I felt that I should at least make an attempt. After all, such as he was, Fo Kofigah was the closest thing to a father that I had had for many years now. I had to think of him as a package that encompassed my relationships with his children. I could not imagine being estranged from all of them forever, especially Emekor.

She had received her A-level results; they were mediocre. She *could* slide into one of the universities if her father decided to pull a few strings, but her chances were really slim. Fortunately, her grades in languages were excellent, and the yearlong course at the Intercultural Centre was due to start in another six weeks or so. She was depending on me to carry out her plan.

'Daavi Shika,' she had said the last time we spoke, 'I took your advice and submitted my application to I.C. for the accelerated translators' course. They have accepted it. When are you moving back to the city?'

'Don't worry, Emekor, I will be back in Accra by then and we can proceed as planned,' I had assured her. But, despite my intention to hold up my end of the bargain, my promise carried no weight without her father's approval. I *had* to find a way to keep the lines of communication open between us.

It was going to be a trying day. Jean had insisted on coming along to Fo Kofigah's with me.

'How can you go to inform him that you're getting married to *me*, yet not have me standing there beside you? In his shoes, *I* would feel offended. If I must go through him to marry you, then I'm going to do it properly. We're in this together, Shika, remember?'

'There's some tension between him and Tassie, that's all,' I explained feebly.

'So? Don't get caught up in their fight. You know how sibling fights go. Stay out of it.'

'Still, it might be wise if we just showed up unannounced, we'll stand a better chance of being received at all,' I said.

'No, that would make it worse. At least call his wife and let her know that we're coming; she will find a way to let him know. He's all bark and no bite, like most bullies. He doesn't intimidate me. Don't worry, chérie, I'm going to slay this dragon, throw you over my shoulder and carry you off.'

We got to Tema around eleven that Saturday morning. Fo Kofigah was out but they expected him back soon. We broke the news of our engagement to Daa Jane and Emekor. After they had congratulated us, I told Daa Jane about the offer I'd made Fo Kofigah to accommodate Emekor in Accra, and how badly he had received it.

She expressed surprise and blamed his reaction on bad timing, the offer coming as it had during Sefa's farewell party and all.

'I myself am relieved that you're offering because I'd been wondering how Emekor would make the long trip everyday, through rush hour, both ways. I'm quite sure your uncle will react differently now.'

We didn't have to wait too long to find out. He walked in while we were chatting. We went through the greeting process all over again, an exercise in diplomacy, for sure. Nothing on anybody's face to indicate any discomfort. Fo Kofigah was almost jovial. He even asked how his sister was faring.

After a few minutes of this chitchat, his wife relayed to him the good news that had brought us to their doorstep so unexpectedly. It seemed to disorient him for a second, but he regained his composure quickly and congratulated us, Jean especially, on doing the right thing. There was no lengthy lecture as I had expected, but he did let Jean know that our family would be performing the necessary investigation into his background.

'This is a precaution, nothing personal against you, you understand? No one can predict the future, of course, but we will do our part. We treasure our Mawusi-Shika very much because we have invested a lot of care and resources into bringing her up to become the beautiful, intelligent woman you came and discovered. I would be remiss in my responsibility as her parent if I didn't conduct this basic background check before giving her to you.

And you are also free to go and ask anybody — ask anyone at all — she has always conducted herself with prudence and respect. In fact, we have a saying, *"When you are going into marriage, ask."'*

I caught a barely-masked sarcastic twist to his wife's mouth as he said this. I did not look in Jean's direction at all but out of the corner of my eye, I saw him swallow hard. He ran his hand across his brow. Twice. My dragon-slayer was sweating profusely.

'Of course,' he replied, 'I have nothing to hide, and I wouldn't have it any other way. May I call you by Wednesday so that we can discuss when my family delegation can come to formally ask for Shika's hand?'

'I'm quite impressed that you already know what is required of you. But don't worry, wait and hear back from me before you jump to the next step. Relax, mon ami, we look forward to welcoming you into our family. Cheers!' he said, raising his glass to us.

This side of Fo Kofigah, I must confess, I'd never seen; but I was glad that I had stuck with him. In spite of all his other issues, his sense of order and responsibility had always been his strongest trait.

Daa Jane had prepared a feast, and it went without saying that we would have lunch before leaving. With all the camaraderie that followed our good news and the delicious meal, I waited until I found an opportune moment to reintroduce the second reason for our visit. Daa Jane must have felt the same. She beat me to it.

'Now that Shika is returning to Accra, that will solve Emekor's problem of going up and down to school. Shika tells me that they are willing to have her come and stay with them whenever she needs to while she takes the course. It is such a generous offer and an answer to prayer, don't you agree?'

For the second time that afternoon, Fo Kofigah skipped a beat. This time his comeback was a little strained as he tried to regain his composure.

'Well, let them first get married, and then we shall see. After all, Shika hasn't yet returned to Accra, has she?'

'The girl starts school in six weeks,' she reminded him.

'As I said, we will discuss this and give them an answer. Later. John-Mark, thank you for the offer. We will certainly think about it and let you know.'

There seemed no point in pushing the matter. The temperature in the room immediately dropped and, just as it was about to turn really awkward, we took our leave, despite Daa Jane's insistence that we stay a little longer.

Before we made our escape, Fo Kofigah promised to get back to Jean.

I called out to Emekor and she walked us to the car.

'I heard everything. I was listening from the kitchen. Daavi Shika, is there any hope at all? I feel like a prisoner,' she said. She sounded really disillusioned.

'Don't be so negative. Your mother will talk to him, she seemed sure that she could bring him around. Don't tell them, but I'm starting my new job at the beginning of next month so I'm moving back here even sooner than I had expected. Everything will sort itself out, you'll see.'

'But that's only about three weeks away! In that case, I'm relieved. At least we'll have a few weeks to convince him together before classes are due to start.' She hugged me tightly before Jean and I drove off.

We decided that considering that I had to be back in a few weeks, I should cut this visit short and return to Togapeme to break the news of my impending departure to Tassie and prepare for my final return. Jean would have to travel for work the week before I was due to return; but he said that he would come to the village that final week to move me back to Accra.

His assignment was to notify his people pronto and have them ready to come down as soon as we got the go-ahead from my family. Despite Fo Kofigah's long speech, we were quite optimistic that we could have the initial *knocking rites* performed by the end of the month. It was necessary for us to at least do that much before starting to officially live together.

True to his word, Fo Kofigah immediately began digging into Jean's background. Jean updated me on developments when we spoke during the following week.

'A retired Lieutenant Colonel Sosu contacted us to request your criminal record and verify your marital status,' the consular officer at the Canadian High Commission had told him when she contacted him to obtain his permission to disclose that information.

Everybody was relieved that I had finally found a man. The receptivity to his foreign race was mixed, but those who take issue with it were few and insignificant, and so our plans went forward without a glitch.

It seemed that it would be more prudent to have the ceremony in my uncle's home in Tema instead of my hometown, being that we had buried a close relative in Togapeme barely two months ago and were, technically, still in mourning.

Tassie resigned herself to my desire to have the ceremony performed in her brother's house. She even agreed graciously to travel down and sit with him to represent my maternal side, to officially receive Jean's delegation. My father's family had been duly informed and they also were sending two or three representatives to join my delegation.

Jean had managed to get his people in Lomé to agree to drop everything and travel down to represent him. They would be bringing along *their* own indigenous Togolese 'relatives', who were familiar with Ewe marital rites, to stand with them.

I had thought that we would be permitted to be absent from the ceremony and to have the whole thing videotaped for us so that we could watch it later, like I had seen other people do before. But Tassie quickly set me straight.

'It is not an option; we don't do that where *we* come from. We are *not* going to perform some modern adulteration of the proper rites; both you and Jean will have to be present that day. His relatives have to see you, and our relatives also have to see his face, otherwise you two might as well be ghosts. How else will people be able to make the connection between the two of you?'

The renovation of the church sanctuary had been completed and Tassie had gone back to being the organist. I hired someone to drive her around so that she could cut down on her long hikes about town. When I was sure that there would be caring people around her, I was able to focus on my upcoming move. So I began, with Irene's help, to tackle the cleaning and airing out of Sefa's room early that final week.

'I don't like the idea at all,' Tassie grumbled when I told her my intention. 'I won't feel his presence anymore if you move things around.'

'I'm not moving anything, just the bed. Then, I'll bring the piano in to replace the bed so that you can relax in here everyday. It will be very comfortable and beautiful, you'll see.'

First thing on Wednesday morning, the house painter came in and transformed Sefa's room into a more suitable palette. We moved the bed out, rolled the piano in, brought in shelves of books, and voila! A library was born. Sefa's sports trophies were everywhere; there were so many of them! Along with many family photos, which we strategically placed around the room, they added a shiny touch to the décor.

And when Tassie walked in and saw the new space, she looked at me with tears in her eyes and said, 'Oh, Shika! Look how beautifully it turned out! You have given me back my peace.'

Then I knew that I had done the right thing.

THIRTEEN

Friday morning, by daybreak, Jean's family delegates have already arrived at my uncle's house, where they symbolically seek access to our family by knocking loudly.

'*A-goh*!' They yell outside the front gate.

'*A-meh*!' Upon being granted access with this response, they waste no time getting down to the business at hand.

The mandatory use of otsamis by both sides facilitates the full understanding and maximum participation of my foreign in-laws. They present the required drinks — one bottle of Baron's Aromatic Schnapps and one bottle of Castle Bridge London Dry Gin — and state the reason for their early morning visit.

Only those who need to be present are here. Delegates from my paternal and maternal sides, who know what they are doing, properly confer with Jean's delegation and perform the rites that will establish that he and I are now promised to each other.

'And now, after having travelled all this way, we cannot consider our mission to be accomplished if we do not identify the flower that our son has come to pluck from your garden.'

I have been waiting within earshot but out of sight while the families conduct the proceedings, but this request from the head of Jean's delegation is the cue for me to come out and be introduced to them. I join a line-up of other female relatives that includes two of Fo Kofigah's daughters-in-law and Emekor, and we file out and greet everyone. Then we stand and wait.

'Jean-Marc,' says Tonton Kouakou, the otsami of Jean's entourage, 'Efo Kofigah Sosu has this lush garden with these four exotic flowers on display in it. Identify for all of us the specific flower that you came to pluck, so that there is no confusion. Then, if we see her standing in some corner with another man, we will recognise her as "Jean-Marc's own flower" and defend her honour in your behalf.'

Jean stands up. He removes his glasses and wipes them, then puts them on again. He inspects each of the girls closely, as if he isn't sure which one is his own flower. When he gets to me, he twirls me about several times, looks behind my ears, stares at my hands, and finally puts his stamp of approval on me by raising my right hand.

'Look carefully, Jean-Marc,' Tonton Kouakou keeps a poker face and continues his flawless execution. 'Now that you have not only scrutinised her from head to toe but also sniffed her perfume to verify her identity, are you absolutely sure? Because, Lomé is far but Canada is even further, and we will not be able to turn around if you discover in the middle of our journey back that you plucked the wrong flower. So, let me ask you again: Jean-Marc, is this one, the one they call "Mawusi-Shika", the flower that you saw in Efo Kofigah's garden? The one that we have been sent from Lomé to come and help you pluck and take away to Canada?'

'I'm very sure, Tonton. She is the one.'

I turn and face D'Amavi, who is acting as my otsami.

'Mawusi-Shika,' she says to me, 'do you know this man?'

'Hm, he looks familiar, auntie,' I respond, setting my face like flint. If anybody is going to be responsible for ruining this concert, I'm not going to be that person.

'Look closely. Is this Efo John-Mark — the one also known as "Jean-Marc" to his people — the bee that has been buzzing through Efo Kofigah's garden by heart, sometimes several times a day, looking at you and admiring your petals? The one that you directed to come to your family to request permission from us before you would allow him to, erh, stroke your petals?'

'I recognise him; yes, this is he.'

'Where is the engagement ring? Efo John-Mark, come and place it on her finger in front of us and let us make sure that it fits; then your business here will be done.'

The gathering erupts in laughter and applause.

After providing our guests with refreshment, we send them on their way.

The two sides have already agreed that the traditional ceremony will be performed in the afternoon the very next day. Jean and I have also decided to take the process all the way and include the civil marriage ceremony. In as much as we would have liked a big church wedding, it is out of the question so soon after Sefa's death.

So, after consulting with all concerned parties, Jean and I fulfilled all the mandated requirements and booked the appointment for ten o'clock.

Setting the dates back to back is a concession that my family has been generous enough to make for the benefit of Jean's entourage, so that they don't have to travel back and forth. It would have been unnecessary and rather inconsiderate to stretch out the various rites over several weeks.

Today, Saturday the twenty-eighth of October 1995, Jean-Marc Charbonneau and I, dressed in proper business attire — he in a navy blue suit, and I in a simple white dress with complementary hat and pearls — have arrived at the municipal building. We are accompanied by Tassie, Fo Kofigah, and two representatives from Jean's entourage. Standing face to face before an official from the Registrar General's Department, we raise our right hands to heaven and swear an oath before Almighty God. Then we sign the document that legally makes me his wife.

By noon, the women have gathered at my house to help me prepare for the afternoon celebration — Miyo, Sweetie, D'Amavi and Tassie.

Sweetie's seamstress has gone all out and created coordinating outfits befitting the occasion for Jean and me. We reserved for a different occasion the lace that Sweetie gave us, opting to go instead with the more traditional *kente* cloth of my Ewe tribe. Miyo has also brought the beautician to the house to do my hair, nails and makeup — she's footing that bill.

After the beautician has completed her work and I have put on my outfit, Tassie sends the other women from the room.

'I have to apply one final touch,' she tells them. 'We will come out in a minute and surprise you.'

She pats the bed for me to sit down. I have my box of coral beads in my hand, waiting for her to help me put them on. But she shakes her head and takes the box from me.

'No, Shika, not today. Take those with you and wear them for him tonight or tomorrow. Today, you are wearing these.'

Then she opens her bag and pulls out a small bundle tied in an old silk scarf, which she places in my cupped hands. It's much heavier than it looks. She carefully unknots the scarf to reveal several layers of delicate tissue. When she peels back the wrapping, my eyes almost fall out of my head at the sight of the most intricately crafted gold jewellery that I have ever seen.

'I promised your mother that I would live to see this day and make sure that you wore these. Your father had them custom-made for her when she gave birth to you. Shika, this is your inheritance.'

She drapes the necklace about my neck and fastens the bracelet around my wrist. I walk to the mirror and put on the earrings with shaking hands; then she takes my hand and twirls me around.

'Oh, look at you! It's Lebene, back in the flesh at the same age. If only she could see you now!'

My heart is melting. My joy and pain collide and begin to spill out at her mention of my mother.

'No, my child, no tears today,' she says, 'I forbid it! Not even tears of joy. You will ruin your makeup; then Miyo will kill me for causing you to destroy her investment.'

She places her cheek next to mine and fans my eyes with her hand. Then we stand for another moment, smiling at each other in the mirror.

'Let's go,' she whispers and kisses my cheek, 'he's waiting for you.'

All the women in my family surround me in Fo Kofigah's living room, ready to bring me out to the front lawn, where my knight has been waiting patiently. They tell me that he has been standing with his hands held together behind him, legs astride like a true warrior, ever since the drums began to roll. I too have been waiting a long time for this moment. Now, I'm finally ready.

Waving their white handkerchiefs and singing joyously, the women dance *boborboh* to the beat of the drums and escort me to him.

He takes a step forward, and then he salutes me by raising both of my hands and bowing his head to touch his lips to them. He seats me, then retains my hand and keeps his eyes fixed on me as he takes his place beside me. This man will not take his eyes off me and my heart will not stop fluttering. All other eyes are on us.

It's heart-warming to see how his people have gone out of their way to honour my heritage by showing up all decked out in the ceremonial fabric of my tribe, the two women sporting artfully designed *slit-and-kaba* outfits with matching *dukus*, and the men in four-piece *agbadas*.

We have strictly limited invitation to close family and friends, as it would be inappropriate to put on an ostentatious show while we are still in mourning. Jean, I know, wanted to show the whole world that he is finally marrying me, but *I* am quite content that we have scaled the ceremony down.

Nonetheless, all the important steps have been followed to the letter. His entourage has returned today, ready to put on a record-setting display, judging from the number of boxes in which they transported the various items that they have included in my dowry.

There is no cutting of corners in their presentation — no second-rate fabrics or inferior beads included in my trousseau, no cheap bottles of liquor with which to offend my relatives. In addition to the mandated ceremonial drinks, they have raised the bar by also throwing in, just for effect, one case each of Château Léoville-Las Cases, Highland Park 30 Scotch, and Baileys Irish Cream. Everything is top-notch, in good taste and definitely above reproach.

After they are done with the process, Osofo Addo addresses the gathering briefly. Then, all the married couples take turns blessing us with their nuggets of wisdom. After we have kissed each other to everybody's satisfaction, we are ready to feast.

By seven o'clock, the real party has begun. When Jean and I open the dance floor, he thrills me with a special surprise to the cheers of everyone present. My chevalier and his entourage have secretly taken lessons in our complex *agbadza* dance so that they can properly serenade me, and this earns my appreciation better than any of the gifts they have brought to impress me with.

'Encore, encore!' Our guests have still not had enough, so Jean and I give them one more dance. And then we stand there smooching each other while they applaud and whistle. We rock each other back and forth for the longest time, until our hearts begin to beat in sync.

Then, Jean whispers in my ear and I nod.

The car key is already in his pocket. Our guests already have full access to our houses — Tassie and D'Amavi will be staying in my house for a week — and the party in our honour is well underway.

To the accompaniment of the escalating beat of the talking drums, and more cheers and whistles from our loved ones, we make our triumphant exit through a shower of confetti and drive off to Hippo Lodge, the place where we first recognised each other, to bring to fruition what we began cultivating there six years ago.

And in the morning, after we're finally able to crawl out of bed, we spend another two hours in the hotel spa, where our limp, aching bodies are massaged and coaxed back to life. We will be requiring every bit of energy in order to make an urgent, three-hour drive later this afternoon.

So as to keep my word to my husband, and in order to preserve his sanity, it is necessary that we make this five-day pilgrimage to a small piece of paradise that is tucked into the side of a mountain peak. There, a giant tree has been waiting for us since the day we first sat at its feet. This tree will bear witness to our long overdue appointment with a tropical waterfall that will not release us from its spell until it has exacted its due.

FOURTEEN

It was very important to me that I keep the promise I had made to Emekor. I was initially worried that Jean would consider it an unacceptable imposition for us to accommodate her so soon after we got married, but he reminded me that he had come into this relationship with both eyes open and married me along with whatever I came with, which certainly encompassed opening our home to Emekor.

That arrangement was a feat in itself, considering how resistant her father had been from the beginning. Tassie revealed to me later that Fo Kofigah decided to let go of his stranglehold on his daughter only after his wife resurrected the ghosts of his other skeletons.

'You should have seen how Jane twisted his arm before he caved in.'

Apparently, their thirty-eight-year marriage had other secrets besides Emekor's conception, and even though Daa Jane had left those skeletons buried all these years, she occasionally dug them up and used them as leverage.

Emekor began staying with Jean and me the week she started her professional course at I.C., just as I promised her that she could. Classes were held on Tuesdays, Thursdays and Fridays, so the driver dropped her off at our place every Monday night and I took her back to Tema every Friday night.

Daa Jane, not surprisingly, was relieved that her little girl had finally ventured out into the world.

'It will give her more independence before she actually goes away to the university. After all, she isn't exactly a child anymore,' she told me the first week.

I thought of Sefa regularly and with much fondness, marvelling at the countless ways in which his memory was being preserved.

But his mother wanted nothing to do with the house he had left her.

'I have no plans of coming to the city for extended periods of time; and when I do, I won't want to stay in that house all by myself,' was all she would say about it.

'And you won't have to, you will always have a room in our home,' Jean assured her.

But I suspected that there was more to her dislike of that house than its size. When I was getting ready to lease my house, I dug a little deeper; and that's when the truth finally came out.

'I told him not to buy that house in Nuinui, but he didn't listen to me. Maybe if I had had the courage to tell him why, he would have made a different decision.'

'Tassie, what is it about Nuinui that makes you hate it so much?'

'Because, Shika, before there was any real estate development there, long before they even gave the town a name, I knew it for one thing only. That is the beach where my beloved Elorm's body washed ashore. You can see the exact spot if you look out of Sefa's bedroom window.'

'Oh, Tassie, Tassie! If you had told me, I also would have tried to talk him out of it instead of going to join him there.'

'It wouldn't have worked, my dear. As soon as he mentioned Nuinui, I feared that I had already lost him. It was as if something were drawing him there.'

Uncle Elorm, an ace competitive swimmer during his college years, had suffered a seizure while swimming in the ocean on that Independence holiday, while his pregnant wife and his toddler lounged on a popular beach. He vanished right before their eyes.

Tassie immediately went into premature labour. Two days later, the tide returned Uncle Elorm's body to an isolated beach ten miles away. The autopsy showed no water in his lungs. In the same breath, they told Tassie that her husband's body had washed ashore and that she had lost the baby.

My mother left all those details out over the years when she was filling me in on our family history. I suppose it would have been too much for a child to process.

'That settles it,' I told Tassie, 'I will put up Sefa's house for lease.'

'With the income that comes in from that and his other business ventures, I will sponsor the building of a chapel at Bremen Clinic in honour of my son. And I will also set up a fund that will award annual scholarships to the youth of Togapeme to further their education.'

Jean and I quickly made the necessary adjustments to propel us into our new life. He constantly assured me that he loved me for myself, and although I carried myself as if I actually believed it, something was still missing. I tried to mask it well, but I had already begun to feel the societal pressures that come to bear on a childless, married woman. There were constant reminders everyday.

'And how many children do you have?' Complete strangers would boldly ask me this as soon as they saw my wedding ring — it made no difference to them whether I was alone or with Jean — and it didn't matter where we were. The question was always directed at me and never at my husband, even when we were standing together. I accepted that those occasions were unavoidable, and I certainly saw no malice in the curiosity of strangers, however inappropriate their familiarity.

Even though my family did not put that kind of pressure on me, I knew that Tassie was probably getting concerned, so it was quite a relief when she finally broached the topic.

'I'm only going to ask you once, because I want you to know that I'm here if you need someone to discuss this with,' she said. 'Are you having problems conceiving, or is your husband?'

'Tassie, I'm the one with the problem. We will go to consult a specialist soon. Maybe there's something they can do for me.'

But there was no such plan. I just didn't have the heart to tell her the truth.

We had already been to two fertility doctors — as soon as we returned from our honeymoon, just to be sure — and there was nothing they could do. All I got from those visits was a battery of painful tests that revealed once and for all, the irreversible effects of the hack job that I had endured more than fourteen years ago.

'Although your ovaries are intact and you are technically fertile,' the first specialist told me quite bluntly after the test results came back, 'your fallopian tubes are completely blocked; but even worse than that is the fact that the lining of your uterus is permanently destroyed. Your womb does not have the structural integrity to bear the weight of a growing foetus.'

'If you want to produce a child who has your blood running through his or her veins, then another woman is going to have to carry it for you,' the second doctor clearly spelt out to me after going over the report.

This confirmation of my worst fear dredged up the painful memories I thought I had left behind, and killed what little hope I had hung on to until now. The irony that I wasn't even barren, yet would now have to live under that curse, was a bitter pill which left me wishing I hadn't even bothered going to find out the details at all. The news threw me into a dark abyss that would have sucked me in and pushed me down, had it not been for my husband's vigilance.

For the entire first month of our marriage, following this devastating report, I crawled into a shell and would not accept calls from anyone. All I did was go to work and return home. I did not even go to church. Everyone assumed that Jean and I were enjoying our new status, so they left us alone. This gave us the time we needed to come to terms with our reality.

But there is a saying that *'the bug that stings you is from your own cloth'* and sure enough, the sharpest darts were those thrown by people with whom I had to interact regularly — mostly female co-workers who felt that by virtue of our common gender, it was now their place to not only monitor my personal business but also give me unsolicited advise regularly, never mind that I had just started working with them and they hardly knew me.

There were even instances that I was sure had been deliberately orchestrated by these malicious busybodies to confront me over the absence of a pregnancy after only a few weeks of being married, as if I possessed within my person the power to command its immediate manifestation, or else owed them and the entire world an explanation for my deferment of their expectation of me.

Lying there on those long nights, with his arm securely around my waist, I waged my own inner battle while pretending to be asleep. I went back several times to my in-depth conversation with Emekor about marriage, and wondered what my outlook would have been, had I had the misfortune of marrying anyone else but this man, and been faced with having to now live under this cloud. How different my expectation of marital bliss would have been!

Although I had come to admire Jean's many good qualities over the years, it took being married to him and going through this crisis together for me to fully appreciate the magnitude of his character. It was as though he carved out a place in his soul and tucked me there so that the pain could not get to me unless it first contended with him. And it was only then that I understood what Osofo Addo had meant during our informal counselling sessions, when he told Jean in front of me, 'your primary role in this marriage is to be Shika's covering. If you have any doubts about your ability to be that to her, then you should not marry her.'

By the time we emerged from this trial, something within my spirit was definitely settled. Strangely, I even felt more secure in my femininity. Yes, Jean-Marc Charbonneau had covered me and in so doing, proved his measure as a man all over again.

This man loved me fully and completely. Of that I would never be in doubt.

The challenge of trying to bear this cross with dignity also gave me greater appreciation of Tassie's fortitude forged over many years of carrying the same cross. I found myself attaining new heights of grace and maturity under her tutelage. We went faithfully to Togapeme to visit her every other weekend.

Jean was completely in love with our village, and he soon began talking about building a house there. His enthusiasm gave me fresh appreciation of its raw beauty; it quickly became a haven where we went to recharge. And the fact that we kept our promise to reward each other at the waterfall during each visit only deepened our passion, both for Togapeme and for each other. There was definitely something magical in the atmosphere.

Even when Jean was away on business, I went alone to the mountain. This one-on-one time with Tassie was invaluable. She was fully tuned in to my emotional deficits, but she seemed to be permanently plugged into a source of strength that I was, perhaps, too inexperienced to access on my own; and so, I in turn tapped into her as *my* reservoir. Slowly, her calmness began to rub off on me. It seemed to flow intuitively, and I benefitted from the constant outpouring from her generous spirit, more than I could ever hope to give back.

She taught me many practical things about life and relationships.

'Shika, you are too old fashioned, too hard on yourself,' she told me more than once. 'Stop trying to prove that you are strong and capable; allow your husband to pamper you every once in a while. It's okay, and he would like that. Really.'

'What about my friends, Tassie? I don't want them to feel that I'm treating them differently now that I'm married.'

'And why not? Where's the logic in your thinking? You *ought* to treat them differently because you now have different priorities. It doesn't mean that you would leave them by the roadside to die if they really needed you.'

'I just don't want to lose them. We've been through a lot together.'

'That will never happen. You give them so much of yourself that they would be idiots to lose you. But they ought to expect a decrease in your availability. You can no longer have duplicates of each other's house keys, or be showing up unannounced for dinner every Sunday, if that has been your arrangement until now. *You* must take the lead in establishing those new boundaries; then, they will learn to respect you and your husband. And only then will you all be free to fully mature into strong, independent women. That would be your greatest gift to yourself and to them.'

'Hm. I never thought of it like that.'

'Of course not, dear! But believe me when I tell you that *"familiarity breeds contempt"* as I've had forty extra years in which to learn this the hard way. You will see that as soon as you outline your perimeter, they too will set up theirs, which they won't realise they need to do until you show them how. And everybody will be healthier and happier for it, you just wait and see.'

*

Several weeks went by before I got together again with Miyo and Sweetie. And when we finally did, my concerns proved invalid. I invited them to dinner the week before Christmas; they were my very first guests in my new home.

They couldn't get over the fact that my husband himself had taken charge of preparations so that I could focus completely on them from the moment they walked in.

'Ei, Mawusi-Shika Amenyo! Look at how this man stops by every three minutes to rub your shoulder or touch your head. What will he do next?

Bend down and suck your toes in front of us?' Sweetie whispered loudly when Jean left the room after stopping in to say hello to them.

'And he's doing all this romancing while popping in and out of the kitchen to check on the chef. What are they preparing for us, anyway?' Miyo said.

'Hm, the main dish is some special pie from his hometown; it's called *Tourtière du Lac-Saint-Jean*. You'd better praise him after you taste it oh; he spent all day yesterday shopping for ingredients and coaching the chef.'

'You were smart to get a male chef and not some floozy who would have come to steal your husband,' Sweetie said.

'This guy is very good,' I said, 'but I only need him once in a while, or when we're expecting guests. Jean actually does most of the day-to-day cooking; he gets home before I do and he loves to cook. His parents used to own a restaurant before they passed away; as for me, I'm not complaining.'

'Considering how much you hate the kitchen, this is like winning the husband lottery,' Miyo said. 'In fact, it makes me want to run outside at once and find myself a man too.'

'Eh? Anyemiyoo Mensah! That I should ever inspire you to utter those words! My work on earth is done.' I laughed, raising my right hand in victory.

Just then, Jean beckoned to indicate that dinner was served. He stayed and dined with us before escaping from the avalanche of compliments over his hospitality.

'I will get out of your way now so that you ladies can finish catching up over dessert,' he said.

'Well, don't run off before we've at least drunk to your health. To Monsieur and Madame Charbonneau,' Miyo said, raising her glass of wine.

'Here's to a long, happy marriage, and more delicious dinners like this,' Sweetie added.

I looked at them warmly as they toasted us. We were right on track and there was no cause for concern.

'So, what have I missed these past few months?' I asked them when we were by ourselves once more.

'Hm,' Miyo grunted. Then she pouted and glanced sideways at Sweetie, who had suddenly become quite fixated on her dessert.

'Hm — what? You've both suddenly gone mute?'

'Erh, I'll be right back. Powder room,' Miyo said before escaping around the corner.

'Sweetie?'

'Mawusi-Shika, Sammy did propose.'

'O Lord! No, Sweetie, no!'

'Yes, Mawusi-Shika, I accepted. It's done. This opportunity is just too good to pass up and I've invested too much of my life in him to walk away now, just when it's about to yield a bumper harvest.'

'I see. So, as usual, this is just another balance sheet to you; you've counted the cost and this is how you want to live for the rest of your life? Make the lie official and permanent?'

'What lie? Sammy and I laid all our cards on the table. If there's one thing we've always had in common, it's that ambition. I was firm; I told him that we needed to move beyond the nonsense and understand each other well in order to make this thing work.'

'Eheh?'

'Mawusi-Shika, the man wept like a baby. He told me how a wicked housemaster had molested him and several of his classmates during their boarding school days. He said he had thought that he would be able to simply file away the experience, along with other unpleasant childhood memories, and just move on into adulthood.'

'Oh, here it comes. He fed you the 'born-this-way' propaganda imported from the West, right?'

'Actually, he didn't — not at all. He fully blamed the boarding school *homoing* for his impotence, despite feeling attracted to me.'

'*Impotence* — is that the new name for it?' I was trying hard to keep the sarcasm out of my voice, and failing.'

'Look, I'm not in denial. All I'm saying is, I can relate to him completely. Rape is still rape, even when it happens to a boy. And as hard as it is for us girls to process, can you imagine a twelve or thirteen-year-old boy having to deal with it?'

'And you believed him, of course, because as for you, no man can resist you. Right? But what about all his clandestine activities all these years?'

'After being repeatedly sodomised by a grown man, an authority figure who was supposed to be protecting him, why should anyone be amazed if that is his only point of reference? And who says the rest of us get to choose the manner in which rape affects a boy later in life, especially when we all but stand by and allow it to happen?'

'Eish, Sweetie! Are you turning soft in the head?' I was truly worried about her state of mind. I leaned forward and looked at her very intently. 'How is what happened to Sammy Dompey your fault or my fault? And what difference does it make to you how he became who he is? He *is* who he is, and you will never have a complete marriage. Unless you're planning to allow him to cross the line and do whatever he wants to your body. Really, is this the occasion on which to finally discover that you possess a compassionate bone?'

'*Compassionate*? Please! Let's get real.' She moved closer, as if that would make her words more convincing. 'Listen, this man is going to become the president of this country one day, with or without me, mark it on this wall. He is set on this course, and only death will deter him. And why shouldn't he be able to pursue that dream simply because he is unable to make love to a woman in the preferred manner? Do you realise what kind of power he will wield when he makes it all the way to the top?

Can you imagine? Me,' she pounded on her chest, '*me* — daughter of an illiterate yam seller from an obscure village that was named after a bead — becoming the wife of the president or vice-president of this country? Even if he were to end up as just an ordinary minister, why should I deny myself of the level of access that it would give me? And have you never heard of a prenuptial agreement? We're both going into this fully aware of what each of us is bringing to the table and what we want out of it.' She was almost halfway across the table by now, eyes glistening, and all but drooling as she tried to reel me into the tantalising picture she was painting.

'Ah, great, she has brought you up to speed?' Miyo said. She had returned in time to witness our intense interaction.

'So you approve of this madness then, do you? You didn't try to talk some sense into her when she told you?' I asked Miyo.

'And since when has that tactic worked on Ahuofeh Sweetie Bediako?' Miyo fired back.

'Look,' Sweetie continued, 'as for me, my father was not a rich man like yours,' she began.

'Hey-hey-hey!' Miyo cut in, 'leave her father out of this; the man is already dead. Allow him to rest in peace!'

'Sorry, Shika, I take that back. Look, all I'm saying is, an opportunity like this comes around once in a lifetime to someone from my background. And you want me to pass it up because of a minor thing like what? *Love*? Will that put food on my table or keep a roof over my head? *Sex*? Well, that's what Bronze is for, remember?'

'Okay, wait! Wait — so, that arrangement *too* will continue even after you tie the knot with Sammy?' I sought clarification.

'Ah, Shika, you too! What kind of question is that?' Miyo said. 'What do you want her to do under the circumstances? Have you already forgotten how she ended up in this situation?'

'No, my memory isn't that short,' I said. 'Actually, I remember quite well. It was because of this same relationship with Sammy that Bronze broke up with you "without giving me the chance to defend myself" as you've said before a million times.'

'To add insult to injury, after I placed a call all the way to Illinois and explained the situation, and he claimed to believe me, he casually proceeded to marry another woman anyway,' Sweetie said.

'Oh, and lest we forget, it was "just for papers"; yet, he *still* went ahead and brought her home,' Miyo added.

'And then — this is the best part — when *she* decided that she would not stomach his controlling family, and fled back to her country with her tail between her legs, he confidently assumed that we could just continue from where we left off, as if nothing had happened. Just like that!

Well, guess what? The joke is on him now because this arrangement actually works perfectly for me. If Bronze chooses to remain my *boy-boy* for life, that's *his* problem. For a husband, I'm looking for a *real* man who can make his own decisions, not some *koliko* whose only asset is that he has "doctor" attached to his name.' She was all but exploding. I dared not interrupt her tirade. 'Men have been using and discarding women for centuries to further their ambitions,' she continued. 'That was before I was born. Now I, Ahuofeh Bediako, have arrived and I'm turning the tables. And you find this confusing?' She sucked her teeth and manoeuvred her neck for emphasis.

'I beg oh! Don't let me upset you,' I said in a more subdued tone in order not to set her off again. 'Obviously, you've thought this through very carefully, and *I'm* coming into the picture after you've already made all the necessary decisions — but I've still got to ask you: what about Odum?'

'Odum is going to be just fine,' she said in a slightly shaky voice. 'I'd rather die than allow Sammy to have access to him.'

'Are you seriously suggesting that he's capable of harming your son?' Miyo asked.

'And if you can't trust him with your son, should you even be entertaining the thought of marrying him? That part, I honestly do not understand,' I said.

'Don't put words in my mouth, I'm not saying that he would do anything to Odum; but I don't intend to gamble with my son's wellbeing; so, just to be on the safe side, I will delay the wedding until after Odum is safely out of this country. The one promise Bronze has been able to keep is that he would always be there for Odum. In fact, he's been mentoring him through the American college application process and is working really hard to get him a scholarship outside. As soon as Odum sits his finals, he's out of here.'

'And for the record, both men still think that Odum is your brother, right? I'm just checking,' Miyo said, holding up her hands, 'so that I can think ahead for you from a legal standpoint.'

'And why would I empower them with that much information? Neither of them has earned the right to know more than the rest of the world does.'

You had to hand it to Sweetie! As always, there was a method to her madness. The law of self-preservation drove her impulses and although I did not agree with her decision, the rationality of her outlook, as cold as it was, defied moralisation.

Now she and Miyo had me even feeling guilty for not empathising more with Sammy.

It caused me to pause and wonder:

How many boys have carried the effects of childhood sexual abuse into adulthood, just as we have, and are trying to live regular lives? There must be many men like Sammy who will go to any lengths to be accepted in our hypocritical society where doing any less is sure to adversely affect their social standing.

In this same society where it is not frowned upon for a married man of forty to deflower a seventeen-year-old girl and then keep her as his mistress or second wife, being married is still the most honourable social institution, and it covers a multitude of sins. Everyone's father was a gallant gentleman in his youth, supposedly, and everyone's mother arrived in the honeymoon chamber still a virgin, of course. We are all co-conspirators in perpetrating fraud under the cover of marriage.

But in this case, how can it even be considered fraud when the two parties are in cahoots with each other, and we the observers are enablers? After all, aren't Sammy and Sweetie doing the heroic thing by electing to sacrifice themselves to appease our collective conscience? In this collective, their individual truths are irrelevant. Rather than judging Sweetie, perhaps I ought to rejoice over her impending union, because she is, in fact, about to do the honourable thing. After all, as the saying goes, 'Muddy water also can be used to put out fires.'

Accepting this truth quickly cured me of the delusion that Sweetie somehow needed my help to run her life. Truth be told, she was one of the most adaptable people I knew, and there had even been times when I secretly envied the independence she exercised in permitting herself to make her own stupid mistakes.

Sweetie had mastered the art of survival — there was no denying it — but it was still dizzying to see how far she was willing to manipulate her circumstances just to make sure that she didn't remain a victim.

As for Miyo, I clung firmly to the belief that she was poised to finally confront the demons from her childhood that had kept her emotionally stunted until now. Sefa's passing seemed to have been a turning point for her.

She and I had had a heart to heart talk when she came up to Togapeme to deliver his will.

'So, during his last days in the city, when I was spending the weekend with Jean, what happened?' I asked.

'The thought of losing him forever released something in me,' she told me. 'I was no longer afraid to admit it to myself or show it to him. It was as if knowing that he was going to die all of a sudden made me feel emotionally secure. This thing between us, as soon as I knew that it no longer required consummation, I was able to let go of my fear of it.

Suddenly, I couldn't imagine letting him go without admitting to him that I'd always loved him.

I came and stayed with him that entire weekend. I read to him, laughed with him; and then I would lie in the bed with him and he would cradle me until we fell asleep. And you know what? Not even once since then have I had the nightmare. His touch took away my nightmare, Shika. *That* was his gift to me. I only wish that I had accepted it years ago. How much pain it would have saved both of us! Now I don't know if I will ever love another man.'

'Hush! Don't say that. It won't bring him back. And you're going to have to find a way to move on.'

I had held her while she sobbed softly. Sefa truly had loved this girl like no one else ever would; and in the end, it had melted her frozen heart. I marvelled at the potency of his love and thought, thank God, maybe she can finally begin to really live.

Now, listening to her tell us that she had been corresponding with Winsome Addo, I could already see the transformation in her demeanour.

After Jean and I left for Hippo Lodge on our wedding night, our guests had apparently continued partying for a few more hours, and it was then that the junior pastor got the chance to reconnect with Miyo.

'He's working on a book, you know. He told me all about it, and I think I can really help with his research; I gave him my card,' she said.

'Ei, you mean the *real* business card?' Sweetie said.

'Well, yeah! It's business, not a social situation; so yes, I gave him my true contact info. Besides, how could I pull that stunt on him? The man is an osofo, for God's sake!'

'So, how is this research coming along?' I said.

'Quite well, actually. Kojo will be coming into town next week, and we will go for lunch to discuss the book.'

'*Kojo*? Who is Kojo?' I asked.

'Reverend Addo! That's his *day name*. I wasn't going to call him "Winsome" and he thought that addressing him by any of the priestly titles was too formal,' she explained.

Sweetie and I looked at each other.

'Ei. *Kojo*. Hmm,' Sweetie said.

The remainder of the evening saw us easing back into our comfort zone. Just a slight shift in perspective was all that would be required to fully navigate our friendship into newer waters, but not tonight. Tonight, we were going to finish enjoying the remainder of what was already familiar to us, this organic ebb and flow that had kept us connected and allowed us to stay afloat all these years.

*

After that dinner, we found a new rhythm. Sweetie hired a tutor to shepherd Odum toward a bright future, far away from the threat posed by her looming marriage of convenience to a man she did not fully trust around her son. Yet, this mistrust was not enough to curtail her ambition. She was going to marry Sammy Dompey, do-or-die, in hopes of one day becoming First Lady of this great and noble land.

I continued to support her the only way I could — by being there for her, and allowing her to use me as a sounding board for her outrageous ideas — not that my honest opinion made any difference.

FIFTEEN

Work was Miyo's go-to therapy when all else failed, and she had begun enjoying her fulfilling professional life more than ever before. In fact, a recent promotion placed her next in line for a very sensitive position of real influence in highly visible international circles.

She began travelling constantly, and she knew that she could depend on me to call or stop by to check on Tati and Oko whenever she had to be away for more than a week.

And so, it was during my performance of the duties of emergency contact person that I found myself in the middle of their family drama one Friday night. Miyo had left at the beginning of that week for a three-week long conference in Addis Ababa.

'It helps to know that there's someone trustworthy close by,' she said to me before she left. 'What would I do without you, Shika?'

Auntie Tati was turning sixty in a month and had planned a very lavish celebration in a few weeks. I called her on Wednesday evening to check on her and made her a promise.

'I'll stop by on Saturday afternoon so that we can discuss ideas for your birthday party,' I said.

But then, right after my evening shower on Friday, as I was getting ready for bed, Miyo telephoned me from Addis.

'Have you heard from Tati? I can't reach her.' She sounded frantic.

'We talked a couple of nights ago,' I said, 'and I told her that I'd stop by tomorrow. Why, what's up?'

'It's around midnight here. I just returned to my hotel room and there is a message from her; she must have called a couple of hours ago. It's very garbled, and then it cuts off abruptly; but she sounded quite agitated. Shika, I'm really worried. I haven't heard my mother sound like that in a long time!' Miyo was in a state of complete panic. She wanted me to investigate and let her know what was going on.

'Jean, honey!' I called out through the bathroom door while throwing on my clothes. He was in the shower and I couldn't wait. 'I'm running to Mrs Mensah's to check on her, Miyo can't reach her. I shouldn't be too long.'

'Okay, call me when you get there.'

I tried Tati's number before I headed out. No luck. Bujuazee was just fifteen minutes from us. I made it there in ten. Her night watchman let me in after he recognised me.

Nothing seemed to be out of place, except that the courtyard was a little tight today. Tati's Jeep was parked in its usual spot, along with a sports car that I had never seen before. I parked next to the sports car, the watchman shut the gate, and I went to ring the doorbell.

After waiting almost five minutes, I headed toward the side of the house. I noticed deep tire grooves in the manicured lawn, going all the way around to the back of the house. Curious and a little concerned, I paused at the corner of the house, leaned forward and looked into the backyard. I heard what sounded like the slamming of a car trunk, some other muffled noises; but I couldn't see anything from where I was standing, and I was reluctant to step into the unknown.

Retreating slowly, I went back to the front door and banged several times.

I called out loudly, '*Koh-koh-koh*! Auntie Tati? Auntie Tati, are you there? It's Shika!'

More noises, from inside this time. A door slammed. Quick footsteps. Tati opened the door and stuck her head out.

'Ah, Shika, it's you.' Then she let me in.

'Auntie Tati! Is everything okay? Miyo is really worried; she said you called and left her a message but she couldn't hear anything you said. And she can't get hold of you,' I said as soon as I stepped inside.

'Yes, we're in the middle of a power outage — it's our turn on the load shedding roster tonight through Sunday night.'

She had a backup generator and I could hear it running, so that excuse made no sense to me.

'Auntie Tati, what has happened? Your wrist, it's swollen!'

'Ah, it's nothing.'

We were interrupted by a commotion at the gate. She peeped through the curtains, then the blood drained from her face and I saw panic in her eyes. She rushed off to the dining table and rummaged through her handbag. Then she counted out some money and folded it into her hand.

I came up to the window and looked. It was the watchman; he was in the process of granting access to two policemen.

'Ei, it's the police! Auntie Tati, did something happen?'

'Here,' she said, shoving the money into my hand, 'make them go away, Shika!' She was fidgeting nervously.

'Quick, tell me what happened before they get to the front door!' I held her by the forearms to get her to stand still and focus.

'The servants had just left at the end of the day and the watchman hadn't arrived yet. There was a commotion — erh, a sound. Yes, there was a noise outside. I thought it was a burglar, so I panicked. I shouted, 'Thief, thief!' Maybe someone heard me shouting and called the police. That must be why they're here.'

'Okay, just stay calm. Wait.' I quickly pulled out my hankie and wiped streaks of dirt and sweat from her face; then I pushed her hair from her forehead. I made eye contact with her to reassure her.

She inhaled, walked to the door, and opened it just as the policemen stepped onto her porch. I stood to the side, close enough for them to see me but far enough so that I did not get in Tati's way.

'Ah. Inspector. Sergeant,' Tati said, nodding at them, 'good evening. How can we help you today?'

'Good evening, madam, we are investigating a report of possible gunshots coming from the direction of this house,' the inspector informed her while the sergeant scribbled away on a yellow notepad.

'But I have been here all day, I would have heard something,' Tati said.

'Madam, do you own a firearm?' he continued.

'There is no registered weapon in this house. Do you want to come inside to search my house?'

'No, Madam, that won't be necessary. We did not bring a search warrant; we are just here to investigate the report. What about your guest?' The inspector leaned sideways to look at me.

'She can speak for herself,' Tati said and stepped aside.

'I don't own a firearm and I didn't hear anything,' I said.

'All right madam, we'll just look around the backyard a little and leave,' the sergeant said.

Tati gave me a sharp kick in the calf from behind the door.

'Oh, inspector, will that really be necessary?' I said, stepping out onto the porch. I held his arm and guided him away from the front door and off the porch. 'You see, we are about to have more guests. Can you imagine what it will look like when they come and meet policemen here? These foolish people who just get up and call the police for no reason, they don't know how inconvenient it is. My uncle is a senior military officer — a lieutenant colonel, in fact — so I fully empathise with you. Anyway, don't let your trip down here be in vain. Here is something for your trouble, just something small to quench your thirst on this hot evening. Thanks for coming to check on us, eh?' I discreetly shook his hand and concluded our transaction.

When I came back inside, Tati was sitting at the dining table still looking pale. Her wrist had really puffed out now, and I was quite sure that she had sustained a fracture.

'I can drive you to Army Hospital. You really ought to have this looked at,' I said, but she was adamant that she could take care of it herself.

'I don't want them asking me what happened and throwing stupid questions at me, I'm not in the mood for any nonsense today.' She sounded weary.

'Auntie, I'm going to make some tea, and then I'll call Miyo. She's almost out of her mind with worry and I promised to let her know that you were okay.'

She didn't argue, only placed her elbow on the table and leaned her head on her good arm. There was no fight left in her.

I used the kitchen phone and called Jean.

'Tati hurt her wrist in an accident. No, you don't have to come over; it's under control. I'll let you know how she's doing in another hour,' I whispered.

Then I dialled Miyo's hotel and updated her.

'Tati's arm looks broken. She's refusing to go to the hospital. I'm about to call Sweetie to see if she can bring Bronze over,' I said.

'Did she say what happened?' Miyo asked.

'No; but somebody called the police before I got here, something about hearing gunshots. I was here when they came.'

'O my God! Did they find the pistol?'

'*Pistol!* What pistol?'

'Erh — never mind — let me talk to her, please.'

'Whatever it is, she's not saying. Go easy on her, she seems to be in shock,' I whispered, before carrying the phone into the other room and handing the handset to Tati.

She didn't talk much, only responded to Miyo in her language for about a minute. Then she handed the phone back to me.

'I've told her that Sweetie will be bringing a trusted friend over to take a look at her wrist so that she doesn't have to go to the hospital,' Miyo said. 'I will call sweetie from here; please go ahead and call her too, in case

I'm unable to get hold of her. Tati should be fine after that, since Shayo is spending the night.'

'Shayo is here?' I asked.

Knowing the nonnegotiable conditions that governed Tati's relationship with her youngest daughter, this news came as a surprise.

'Oh, you haven't seen her? Tati said she was there. Thank you, Shika. Call me after Bronze comes and leaves, eh?'

I placed the call to Sweetie and gave her the lowdown.

'Yah, Miyo just called but we didn't talk for long,' she said. 'Luckily, Bronze is here; he was just getting ready to leave. We're on our way.'

'Sweetie's on her way with the doctor,' I told Tati when I brought her the tea.

She just nodded.

'Shayo is upstairs? Maybe she can help you clean up before they arrive,' I said.

'She's in the shower, and I already had a bath earlier this evening. I'm going upstairs to lie down.'

'In that case, we'll just use some ice for your wrist and I'll get you a hot towel for your face and neck; how about that?'

I brought some ice up to her bedroom. Then I got a bowl of warm water and a face towel to wipe her neck and arms before applying the ice to her wrist.

Auntie Tati did not make a sound. I almost wept at the sight of this magnificent woman just sitting there limply and surrendering to my kindness, which, although necessary and well intentioned at this moment, still seemed to obliterate the last vestige of what had once been her dignity.

When a door slammed down the hall and I heard footsteps, I knew that Shayo was indeed here. This fact caused my heart to beat loudly in my chest, but I refused to question its significance. It was sufficient that she had shown up when her mother needed her most.

She came and got the towel from me.

'Oh, Shika, thank you so much! Here, I'll continue,' she said and took over the process.

The last time I saw her was at Sefa's funeral, so she congratulated me on my marriage and enquired after my aunt.

'Why don't I go downstairs and wait for Sweetie and the doctor,' I said after the niceties were over.

I really looked around me for the first time that evening while I sat at the dining table drinking my tea. That's when I noticed a significant detail that would stand out only to someone familiar with the heartbeat of this home — its strict adherence to the predictable — which was not only necessary for maintaining a safe haven for Oko but was, in fact, essential for his survival. And if anything were going to be out of place, it wouldn't be Tati's blue and gold, Russian angel wood carving. Yet there was its usual place atop the curio stand, glaringly vacant, with only a few shards of blue and gold flecks of paint attesting to the prominent position it had always held as overseer of the entire downstairs, until today.

When I heard a vehicle pulling up, I quickly ran upstairs to inform Tati and Shayo that the doctor had arrived. Mother and daughter were sitting on the bed. Tati was propped up and Shayo was still applying the ice to her wrist.

As I quickly scanned the room, my gaze fell and lingered for a moment on the remnants of the blue and gold angel, which was partly sticking out from underneath the bed, with half of its head completely shattered. I returned my gaze to Auntie Tati.

'Sweetie has arrived with the doctor,' I said, 'shall I just send him up?'

'Please, Shika, that would be best. Thank you,' Shayo said.

I escorted Bronze upstairs, and then I went back downstairs to sit with Sweetie.

We did not exchange a word. Our heavily coded silence was all that we required to convey to each other the gravity of the situation.

About thirty minutes later, Bronze returned downstairs accompanied by Shayo. Shayo said hi to Sweetie and thanked her for bringing Bronze.

'Is Auntie Tati going to be okay?' Sweetie asked.

'For now, yes,' Bronze said. 'I have bandaged her wrist; that ought to get the swelling down overnight. But I want her to come to the clinic no later than nine in the morning for x-rays. We have to determine the full extent of the injury so that we can properly set it. However, someone is going to have to drive her there.'

'The driver is off this weekend,' Shayo said, 'and I'll have to stay with Oko. Shika, do you think you might be able to help again?'

'Sure. I'll pick Tati up by eight-thirty, no problem.'

'Thank you, thank you! And don't worry, I'll call Miyo and update her. Please go home and catch some sleep! We greet your husband, eh? Good night.'

We dispersed.

I hurried home. It was way past midnight by the time I plopped into bed and cuddled up to Jean, who had long fallen asleep. In the morning, I left him a note and was gone again before he woke up.

Tati looked much better and her mood was quite improved. Six hours of Valium-induced sleep had restored colour to her face; the bright orange lipstick also helped. She even greeted me with a cheerful peck on the cheek before we drove off to Bronze's clinic.

While Tati was being treated, I called Miyo in Addis. I asked her if she was thinking of cutting her trip short to return home, but she was very firm in her resolve to complete her mission.

'There's no urgency, and I can't afford to be taking these types of chances if I want to be taken seriously at work. On top of that, something really important came up just before I left town and I've already planned to stop briefly in Paris to take care of it. Shayo says she can stay with Tati and Oko for a while, at least until I return. She should be able to handle anything else that might come up.'

'With everything that's going on, is the party still going to take place as planned? Maybe you should buy some time, postpone it for a week or so,' I suggested.

'No-no-no! We're sticking to the plan. My mother is celebrating this birthday; everything's already in place and nothing is going to throw us off track. I also spoke to Manye just this morning and it's likely that she *will* come home after all. If she's able to adjust her itinerary, she may even get there ahead of me; if not, then we will plan to come down together.'

'Oh, I see,' I said.

Manye had not been home in many years and for her to return from her self-imposed exile meant that whatever had transpired in their mother's house last night must have been significant enough to warrant a truce. Taken together with Shayo's sudden change of heart, I felt an unpleasant sensation down my spine. I wasn't even sure that I wanted to be privy to any details, and instinct told me that the less I thought about it, the better it would be for me. But as I drove Tati back home, I couldn't help wondering what the full sequence of events had been the previous day.

At any rate, it was only prudent to step back and let Shayo handle their family matters. So, I gave them the space they needed, only calling every few days to check on Tati.

Shayo called me one afternoon a few days later and stopped by my office during lunch to drop off the invitation: *Come celebrate with Tatyana Mensah as she begins this most glorious diamond chapter of her life.*

Jean and I were away in Togapeme the weekend Miyo returned to town; so, although I spoke with her at work during the week, the next time I saw her was at her mother's party. We passed through the house to say hello before joining the other guests outside, and found Miyo in a teasing mood.

'Shika, Jean! You're beginning to look alike; I love the coordinating outfits.'

'Addis must have been good to you — you look well, Miyo,' Jean said.

We chitchatted briefly about her trip and she said 'thank you' again for coming to her mother's aid.

I had been looking about me expectantly, so when I saw Jean staring with his tongue almost hanging out of his mouth, I didn't need to turn around to know what had so captivated him — the effect was always the same on any living organism. But I was still startled to hear that recognisable voice, long missing from these parts, addressing me in a familiar manner.

'Ei, Shika Amenyo! Ah, pardonnez-moi, c'est "Madame Charbonneau" maintenant, non?' I turned around to see Manye, closely followed by Shayo, in the middle of the staircase.

'Manye! You did come! Oh, it's so good to see you,' I greeted her fondly, and introduced both sisters to Jean. After exchanging pleasantries for a few minutes, Jean and I went outside to join the other guests who were waiting for Tatyana to make her grand entry.

When we walked into the backyard, I couldn't help looking on the ground for the tire tracks from last time, but there was no trace of anything unusual. All the hedges and flower bushes had been freshly trimmed and the lawn evenly manicured. I could barely recognise my surroundings.

The yard had been transformed into party central with the installation of a giant canopy that was festooned with blue and silver balloons, and satin ribbons. The VIP table was on the far end of a parquet dance floor with a live band on the other end; and arranged along the sides of the dance floor were ten round tables that featured clearly labelled place settings for sixty guests in all. Everything was laid out tastefully under the canopy.

We worked our way around the gathering and said hi to a few familiar faces while we searched for our table. Sweetie was here with Sammy, and sharing their table was Osofo Winsome Kojo Addo. We stopped at their table to greet them.

With a mischievous twinkle in her eye, Sweetie pointed us in the direction of our table, which was across the dance floor from theirs. As we crossed the floor to take our places, I understood the reason for Sweetie's look, and almost tripped. There, sharing our table, sat Bronze. Without skipping a beat, we exchanged greetings. I introduced him to Jean; and then we all waited on the edges of our seats for the guest of honour to appear.

As soon as she stepped out into the open, the band struck the first note. Auntie Tati sauntered out in true regal fashion, hanging onto Oko with her good arm, her three daughters following closely. They danced their way to every table, greeting each of us personally, before finally making it to the VIP table.

Her ensemble, which was probably styled deliberately to hide the cast on her arm, was a stunning, asymmetrical affair made of white satin overlaid with embroidered silk organza. The whole thing was topped with an intricate turban. And punctuating her person in all the necessary places was a king's ransom's worth of custom-made *Korli beads* trimmed with gold. In effect, her wardrobe was no less than I expected.

This woman who had come so far and endured so much, truly needed this moment in time to record the fact that she was still here, and standing tall. In the simple act of climbing up to the VIP table accompanied by *all* her children, I got that message.

And when Osofo Addo stood up and said a prayer to launch our celebration of her — she who had systematically rejected all forms of religious symbolism over the years — I knew that something had caused a major shift in Tatyana Mensah's consciousness.

As the party progressed, I watched the joyous interaction between Tatyana and her children and realised that this — their happiness and cohesion, which she had been willing to almost die to secure — was her legacy.

With Champaign glasses in hand, we followed Tatyana to a freshly dug flowerbed in the far corner of her garden, where she planted a tree to symbolise the beginning of her new season. And when Miyo raised her glass and proposed the toast, I could not help thinking about her mother's journey up to this point.

'Mama,' Miyo said in a voice that trembled at the impact of that rare utterance, 'anything you ever endured or gave up was a sacrifice, a strategic surrender deliberately offered as down payment toward what now lies ahead. We will never lose sight of that. To the most resilient woman in the world, our mother, Tatyana Mensah!'

'Looking at the quality of friends I have here today,' Tatyana responded, 'I wish that I had been surrounded by the same calibre of people twenty or twenty-five years ago. Yes, I feel fortunate today, but my children are more fortunate because they will have you all in their lives tomorrow. Let us drink to our friendship.'

I looked around at all the familiar faces. We raised our glasses and smiled at each other in recognition. Tatyana was standing in for all of us, the forgotten ones. We, who had no designated safe havens where we could carry our vomit for other people to clean up for us — who were too urgently needed to afford to pause for occasional maintenance, too dignified to succumb to emotional fatigue — not for us the overpaid charlatans disguised as therapists, who would only poke at our scabs and suck our money. No. We, the unbreakable ones, *we* ourselves were all the therapy that we needed.

'To Tatyana!' I placed my glass to my lips, closed my eyes and drank.

SIXTEEN

As the weeks turned into months and those months rolled by, the gnawing feeling of emptiness in my gut gradually subsided, along with the sense of hopelessness that used to accompany it. The rhythm of my life was no longer being determined by the ticking of my biological clock; and for the first time since becoming an adult, it felt enough to be Mawusi-Shika Amenyo. That I was now known also as somebody's wife was just another layer added to my identity, and not the entirety of it.

It was in this state of newfound contentment that I marked my thirty-third birthday, and also approached the anniversary of Sefa's passing. As was customary, our family marked that occasion with a memorial service in Togapeme, after which we unveiled Sefa's tombstone. Then we made the short pilgrimage to Bremen Clinic. There, surrounded by our guests who had travelled up the mountain to support us, we held a ribbon-cutting ceremony to mark the completion of the Sefanam Memorial Chapel that his mother had funded in his name.

At the repast that followed, Tassie announced the first two winners, one boy and one girl, of the Sosu-Gameli Memorial Scholarship.

'Our small district is honoured that such an outstanding young man had deep roots in this area,' said the M.P. for our district, who was the guest of honour. 'We thank his mother, Daa Nenor Gameli, for cultivating this solid tree that is now bearing such diverse fruit for our community. The name "Sefanam Sosu Gameli" will live on as a shining example of what is possible to the young men and women of this country.'

*

A couple of months after Sefa's anniversary, I went to check his postal box after having neglected it for several months. He had already paid for the box for a two-year period that was about to expire. There was no more mail coming in, the traffic having dwindled and eventually trickled off several months ago.

So I checked the box one last time and there it was, a thin envelope from Paris addressed to me. Marked 'urgent'. But, who sent it? And what could it possibly have to say that I would want to hear now?

I drove all the way home before sitting on the bed and opening it. With each sentence, my flesh broke out in goose bumps:

Dear Mademoiselle Mawusi-Shika Amenyo,

I have been informed that you are the appropriate contact person in an urgent official matter that pertains to Madame Yaaba Delouve, also known as Yaaba Koomson, who is a client of mine.

I quickly glanced at the bottom of the letter to see who had written it. I did not recognise the name 'Philippe Sauvageot' or his address, but my pulse raced uncomfortably as I shot through the rest of the letter:

Should you be interested in pursuing this matter, please contact me at the address and telephone number listed at the bottom of this letter. You may also contact Madame Cécile Volmer of EMADA directly. There is a case file under the name 'Yaaba Delouve'. Madame Volmer will be expecting to hear from you.

Philippe Sauvageot's return address seemed to be some sort of facility, and the other contact person, Cécile Volmer, also appeared to be an official person. And then, although Monsieur Sauvageot had referenced the name 'Yaaba Koomson' so that I knew to whom it was referring, there was the other name in the note. I could feel the hairs standing on the back of my neck.

Jean came and found me sitting there like that, deep in thought, the letter in my lap.

'What is it, chérie?' he asked.

I just looked down at the letter. He picked it up and read the first paragraph.

'Who is this Yaaba Koomson and do you know what this man, this "Sauvageot" is talking about?'

'Yaaba is an old girlfriend of Sefa's. I didn't know that they had stayed in touch. Even after his death, she won't leave him alone! Jean, this girl is a real devil. I don't want to have anything to do with her.'

'This does not look too good,' he said after reading the entire letter. 'We're lucky we have our trip coming up in less than two weeks.'

'Are you suggesting that we go through there during our short vacation?' He must be out of his mind, I thought.

'But of course! We have no other choice. Don't you want to confront, once and for all, whatever secrets remain so that we can move on and not look back? This note sounds really important. We are going, yes?'

'I suppose so. But, EMADA — what is that? What could they possibly be overseeing on Yaaba's behalf, and how did they know where to find me?'

'I cannot imagine either, chérie. Do you want us to call these people to find out what they want?'

'Perhaps not,' I said. 'Whatever the issue may be, we should probably wait and deal with it face-to-face. That way, we won't be privy to any details that could come to haunt us down the road if we should change our minds midstream.'

'That's the more reason why we should go and find out. Spending a few days in Paris is really not such a bad idea. We can do some shopping.'

I reluctantly agreed and we decided the matter then and there. We made the necessary adjustments to our travel plans to allow for a three-day break in Paris on the front end of our trip.

Barely an hour after checking into our hotel, we were standing on Rue Paul Vaillant Couturier in front of the EMADA address that was referenced in the letter, looking up at their sign spelt out in no uncertain terms: Enfant Mondial Agence de L'Adoption. After taking the lift to the fifth floor, we landed in a reception area. In another minute, we were sitting in front of Cécile Volmer in shock, hanging on to each other for support, as we prepared ourselves to confront the 'urgent official matter' that had brought us so far out of our way.

After we had told her about the letter sent by Philippe Sauvageot and shown her our passports, Madame Volmer took her time to explain the details to us as delicately as she could. Her diplomacy, however, could not lessen the impact of the information she delivered.

'Madame Yaaba Delouve has an eighteen-month old child. The baby's name is Bijou,' Cécile said. 'My office was contacted as soon as the mother got institutionalised, and we immediately placed Bijou in foster care. You, Mademoiselle Amenyo, were identified as the next of kin in the paperwork. Bijou becomes eligible for adoption the moment her mother dies.

So, should you decide to accept this child, it would just be a matter of custody transfer, already authorised and signed by her mother. But you must make that decision *before* Delouve dies; otherwise you will have to go through the legal system to adopt the child. That process carries its own set of complications, not the least of which is the inter-country component.'

'Madame Volmer, could we at least speak with Yaaba Delouve before proceeding with this discussion? This is rather unexpected, and we are still reeling from the shock, as you can tell by looking at my wife's face,' Jean said.

'Ah, but there is a letter in the folder. And Delouve is a guest at Maison Saint-Pinel, under the direction of Dr Philippe Sauvageot.'

'*Doctor*? What is she being treated for?' I asked.

'Sauvageot did not mention it in his letter?'

'No. It was just a short note asking if we could come, that's all,' Jean said.

'Well, why don't you read Delouve's letter first, and then we can proceed from there, yes? My office is only overseeing matters pertaining to the child, you understand.'

Cécile then ushered us into a private lounge where she left us to peruse the contents of Yaaba's detailed letter at our own pace, with ample time to fully process this shocker while she tended to another client. She promised to come back to us in fifteen minutes.

I cannot imagine how I would have handled myself had Jean not been there with me. I could barely hold the letter up so that we could read it together. This one too was addressed to me:

Shika, I am so glad that you have come. It means that you believe me. I love Sefa very much, but I have ruined everything. And now, these people are trying to keep me from him by telling me that he is dead. But I know that he listens to you. If I tell you everything, will you explain it all to him?

I dropped the letter and stood up.

'I need some air,' I said.

'We don't have to read it right now, we can leave it for another time,' Jean said.

'I'll just stand here by the window while you read it to me. Please?'

He quickly flipped through the pages with a grim look on his face.

'I have a better idea,' he said. 'Why don't I read it silently, and if there's anything that will affect our decision, I'll let you know. Then we can save the rest of the letter for later. Yes?'

I nodded.

He adjusted his glasses and proceeded to read the letter to himself.

I folded my arms, leaned against the wall and stared through the window, preoccupied with my thoughts…

*

Yaaba Koomson was anathema to Tassie. She had been Sefa's on-again-off-again girlfriend throughout secondary school; kept messing with his heart and trying to throw him off his discipline during sports season by breaking up with him over any trifle. She would leave him and go with another boy, only to come back with tears and excuses — usually after he had just won another athletic victory — to make up with him. And Sefa would fall into her trap, over and over again, whenever she came back and swore to him that this time it was for real.

His mother warned him many times to let Yaaba go for good.

'She's nothing but a loose girl with nothing to offer besides what you see on the outside,' Tassie told him, 'she will destroy your life, Sefa!' But it was of no use. This girl had him wrapped around her little finger.

Tassie even took the problem to her prayer cell and mentioned it by name — Yaaba Koomson, Yaaba Koomson — so that they could pray with her over it. At seven-thirty, every Wednesday night for three months, they prayed over Yaaba Koomson. And then, just like that, Yaaba vanished. She did not come back for her fifth year. Problem solved.

We learnt afterwards that she had left the country and moved to France with her two brothers to try and connect with their French family. Their grandfather, a French seaman of loose morals — but a wealthy merchant, according to *their* version of the story — had dropped many bastards in Takoradi and other seaports along the Gulf of Guinea before he returned to France in the mid 1950s. Their mother herself had never even known him; yet they felt entitled to harbour high expectations of his legitimate descendants.

We secretly thanked God when Sefa moved on and dated a string of other girls. We were pleased with all his choices so long as none of them was Yaaba Koomson. And although Tassie forbade anyone from ever mentioning that girl's name again, Yaaba was never far from our minds. Like dog faeces, the stench of her decadence lingered long after she had scampered away.

*

Jean waved the letter and made an irritated sound with his teeth.

'What madness! Chérie, this winding story has no end,' he said, 'her words are not credible.'

He was not familiar with the history of this sociopathic Jezebel, but I was; and so, I braced myself for what I *knew* had to be hidden somewhere in the letter. I came back to the sofa and sat down again beside him.

'A *baby*, Jean — does she say anything about getting pregnant, or having a baby?'

Jean wrapped his arm around my shoulders and searched through the remaining pages.

I folded my arms and leaned against him, waiting.

'Let's see — ah, here is something. Oh…'

'Just tell me, Jean.'

'She claims that Sefa *is* the father of her child but that he left Europe before she discovered she was pregnant, and so he never knew about the child.'

'I see.' I shook my head to clear it.

I tried to quantify the magnitude of Yaaba's betrayal of Sefa but I was unable to. What had he ever done to deserve such treachery at the hand of this bloodsucker?

'Jean, I can't do this,' I said, 'I just want to go back to the hotel.'

'Are you sure? Maybe we should first go to the clinic and try to see Yaaba, or at least talk to Dr Sauvageot before making a hasty decision. Don't you think we owe ourselves at least that much after coming all this way? If we stop now, the unknown will hold us hostage forever.'

When Cécile returned to check on us, we told her what we wanted to do.

'I believe you have the contact information for the clinic,' she said. 'It's about a twenty-five minute walk from here.'

'We have a taxi waiting,' Jean said.

'In that case, it's only five minutes down the road. Your driver should know where it is. I can telephone Sauvageot's office and set up a priority appointment for you, if you like.'

We gave her the go-ahead. After all, how much of a vacation were we going to have with this thing now hanging over us like a ghost?

Cécile was very accommodating. She gave us the paperwork to take along so that we could take our time and look over it in detail before morning.

'This is a sample of what you would be signing, just four pages. You will find that it is not complicated at all. When you return in the morning, the child will be here so that you can meet her before deciding. Today, go back to your hotel and think about it — pray, consult with your family, sleep on it — but tomorrow, you must decide.'

Ten minutes later, we were showing our passports at the security gate of an unmarked mansion on Boulevard d'Argenson, asking to see the man who had sent the note that was going to change our lives forever, no matter what we decided. A young lady in a nurse's uniform ushered us into an office down the hall where we waited for Dr Sauvageot.

He seemed relieved to see us. Madame Volmer had conveyed to him our lack of information, it appeared, and so he too was very gentle with us.

'You arrived not a minute too soon,' he said, 'Madame Delouve, she does not have much time now. We have been hoping for weeks that you would at least call. This has been a very bad week. She hung on, very worried about Bijou and hoping that you would come, Mademoiselle Shika. Thank you for coming.'

'I only recently got your letter, more than two months after you sent it,' I said. 'What exactly is wrong with Yaaba? And what is this place, anyway? We don't have any information, only what was in your note. We came at once.'

'And Madame Volmer, she did not discuss the mother with us, only the baby.' Jean held my hand firmly while he spoke.

We waited for Sauvageot's response. He looked at us in surprise, turning as white as chalk.

'Pardon me! You mean to say you do not know *anything* at all? Please, come with me at once. I will take you to Delouve.'

He briefed us as we walked down the hall.

'This is Maison Saint-Pinel, a private psychiatric hospital. Delouve, she has a well-documented history of depression fuelled by years of using narcotic drugs. Her malaise is marked by periodic psychotic episodes characterised by delusions of grandeur.

Her relationship with this facility goes back at least five years; it's as if she has a running tab. This last time, she was brought here in very bad shape, suffering from deep psychosis after a failed suicide attempt. We also discovered that she has the SIDA and had never been diagnosed or given any treatments. In effect, her prognosis is not good. I'm sorry you did not know all this.

By the way, here is her file photo. This is what she looked like when she first came to us; you will not recognise her now. Ah, but we have arrived at her room. Please, come in. Let me see if she is aware enough to be able to communicate.'

We entered the death chamber; you could feel it everywhere, could almost touch it. Jean's arm immediately went up around my shoulder.

Of course, Yaaba did not resemble anything close to what I would have expected, given how she had looked the last time I saw her. Her features were completely distorted, her beauty obliterated. In its place was the ghost of someone else, a chassis clothed in diseased skin. Her eyes were fixed ahead but she had no vision.

I stared hard, looking for *anything*, really. And then I remembered. I bent close and searched for it, the small scar on her chin. It was lost in the blemishes inflicted on her canvas by Kaposi's sarcoma, but it was there all right. I settled for that barely visible mark and the photo in her folder as proof of her identity.

'Mignon, Mademoiselle Shika has come after all. You will give her a sexy smile today, yes?' Sauvageot spoke endearingly to her as he stroked her cheek with his gloved hand.

She silently held her position; there was no way to tell if she had even heard him. Suddenly, it slid out of the corner of her eye and vanished behind her ear, the one tear of recognition, of relief perhaps that her wish had been granted.

The scene transported me back to Sefa's final days. I froze.

Jean rubbed the goose bumps from my arm and gripped me firmly to himself. We never spoke to Yaaba. We only stayed a few more seconds before Sauvageot ushered us out. He was apologetic.

'At this stage, she will remain in isolation until the end. But she spent many therapy sessions writing you a long letter in case you arrived too late. I caution you to take anything you read in it with a pinch of salt because she has a rather unrestrained imagination. The letter is with Madame Volmer.'

'I have actually read it, a long rambling account of things that made no sense at all,' Jean told him. 'Now that we know the nature of her illness, it puts things into perspective. But, can you not bring some clarity to the situation? If we are to adopt this child and raise her properly, I'm sure that whatever information you can give us now will greatly aid us in deciding whether we should even take on this huge responsibility.'

'And the medical history would be helpful to know, just in case anything comes up in the child's future,' I added.

'Your concerns are certainly valid,' the doctor said. 'There are privacy laws, of course, but the truth is, this is a highly unusual case. And I have been treating Delouve for years, so I could probably tell you a few details that would explain things better. But it would all have to be off-the-record, you understand. I'm only trying to help you.'

'Dr Sauvageot, you would make my wife very happy, and I would forever owe you a debt of gratitude.'

'How did my name even come up in the first place?' I asked the doctor.

'A woman — some international lawyer — contacted my office before Delouve got admitted to the facility this time,' Sauvageot said.

Jean and I looked at each other.

'A foreign woman, a human-rights lawyer from Ghana?' Jean asked Sauvageot.

'Something like that — a moment, if you please; let me find her name. Ah, here it is: Anyemiyoo Mensah. As I understand it, there was some kind of bank fraud investigation initiated by this lawyer on behalf of a client. She had a client who died, and while settling his affairs, she was alerted by his bank in Amsterdam that there was still activity on his account.

The investigation led authorities to this clinic, because Delouve's bills here, from the very beginning, have always been paid from the bank account in question. But, let me assure you, Delouve is no thief, and this is a reputable facility. The owner of the account in question was Delouve's benefactor, the person who checked her into this clinic the first time, five years ago. He brought her in himself, sat right where you're sitting, and signed the paperwork for me to admit Delouve; and he gave us his bank account information to pay her bills.'

'Are you able to give us the name of this angel, Delouve's benefactor?' Jean said.

'I'm afraid not; that's highly confidential, of course. But I can tell you that he introduced himself as 'an old friend who is very concerned about her' and told us, 'do whatever it takes, no matter how many times she needs to come back here.' And that is exactly what we have been doing on and off for five years. Before this last episode, the last time we saw Delouve was two and a half years ago; and then the lawyer called three months ago.'

'So, how did my name come up?' I asked again.

'Ah, yes! The lawyer informed us that her client had died, and that if I testified at Delouve's arraignment, she could get the judge to dismiss the case on the basis of my testimony. So I did, and Delouve was released into my custody.'

'What about Delouve's tab at Saint-Pinel, how is it being paid, now that the bank account is closed?' Jean asked.

'Oh, the lawyer has taken it over, *she* has been paying Delouve's bill.'

I kicked Jean's foot to prompt him.

'Dr Sauvageot — and my wife's name?'

'A moment, I'm coming to that. The police report on the bank fraud case only described her as *"a destitute, drug addicted prostitute living in a women's shelter"* without any mention of a child.

When we detained her, she got very agitated and kept yelling, 'Bijou! Bijou!' but we didn't understand her. Not until the sedatives wore off three days later, were we able to get her to explain that she now had a little child named Bijou.

By then, the shelter had contacted EMADA and turned the child over as abandoned. When we contacted EMADA and explained the circumstances to them, they of course did a DNA test to confirm the relationship. Then they conducted an extensive interview with Delouve to see if she could pinpoint anyone that they could list as preferred guardian or next of kin. That is when Delouve mentioned you. Everything is arranged with EMADA; as soon as she was deemed legally competent to do so, Delouve signed off on every tiny detail pertaining to the child's future.'

'So, this lawyer, she does not know about Delouve's child?' I asked.

'Not to my knowledge. It was not in the police report, and it never came up until after Delouve had been here for three days. By then, we had already concluded our interaction with the lawyer.'

'Dr Sauvageot, I have one more question. Do you know if Delouve ever lived in Holland? She mentions it a lot in her letter and in much detail, and I was wondering,' Jean said.

'As far as I know, she never did. One of her brothers was a male prostitute who introduced her to that life when she first arrived in Paris at only sixteen years old. He was stabbed in a brawl about six years ago and left to die in an alley, like a dog. She witnessed the whole thing. That likely triggered her first breakdown. As for the other brother, *he* has been sitting in an American jail for many years already, for auto theft.'

'And her name? How did she get the French surname?' Jean asked.

'Now, that! *That* is legitimate. She met a boy about two years after she came here and married him — for citizenship, probably. But it was a valid marriage, all the same. She has been a French citizen for some eight years now. She quit prostitution briefly after she married him, but he got her hooked on drugs. He died, after they had been married five years, from a heroin overdose. She went back on the streets to support her drug habit. Her body cannot take it anymore. I'm sorry, there is nothing salvageable in her story.'

By the time we returned to our hotel, I had a headache. I left Jean to his own devices and took a nap. I stayed in the rest of the day.

That night, we barely slept. All we did was discuss our options and keep obsessing over the implications of either choice.

'How could Miyo know something like this and not tell me?' I finally asked, after unsuccessfully trying to block that detail from my mind.

'There's a reasonable explanation which we would have heard if we had told her about Sauvageot's letter in the first place,' Jean said.

'Or if I had told her that we were stopping in Paris and why, I suppose.'

'Exactly. We'll figure it out by ourselves, but if it will ease your mind, we can call her. Do you want us to call her now?'

'I need a minute to think about it,' I said.

Loyalty and uprightness, honour, family — hah! I thought about Tassie and everything she stood for, all that I had learnt from her. How unrealistic her ideals now seemed in this setting. Although she had been almost broken when Sefa left us without fulfilling her wish that he settle down with a nice girl from a good family and father a child, she had bounced back and found strength from trying to carry on his name. Now, how was I supposed to go and explain this twist of fate to her?

What hypnotic spell did this coldblooded witch cast on Sefa even in childhood that would cause him to *still* be so drawn to her, after everything she put him through? How could his judgement be so off the mark? And what would I tell my relatives when I returned home with a child that was supposedly Sefa's, especially if this child really resembled him? Why must this burden too be mine to bear? Ah, how easy it would be to pretend that I had never received Yaaba's letter, just get on the plane, and continue with my vacation plans. How easy it would be...

And then I remembered. I remembered all those times when *he* had been there for me, and all *my* secrets that he had taken with him. I reminded myself of how much his illness had already robbed from me — from all of us, but mostly from me — and I relented. With this realisation came greater clarity over my place in our journey.

'No, Jean. You're right. This is going to be our decision alone,' I told my husband.

'Then, whatever we decide will be our choice to live with. Be still, chérie. Tomorrow will come soon enough and we will decide.' He drew me close. 'Come, let's try to catch some sleep.'

The next day, we arrived thirty minutes early for our appointment. Cécile was happy to see us anyway. She went over the process with us, stressing that we had to make a decision at once.

'It does not require a background investigation,' she said, 'nor do you need to prove anything beyond your identities, and your passports are sufficient to meet that burden of proof.'

We were leaning in the direction of accepting custody of the child, anyway. We had returned to EMADA that morning, knowing full well that we couldn't simply walk away without her as if none of this had occurred.

But I was still plagued by last-minute jitters. I mostly worried about whether Jean would be able to bond with a child that did not share any of his physical attributes; I obsessed about how people would react to the three of us together in public. As usual, I was consumed by other people's opinions of Jean and me, opinions that ought to have no power to affect our current existence or impact our future. Yet there it was, my insecurity, the most prominent barrier to one of the most important decisions Jean and I would ever make.

I looked at the papers on the table. Just a few typed pages to determine a child's fate, only one set of signatures required and this thing would be done.

'Can we meet the child now, please?' Jean said.

'I will bring in the baby now,' Cécile said. She left.

I just stared ahead. I tried to picture her, but her image eluded me. Would she feel any connection at all to me, or to Jean?

The door opened. I gasped for air as a final moment of panic grabbed at my throat. What if she was the spitting image of her mother? How would I be able to love a child that looked anything like the monster that had birthed her?

Jean squeezed my hand tighter as Cécile entered, jabbering to the little parcel in her arms.

We turned around.

I swallowed.

'Mon dieu!' Jean swore. He saw her a split second before I did, but see her I did.

'Oui-oui. Isn't she beautiful?' Cécile kissed her cheek.

'Yesu Kristo!' I whispered in shock when I also saw her.

There was no doubt about it — from the crown of her curly head, past the glint of her few teeth peeking between her heart-shaped lips, to the tip of her ballet shoes — this child was half-white! She could not be Sefa's.

I leaned back slowly and closed my eyes.

I briefly went back to eighteen years old, and then fast-forwarded through everything that had happened since.

All that had shaped my understanding of normalcy, of loyalty to family, had been nearly stripped away in just two days. I lost my centre of gravity, even questioned my own capacity for humanity. How close I had come to being sucked into the depraved mind of Yaaba Koomson! I was truly, emotionally burnt to a crisp.

Finally, here was this clear glimpse of the hand of God reaching down and salvaging the tiniest but most symbolic remnant from those ashes, and it was the answer to everything. My outstretched hand had been acknowledged, my supplication received. I buried my face in my hands and allowed the tears to shake me one last time — for innocence completely and irrevocably lost, but also for the restoration of my sense of balance.

When my tears subsided, I raised my head to see Jean holding her to his heart. *He* had tears running down his face too.

'Come, Mawuena!' I stretched out both arms and embraced my gift.

SEVENTEEN

'Look!' Jean reached over the baby and patted my arm urgently. We had just taken off on the last leg of our flight back home. I had turned on the cartoon channel for Mawuena and finally plugged in my headset when he reached over the baby's head with a local newspaper. It seemed that much had transpired during our brief absence.

I removed my headset and craned my neck in order to read the first paragraph of the lead story:

> *Police have retrieved a Mercedes Benz out of Tefre Lagoon near Tarkwa, after local fishermen reported seeing the partially submerged vehicle at dawn on Tuesday, December 31. Authorities have identified the vehicle as belonging to one Dr Tawiah Mensah, an Accra civil engineer, said to be the father of prominent human rights lawyer, Anyemiyoo Mensah. The vehicle was vacant.*

'Miyo's family made the news? O my God, Jean!'

'Yes, and not in a good way.'

The details got worse as we continued reading the report:

> *The Office of Criminal Investigations (O.C.I.) is trying to determine when Dr Mensah was last seen and by whom, as there appears to be some discrepancy over his last known whereabouts. Mrs Tatyana Mensah, his wife of thirty-six years, told investigators that she had not seen him in more than a year as 'he has been living with another woman in Nungua.' When questioned, the other woman, who identified herself as 'Dr Mensah's second wife' said, 'It is not unusual for him to be absent for weeks at a time since he goes on trek regularly to Tarkwa.'*

Lawyer Anyemiyoo Mensah was not available for comment. Police are treating this as possible foul play. Anyone with information is asked to contact the O.C.I. hotline.

'Don't panic,' Jean said. 'Let's stay focused; we will call her as soon as we land.'

I called Miyo as soon as we got home. She was her usual controlled self, but knowing her as well as I did, I could detect the strain.

'I'm at Tati's. It's been a really long week,' she said. 'I had to take an unplanned leave to handle this emergency. They will begin dredging the lagoon early next week.'

'And Tati? How is she faring?'

'It's been a nightmare but what can she do? It was a major nuisance when the news first broke, because the press and the police kept harassing her with questions. But things have since calmed down. Now that they are all aware that he wasn't living here anymore, they've shifted their focus to where it needs to be. But let's talk about more pleasant things. How was Canada?'

'Well, it was quite a trip; a lot happened, too much to tell you over the phone. We're going to the village this weekend. Focus on taking care of this issue, I'll call you when we return, eh?'

*

Tassie had already heard the good news about our addition and was expecting us in Togapeme that weekend. Even before leaving Paris, Jean and I decided that it would be too risky to just spring the baby on her. So we called her as soon as we arrived in Montréal and broke the wonderful news to her.

'We have adopted a child and we're bringing her home,' I said.

'We want to give her an appropriate Ewe name that speaks to the manner of her arrival in our lives, so we're thinking that "Mawuena" would be perfect,' Jean said.

'Ah, the Lord has given indeed — that's exactly what I myself would have chosen for this precious gift,' Tassie said. 'Her name will convey blessing every time someone utters it. Yes, "Mawuena" is her name! I cannot wait to meet her. And don't worry dear, I have the perfect nanny in mind.'

When we arrived in the village on Friday afternoon, she was waiting for us on the porch, all spruced up as if she were receiving a dignitary in her home. And as soon as Mawuena saw Tassie, she stretched out her arms and leaned toward her. And when Tassie also reached out and carried her, it was as if they had already known and trusted each other for ages and were reuniting after a long separation. Jean and I stood back in awe, watching their interaction. We might as well not have been there. The weekend was going to be special.

Tassie floated about the house all afternoon, unable to focus on anything besides her new role as 'gammar', with Mawuena trailing her like a puppy. She finally got the chance to sit and chat with us briefly after Mawuena turned in.

'I spoke to the nanny; she will come by early in the morning so that you can meet her. Her name is Melody and she's about forty-five. Her grandmother was my father's eldest sister.'

'We're related then? How come I've never heard of her?'

'Oh, they attend every family function; you'll recognise her when you see her. Her grandmother married a man from another town and moved away decades ago; that entire line did not grow up around here. Anyway, tomorrow you can get to know her better, discuss the terms, and decide what you want to do. By the way, before I forget — I hope you don't mind — I have spoken to Osofo Addo about christening Mawuena tomorrow, just something quick. Then you can take your time and plan something bigger in Accra. Osofo Addo is approaching the end of his extended term with us. He said he would be honoured to officiate.'

'We're not really planning to organise anything in the city, nothing like that. We haven't even discussed it. Jean...?' I said.

'Of course — it's a good idea. Thank you, Tassie,' Jean said.

So, on Sunday — with Tassie by our side and in the presence of the congregation — Reverend Winsome Kojo Addo, our trusted friend and confidant, christened our child.

'Mawuena Charbonneau, who was destined to be in this family, has now arrived. We receive her as such — God's gift to our brother, Efo John-Mark Charbonneau, and our sister, Daa Mawusi-Shika Charbonneau. Little Mawuena is also the beloved granddaughter of our own church mother, Daa Nenor Gameli.'

*

Miyo had left for Tarkwa by the time we got back to Accra. She was not picking up her car phone so I left her a message to let her know that I was thinking of her.

I also called Sweetie to touch base and find out if she had been following the investigation into Tawiah Mensah's disappearance. Jean and I tried to keep up with the case, but the police had hardly made any progress.

'Sammy offered to pull some strings, but you know our Miyo — she's doing everything by the book, as usual, and won't let anybody help her,' Sweetie said.

'I can't even begin to imagine how complicated and expensive it's going to be to secure the equipment needed to dredge a lagoon. I mean, who does one even call to say, "Look, come and dredge this lagoon for me?"'

'That's not even the problem. That Shayo is seriously connected, and she has already secured the equipment and manpower required, but everything is on standby.'

'What's holding up the process?' I asked.

'The amount of government red tape that *even* the police have to go through just to get the go-ahead to dredge the lagoon is mindboggling. Everybody positioned at any point in this process — from the insignificant office clerk making the photocopies, all the way to the guy whose signature is required on that last page — wants a bribe, paycheque aside.'

'How ridiculous! Do they think this is a diamond excavation?'

'Who says there's any logic to their calculations? Anyway, how was your trip?'

'Hm. Plenty to boss you, oh. Are you sitting down?'

'Ei, Mawusi-Shika Amenyo! What did you go and do? Tell me, I'm sitting.'

'We brought a baby home.'

'You're pregnant!'

'No. We adopted the most amazing child you ever saw. It was love at first sight!'

'Ei, wonders will never cease! And I thought that *I* was the impulsive one. Good for you, my dear! I think I'm going to prefer this new, bolder you. So, tell me — girl or boy? And how old?'

'She's eighteen months old and her name is Mawuena.'

'Wait, let me guess what that means: "God something-something", right?'

'Yes, "God has given"; Sweetie, she's truly a gift from above.'

'Ei, Mawusi-Shika! I can't believe this oh! I think I'm going to cry!'

'Oh, Sweetie! Real tears? Challey, stop sniffling! You're scaring me.'

'*Ayekoo!* Well done. I'm so happy for you.'

'Thank you, that means the world to me. And don't worry; you'll get to see her soon. Anyway, how's *your* baby?'

'He graduates in exactly three weeks. But he already accepted the full scholarship to attend Northwestern University.'

'Then, Bronze's guidance in this process was very useful?'

'Please! Let's not get carried away. You know he owes me big-time. Besides, it was my son who did all the hard work; we just didn't know how to access the opportunities that existed. As soon as Odum leaves town, I can relax.'

'And then we have a wedding to plan?'

'Yes, and *then* we can sit down and plan my wedding. But next Saturday, the graduation party is happening live at Extravaganza Party Hall. Bring your man and your baby.'

'My man will be out of town, but you will definitely be meeting Mawuena.'

Miyo returned to town at the end of the week. Every inch of Tefre Lagoon had been thoroughly dredged. Tawiah Mensah was not in that lagoon.

'So what now, Miyo?' I asked when she called to say that she was back in town.

'Life goes on, Shika. We will make whatever adjustments we need to make and move on. Gosh, that sounded like something *you* would say! Anyway, Sweetie has called me at least four times since I came back last night to ask if I'd seen you or been to your place yet. What have you been up to?'

'We adopted an eighteen-month old baby girl and brought her home. Her name is Mawuena.'

'Oh, are you kidding? Well, congrats! I'm not that familiar with the Canadian system, but I hope you guys thoroughly went over all the paperwork before signing anything.'

'We were very thorough.'

'Good. Oh, wow! So when do we get to meet Mawuena?'

'I'll bring her to Odum's graduation party. Will you be there?'

'Of course.'

*

Emekor was also done with her course by the time we returned from Canada. And in a move that completely floored me, she had taken the initiative, during my short absence, to commit to an apprenticeship with a local dressmaker not far from my house. This had nothing to do with the course she had just finished; it was a complete deviation from her stated plan of action and sure to incite her father's wrath.

'Ei, Emekor! I turn my back for just three weeks, and you pull this stunt on me? I thought the agreement was that after the one year, you would either enrol in the university to study design, or you would register for level two at I.C.? When did you change your mind?' I asked her.

'Daavi Shika, as you know, I really just want to make clothes, but Papa acts as if it's the end of the world if I don't attend one of the two or three major universities in this country to study something academic for which I feel no passion. In effect, I should go and waste three or four years getting a design degree. Is it so wrong for me to want to develop my talent out in the field instead of inside the classroom? Daavi Shika, can't you please make him understand?'

'Ah, so why didn't you just wait for me to return so that we could discuss it before you went and committed to something else?'

'As the level two enrolment deadline was approaching, I had to quickly make up my mind.'

'Why didn't you at least discuss this with your mother?'

'But I did. In fact, it was *she* who suggested to me that it would be a waste of money to register to study design in a university when I could just learn directly from a seamstress. She even suggested that I look for one near your house so that I can continue staying with you. So, although I had already filled it out, I decided not to send in my application to the university; and after the registration deadline passed, that's when I went and talked to the seamstress.'

'Then if your mother is aware of all this, she must have informed your father, as he will be expecting an update now that the year is up.'

'That's the problem — she hasn't told him anything! When I asked her if she had told him, she said to leave it for *you* to handle because *she* wasn't going to touch this one.'

'He'll blame me for your decision simply because you've been staying in my house. You've placed me in a very awkward position; but you're almost twenty-one and I will *not* be assuming the blame for this one, I'm sorry.'

'Daavi Shika! Are you're abandoning me now?'

'Don't say that, you know that's not true. And to prove it, when I drop you off this week, I'll even sit with you before your parents so that you or your mother can break the news to your father. That way, it will be on record that this was *your* decision, and not mine. And then we can proceed from that point.'

'My father will disown me, and then I'll end up on the streets; I can see it already.'

'You're being melodramatic; he's not that crazy. I said I'd go with you, didn't I?'

When we walked into the house, her parents were relaxing in the living room. After we greeted them, I sat on the edge of the seat, while Emekor stood defensively behind it like a bodyguard, holding her hand luggage to her chest as if it were a shield.

'Fo Kofigah, Daa Jane — a year ago, I volunteered to help Emekor by providing her with accommodation in Accra so that she could attend classes at I.C. I'm happy to report that she has completed the level one certificate course successfully. And today, I'm returning her to you whole, just as she was when she started this process.'

'My love, you have heard what Shika said.' Daa Jane was playing the role of unofficial otsami.

'Well, you have done what you said you would do,' Fo Kofigah said, 'and we are grateful. So now we proceed to the next step.'

'Ah, Shika — you heard your uncle,' said the otsami.

'Regarding that next step,' I said, 'Emekor says she has been thinking about it seriously; and when I returned from my recent trip, she informed me about her decision not to continue in this program.'

'Your uncle says he has heard everything you said. So what is Emekor going to do next, if not this?'

I looked up at Emekor's face to give her a cue, but she stood stiffly without looking at me. The judiciary atmosphere, rendered even more rigid by Daa Jane's role of courtroom interpreter, had only made the tension worse. If I didn't speak up for Emekor now, her wishes would remain unheard.

'She does not want to go to the university either,' I said. 'She wants to study dressmaking with a local seamstress. She says she has discussed this with you, Daa Jane, and that you have given her your approval.'

I turned to Daa Jane for support. I waited for her interpretation; but even that inadequate sign of engagement had been completely shut off. She offered nothing, just sat there with perfect posture, like Lot's wife.

'Emekor, you don't want to go to the university? Fine,' Fo Kofigah finally said. 'You want to learn dressmaking? No problem. So, pick any established dressmaker in *this* city and your mother will go there and arrange an apprenticeship for you. You see? It isn't that complicated, and I haven't bitten off your head, have I? If only you had been honest from the beginning, you could have been ahead by a whole year already; instead, you went and wasted your time and my money taking that French course.'

'Emekor — talk!' I tugged at her arm to get her going.

'I have already spoken to a woman near Daavi Shika's house about starting my apprenticeship there,' she said in a shaky voice.

Her father adjusted his position and took a sip of his cognac.

'Ah, is that so? If Shika wants to parent you in her house so that you can execute your revised plan — since she is now a millionaire, and has suddenly become an expert in parenting after only one week — then, why don't we give you our blessing right now? And then, you can properly move out and go and live with her fulltime; you would not even need to carry your luggage upstairs. That way, we will all be on the same page, and everybody will know that Shika is now your father and mother. She will usher you into adulthood, and be fully responsible for the outcome of your life.'

'Oh, Fo Kofigah! That was never my intention. Daa Jane!'

But my righteous indignation did not impress either of them. Their features remained set in stone. It was quite clear that if I did not extricate myself, I was going to be recast as the villain here.

'Emekor, your father is right. My help was contingent upon a specific understanding of how you wanted to proceed; it was not meant to substitute for the guidance of your parents.'

She did not utter a word. Just picked up her luggage and, summoning the same composure as her mother, she dragged her bags up the stairs. She did not look at me.

I suppressed the crippling sense of failure that washed over me. How fortunate that the nanny had arrived from Togapeme just that morning, so that I had not needed to bring Mawuena along. I would not have wanted to expose her to such toxicity. And it was just as well that the front door was still open. The air in this house was no longer sufficient for all of us. And so, I gripped my keys tightly, stood up, and said goodbye. But these pillars of propriety could not be moved.

I let myself out.

The drive home was exhilarating. My family dynamic had shifted drastically in just ten minutes; yet, even if I could, I would not have reversed the clock. Some people are so fused with their baggage that progress is impossible, as what it requires of them would cause them to shatter beyond redemption. Besides, I should not have expected to execute well what I was not equipped to even attempt. This revelation did not kill me.

*

Odum soon left for college and a month later, Sweetie began planning her wedding. She imported the lace for her traditional attire from the Orient, but she was planning to have the outfit custom-made locally.

'I'm looking to the future. After all,' she said, 'it's important for me to establish a reputation from the very beginning as a patron of local businesses. They really dig into those insignificant things when they are looking for something with which to ruin your political aspirations.'

Our Sweetie was on her way to doing what she felt called to do — firmly rerouting her family's destiny away from poverty and toward a definite purpose.

The Mensah household underwent a major transformation following the disappearance of Tawiah Mensah. It was as if the sky parted and the sun began to shine in the middle of the night. Auntie Tati cut down on the booze and, as a result, she lost about twenty pounds. She got fulltime live-in help specifically to care for Oko, and took to driving herself around town more often.

And Miyo — our Miyo remained true to herself. She continued to move mountains, fighting for the overlooked and forgotten among us who, but for her advocacy, would have fallen through the gaping craters created where our social norms collided with the expectations of civilisation.

Last year, her birthday had fallen while she was on mission and she had not really celebrated it. So, this year, she decided that she would be spending that entire weekend, when we would have traditionally gone out on the town, entertaining us.

'It's about time I started a new tradition,' she said. 'So, on Sunday, you're all invited for lunch at *my* place. And just so there are no surprises, I'm letting you know now; I will have a new guest — Reverend Winsome Kojo Addo.'

As to this matter between her and Osofo Addo, she did end up penning the forward to his book, which got published at the beginning of the year and instantly became a bestseller; and they have remained friends ever since.

'We have an understanding,' was all she said the last time I tried to fish for an update, and then she cast me one of her side-glances, as if to say, 'eheh?'

'Miyo, will you ask Tati about the nightmare this year?' I asked her.

'You know, I've decided that as my gift to myself, I'm ready to let go of the need to know what my nightmare means. It seems to be over. Why bring it up now when my family is the happiest it's ever been? It could potentially devastate my mother. Quite frankly, I think I can live without knowing.'

*

As for me, I have more than enough on my plate to occupy me these days, which is how I like it. I'm busy with my new family, and I continue to marvel at the effect Mawuena's presence is having on our lives. We are waiting for my husband's contract to expire; then we will be free to exercise some other options. We have big dreams for Togapeme.

As soon as Daa Melody moved in last year, we realised that we had outgrown Jean's bungalow, so we quickly sold my house and moved into a bigger one, where we have now spread out quite comfortably.

For months, I had suppressed the urge to quit my job before the end of *my* contract, although I really didn't need the money anymore. I had not told anyone at work about the adoption, but dogs have an insatiable compulsion to dig up anything that looks like a bone; and the female of the species are particularly adept at sinking to new lows to unearth anything that they think they can use to hurt one other.

After it leaked out that I had adopted a baby, it gave the water cooler witches at work a new aspect of my life with which to find fault: 'That Shika Amenyo has now gone and bought herself some stranger's child. Now, she too can consider herself to be a *real* woman; fancy that!'

Except that, this time, they were picking on the wrong person. Yes, a *real* woman, one fitted with a flexible spine, had replaced the previous Shika Amenyo. I was determined to win this battle. And so, I stayed until the timing was right before I resigned.

I think of Emekor often. I have sent her letters and cards assuring her of my affection and my continued availability, should she ever find that she needs me. She is yet to respond.

I think of Kobla less often, but every now and then, I *do* think of him. But I no longer bring his tracts home from the post office, I just drop them in the wastepaper basket at the entrance when I'm walking out; and I have chosen to tear his contact information out of my address book. I only made that decision after carefully weighing it and knowing that I could live with it.

For now, this is what I need to do for *me*. Maybe, in time, these stiff places in my life will also become pliable.

EPILOGUE

I have not visited Sefa's tombstone since its unveiling, but today is special — he would have turned thirty-five today. Besides, it's going to be a while before I can do this again.

Most of the other markers are overgrown with weeds. Not this one, though. Tassie regularly maintains it by pulling out the weeds with her hands whenever she stops by. She visits his grave every Sunday evening.

The slab is wide enough for me to sit down and talk to him:

'Sef, I could not take this next step without letting you know. Jean, Mawuena and I are moving to Canada for a couple of years. It was never part of Jean's plan to move back there — we have already acquired a parcel of land overlooking Paradiso Waterfall, so that he can fulfil his dream of owning a restaurant here — but he is once more choosing to put his life on hold for the sake of my happiness. And although I am trying not to dwell on the negative, I don't know if we are making the right decision.

Worse than that, we haven't even told a soul the real reason why we have to leave so suddenly — it is too sacred to share with anyone. But we cannot wait any longer, so I have come to say "bye for now, thank you for everything" and also to let you know that your life was not in vain.

Because your life gave hers purpose, your mother is changing the future for many young people in Togapeme; and because of your tenderness toward her, Miyo is slowly learning how to allow another man near her heart. Sef, were it not for your graciousness toward Yaaba, who deserved nothing from you, Jean and I would not have Mawuena today.

Most of all, it is because of the gift, with which you so generously blessed me, that I can now afford to have restored to me all that I thought I had lost. Jean's sister, Colline, has found me a woman in Montréal. I don't even know her name — or anything else about her, for that matter — but this stranger will complete my healing by bearing my other children for me. So you see, Sef, I cannot postpone it. For now, I *must* go.'

GLOSSARY

Visit the book club at www.MariaKwami.com/BookClub.html

to access interactive features.

»

Names of people and places

Adokor

Ga name for the second born girl of that family.

Afi

Ewe name for a female born on Friday. Also 'Afua'.

Ahemekrom

Fictional. In Akan, it means 'beadtown'.

Ahuofeh

Akan word for beauty.

Akan

A large ethnic group in Ghana and Ivory Coast comprising subgroups like the Ashanti, Akwapim and Fanti . Also refers to a person from this group, and the language.

Amavi

Ewe for 'Little Ama'. Ama is the name for a female born on Saturday.

Amenyo

Ewe name meaning 'good person'.

Anlo

An Ewe group occupying the southern part of the Volta Region along the eastern coast of Ghana. Also refers to their specific dialect.

Anomar

From 'anomaa', the Akan word for bird.

Anyemiyoo

Ga word for sister. Used here as a girl's name.

Atiawu

Fictional. Ga word for cashew nut.

Bediako

Akan name meaning 'came to fight' or 'warrior'.

Bujuazee

Fictional. Coined from the word 'bourgeoisie'.

Dodzi

Ewe name meaning 'take heart'.

Dompey

Akan word for bone. Used here as a name.

Elorm

Ewe name meaning 'he loves me'.

Emekor

Ewe name meaning 'it is apparent'.

Eno

Originally an Akan honorific for an old woman. Commonly used as a name or nickname for a girl who resembles or is named after her grandmother or great-grandmother.

Efik

An ethnic group in Cross River State, Nigeria.

Ewe (pronounced 'eveh')

An ethnic group occupying the Volta Region along the eastern border of Ghana down to the coastline, as well as parts of Togo and the Republic of Benin. Also refers to the language or a person from that group.

Fanti (also Fante)

An Akan subgroup that occupies the Western and Central Regions along the western coastal area of Ghana. Also refers to the language or a person from that group.

Ga

Part of the joint Ga-Adangbe ethnic group that occupies Ghana's capital province, Greater-Accra Region, and part of the Eastern Region. It also refers to the language or a person from that group.

Gameli

Ewe name meaning 'there is time'.

Hadiye

Girl's name meaning 'gift' in Arabic.

Hassana

Girl's name meaning 'beautiful' in Arabic.

Ibibio

An ethnic group in Cross River State, Nigeria.

Klenam

Ewe name meaning 'shine'.

Kobla

Ewe name for a male born on Tuesday.

Kofigah

Ewe for 'Big Kofi' or 'Kofi senior'. Kofi is the name given to a male born on Friday.

Kojo

The name for a male born on Monday. Used by multiple groups.

Kouakou

Francophone version of Kweku or Kwaku, a male born on Wednesday.

Lebene

Ewe name meaning 'cherish'.

Manye

Ga word for queen. Used as a girl's name.

Mawuena

Ewe name meaning 'the Lord has given'.

Mawusi

Ewe name meaning 'in God's hand'.

Mensah

Name given to the third son born to a woman; commonly used as a surname by several ethnic groups.

Nenor

Ewe name meaning 'destiny' or 'may it be so'.

North

Northern part of Ghana, encompassing the Northern, Upper-East and Upper-West Regions, predominantly Moslem in population.

Nuinui

Fictional. It means 'watery' in the Ga language.

Oko

Ga name for the older male in a set of twins.

Oxford Street

A real busy shopping district in the old coastal town of Osu.

Rahmah

Girl's name meaning 'mercy' in Arabic.

Sefanam

Ewe name meaning 'God has given me peace'.

Shayo

Ga word for mother-in-law. Commonly used as a name for a girl who resembles her paternal grandmother.

Shika

Anlo girl's name, also Ga girl's name meaning 'gold' or 'wealth'.

Sosu

Ewe name meaning 'son of God'.

Tawiah

Gender-neutral name for a child born after a set of twins or triplets. Used by multiple ethnic groups.

Tovidzi

Fictional. In Ewe it means 'peak of a small mountain'.

Togapeme

Fictional. In Ewe it means 'home of the big mountain'.

Windy Bay

Original English name of Winneba. Known locally as Simpa, it is a real coastal town and old seaport in the Central Region of Ghana.

Yaaba

Fanti version of 'Yaa', the name for a female born on Thursday.

Yao

The name for a male born on Thursday. Also 'Yaw'.

»

Unusual words and phrases

A-levels

General Certificate of Education (GCE) Advanced level exams taken after seven years of secondary education to obtain a GCE A-LEVEL certificate and gain entry into the university.

abobi

Fried anchovies and other tiny fish. Also known as 'Keta schoolboys' after the coastal town known for this delicacy.

abolo

A white fluffy cake made by steaming a paste of fresh corn dough sweetened with other ingredients, in leaves. Typically eaten with fried anchovies, grilled tilapia and fresh salsa.

agbada

Traditional embroidered men's formal attire consisting of trousers and long-sleeved collarless shirt. The full set includes a loose-fitting smock that is worn over the two main pieces, and a matching embroidered cap. The smock and hat are typically discarded to allow a man to let loose and dance, if the weather gets too hot, or for a less formal look.

agbadza

A graceful, traditional Ewe dance marked by flexible bending of the waist in sync with bending the arms at the elbows.

a-goh! a-meh!

The callout-and-response sequence that is rendered upon approaching a private residence or the designated location for traditional business.

akple (also banku)

A soft pliable paste made by using a wooden paddle to stir a mixture of fresh maize flour and cassava starch in a pot over fire until done, then it is rolled into serving sizes. Banku is a variation of the same paste but is made with fermented maize dough instead of fresh maize flour. Eaten with okro soup known as 'fetri-detsi', or with smoked tilapia and a sauce of fresh ground peppers, onions and tomatoes. This is a staple dish of the Ewe people.

aliha

A local beverage of the Ewe people; made from maize.

alomo

Romantic interest, lover.

ashawo

Widely used in West Africa, originally a Nigerian word for prostitute.

atuu!

An expression uttered during a hug or embrace. The full expression is 'awaa-waa-atuu!'

ayekoo!

An expression of congratulations.

boborboh

An intricate Ewe dance.

bofloat

Donuts.

boy-boy

Pidgin English for errand boy or messenger.

book-long

Pidgin English for a bookworm, intellectual or academic.

boss; bossing

Slang expression meaning 'tell me the latest'; a chat session.

bottom-power

Using one's sexuality to progress.

boys' quarters

Servants' wing of a house.

bush person

An ill-mannered person; a hillbilly, one who exhibits ghetto behaviour.

bushiatics

Ghanaian slang word coined to describe typical behaviours exhibited by a bush person (see above), such as bad manners.

challey

Variation of 'Charlie', it means friend or buddy.

challey-wotey

Literally means 'Challey, let's go' in Ga. Slang for rubber slippers/flip-flops.

chenchema

Slang for 'second-hand'.

chief-mourners

The closest family members, in-laws, clan heads, and rich-and-famous relatives of a dead person. Their names are listed in the obituary so that the public knows whom the dead person was related to. These people sit in the V.I.P. section during the funeral.

chop-bar

An accessible restaurant frequented by the working-class, where one can find affordable but delicious local dishes.

chop-box

Pine box used by boarding-school students to store non-perishable supplies such as canned foods, cereals, soaps and detergents.

chop-money

Spending money or allowance, usually given by a man to a woman with the expectation that it will be used for food and supplies for the home.

colo

Abbreviation of the word 'colonial', it means 'old fashioned', 'outdated', or 'out of touch'.

Common Entrance

General Certificate of Education (GCE) exams taken at the end of primary education to obtain a certificate that is required to gain entry into a secondary school.

comport

Used as boarding-school slang to mean 'accept a romantic proposition' or 'agree to date someone'.

daa

Ewe honorific for any married woman, or any middle-aged woman. English equivalent would be 'madam' or 'missus'.

daavi

Ewe honorific for any unmarried young lady in one's society, including one's older sister, a slightly older cousin or a young aunt. It literally means 'little mother' or 'miss'. Also used commonly to refer to any female food vendor believed to be of Ewe extraction.

dadaa

Ewe word for mother.

dadaba

Daddy's-boy or daddy's-girl, spoilt brat.

day name

Common to almost all Ghanaian tribes. Every person is automatically assigned a name that corresponds to the day of the week on which he or she was born. There are seven male and seven female names, with multiple variations depending on the particular tribe. Thus, every child is born with that basic identity already in place.

drinks

Alcohol is symbolically used to transact any traditional business and to perform customary rites. Requesting a woman's hand in marriage from her family head is marked by the practice of bringing along specifically mandated alcoholic beverages. To break an engagement or to initiate a divorce, the plaintiff's family representative, accompanied by at least one witness, returns the mandated alcoholic beverages.

duku

A woman's headscarf. Various dialects.

EMADA (Enfant Mondial Agence de L'Adoption)

Fictional. French for 'Global Child Adoption Agency'.

efo, fo

Ewe honorific for any grown man, including an older brother, cousin, or uncle. 'Efo' is typically used in a formal setting and abbreviated to 'Fo' in a more familiar setting. The English equivalent would be 'mister' or 'sir'.

fetri-detsi

Okro soup made with palm oil, seafood and meat. Eaten with akple or banku. A staple dish of the Ewe people.

fufu

A thick paste originally made by pounding cooked starchy vegetables such as plantains, yams and cassava in a mortar with a pestle. These days, there are all sorts of fufu powder mixtures on the market, which are even microwaveable.

haabah!

Ghanaian expression for 'gosh!', 'goodness!', or 'for Pete's sake!'

hoh!

An exclamation indicating disbelief.

homo

Boarding school slang term for a freshman or new student. The noun supposedly derives from the scientific term 'Homo sapien' but it is also widely assumed to have sexual connotations because of the extent of bullying that male juniors are often subjected to. The verb refers to bullying or hazing including physical and sexual abuse, in extreme cases. However, this topic is treated with a lot of secrecy and denial and is seldom discussed publicly.

huu

Slang for 'nothing'.

juju man

A witchdoctor, someone who practices black magic or voodoo.

kanami

Ewe word for fried fish.

kelewele

This delicacy is made from wedges or cubes of ripe plantain, which are seasoned with ground ginger, onion and red chilli peppers, then deep-fried in a wide skillet over a log-fire by the roadside, in the evenings. It is sold wrapped in paper, which soaks up the oil. This is a popular Ghanaian fast food. May be eaten with roasted peanuts.

kelewele junction

Any neighbourhood corner where a kelewele seller has set up shop.

kenkey

A solid, heavy cake made from a paste of fermented corn dough mixed with cassava starch, which is wrapped in cornhusks and steamed for hours. It is served with fried or grilled fish and a black pepper sauce, or hot salsa, and is a traditional staple dish of the Ga tribe. There is also a Fanti tribe variety that is not as fermented and is wrapped in plantain leaves instead of cornhusks. Sold by roadside vendors.

kente

An intricately patterned fabric made by weaving brightly coloured silk and cotton fibres on a loom. The most popular variety is the Akan kente cloth, but there is also an Ewe tribe variety. Reserved for special formal occasions, its designs and patterns are not random. Each motif, logo, or colour combination, is symbolic and assigned a specific occasion for its appropriate use.

knocking rites

Preliminary visit to state a man's intention to request a woman's hand in marriage, and set the date for the engagement. A delegation of the man's family knocks at her parents' gate at dawn (see 'a-goh!').

koh-koh-koh

Knock-knock!

koliko

Puppet. Also used to refer to a wimp or a follower.

koobi

Cured fish or dried salted tilapia used to season vegetable stews.

Korli beads

Expensive beads used in formal jewellery.

kuluulu

Slang for 'conspiracy', 'plot' or 'underhanded behaviour'.

kwasiasem

Akan word for 'nonsense', 'stupidity', 'bullshit'.

light soup

Delicious spicy soup of thin consistency and pale colouration reputed to be a fever cure-all.

ma chérie

French for 'my darling', 'my beloved'.

mamaba

Mama's-boy or mama's-girl, spoilt brat.

mami-water

West-African term for 'mermaid'.

milo

A popular brand of chocolate beverage.

mon coeur

French endearment meaning 'my heart'.

O-levels

General Certificate of Education Ordinary Level exams taken after five years of secondary education to obtain the GCE O-LEVEL certificate. After that, there is an option to advance through two more years of secondary education if one aspires to enter a university (see A-Levels).

obroni

Akan for 'Caucasian' or 'white person'.

on-the-body

Illegal transportation of narcotics or other contraband by hiding them on one's body or in one's body cavities to elude detection by customs and other official authorities.

osofo

Ghanaian word for priest, reverend, preacher or pastor.

otsami (also okyeame)

An interpreter, spokesperson or linguist. Every tribe in Ghana utilises the services of otsamis during traditional customary ceremonies. Their role nowadays is largely ceremonial and flamboyant, and requires record-setting oratorical prowess. In less public settings, traditionally-minded folk sometimes communicate with each other over a serious matter through the use of an informal intermediary also referred to as an otsami, who serves more as a witness than an interpreter.

palaver-sauce

A leafy stew made with cocoyam leaves, palm oil, ground melon seeds smoked fish and meat. Any leafy green such as spinach or kale can substitute for the cocoyam leaves. The ground melon is optional.

palm nut soup

A thick, bright-orange soup made from the fruit of the palm. Eaten with fufu.

palm-grease

Slang for bribe.

pikinabodo

Pidgin English for 'illegitimate child' or 'bastard'.

portmanteau

French for 'suitcase', used widely among English speakers in West Africa.

Poutine

A French-Canadian dish. Fried potatoes with gravy and cheese curds.

pswii!

A verbal expression of disdain. There is a tooth-sucking equivalent.

puna

A yam variety, slightly yellower and more delicious than others.

school-mattress

Ghanaian boarding-school slang for a 'loose or promiscuous girl'.

SIDA

French for HIV/AIDS. Le syndrome d'immunodéficience acquise.

slit-and-kaba

A traditional outfit worn by Ghanaian women on semi-formal or formal occasions. The slit is a fitted full-length skirt (with a side or back slit) worn with matching, intricately designed blouse known as a kaba. Generally, the more formal the occasion, the more intricate the kaba.

smoked fish

Fish that is preserved by grilling with dry heat in a special appliance known as a smoker. Used in soups and vegetable dishes.

supi

Boarding school slang word for lesbian.

tassie

Ewe endearment for auntie.

tin-cutter

Pidgin English for can-opener.

tonton

Francophone endearment for uncle.

Tourtière du Lac-Saint-Jean

A traditional French-Canadian meat pie.

tro-tro

Minivans and minibuses used as low-cost mass transportation. 'Tro' was a Ghanaian coin equivalent to two-and-half pence.

Tuu tuu gbovi; Tuu tuu gbovi...

An old Ewe lullaby/folksong. Popular in Benin, Togo and Ghana.

twapia (pronounced: chua-pia)

Chewing sticks derived from the wood of medicinal plants such as the neem tree, usually pre-cut and sold in bunches at the market.

two-two

The act of prostitution or soliciting a prostitute. It refers to both parts of the transaction.

waakye

Rice-and-beans. Served with tomato stew or gravy containing meat, boiled eggs, or fried fish, and topped with hot pepper sauce.

wele

Cooked cowskin that is used to flavour waakye stew and other soups.

woezo, mia woezo

Ewe word for welcome. Mia woezo is an expression used in the plural to welcome a group of people.

water

It is a mark of politeness and good culture to refresh one's guests with water to drink as soon as they arrive, whether they are thirsty or not.

wrapper

A two- or three-yard piece of fabric (depending on the girth of the owner) that is used as a wrap-around skirt, a shawl, or to tie a baby to one's back.

»

Proverbs and idiomatic expressions

A crab does not give birth to a bird.

Equivalent meaning is 'like mother like daughter.'

All things are lawful for me, but all things are not expedient

The fact that an act is legal does not mean that it is therefore beneficial to indulge in it. Biblical, 1 Corinthians 10:23.

Muddy water also can be used to put out fire.

Every person is good for something, however unqualified or useless that person may appear, and however insignificant the task.

Swept away their footsteps

A spin on the Biblical passage in Luke 9:5, this old-fashioned practice means 'good riddance to bad rubbish'. In this case, the owner of the house sweeps away the dust of the visitors who came to offend her.

The fact that a horse is crazy does not mean that its owner is also crazy.

A leader is expected to exercise better judgment than the rank and file.

The louse that bites you is hidden within the folds of your own cloth.

The one who hurts you the most is always someone close to you.

When a single tree tries to withstand the force of the wind, it breaks.

A person should not go through a challenge alone, lest it overwhelm him.

When you are going into marriage, ask.

One must not jump into any contractual commitment without performing due diligence.

Your ship is about to sail home.

Your luck is about to change for the better.

www.ingramcontent.com/pod-product-compliance
Lightning Source LLC
Chambersburg PA
CBHW060421030726
47495CB00003B/681